MW00694875

BLACKWATER
SECRETS

BLACKWATER
SECRETS

GWEN HUNTER

BellaRosaBooks

BellaRosaBooks

BLACKWATER SECRETS
ISBN 978-1-933523-02-6

Copyright © 2007 by Gwen Hunter

All rights reserved, including the right to reproduce this book or portions thereof in any form whatsoever. For more information contact Bella Rosa Books, P.O. Box 4251 CRS, Rock Hill, SC 29732. Or online at www.bellarosabooks.com

This book is a work of fiction. Names, characters, places and incidents are products of the author's imagination or are used fictitiously. Any resemblance to actual events or locales or persons, living or dead, is entirely coincidental.

First Printing: January 2007

Library of Congress Control Number: 2006909402

Printed in the United States of America on acid-free paper.

Cover painting by Joyce Wright – www.artbyjoyce.com
Book design by Bella Rosa Books

BellaRosaBooks and logo are trademarks of Bella Rosa Books

10 9 8 7 6 5 4 3 2 1

It's never too late to chase your dreams.

BLACKWATER
SECRETS

1

PLANES, CHUTES AND PAPARAZZI

She didn't want Lake Pontchartrain, shining in the sun, to be the last sight she saw in this life, but unless the pilot was good—very good—it would be. Looking out the window of the 727, water sparkled, appearing pristine beneath her. Beautiful to look at from this vantage, where the remembered chemical stink of the dead water couldn't be smelled, where the rainbow effect of decades of spilled gasoline and oil and the scum growing on the surface couldn't be seen.

News reports said the lake had been cleaned up but she never believed it. She hated it. Hated this lake, the buildings huddled like beetles on its rim, the ships plowing their way out toward the gulf, hated everything the view below represented. She was a fool to have come here. But then, she'd been a fool quite often lately. There'd been ample proof of that.

The flight attendant, a slim young man with Humphrey Bogart eyes, checked the passengers to see that their seats were upright and locked, seatbelts cinched tightly, and made certain they all had a pillow or blanket to burrow their faces in. He was terrified, but trying not to show it. Too bad the airlines hadn't thought to provide parachutes. He was awfully young to die today.

She wasn't usually this morbid. She wasn't *ever* this morbid. A sudden flush of anger shot through her, and she forced a smile onto her frozen features. If she died, she would not be pulled from the dank water, face etched with fear. Instead she gestured to the flight attendant on his way back to the galley. "Do we get complimentary drinks when we land? I think I may need one then. A double. What do you recommend?"

He stopped, surprised, and an answering smile fought the fear in his famous-looking eyes. "Mrs. Stone, if the airline doesn't offer you one, I'll buy you one myself."

"It's a date." He nodded firmly, as if making a pact, and hurried away.

Moments later, she bent forward against the seatbelt and pulled the sandals off her feet, tucked them into the neckline of her silk shell. With deft motions, she pulled her raincoat closed, buttoning it over the carry-on tote and camera bag slung over her shoulders, the bags and spike heels hidden beneath it.

The 727 was descending. If the old bird survived this landing without landing gear, these shoes would not be left behind. Resting her face in the rough fabric of the USAir pillow, she smelled the stale scent of cigarettes and the last patron's hair spray. White Rain? Alberto? And the fragrance of her own sweat.

"Jesus, Mary and Joseph," she whispered, mostly in prayer. "Jesus, Mary and Joseph."

The landing was brutal. Metal shrieked, a grinding squeal. Braking engines roared, vibrating through her bones. She was forced forward, bouncing with the jet, the safety belt cutting into her. She forgot to breathe. The sound crescendoed, beyond anything she could ever have imagined. Someone was screaming nearby.

The seat beneath her lifted and fell again slamming the breath from her. Her face banged onto her knees through the thin pillow, the impact drawing mucous and tears. The jet skewed to one side, throwing her against the armrest. There was the coppery taste of blood. Beneath it all she could hear herself whisper through clenched teeth, "Jesus, Mary and Joseph. Jesus, Mary and Joseph. Hail Mary full of grace." Catholic schoolgirl prayer.

An eternity later, the movement of the jet slowed. The engines changed pitch. Deeper. Softer perhaps, just a bit. The screaming of the jet's skin against the tarmac grew to basso profundo and eased away. The forward momentum slowed.

A silence louder than the roar buffeted her ears. They had stopped.

Slowly, Geneva raised her head, licked her lips. Jack was beside her, pulling at the buckle of the safety belt. She stood, her raincoat swirling around her, hidden carry-on baggage bumping beneath the long folds. Barefoot, she stumbled up the aisle, daylight from the open hatch blinding her.

She turned to Jack as he gripped her beneath the arm. "That

drink?"

"Bottomless Margaritas, Mrs. Stone. Enough to swim in." His eyes were manic and she grinned at him. "Wipe your face when you get to the bottom," he advised. "Your lips are all bloody." He lifted her, fingers cruel beneath her arms as he and another tossed her from the 727 onto the emergency chute.

The world danced a sickening pirouette as she skidded off the rubber slide into the waiting arms of the rescue worker. With bruising fingers he, too, lifted her, and with an ungentle shove sent her stumbling, barefoot, toward the terminal.

She had survived the landing.

Dizzy from the rough arrival, she fought for balance and sucked wet air.

Geneva had prided herself for nearly twenty years that her tolerance for stifling New York summers was the one positive holdover from her youth. The first breath of New Orleans' August air was an insult, searing her lungs, assuring her that any real tolerance to southern humidity was long gone. Jet fuel exhaust, the sour miasma of Lake Pontchartrain, and the sudden stink of her own sweat enclosed her like a fevered wet fist.

Raw silk slacks, already creased from the hours of flight time and the three hour holdover in Atlanta, wilted. Her silk blouse stuck to her back beneath her raincoat like loose snakeskin needing to be shed against some handy rock.

Shoving damp blond strings off her forehead, she wiped blood from her lips and licked at the smear before slipping her sandals from inside her blouse and onto her feet. Her bare soles were already blistering on the hot tarmac.

She pulled off her raincoat, fighting the heat. The heavy camera bag—which she had refused to relinquish to the exigencies of the landing—she slung over her shoulder again as she slogged her way to the terminal. Her soles sank in a line of tar in the concrete, and with each step after, they adhered, leaving a trail of gooey black footprints.

But she was alive.

She waved at a small boy running past and he waved in return, giving the thumbs up signal. She returned it and laughed. *She was alive*. She wanted to cry, but laughed again instead.

"I should have stayed in New York," a woman muttered

beside her, mascara streaking her face. "I should have stayed in New York."

"That's what I thought," Gen said, "but then I'd have missed all the fun." The breath and the words parched her lungs.

The woman looked at her as if she thought Geneva was crazy, then quickly turned away.

Perhaps she *was* crazy. She had been more than a little wired for days. The mascara-smeared woman pushed past her and ran with the flow of passengers.

The terminal loomed ahead. *Twenty-nine years is too long.* There were no bridges left to mend in this godforsaken, parboiled place, only bad memories and the ghosts of the past. God only knew how her father would react. Sweat now ran like spiders down her back, and she stretched her shoulder blades to relieve the itch.

It was insane. And it was all Barry's fault. She laughed again, feeling black despair gather in her chest, the despair that had sent her running from New York and the paparazzi and the fact of the lie that was her marriage. The laughter died. Twenty seconds in Louisiana and the last dregs of her good humor had evaporated. Not even her legal separation and impending divorce had accomplished that. Tears, once an unfamiliar sensation, prickled her eyelids. She would *not* cry. She would *not*. Geneva took a deep breath of the fume-laden air.

Grimacing, she clenched her toes against the slippery leather of the sandal bottoms, managing to make the last few yards to the air-conditioned lobby as passengers from the plane's nether regions merged around her, running for the building. Icy air hit her face and dried the sweat already trickling down her temple. She shivered in the sudden delicious cool and licked salt off her lips. A remembered taste from childhood. Her tears faded and she shook her head. It had been this way for days now. Despair and hilarity in equal parts.

Once inside, she pulled off the ruined sandals, holding them out to the U.S. Airways officer standing just inside the building. If he had been about to badger her for refusing to leave her possessions on board, the sight of her sandals stopped him. His face fell as he took the delicate shoes by their thin ankle straps. "I'm just glad I didn't have to walk across the hot concrete in my bare toes," she murmured.

"U.S. Air—"

"Did an exceptional job." She smiled warmly and watched the man's discomfort clear instantly. "The captain is my hero for life. Honest." She held up a hand "Honest Injun" style, a politically incorrect gesture she hadn't made in decades. It was this place. Had to be.

Sticking the offending hand into a pocket, Geneva looked back out at the plane. It was a wounded bird nestled in a bed of foam, surrounded by fire trucks and workers in bright yellow fire retardant suits. A long scar gouged the runway behind it. A trace of fear remembered from the long descent fluttered through her. Geneva clenched her jaw. She never gave in to fear. Never.

"It was my first belly landing, and I expected it to be much worse." She laughed, pleased that the sound was steady and calm, taking the opportunity to check the man's name badge as she touched the black goo cooling on her shoes. "But perhaps bogging down the belly of the plane in strips of melted tar is a Louisiana safety technique."

"Designed just for this kind of emergency, ma'am," he said with a twinkle. "Not even landing strips can handle the kind of heat we've had this week."

"Please pass along my compliments to both the captain and flight crew, Mr. James. And if you would be so kind, would you remind Jack, the flight attendant with beautiful Bogart eyes, that he owes me a Margarita big enough to swim in?"

Mr. James looked nonplussed a moment and then understanding dawned. "You earned it, ma'am. I'll make sure to remind him."

"Again, my compliments to the flight crew, Mr. James," she said, leaving her ruined shoes dangling on his fingers. She almost added, *I'll pass along my compliments to Mr. Stone*, but caught herself at the last moment. Old habits die hard. James turned his attention to another passenger, one a bit more cranky, now that she was safely on the ground.

"Aunt Gen!"

Geneva turned at the sound of the fresh voice. "Keri!" She held out her arms, enfolded her niece, and hugged her tightly, thinking fleetingly that perhaps there were compensations to be found in this trip after all. With a hand beneath the girl's pointed chin, Geneva tilted back the black head of hair and smiled down into the gamine face. "You beautiful child! And so tall! Look at you. You've grown into a beauty. You are a sweetheart to meet me."

"The landing gear got stuck. And we were all scared to death."

"I'm absolutely fine. Not a scratch on me." Gen tucked a strand of greasy blond hair behind her ear, remembering to check her earrings. The diamonds were still in place, and suddenly she was feeling better, calmer, out of the fetid air and the stink of near disaster, Keri in her arms. She kissed her niece on the forehead.

"Some dramatic entrance, Aunt Gen," her tall, dark nephew bent across Keri and kissed her cheek. "You look great, especially for someone who just went through a crash landing in a 727."

"Destan! I look awful and smell almost as bad," she added in mock whisper. "But you are a darlin' to say so. Look at you, nearly six feet, are you?" He blushed and Gen hugged her lanky nephew and linked arms with both teens, as they relieved her of camera bag, raincoat, and the shoulder bag she had forgotten she carried in the slippery departure. After she released Destan, she could feel the bruises left in her skin by the spikes of her ruined heels. She might be sore for a few days. . . .

"Barefoot through the terminal, *Ginny?* Such gauche behavior for a Deveraux," a strange voice teased. Gen looked up, startled at the sound, the almost-familiar accent on her name as she found him. Time dilated and slowed.

He leaned against a support pillar, one leg bent, booted foot flat against the column. Dark slacks, crisp white shirt, sleeves rolled up. Whip-cord strong arms crossed over his chest.

Coiled strength. Lean. Lethal-looking.

She met his eyes. Black eyes crinkled in a sun-worn olive-skinned face. French-black hair, black as Destan's, black as a bayou in starlight, fell negligently over his forehead.

She remembered the feel of that silky hair sliding through her fingers. The salty taste of his skin. Cold ran down her body, a shock, like icy water.

"*Ginny,*" he said, the sound French with a soft G, almost *Shennay.* "Me? I can't see you, *pas you,* being so . . . *chokay.* . . ." A flash of white teeth in a dangerous smile.

"Starnes," she breathed. The blood drained from her face. Her feet were frozen to the frigid floor. Her skin prickled as if thousands of tiny hairs lifted. *Starnes Templar.* . . .

He raised long fingers to tip an imaginary hat, his face grave. She started forward, lifted a hand as if to touch him.

"TV cameras are outside," Keri said. Time snapped back in place with an almost audible pop.

Gen blinked, looked down at the girl, away from the vision of her past, her niece suddenly remembered. "They're filming the landing and interviewing the passengers," Keri said. "Sure you don't want to put on some shoes? Uncle Barry won't like—" Destan elbowed Keri to silence and the teens exchanged a guilty glance.

Shoes? The conversation came back to her, along with her despair. A fragile smile covered her reaction to Barry's name, to the sight of the man nearby. "The floor feels *wonderful* on my bare feet," she assured them. "Besides, I'm only a photographer now, not a socialite, *not* Mrs. Barry Stone. I can afford to be eccentric," she said, excusing the aborted comment about her almost-ex-husband. "And your Uncle Barry is no longer around to decide what I should do."

Putting her forehead down to Keri's, she added, "You don't have to be careful about using his name, you know. I'm divorcing him, not dying of Barry-cell leukemia." The teens grinned, relieved.

"I'm so glad you're okay," Keri said, hugging her, voice muffled in Gen's shoulder.

"You may as well know." Destan looked at his sister. She pulled away, shook her head 'no', but he ignored the silent advice and plowed on. "We called Mama. Uncle Starnes said we had to."

Uncle Starnes? *Uncle* Starnes? When did that happen? Gen looked up, meeting the amused, dark eyes.

"Yeah. He brought us to get you. Stayed with us all afternoon while the plane circled and landed."

"And? You called Lily . . ." Gen prompted, her own eyes looking away from the dark form.

"So, anyway, the Old Man answered the phone."

"You didn't." Dread washed through her.

Keri looked miserable as she added to the narrative. "We had to tell him."

"Had to," Destan reiterated. "Mama would have been pissed if we hadn't called and you had gone down in flames, smeared all over the runway." Destan was delighted with his vision, eyes alight and dancing.

"Mama won't like you using that word."

"Mama isn't here," Destan countered his sister.

"I don't suppose it occurred to either of you that your grandfather didn't know I was coming."

"We figured that out." Destan said with a devilish grin, flash of white teeth in his olive-skinned face.

So like Starnes. Why had she never noted the typical Louisiana coloring, the French-y similarity before? It had been years since she thought of Starnes, and now suddenly, she was seeing him everywhere. His lithe form pushed away from the pillar, moved closer. She felt her breath catch, her eyes locked to his.

Rebound attraction, the rational part of her brain whispered.

"So you may assume he saw your dramatic entrance, *Ginny*," Starnes said. "In full color on the new wide-screen TV at the foot of his bed."

"And he'll see you walk out of the terminal without shoes," Keri said, grinning at the thought.

"He'll be pissed," Destan added with teenaged jollity. He dropped his voice and set his face in stern lines. "It is *not* the way *we* do things." It was a good impersonation of her father. The fact that it also sounded just like her near-ex wasn't lost on her either. Funny, she had never noticed how alike the two men were until she was about to lose both of them. Suddenly she was seeing resemblances in everyone.

"Jesus, Mary and Joseph," she whispered.

"And he'll be making Mama's life a living hell till we get back with you," Destan said. "He can be a real devil. I know now why you and Mama never came back once you left the estate."

Geneva sighed. It wasn't the entry she had planned, worried over, and lost sleep over in the two days since she had made the agonizing decision to come home. "Except for the ones I was wearing, all my shoes are in my luggage. On the plane." She looked down at her bare feet and wiggled her painted toes. Touching the shoulder tote, she said, "This is it baggage-wise, until the airline releases my luggage stored in the belly of the plane."

Geneva took in the cameras up ahead, the mobs of passengers and frantic families with microphones stuck close to their faces, the shouted questions and near hysteria. She had been trying all her life to rid herself of the hated image of her father and the terrified girl who had run away from him so long ago. And now she was walking back into his life and his disapproval with bare feet. A breathless sensation she hadn't felt since childhood gripped her a for moment. Fear of her father. Of his swift, unpredictable anger. His wide leather belt. Her father who lay dying.

"*Hésitant, Ginny?*" Starnes' voice drawled, challenging.

She jerked, saw him again, just ahead and to the side of them, standing alone, apart from the Deverauxs as always, amused crinkles at the corners of his eyes.

"*Pas ma Ginny.* She fear nothing." His black eyes seemed to be saying something else, hold another meaning. Seemed to pull her in.

Gen sucked in a deep breath, her eyes locked to his. "Jesus, Mary and Joseph." She paused, needing something far stronger than the mild swearing. *Maybe the old goat will die before I get there.*

Starnes cocked a mocking brow and she realized she had spoken aloud. Destan and Keri giggled and urged her on toward the TV cameras and press waiting at the end of the terminal, Starnes falling in behind. Gen had known on takeoff, when she looked out the window and saw the afternoon sunlight dappling the New York skyline, that this trip south was a mistake. The landing from hell was further persuasion, the tar clinging to her ruined sandals like black glue had convinced her. And now the press. It was all one gigantic nightmare. And Starnes. . . . She could feel him behind her, the heat of his body seeming to blaze.

She would go on TV—in what might make national news if this was an otherwise uneventful day—looking like a sweat-smeared zombie from some C-grade movie. She hated this place.

Destan cleaved the way through the press like a football fullback, one elbow up to shove aside bodies, the other hand raised to push away microphones. Yet, one woman, more vicious than the rest of the pack, managed to pull Keri from Gen's grasp. Using the girl as ransom, she shoved a fuzzy microphone into

Gen's face.

"Mrs. Stone, is it true that you left your husband for a younger man?" she demanded.

Gen actually laughed. "Print what you want! You always do!" *Almost anything would be better than the truth.* "It'll be better fiction than most of the stories about me."

Keri jerked her arm free, slammed her heel down on the woman's instep and moved with Gen after Destan. Starnes lifted an arm, elbowing a cameraman back.

"Good move, girl. You should be a bodyguard," he said.

"Stupid witch," Keri said, ducking under another mic and breaking free of the mob. "I think she bruised my arm. How can you stand these people, Aunt Gen?"

"They aren't people. They are parasites," Gen huffed, now following her niece and nephew into the parking garage. "Leaches." She had started to sweat again and knew her deodorant had totally failed her. She was loosing her breath in the heat and fumes, her head pounding. Someone had stepped on her bare foot in the passage through the press. "They are scarabaeids."

Starnes jogged ahead, his gait uneven, and vanished into the gloom. Behind them, several of the media turned and began to follow in a tangle of bodies and cameras.

"What's a scarabaeid?" Keri asked and guided her to one side, around a large woman who should never have discovered Lycra, especially in such a vibrant purple shade. Gen had no idea that boas and mules even came in that shade of grape. The smell of exhaust stung Gen's eyes, or maybe it was the sight of the stretched-thin Lycra. Keri glanced back and rolled her eyes, making an awful face.

Gen managed to laugh at Keri's antics. She loved her niece like the daughter she never had. "Dung beetles are scarabaeids," she said. "Most *men* are scarabaeids. Your Uncle Barry is a scarabaeid of the first order. President of the Scarabaeid Society."

Laughing, Keri aimed Gen at a long white Lincoln, its engine idling. She tossed the baggage into the trunk as Destan climbed into the front passenger seat. Keri got in the back seat with Gen. The upholstery was velour, soaking up sweat like a sponge. The AC on high brought back her shivers.

The Lincoln peeled down the exit ramp like a race car, taking the turns with abandon as the press raced toward the parking site on foot. Gen cinched the safety belt in self defense. Destan tuned the radio to a rap station. She thought her head would explode. "Uncle Starnes, Aunt Gen looks a little green. Slow down," Keri said.

"Can't. Got company. I have a feeling *Ginny* doesn't want *them* following us to the estate."

Uncle Starnes? That familial title again. It was unnerving. Swallowing her nausea, Gen turned her head. Behind them was a news van, the distinct MSNBC logo painted on the side. The woman who had waylaid Keri was in the passenger seat, a compact open before her face, touching up her makeup. Even from this distance, Gen could see the sweat glisten on the woman's skin. Starnes took another turn, tires squealing. "Drive," Gen said.

On the straight length of down-tilted concrete, Keri stretched across the front seat and turned off the radio. "I'm telling you, Aunt Gen looks like she's gonna puke."

Destan glanced back at her but said nothing as Keri dropped into her seat and buckled up. The radio stayed off, however, and Gen thought she detected a slight decrease in acceleration. Speed was really a waste of time as the ticket booths were just ahead with lines of cars waiting to pay. Destan cursed, a new teenaged trait Gen hoped he would outgrow. Lily would have a fit if she knew her son used that kind of language. The car came to a stop. Starnes' tanned fingers tapped gently on the wheel, his impatience clear in the rhythm.

The news van roared up behind them as a camera man and the female reporter jumped out, mic in hand. She rapped on Gen's tinted window with force, and Gen wondered what would happen if she opened the window and threw up all over the woman. Would it still make the evening news?

A new toll booth opened to the left of them and Starnes gunned the engine, swerved hard, taking the first spot and handing the teller correct change. Three more cars pulled in behind them before the reporter could get back into the van. They lost sight of the press in a sea of slow moving vehicles, as Starnes, pushing the Lincoln, chuckled softly.

2

PROUD PLEASURES AND BON À RIEN

The feeling of nausea passed. Gen settled deeply into the velour, resting her head against the seatback. Home. She just wanted to go home. She wanted skyscrapers and rooftops and great canyons of thoroughfares. She wanted joggers in spandex walking pouffed-up poodles and bag ladies pushing shopping carts and winos snoring in doorways and the ever present roar of traffic and turbaned cabbies who spoke little English. Gen glanced once at her watch. Five P.M. Two hours circling and a belly landing and ruined shoes . . . and seeing Starnes.

She closed her eyes against the glare of the hazy Louisiana skyline, low and obscure, brown with smog, instead of multistoried and grand. She was ten times a fool for coming here.

Her head ached in distant waves of pain that foretold a massive migraine, her breasts hurt where the spike heels had bruised the flesh, her feet hurt. Gen lifted both feet into the light and studied them. They were filthy—black around the heels, the color like an outline, and her polish was chipped. She had paid good money for that pedicure. Like the shoes, it was ruined. And the silk she wore was stained and her hair was— "Turn there," she ordered, pointing.

Surprised at the imperious tone, Starnes made a hard right and pulled into the airport hotel. "Pull up over there," she ordered again, pointing to the lobby entrance. When he complied, she opened the door and stepped out. "Park. Pop the trunk. You can come in to wait. I won't be long." Grabbing the small tote from the trunk, Gen moved into the hotel lobby. Booking a room was a snap. By the time the kids decided to join her, Gen had paid, signed, and taken the plastic card-key in hand. Starnes was nowhere in sight.

Halfway up to the third floor, elevator music soothing her

ears, Gen realized that she hadn't said please. . . . She had ordered him around like a paid servant. Guilt sparked for a moment, before she banished it. She could apologize later, after the shower she couldn't live without.

Keri took the camera bag, and together the trio traipsed down the third floor hallway to the small suite she had taken. Geneva made her living flying to photographic shoots all over the globe, and had learned that lost luggage was a more common phenomena than the airlines liked to admit. While she didn't have an extra pair of shoes, she did have toiletries, underclothes, headache meds, and a change of outerwear for emergencies.

Keri sat on the bathroom's toilet seat and chattered about learning how to ride a horse in the last week, and how the Old Man was teaching her to play chess, and how he promised to leave her a horse in his will. Listening above the roar of the spray, Gen showered off the stink of fear and nerves. Beneath Keri's prattle, Gen could hear her unvoiced complaint. *How could Mama keep us away from our grandfather all these years? He's a pretty neat guy.* But Lily and she had never told the kids the truth about their pasts, the secrets that had kept the sisters away for nearly thirty years. John Deveraux was not a 'pretty neat guy'. Never had been, never would be.

Half an hour later, showered, medicated, and dressed in tailored jeans and a chambray shirt, with wet hair tickling her collarbone, Gen and her entourage left the room, having paid for the entire night. She figured that if things went sour at the estate, she could always spend the night here.

Starnes had waited in the lobby, nursing a cup of coffee, his face unreadable. "Thank you," she said to him the moment she saw him, uncomfortable at her earlier manner. "I meant to say please when I asked you to turn in. And I appreciate the shower."

"Asked?" he said, his tone bland. As if considering, he stood and set the cup on the small table. "No problem, Miss High and Mighty Deveraux," he drawled, his eyes gleaming wickedly as he turned away.

"Miss High and—" Gen stopped, her lips parted, Starnes pulled out the car keys, moving to the parking lot. She watched him walk away, the kids following him into the sunlight. "Miss High and Mighty, my pale rear end," Gen whispered at the childhood nickname.

Even twenty-nine years ago Starnes Templar had been difficult to read, a feral French kid from the swamps, eyes glittering with rage, energy, and impetuous, hungry need. Now the savage, stormy nature of the wild Cajun teen had been harnessed, restrained, hidden beneath an urbane layer of social graces and well-schooled dignity. But that wicked glint in his eyes as he insulted her had ruptured the thin skin of civility, exposing a turbulent current, just as raw, just as rough as the bayou which had spawned him.

His slacks hung low on his hips as if they had been tailored for him, his lean body moving smoothly across the parking lot. Gen readjusted the position of the heavy bag on her shoulder and followed.

There were no news vans waiting beside the expensive white car, which had been Keri's constant worry, and the time watching afternoon soap operas had cooled Destan's adolescent need for rap, making the rest of the trip to the estate much easier to bear. The Deveraux Estate was over an hour's ride from New Orleans, deep into some of the finest horse country in the world. Gen slept the whole way. She woke to feel Keri shaking her shoulder.

"We're here, Aunt Gen."

"I'm awake," she mumbled, shoving hair out of her face and sitting up in the seat.

"I didn't know you had curly hair," Keri said, surprised. She lifted a hand, touching a blond curl.

"*Une jeune fille.* Her hair like that when she was a little girl," Starnes said, a trace of humor in his voice. And perhaps a hint of an ancient caress in the eyes that crinkled at her through the rearview. A trace of the icy shock she had felt when she first saw his face quivered down her spine.

"Humidity and lack of a hair dryer," Gen said, tasting sleep-induced dry-mouth. "I normally blow the curl out." It had been years since she had seen herself with curls, and now they hung into her eyes, just like they had as a teen. She gathered her meager belongings and stepped from the car, deliberately stretching her tired back and then rearranging the raincoat and tote and reaching for the camera bag before looking at the house.

Warm Louisiana soil was dusty beneath her feet. The weight of the camera bag pulled at her shoulder. Late afternoon sunlight dancing through shadows of live oaks lit the old house in a lacy pattern, and she stared at it through her curls. Twenty-nine years fell away, leaving Geneva feeling frozen and paralyzed in the wet heat. New York, her life there, the person she had created and grown into melted away as if they had never been.

An old two-story French-Georgian home, the Deveraux Estate house, stood in a grassy glade of azaleas, climbing roses, and impatiens in long winding borders. Silk drapery closed off the downstairs windows, pale green against the white-painted wood trim and rose brick. The architect had been lavish in his use of fluted wood, and carved black shutters were secured with ornate wrought-iron braces at each long, narrow window, while above, extravagant dental moldings stood in soldierly relief beneath the roof overhang, as if at parade rest.

Behind her a motor purred to life, the sound slowly fading into the distance. A horse called out a whinny. Hoof thumps reverberated hollowly.

Her eyes on the house, she spotted the ancient horse-ties that once held the mounts of visitors until a handy groom could take over. Though painted black, they still stained the brick in long rusted lines like tears down the old walls. Two-hundred-fifty-year-old live oaks, sinuous limbs dripping moss like dusty lace, cast serpentine shadows over the green of the lawn.

Peeking from the side was the old Victorian-style playhouse with its deeply patterned moldings and carved wooden door, lace curtains and window boxes. The tip of its cupola was obscured by a massive limb, but she knew that the weathervane of a galloping horse would be pointing into the faint breeze.

A horse cried out again. In the distance stood the barn, the stalls' white-painted half-doors closed. It was too far to see if horses stood in the open windows, but the familiar scent of horse and manure brought a lump to her throat, and the humid air held the sounds close. New York seemed far away and unimportant, like a dream only half remembered upon waking. And the strange thing about seeing the estate again was that she felt more free than she had in decades.

With a shaking hand, Gen shoved curls from her forehead, hitched the camera bag higher on her shoulder and walked toward the house. Dust beneath her feet became shell-shaped stepping stones as the house grew closer.

Lily had come out on the uncovered front porch. She stood, one hand shading her eyes as her engagement ring glittered in the wavering sunlight, her face in shadow. Lily was all the things Gen was not. Rounded where Gen was angular, full-busted where Gen was boy-slender, sensuous where Gen was sleek. A dark Aphrodite to Gen's blonde Diana. They were as different as two sisters could possibly be and still share the same genes. And neither had ever expected to be on Deveraux Estate land again.

Full lips smiling, Lily took Gen's raincoat and tote. The kids' voices echoed from the barn; Starnes had vanished, perhaps with the engine she had heard, and the sisters were alone. He hadn't said goodbye. Gen wondered if he was still mad. He used to get mad when she would order him around. . . .

"Barefoot?" Lily asked, one dark brow lifted.

Gen looked down and wiggled her toes. The black rings had been difficult to scrub off, but worth the extra work. "First time in years. I had forgotten how good grass feels. Prickly."

"And such an entrance, sister-mine. Plane crash, national media. All the drama. Remind me to beat you within an inch of your life for that one."

Gen smiled up at her sister, noting the stress puckering between her eyes, the shadows of fear that hadn't yet faded. "I'm okay, Lily."

"If you can drag your feet off the lawn, I thought we'd have a glass of tea on the back porch."

"Why? Did the Old Man tell you to make me stay outside?"

Lily laughed. "No. But he's taking a nap and I thought we could visit before he wakes up. He sleeps so lightly, wakes at the slightest noise, and the doctor insists that he get his rest. Not easy with Destan and Keri here."

She led the way around back of the house to the screened porch that had been added nearly twenty years before. Gen had never seen it. She stood in the grass, taking in the cypress supports and the dark mesh screening. Windows that converted the porch into a sunroom for winter had been removed and stood beneath a canvas secured with bungee cords, hidden behind tall azaleas.

Without looking at Lily she asked, "Is he still mean as a snake? No, don't bother to answer. He'll never change. He was born mean and he'll die mean."

Lily ignored her comment and the bitter tone even Gen could hear. "I have mint tea if you like. Made by Della, just the way she used to. Or coffee if you prefer."

"Playing hostess? You've only been here four days longer than I have."

"Being polite."

Gen laughed and looked at her sister. "I'm being bitchy, aren't I?"

"I went through the same thing when I got here. It wasn't easy coming back. The kids love it here," she added sadly. "They don't say so outright, but I hear the questions in their voices. They want to know why. . . ."

"So much for lifetime vows."

"Everything changes, sister-mine. Everything changes."

"The old man didn't. Hasn't. Won't. I'll have the tea," she added when Lily didn't reply.

Lily just smiled, opened the screen door and held it for Gen.

It wasn't the Big House, it was only a screened porch she had never been in, yet, Geneva could see the old kitchen and breakfast room beyond, the beaded-wood walls still painted white with green trim, grape leaves stenciled at ceiling height, with two-dimensional clusters of green and red grapes clinging to the stems. She spotted her mother's crystal goblets behind high glass cabinet doors, and a silver punch bowl and ladle. Old belongings in new places.

Gen could almost see her mother standing at the center aisle, giving orders to take down the crystal and polish the silver. Unexpected grief welled up.

Della bustled onto the porch, her width filling the doorway, breaking the spell. She paused, her eyes on Gen and Lily, a tray of sweating glasses before her, her face wreathed in a jubilant smile.

"Lordy, Lord-a-Moses. I got my two girls back together again. Praise be." She slid the tray onto the table and gathered Geneva into her arms.

Hugging Della, Gen buried her face in the big woman's shoulder, let her burdens slide to the floor and closed her eyes.

Della smelled of baking and Avon Roses Roses perfume and Baby Powder. She smelled like all the good things that Louisiana represented, the few good memories Geneva had of home. And then she caught herself. Louisiana was *not* home. Not now. Not ever again.

She moved back from Della's grasp. To lessen the seeming rejection, Gen stared at Della and stroked the old woman's face, the way she had as a child, palms on either side of the wide black cheeks. "Della, you haven't changed. Not one whit. Still the buxom beauty." Della snorted, pleasure evident in her dark eyes. "You haven't found you a man to replace that husband of yours?" Geneva asked.

"One man in a lifetime is a gracious plenty, child. I done buried one, what I need another man for? More trouble than they's worth most times. Sit yourself down and drink some tea," she said, pushing Gen to a chair and flipping a switch that started the ceiling fan's slow rotation. "I 'bout had me a conniption fit when I seen you slide down that ramp and hit the pavement, that plane on its bottom-side and all. Here," she placed a napkin on Geneva's leg and a glass in front of her, "you drink some this tea and get back your strength while we talk a spell. Lily, I got you some tea without sugar brewing on the stove like you ask't for, but how you drink that nasty stuff with all them artificial sweeteners is beyond me. Here's you a glass 'til it be ready, that nasty stuff. My Geneva here drinking hers like God meant it to be drank, all sugared up just fine."

It had been years since Gen had swallowed sweet tea, but it was delicious, cold and sugary and just minty enough, with a crushed mint leaf drowned in the bottom of the glass. She wouldn't have admitted to drinking unsweetened tea for love nor money, not with Della smiling across from her, settling her bulk into a cushioned chair and drinking down a big gulp of her own tea.

"Now. You tell old Della why you done left that good looking man you married."

Geneva choked and started coughing.

Ignoring the ruckus Gen made as she spluttered into her napkin, Della went right on. "I was shamed to my soul to see your face all over the *Enquirer* in the checkout line, you with that *boy-toy* of yours. He must be all of twelve years old. And you can't tell me he ain't at least part black. He too pretty to be white all together."

Della shook her finger in Gen's face. "The Good Lord mean for black folks to be sleeping with white, then He'd a made us all tan. And if you robbing the cradle with that child, then you ain't no child I raised up, no ma'am. I taught you better, I did."

Lily watched, her black eyes falsely innocent, as Gen composed herself. Glaring at her sister before answering her old nanny, Gen said, "Joachim is my assistant and protégé, Della. You've seen pictures of him a dozen of times. I can't help it if the *Enquirer* decided that I was sleeping with him. They agreed to print a retraction, and it'll be in next month's issue. Besides, Jo is *gay*, Della, I told you that. He has a significant other . . . or two or three."

Della shook her head. "Right is right and wrong is wrong. Period. That boy should be shamed, doing abominations in the sight of the Lord."

Geneva had no intention of discussing alternative lifestyles with Della. "I am not sleeping with him."

"You ain't?"

Lily hid her amusement in her tea glass, sweet with sugar or not. Lily had to have known this was coming. She was enjoying it too much.

"No. I ain't."

"Don't you be getting sassy with me, missy." Della's dark eyes glittered dangerously.

"I am not being sassy. I am standing up for the truth in the face of lies just like you taught me to."

"And don't you be quoting me back at me. Good. I knew you wasn't sleeping with no boy. I done told Esmee that, and I'm proud you be confirming it for me." Della bobbed her head once, smartly, and drank most of her tea in one satisfied gulp. "I know you a good gal, you is."

"And Jo isn't black, Della. He's half Thai, half Puerto Rican, his mother is from Thailand and his father is in the Navy."

"Bet his daddy be shamed 'bout him, too. Right is right and wrong is wrong," Della said, and that closed the dual subjects of race and homosexuality. "Now you tell me about your Barry."

Gen looked down at her tea, letting the silence stretch. She had told no one about Barry except her attorney, and then it had taken all the strength she had just to say the words without sobbing like some heartbroken teenager. She couldn't find the words to explain now. She couldn't even find the words to lie, not even enough to satisfy Della. Barry had done the unspeakable, and the words lodged in her throat now, just like every other time she had thought she might open up and let out the misery. After all, as Della had said, right is right, and wrong is wrong. And Barry had done wrong.

Della patted her hand, her plump fingers moist and chilled from the tea glass. "Never you mind, child. Never you mind. You tell Della when you can. I can see it hurt too much just now."

The lump in Geneva's throat grew and she drank tea, forcing chilled liquid past the pain. There were compensations to being home. Della and Lily made the broken vow worthwhile. If only she didn't have to see the Old Man, then it would be fine. Once again she cursed the fact that he had chosen to die slowly of cancer instead of some massive stroke or heart attack or being hit by a bus. But then, he had never done a single thing in life the way the girls wanted, so why should he die as they wanted?

A cat appeared from nowhere and jumped into Gen's lap. She was so surprised that her pain vanished. "A *cat* !"

"That be Princess. She a tabby, and she showed up down to the barn last year. She took up with Mr. John when he got sick."

Princess rubbed her head under Geneva's chin, a soft purr rumbling. The sound was soothing and Gen rubbed the cat down her long length as she preened, then rolled over in Gen's lap, exposing her belly for all the world like a submissive dog.

"Seem like she know when people be hurting and she jump up and rub on them like that. Curious thing is, most folks seem to like her, even Mr. John. I thought he'd a killed a cat soon as look at one, but he took to Princess just fine."

"She sleeps on the foot of the Old Man's bed, believe it or not," Lily said, contributing to the conversation for the first time in minutes.

"I gots your old room fixed up for you, Ginny, child."

Gen blinked tears from her eyes and stroked the cat, who batted her hand with four paws and wriggled deeper into her lap. "I don't want to stay in the Big House, Della. I took a hotel room near the airport for the night."

Without looking up, Gen could hear the censure in the silence. The overhead fan ticked unsteadily, like a drunken clock. Late sun slid in under the eaves, brightening the porch.

Della drummed her fingers on the tabletop. She said, "No child a mine be staying at no hotel. No ma'am." Her words were firm and rigid, set in Della's right-and-wrong tones, her belief system like a post in concrete.

"I'm not staying here, Della. I'm just not." Geneva had not intended to drive back into town and stay at the hotel, not really. But during the last few minutes of conversation, she had found inside herself an ancient misery, a loathing of staying here. Loathing born of fear and too much time and . . . . She couldn't sleep under the same roof as the Old Man. She simply could not.

She wondered why Starnes hadn't waited. He could have driven her back. She could have ordered him to. A half smile pulled at her mouth. He didn't take kindly to orders. Some of their best fights had been over her orders. She hadn't seen him in twenty-nine years, and suddenly she missed him. Had to be rebound attraction. Had to be.

"She could stay in the guesthouse," Lily said. Gen looked up. "I thought about staying there, but decided that the possibility of rats wasn't worth not breaking our vow."

She remembered the guesthouse, a square of a place, not much bigger than a deluxe hotel room in New York, no kitchen, no phone, and not much of a bath, if she remembered it right. But the small house stood alone at the edge of the lawn, and it had its own lock and key. And it wasn't the Big House. "I could stay there. Maybe."

Della snorted and poured more tea from a glass pitcher. "That old place been closed up for near 'bout two years. And my knees got the rheumatism, so don't you be thinking I'm gonna clean it up for you. No ma'am. Ain't right, you staying there when you should be sleeping in your room." But her tone was accommodating, and Gen knew that Della had already half-agreed to the compromise.

"The guesthouse or the hotel, Della. I can't stay here."

Della sighed, her belly moving ponderously with disgust. "I get me a cleaning girl to come out in the morning and give the place a going over. Till then, you just have to deal with the dust. And I ain't making no promises 'bout no mice and no roaches. Place been sprayed last spring along with the Big House, but it ain't been lived in. Probably a mess and a half."

"I'll survive. The room I took in New York when I first left home had rats the size of small cats, and roaches almost big enough to eat the rats. Besides, no rat is much of a bother after you've seen a rabid nutria or two."

Della laughed and launched into the tale of the sisters and the twenty-pound, mating nutrias she had "saved" them from back in the late sixties. "You babies so young you be thinking they crazy with the rabies and they just making baby nutria is all. Hee heeee," she slapped her thigh, "Funniest thing I ever did see. It shor-ly was. Ahhh. It a proud pleasure to have my babies home at last." She sparkled, looking from Lily to Geneva as she fanned her glistening face. "It be a *proud* pleasure."

◆ ◆ ◆

Starnes stepped into the johnboat and paused as pain from the old injury shot down his leg and up the length of his spine. Lightning agony. He balanced on one foot as the slim, shallow-draft boat waffled in the still water and the muscle spasm slowly began to recede. He had managed to walk without a limp all afternoon, but the discomfort was growing now.

Standing on one foot, he caught the faint stink of polecat and dead fish, common scents on the bayou, ordinarily scarcely noticed. Today there was something unpleasant in the smells. He wrinkled his nose at the reek.

Carefully, deliberately moving with a calm he did not feel, Starnes eased into the boat with his full weight and the pain finally subsided to its customary, bearable level. Stowing the last of his gear, he settled into the bottom of the small craft. There was more room than usual in the hull. No camping gear. He had decided not to remain in the basin overnight, planning to return home to the answering service and possible messages. Stupid, when Serena had been on her best behavior for so many weeks and there were no pressing cases, but there you have it. The very fact of her uncommonly calm temperament was unsettling.

Starnes scratched at his twelve-hour-beard, the skin itching as tough bristles pushed through to the surface. Pulling his weekly cigar from his pocket, He peeled the cellophane off the greenish-brown tobacco. With his bush-knife, he trimmed the end of the Griffen Corona. Lighting the thin cigar was pure ecstasy, the first whiff of smoke like burning bliss in his lungs. The heady scent of the tobacco overpowered the lesser bayou smells. The smoke displaced the dregs of his anger, and a measure of peace came over him as the aromatic leaves caught. He gripped the cigar in his teeth, pulling strongly on the fine tobacco, sheathing the bush-knife's twelve-inch blade, and braking open the 12-guage shotgun. Both barrels held rifle-shot, and two extra shells were in his front shirt pocket just in case.

The day was nearly gone; the afternoon glare so bright it blinded. Soon the light would change to pale pink, then red, the light spilling across the bayou like blood. Beneath the dock, fish nosed at the surface of the water, making rings that glistened like silver. Almost against his will, Starnes glanced back at Serena's rooms, the small apartment added onto the house fifteen years ago. The lights were off. No music moaned from the speakers he had installed for her. Either his sister had slept all day—a rarity—or she hadn't bothered to come home last night.

Starnes turned away from the darkened house. *"Bon à rien,"* he muttered, the old, helpless feeling rising in his chest. *Good for nothing* . . . the words the judge had used the last time he turned Serena over to Starnes' care.

He re-secured his supplies; easel and paints were loaded in the pirogue tied behind his johnboat, along with fishing gear, late lunch or supper, a six-pack of beer, and a gallon of fresh water in an ice-filled chest. Prudently, he wrapped the shotgun and extra ammo in a waterproof case. They would do him little good against pesky alligators if they happened to get soaked. Another case protected camera and film, which he used if the weather changed, forcing him to finish a painting at home.

As was his usual practice, Starnes was heading into the swamp to paint, leaving behind all his civil cases, legal minutiae, and personal, family problems. Three days a week he forgot the world and disappeared into the Atchafalaya River Basin in search of wildlife and exotic flora to paint. Three days to call his own. Three days he owed to no one, not even Serena.

And certainly not to Geneva Deveraux Stone. He was a fool to have gone to the airport today. Twenty kinds of fool. He sucked a deep breath of fragrant smoke into his lungs, fighting his anger.

With a single, quick motion, he pulled the starter cord. The twenty-five horsepower motor roared to life and he tossed the mooring line onto the dock, pulled into the black water and moved with the current down the bayou. Tugging the rim of his hat down over his brow, Starnes adjusted it against the slight breeze and the blazing light. Smoke curled beneath the rim and into his eyes, burning a moment before the wind whipped it away. Though it was late, he intended to paint, and if a whispery voice kept insisting he do something else, be someplace else, especially tonight, he would ignore it.

There was always the problem of Serena, intruding into his thoughts, his free time, costing him money, sleep, and peace of mind, but today there was also Gen. Despite the old anger, a strange frission of warmth stirred through him at the thought of her, a sweeping heat. A schoolboy reaction, full of unsatisfied lust and old dreams. There were some things he had never been very reasonable about. Perhaps Gen headed that list. As the current strengthened, he sucked deeply on the cigar, its glowing tip lighting the way into the wilderness wetlands as the muddy water began to glisten with pink light.

Starnes had earned the right to paint, with seven high profile, successful civil lawsuits against five national companies, as well as a host of smaller claims. At thirty percent plus expenses, he had enough invested to live any way he wished, work only when and for whom he wished, and paint three days a week. He had made his name as an attorney in the civil courts several times over. Now he had begun to find success in his wildlife paintings as well, making a name in artistic circles, following a small showing in a New Orleans art gallery. He deserved his time off. And yet, today, in a special waterproof case, he carried his pager and cell phone. And resisted the urge to turn them off or toss them overboard.

Starnes wasn't sure if he hated himself more for bringing the pager and phone with him, or for going to paint without checking Serena's rooms or calling to see how Gen was doing. She had been white as a sheet when she entered the terminal. "*Bon à rien,*" he said again, this time thinking of himself. "And twenty kinds of fool."

In the distance he heard a loon cry, the call piercing over the low roar of the small craft, and clenching the Corona firmly in his teeth, he laughed, lips moving on the damp tobacco. It was fitting. A loon and Starnes Templer on the water together. He checked his pager and the phone as he advanced slowly into the wastelands. There'd been no calls. Feeling as if he was missing something vital, Starnes gunned the little motor.

Two hours later, the johnboat tied off upstream, the sun beginning its final descent into the marsh around him, Starnes studied baby gators hiding among the rushes. They poked thin snouts above the water, trails of their breath making miniature furrows across the surface, then ducked down, paddling quickly to another location to breathe again. On shore, almost hidden in the lengthening shadows, the mother gator watched him with half-shut eyes, unmoving, gauging this menace-in-a-pirogue.

She was only five feet long and skinny, not much of a danger to him had he been in the johnboat. But even her small length could capsize a pirogue should she decide he was a problem. Belly-down in the black mud of the shore, lying beneath a snowball tree in full bloom, she was the femme fatale of gators. Brownish-green scales like armor, several wicked teeth visible along the curve of her lip, eyes a slow, seductive, half-hostile stare, delicate white snowball petals scattered across her. She looked like a bride on her wedding day.

Starnes had taken a dozen shots of her snoozing in the mire, the reptile watchful but unafraid, before he spotted the tiny gators in the shallow water. Now he had a full roll of 35mm film of the fast-moving babies, and mama gator was getting antsy. The tip of her tail swished once through the mud, splattering the water. Starnes interpreted this as a warning, like shots across the bow in a naval battle. If he didn't want to rile her further and risk standing knee-deep in the slow-moving muddy bayou, legs and feet in her territory with no protection but a pair of old cowhide boots, he figured he better move on. He wasn't afraid of gators, but he wasn't stupid either.

The tail swished again, this time with more force. Starnes dropped his camera into the waterproof bag, stowed it in its special canister, stuck his old hat on his sun-heated head, lifted the pole balanced along the length of the small boat, and pushed away from shore, all with an economy of motion and grace that did nothing to further alarm the mama gator. As he pulled away, the indolent alligator settled deeper into the mud and closed an eye slowly, as if winking. A sensual femme-fatale farewell. Or maybe she was just sleepy. "*Bonne chance, mamselle*," he said softly.

It took a lot of practice and excellent balance to pole a pirogue, and even among the Cajun French still surviving in bayou territory it was nearly a lost art. Young people these days didn't need to know how to move a boat with muscle power and a stick, preferring johnboats or those huge wooden airplane propeller-driven airboats that made such an awful noise. He'd like to see one of those things sneak up on a sleeping gator.

Poling was second nature to Starnes. It was accomplished standing, legs braced, arms moving with smooth, regular strokes, shoving the pole into the deep mud until the far end hit something that might be called bottom, pushing the boat along, weight distributed carefully. When the pirogue slid past, its motion pulled the shaft free of the sucking mud. If a pole-er were foolish or tired enough to lose his grip on the long spar, leaving it behind standing up in the mud, he was just up a creek. Literally. Swimming or wading after a lost pole wasn't always a wise move.

Overhead, a jet screamed by, landing lights bright against the plum-colored sky, descending toward the local airstrip. It was smaller than the 727 Gen had flown on. A corporate jet with only a few seats. Gen's plane had been filled with commuters and vacationers and businessmen not wealthy enough to travel by private jet. He could still see her, blonde hair flying as she jumped out the doorway onto the long rubber chute. She was not a part of his life anymore, hadn't been in twenty-nine years, give or take a month. Yet, Gen once was everything he had ever wanted. The one woman he had begged God for, and then lost to another man. Another life. *Gen.*

Around the next bend was his johnboat, tied off to a low-hanging branch, the current of the bayou here enough to keep the boat parallel to shore and make a small wake as it slid past the bow. Stepping onto the low bank, Starnes tied the pirogue to the johnboat's stern, and stowed the camera case safely in the side wale. *Gen's camera*, he remembered. The one she had gifted him with when her father had given her the fancy new Nikon for her sixteenth birthday. What in hell was he still doing using her castoffs?

Starnes sighed. Gen was home. Had been on Louisiana soil less than half a day and already he was angry at her. And what was he going to do about it? About her? He lifted his pager from the dry-packet where he'd left it when he poled upstream and checked the LCD readout. Two messages. He expected neither one to be from Gen. Remembering Serena's dark apartment, he knew who had tried to reach him. It was the Sheriff's Department, both calls. Two more were on his cell phone.

Straddling the bench seat of the johnboat, he punched in the number, identified himself and waited as the dispatcher connected him. Instead of a hello or a name, the voice on the other end drawled, "*Alle est fou*, your sister. Caraaaazy in her head, she is for sure. *Ça c'est honteux.*"

Gut tight, Starnes said, "What she do this time, L'ron?"

"Mebe you best come down to the station *dis* time," the deputy said, accenting the heavy Cajun of his forebears. "Serena a pretty girl, but she need to keep her clothes on more, yes. Like when she in Catholic church for Mass." As if L'ron could hear the frustration building in Starnes' chest, he laughed. "*Ça fait pas rien*, bo. I got her dressed and down to the station, sleepin' it off in back. No harm done, no charges filed. This time."

The breath wheezed out of Starnes in relief, only to hear L'ron add slyly, "But the good Father, he want you to come talk to him 'bout her. Soon."

3
J'AI PAS FOU, NO ME

Starnes tossed the bag of fried boudin balls onto L'ron's desk, and set a sweating six-pack of iced home-brewed beer beside them, no labels, just plain brown mismatched bottles in an old root beer box. Grease had soaked through the bag in circles, and the mouthwatering scent of fried peppers, dough, whole-hog meat, and rice that comprised the balls filled up the room.

"This a bribe?" L'ron drawled, his hazel eyes narrowed in amusement.

"My dinner. Still hot from Old Lady Foulcard's big iron kettle." Starnes pulled a slatted chair across the worn-out linoleum and sat, throwing one booted foot onto L'ron's desk and twisting open the top of a beer, which he half-drained in a long pull. "You welcome to join me though. Hate to eat alone. Does something to my digestion."

He pulled his sweat-damp hat off and tossed it to the desktop. Lifting a boudin ball, Starnes cradled it in a paper napkin and handed it to Sergeant L'ron Rebardi. *"Tchens, prend lé."* Here, take it.

"I'd hate to ruin *l'estomac* of the parish's finest attorney-at-law," L'ron said, biting into the still-warm crust and sucking in the juice-filled rice and spiced meat. As Starnes had closed the door when he entered, L'ron opened a beer, poured the iced dark brew into a plastic cup sitting on his desk, and sucked the foam with an appreciative glance. The empty went back into the box. "Heaven inna bottle," he said after the first taste. "Sheriff and Captain Freyouz are working up some crispy critters and I can't leave the station tonight. Supper was delivery pizza or tacos from Bessie's Hot Tamales." He stuffed the rest of the boudin ball into his mouth and moaned with pleasure. *"Mon Dieu,* dis good."

"Just feeding my favorite cousin."

Once he swallowed, L'ron said, "So far removed we can't

count back that far, bo. Six cousin t'ree times remove, it was?"

"Third cousins, twice removed. Marry my sister like you should have twenty years ago, and that would be a different story," Starnes said with a boudin-filled grin.

"*J'ai pas fou*, no me."

Starnes swallowed the boudin and drank down more beer. Any man would have been a fool to marry his crazy sister. It no longer hurt to hear one say so.

"Not that I didn't love her, you unn'erstan'. Still do," L'ron added complacently. "Take care a her when I can, protect her when I can," he shrugged slightly, a very Gaelic motion, his eyes on the food. "But a man got to protect his cajones, *oui*? And if a woman be crazy in de head and bite off one man's ding-dong, den she mebe crazy 'nough do it again, *oui*?"

Starnes shrugged. Serena's history was well known in the parish. For a while, in the entire state. When a woman bites off three inches of a man's privates while experiencing a schizophrenic episode, it kinda makes the news. The fact that his sister hadn't done hard time for the removal of Deon Hoffpauir's manhood made it difficult for at least half the parish to forget, ameliorating circumstances notwithstanding. "She was in love with you."

"And sleeping with half the town." L'ron pointed to the bag, questioning.

"Help yourself. They don't reheat well." Starnes opened another beer and finished it off as fast as the first. L'ron finished off his second, again hiding the beer in the plastic cup. Aged with locust-seed pods for flavor, the homemade beer brewed by Foulcard's husband was the best in the parish, the seeds making the beer rich and mellow. But Foulcard paid no taxes, ran an unlicensed brewery, and was therefore technically illegal. Not to mention hard to find, buried deep in bayou country. As a law enforcement officer, L'ron couldn't buy the best beer in the parish. Starnes could. And if the meal could be viewed as a bribe, it was a small one by Louisiana standards.

"Crispy critters?" he questioned. At L'ron's blank look he added, "The sheriff is looking for them."

L'ron's eyes slid away again. Something in the gesture set off warning bells in Starnes. "Report of a burned-out car near Le Cou

Bayou," he said, his voice carefully unconcerned. "Two men inside. Dismember before they burn, they was." L'ron chewed, his attention on the closed door beyond Starnes. "Track lead off to bayou. Small man. Wearing boots. Or woman." L'ron didn't meet his eyes for a long moment.

"Woman?"

L'ron nodded slowly, biting into a boudin ball with intense concentration. "Yea."

"Serena. Was she . . . had she been in boots? Before she took off her clothes?"

"No shoes in confession box. Barefoot she was."

Starnes' tension eased fractionally, watching his friend. "And?"

"And I don't think it her. Not what kill them boys. Sheriff say boot prints, they press in the char, over top of it. Coulda been the killer checking out he work, after-like, or someone else coulda found them nex' day, take a look, then walk away. Petite Serena, not the one take out two big boy like they was. Sheriff Pritchard, he agree. Captain Freyouz, he not so sure. And they find two, t'ree long black hair in de wood nearby. A hat on de ground in de trees."

Starnes looked at the greasy bag, feeling sick. "People, other officers, are saying as how it could be her. Yes?"

L'ron wiped his mouth on a brown napkin and belched. "Freyouz, he mebe problem, *oui*. People talk. That never change." He looked up, his gaze piercing. "You think any mo' 'bout puttin' her in a halfway house? Kind we talk 'bout befo, kind what mental patients stay in?"

Starnes chewed a moment, now the one avoiding L'ron's eyes, despising the way everyone in town always thought they had a right to discuss Serena's treatment and future. He was her brother. And though he once had walked away from that responsibility, he had since shouldered it. Everyone else should just butt out.

But this was L'ron, the cop who both loved Serena and looked out after her. Starnes owed him many times over, so instead of telling his old friend off like he wanted, Starnes swallowed down the decades-old resentment and answered honestly. But even he could hear the defensive tone, the barely restrained hostility in his voice.

"She was doing better. Didn't seem to need a halfway house, and frankly, she didn't want it." He smeared greasy hands and mouth on one of the thin napkins that had come with the meal, fighting the bitterness, the remorse, and the humiliation that these kind of conversations always brought him.

"And then there's the fact that she's slippery as a catfish on a hook. She promised to walk away if I put her in a halfway house."

"You got to do something 'bout her. She outta control again."

Starnes speared L'ron with his eyes and the cop sat back slowly, withdrawing from the fierce gaze. "So what am I supposed to do, L'ron? Shackle her to her bed? I'd get put in jail for that one. Have her picked up by mental health a dozen times a year? Been down that route and it didn't work, she only got worse. Walk off and let her fall flat on her face? Just what the hell am I supposed to do with Serena, L'ron? Tell me."

The cop slowly tilted his head, pondering the dilemma of a family with such a problem. There was no pity in his eyes, no condemnation of the way Starnes had handled his "problem" sister for so many years, just an acceptance of the situation as Starnes had stated it.

And somehow, the cop's matter-of-fact manner brought Starnes a measure of calm. Unexpectedly, his resentment faded. Looking away from the mild hazel eyes, Starnes drank more beer, fulfilling his body's need for action, any kind of action.

As if choosing his words carefully, L'ron said, "Co-dependent, you. Lettin' Serena run you life."

Starnes lifted his brows, amused. He hadn't expected to hear L'ron use a psycho-babble catchphrase. "Been watching Oprah, have you?" he asked, his tone biting.

L'ron looked away, a half smile pulling at his mouth, accepting the rebuke. "Dr. Phil."

Starnes snorted with mirth. Pulling the afternoon's unfinished cigar from its special plastic case, he trimmed both ends carefully with the bush-knife and took his time re-lighting. Because he only allowed himself one imported Griffen 500 Corona a week, it had special significance, and wasn't something he ever hurried. Strong smoke from the full-bodied leaves filled the small office. The sergeant breathed deeply in appreciation, holding in the heady, spicy flavor of the cigar, waiting out the small ritual.

After he breathed out, L'ron said, "Her off her pills again."

Starnes stilled, hands on beer and cigar momentarily motionless. Smoke curled around his fingers like a lover. "She say that to you?"

L'ron half shrugged. "She had a whole t'ree bottle a pill in her purse. Never open, dem, look like to me, but I don't tell that the sheriff, you unnerstan'?"

Starnes pulled on the tobacco, the implication clear. L'ron was protecting Serena from the sheriff's suspicion. Considering her history, that could be a mistake.

"She say she well now, don' need no medication no more." A twinkle abruptly returned to L'ron's eyes and his mouth turned up at the corners. "*Pooyah-ee*, but she one crazy gal. Go to confession and stay for mass. Come out the box buck nekkid, she done, and walk herself right up to Father Tony. Kiss him on the mouth before all the old ladies. They be talking 'bout this one long time come."

Starnes sighed, crumpled the empty bag and slammed it in the trash, as if his problems could be tossed away with the garbage. "And Father Tony called you, you came to pick her up, and took care of her. Like always."

L'ron grinned, his big horse-teeth white in his darkly tanned face. "Like always. Sometime it seem like my part-time job," he agreed, the twinkle firmly in his eyes. "I got to say, Serena, she a fine body for a woman her age. Fine body, *oui.*"

Starnes wanted to laugh, and instead said dryly, "There are some things I don't need to know."

"*Pooyah-ee*, 'nuff to make a priest sin."

Starnes shook his head. "Spare me. Can I take her home now?"

L'ron rose and knocked Starnes' foot from his desk. "Now a good time as any. And, nex' time you want bring a bribe, make it one a those ceegars. Some e-le-gan' smoke that be, yes."

Serena was awake, sitting on the edge of the bunk in the back of the station house, walkman earphones draped around her neck, the tinny sound of some punk group buzzing like angry bees, black hair falling forward across her face like a shroud until she raised her head.

The room in the building housing both the Moisson PD, the Sheriff's Department, and the parish lockup, was for emergencies, times when an officer was kicked out of the house and needed a temporary place to sleep, times when a rare investigation was taking its toll and a man needed a few hours down time but couldn't leave the station, times when an important "prisoner" needed a place to sleep off a drunk without his presence being put on the books. Serena fit the last concept of an emergency, her eyes red-rimmed, hair disheveled, jeans ripped and muddy. She hadn't worn a bra in years, her small breasts still pert, poking out against the old T-shirt she wore.

"Serena?"

She pulled off the headphones. "Well if it isn't my avenging angel and my brother dearest, both here to rescue me." She held up a hand, lady-in-distress style and smiled at them.

Returning her smile, L'ron moved to take the hand. The sergeant assisted her to her feet and tenderly smoothed back her hair. She might be crazy, with the morals of an alley cat, but something about her was still desirable in L'ron's eyes.

Starnes stood in the door, his cigar held in a hand against the doorjamb on the outside, his head inside the room, and sniffed. The smell of smoke was faint, but distinct. Not campfire smoke. Not the cordite of gun smoke, or even cigarette smoke. Something else. Something putrid and oily with a hint of gasoline underlying it all. Human flesh?

He remembered the two crispy critters.

Entering the room, he reached for her purse on the floor at her feet, opened it and poured out the contents onto the small cot. The three bottles of pills clattered to the thin mattress. Blowing a stream of smoke, Starnes lifted and shook each bottle in turn, the sound like angry rattlers in the small room.

Serena abandoned L'ron's ministrations, watching her brother instead, her black eyes hollowed, full lips stretched tight. Starnes opened the bottles, poured out the proper dosage from each and handed the pills to her. Without a word, his sister took them and tossed them back, swallowing the handful dry, from long practice. It was a talent, that.

"Where are your boots?" he asked.

"Lost. On bayou somewhere. Last week sometime," she added, the Cajun accent she had never tried to lose, faint but unmistakable in the rhythms of her speech.

"You been barefoot since then?"

"Sandals," she said slowly, as if thinking. "In the back of Father Tony's car," her eyes lit slyly with the words, "where we left them."

"*Tais-toi!*" L'ron shouted, pulling back his hand as if it burned where he touched her. "You don' say that 'bout the Holy Father!"

"Say what?" Serena shrugged, the movement calculated to move her breasts beneath the thin T-shirt. "I was thumbing down to Byglass Road. He offer me a ride to confession, an I accept. Left them in his car. Ask him, you. Why? You think I meant something else, mebe?"

L'ron turned and stomped from the room, frustrated with Serena's antics. In the outer office, Starnes heard another beer being opened, the soft hiss of escaping carbonation. His sister was enough to drive anyone to drink, even a cop on duty. "Let's go home."

"Don't you want to know what I was doing on Byglass Road?" she asked, her face still hard with calculating amusement.

"No. I don't. What I want is for you to take your medication and stop acting like a. . . ." The word nearly slipped out. The hated word. The word that had destroyed his sister's life so long ago.

Serena's eyes flickered. "Just say *whore*, Starnes. It's what I am."

"It's *not* what you are," he said savagely, the words and the argument an old theme that never seemed to die away. "It never has been. You can't help what was done to you."

"That's not what Daddy said."

"Daddy's been dead a long time."

She smiled sweetly. "Yes. He has been."

Starnes shuddered, the words freezing through him, just as she had intended. Though he tried to control his expression, he didn't quite achieve the wooden look he wanted. He never could hide his emotions from Serena; she pulled strings and he danced, just like always. His sister watched him, her eyes lit with brutal humor. Finally he ground out, "You didn't kill our father."

"Didn't I?" she taunted.

Starnes turned away. "Let's go home Serena."

◆　◆　◆

His breath stopped as he watched the big 727 from New York descend through the murky Louisiana sky, landing gear clearly still captured in her belly. With a quick flick of a finger, he hit a button on the remote and the TiVo blinked on, recording Gen's landing on the ten o'clock news. The landing looked worse—much worse—on film. He leaned closer, his throat constricting as he watched. The Coors can in his hand tilted to one side, forgotten.

The flaps went down, the plane pitched in the air, seeming to bend in the middle. Watching through the airport window, from a distance, he had seen the plane stagger. It must have been a sickening lurch for the passengers. Then, gently, the big silver beast slowed and dropped, wings outspread. And she touched down. It was a beautiful landing, as smooth and clean as if the plane had landed on a down pillow instead of fire retardant foam. He found he could breathe again.

At his feet, Bubba-Boy watched the can with predator eyes, hoping it would tilt just a bit too far and a quick tongue would have a chance to lap up the spill. Bubba liked beer, and upon a rare occasion, Starnes let the big dog have a slurp or two. Spoiled dog.

Moments later, the first passenger stood, clearly outlined in the doorway, caught in the reporter's telephoto lens. *Ginny*, laughing, jumping into the chute, blonde hair flying. She reached bottom, was caught by a fireman in yellow and orange and helped to her feet. Still smiling, she bent, pulled a pair of sandals from her blouse and put them on before making the trek to the terminal. Starnes laughed with relief again, as he had when she first landed, and sat back in his couch. Air whistled from the soft, worn leather.

Unlike the slightly gawky teenager she had been, this Gen was elegant. Poised. His stomach clenched with unexpected memories, and he set the can on the small table at his side, the weeping Coors centered in a series of darkened water rings.

Geneva Deveraux had crash-landed in an airplane, made the evening news, then ordered him around as if he were her servant, still the girl he knew from so long ago. She always had made a spectacular entrance. It was something rich girls just seemed to know how to do, and *Ginny'd* had the ability down pat. When she walked into a room she took it and the people in it over as if they belonged to her alone, even when she was just a kid.

For him, growing up in Moisson, Gen had been a fantasy almost realized for a time and then lost, a flight of self-deception, a childhood dream, like becoming a billionaire, or a movie star, or an astronaut. Something for a poor boy to finally put away. But as he watched her jump into the emergency chute, laughing and unafraid, he realized that he had been deceiving himself. He had never fully put *Ginny* from his mind. Somewhere down inside him, she still ruled, just as she did when she walked into a room.

He hadn't known he was going to pick her up until Lily had barged into the Old Man's sickroom and pulled him out by a sleeve. Told him the kids needed to pick up their aunt and he was elected to drive them to New Orleans. In the hurry of leaving, he hadn't put the idea of Destan's and Keri's aunt together with Gen. And once he knew the news about the plane in trouble had driven from his mind any thoughts about what her return would mean. He had been frantic, trying to hide his own fear from the kids.

And then she had stood there, in front of him, sweaty, disheveled, her feet bare. And she had met his eyes, full on, the power of her gray gaze like being hit by a granite landslide. He punched buttons and watched again the sickening midair jerk and the landing.

Starnes drank down the Coors, his fourth beer of the day, an unaccustomed overabundance, and considered his feelings for Geneva Deveraux Stone in light of the mild alcoholic haze clouding his mind. Okay, so it was obsessive/compulsive behavior to want a woman for so many years. It was nuts.

Starnes laughed softly in the silent room. *Ça c'est triste. So sad.* Just like his sister, he was a little bit crazy. Bubba-Boy whined, clicked her nails on the wood floor to draw his attention. Moving with exaggerated care, Starnes dribbled a small amount of beer on the floor and watched the dog slurp it up as he popped the top of a fifth beer and decided that he could live with that thought. Being a little bit crazy. It wouldn't be the first time he had been called crazy; lawyers all across the state had called him crazy at one time or another.

On the screen, Gen jumped from the plane, hair flying up in a single swooping wave. She was so fresh and alive and so...

normal. Just like he remembered her. Beautiful and bossy as hell.

Music moaned from the speakers in Serena's rooms, soft and mournful. Normal Gen again jumped from the plane. Gen in contrast to Serena, his sister, who wasn't normal.

Starnes turned up the TV's sound. For half an hour as he finished off the last of six beers, he toured other stations, taping Gen's descent from the downed plane and her trek through the mob of reporters. She wasn't the eighteen-year-old child-woman he had known. Maybe she was someone else entirely now. But whoever she was, whatever she had become, she was intriguing, this vibrant woman who threw herself down an emergency chute, laughing and so full of life.

In the distance, his personal line rang, the four muted peels sounding before the machine picked up. Recognizing the female voice as Lindsay, he considered getting up. Instead, he watched *Ginny* take her jump again. And again. Finally, images of Gen firmly in place, he rose and went to the darkroom. The baby gators and their mama were waiting. He had hours of work to do. It was too late to go see Geneva. She needed a chance to unwind from her day. At least that was what he told himself.

4

WORKED ROSES & CUTTING SADDLE

Mosquitoes buzzed threateningly around her head, fireflies traced yellow-green arcs in the darkness, two horses whuffed and blew in the night air, their forms barely discernable as a white star and six white stockings beyond the split-rail fencing. The scent of bug repellent, manure, and distant bayou created a familiar perfume. The sights and sounds and scents of the estate made Gen ache with a quiet pain she had not expected.

She pushed off with her toe, sending the swing creaking a few inches forward and back. Across the expanse of sculpted lawn, a light glowed in a bedroom window of the estate house, a TV screen flickering as someone changed channels restlessly. It was the Old Man's room. Strange to see television in a house where it had always been banned. The sheers on either side of the window fluttered in the breeze proving that the window was open, as always, and most likely against doctor's orders. The Old Man had slept with the window open his whole life. Some things hadn't changed.

Two rooms down, a light came on, stayed on a moment, revealing bright yellow walls and a highboy, and then went dark. Lily's room. Her sister was back in the fold, just where the Old Man had always wanted them both. Gen wouldn't have been surprised to discover that the cancer was a hoax designed to get them home. She would put nothing past the Old Man. Again the light in Lily's room came on, and went off almost instantly.

The room between Lily's and the Old Man's remained unlit. It had once been the nursery, filled with the unrelenting, colicky cries of a baby. Carefully, Gen turned her thoughts away from that room. Now was not the time to remember certain things about the past. Perhaps *never* would even be too soon. Yet, she had to face the Old Man sometime. Tomorrow. And then there would be no respite from the memories. From the past in all its faded misery.

The mosquitoes were becoming unbearable, darting at her eyes, into her nose with each breath, creating havoc at her ears. Slapping her hands, Gen shook herself free of the blood suckers and entered the guesthouse. It was dusty and musty, the air close and stifling. Princess lay on the foot of her bed, sleeping, curled into a furry tricolor mass. Gen stripped off her jeans with economical grace and crawled between the clean sheets she had brought over from the Big House.

Instantly, she was asleep, the calls of night birds entering uneasy dreams, blending with old memories, sounding like a baby and lullabies and ancient fear. When she cried out in her sleep hours later, Princess curled close to her face and purred peacefully, the sound seeming to calm her restive slumber. The tabby was still purring softly when Gen awoke, cat fur tickling her face, a cold nose poking her cheek.

"I guess I should be glad you didn't want to sleep on my face," Gen groaned. Princess jumped from the bed and stretched with a feline grace that made Gen feel old. "Thanks, cat. I really needed that." The cat walked to the door and stood, tail twitching, her eyes glowing-green-orbs in the early, pre-dawn light. Gen crawled from the bed and pushed open the screen door she had forgotten to latch. Less than twelve hours back in Louisiana and already her New York survival skills were forgotten. Released, the cat vanished in the gray light.

Sun-touched clouds hovered over the barn, brightening the dark horizon. For the first time in days, a smile that she didn't have to consciously plant lit Gen's face. The horses were gathered at the barn, snorting and stamping, tails twitching, waiting for breakfast, dark milling forms in the pinkening light. Gen shook her jeans, hoping that any roaches or spiders that had taken up residence in the denim overnight would let go and fly. She would have to remember that she was not at home in her New York loft anymore, bug-free for her to drop clothing any place she liked, but rather, in the bug infested South, where critters were happiest when they lived in your clothes and chewed on tender flesh. Dressed, she scrubbed her face, brushed her teeth, grabbed her only pair of socks, her camera bag, and headed for the barn, bare feet in the crisp, dew covered grass.

The head groom had not yet arrived. Gen threaded her way through the barn by memory, slapping on lights in the tack room. The place was unchanged since she was here last. Same saddles on the same saddle-pegs, bridles above, blankets spread to dry, curry combs and hoof picks and jars of liniment, Copper-Tox, hydrogen peroxide, and various other chemicals lining the shelves on one wall. The huge, stained sink where she had rinsed out rags used to clean saddles and bridles. Where she had bathed the stray dog that time she had braved her father's wrath and brought one home. The dog had disappeared the next day and Gen always assumed the Old Man shot it. He hadn't cared much for dogs, except hunting dogs.

There was one newer saddle, perhaps a decade-old western, designed for range riding. Well-oiled, broken in, tan leather embossed with roses, it was clearly her father's newest seat. He had always bought saddles with roses of one kind or another worked into their surface.

She found her old saddle in its usual place. It was a cutting saddle, a three-quarters seat, called a youth saddle in some circles. It had been modified to tie saddle-bags to the back, and now a canteen and two lengths of nylon rope were coiled there. The saddle had been cared for but not loved. The leather was dark, its roses and leaves barely visible beneath layers of oil and grime.

An old pair of boots, recently oiled, rested beneath it. They looked a little large, but with the socks, not too bad. Gen banged the boots on the worn cypress floor, watching for critters who may have nested in the toes. They were clean and fit fairly well as she slid them over her narrow feet. *Keri's boots, perhaps? Not Lily's. She hated horses and riding. But are Keri's feet so big?*

Gen removed the canteen, looping its cord over a bare peg, and hefted her saddle. Taking two lead ropes with heavy thumb hooks on either end and a thick blanket, she considered the bridles and decided she would have to come back for one the right size. She laid the riding equipment out in the curry room and proceeded to open the stall doors. There were ten stalls in all, left clean from the night before. A quick count showed ten horses in the corral, milling in excitement.

Climbing the ladder to the loft, Gen split open three bales of hay and tossed a third of a bale into each stall's feedbox below before descending. Strange, how the routines of youth came back so easily. On the ground, she checked that each stall had water and found that running water had been installed in the barn at some point. The stalls had basins with clean water and drip-spouts.

While she was inspecting the stalls, a car pulled up behind the barn, ran a moment as a door opened and closed, then the engine died. Heels crunched on the gravel outside and then stomped on the packed ground of the barn entrance. Gen came out of a stall prepared to greet the head groom and met the eyes of a young girl instead. She couldn't have been more than sixteen, with black hair and blue eyes fringed all around with heavy lashes. She was slim, and wore half boots with English riding breeches and a tan tank top. She stopped, surprised.

"I'm Geneva. I used to live here."

The girl's brows went up a notch before she concealed her surprise and moved forward, right hand outstretched. It seemed that family gossip had found its way from the Big House to the help. That was a change. Twenty-nine years ago the Old Man would never have let on to anyone that there was a problem he couldn't handle. "I'm Olivia Pellissier. The head groom here at Deveraux Estates."

Geneva upgraded her age estimate to early twenties when she took the hand. The grip was firm and adult, and fine wrinkles fanned out from Olivia's eyes. "I hope you don't mind. I started without you," Gen said.

"Thanks. Remind me to show you the animal's charts so you can help whenever you want." Olivia hooked a foot across the barn railing and looked the place over, noting the saddle and the curry equipment Gen had left out. "You looking to ride this morning?" she asked with a grin.

"How could you tell? Was it the boots, the avid gleam in my eyes, or the way I salivate every time I see a horse?"

Olivia chuckled, a husky, almost intimate sound. "How long since you rode?"

"Twenty-nine years, give or take a month."

"Ouch. You are going to be one sore lady."

"Long soaky bath, a massage and some muscle rub. I'll be right as rain."

"Don't let me stop you from feeding the animals. I have a few supplements to put together while you finish up. And when you find a masseuse in this parish, let me know. . . . This isn't exactly New York." Olivia flashed a knowing grin.

"Good point," Geneva said dryly, and went back to work. She added a half-can of sweet-feed to each stall and let in the horses. They ran in the semidarkness, each to its own stall, some stopping in the doorway for a mouthful before moving on in. Unless there was a breeding mare, there was no special feed, and even if there was, Gen knew that sweet-feed would present no digestive problems.

As the horses munched, Gen added half an apple and a half-carrot to each feed bin, slicing them into quarters and three-inch lengths respectively. That was enough to keep a horse happy and—well, not exactly fat, but at least well fed—even through a particularly lean winter. As the sun rose outside, Gen looked over the horses for the mount she wanted. Most looked like Standard Bred or Quarter Horses, but there was one long-legged mare who looked like a Tennessee Walker. She was black or nearly so, with a white star and a placid gleam in her dark eyes.

The mare watched Gen as she ate and though she didn't stop eating, she whuffed gently and moved over with dainty steps as Gen entered her stall. If the painted sign on the door was right, this was Shawnee. The mare sighed contentedly as Gen curried her coat and agreeably lifted her feet to have her hooves cleaned, ears twitching peacefully. Once, Shawnee nosed Gen's hair, breathing the human scent as she scrubbed her muzzle over the blond locks. "I love you, too," Gen murmured. So much for yesterday's clean hair. Horse snot and horse spit. She had missed them both.

The sun was up by the time Gen moved out of the barn with the saddled horse, her camera bag looped around the saddle horn. She mounted at the old, pink marble mounting block. The large stone had stood in its present spot for over three hundred years, a notched marble slab brought from France in the early 1700s by the first Deveraux to emigrate to the colonies. The stone had made the trip as part of the ship's ballast, and been unloaded in the port of New Orleans in a raging hurricane; three men died getting it ashore, or so the old family legends went. It had been in the family for centuries.

There had been a time when Gen refused to use the stone to mount her horse. She had been a fire-breathing radical in her teens, and because she could leap from the ground into the saddle back then, she had disdained the use of the stone as a symbol of colonialism, slavery, and chauvinism. Now she was older, wiser, tired, and—God knows—stiffer. She used the mounting block and said an apology to the teenager whose ideals had died a slow and jaded death.

◆　◆　◆

Starnes stood at the window, nude from the waist up, his feet bare on the cool tile floor, worn jeans hanging open at his hips. The sun was up and he wasn't on the water yet. Though it upset seven years of precedent, he knew he wasn't going to paint today. He wasn't even going onto the water today, which was a sad state of affairs since yesterday had been such a bust. He had wasted the light, wasted the whole day, found little worth painting except for his gator-bride.

Later last night, he had found himself in the darkroom, staring, holding the camera in his hands because once it had belonged to her. To *Ginny*. Wasted time. Even the darkroom time had been wasted. Only a few shots of the baby gators had turned out, the rest marred by glare. Almost not worth the use of film, though Starnes knew he could paint from them. He could paint from almost anything.

Music still moaned from Serena's rooms, sounding like John Mark, the one instrumentalist composer they both loved. Mystical strains of Alhambra soughed through the house like pain and old love.

Starnes chugged orange juice straight from the carton and stared into the mottled dark. His head hurt, slightly hung over from the unaccustomed excess of beer the night before. But he wasn't painting today, so it didn't really matter. He was changing a pattern years in the making and he was too honest with himself to pretend that there was a legitimate reason for breaking his habit. Serena didn't need him today. He wasn't staying on land because of her. And Old Man Deveraux hadn't called with a new codicil to his will.

Yet, Starnes was going to the Deveraux Estate.

To see Gen.

Blood coursed through his body at the thought of seeing her. It had been twenty-nine years since he stood in the same room with her. Seen the way the sunlight streaked her hair into spun gold. Touched her hand. Starnes snorted and shook his head, feeling the too-long hair slap wetly against his face. He was acting like a teenaged boy with his first crush. He bet everything in his pockets that the woman hadn't even thought of him once in the last three decades.

Starnes swallowed down another gulp of OJ. It had been in the fridge too long and had a sour bite to it. He drank it anyway, watching the skyline brighten into a gray haze. Typical Louisiana dawn, too hot, too muggy, too full of smog, and the day had just begun. Starnes was grateful for the air-conditioning that blew up from beneath the sink, chilling his feet. The dark hair on his toes stood up from the cold.

In the office behind him, the phone rang. Starnes ignored it, watching a black bird swoop toward the water, and when the answering machine picked up, listened to the message with half an ear. The bird was too far away to determine its species. He had seen it several times and hoped to be in place one morning to capture its breakfast routine on film. When his own voice finished speaking, the tone sounded.

"I know you're not there. I don't know why I called." Lindsay paused and he heard a faint sniffle. She was crying; he'd never heard her cry. Starnes' gut clenched and he absently rubbed the long scar running down his left hip, the ridges raised and hard even after all the years. He hadn't meant to hurt her.

Carefully, he set the empty juice carton in the porcelain sink. In the distance, the black bird landed on a branch and called, hooked beak open against the pale sky. It wasn't a crow, it wasn't a raven. It didn't act like a water bird. He didn't know what it was.

"I need to talk to you. I understand that you don't want to get married. I guess I always understood that. After all, it's not like I was your first fiancée." She laughed weakly, and he could picture her, rubbing her wrist across her nose the way she did when she was upset. "But we need to talk, Starnes. We *have* to talk. So call me when you get in, please. Okay? And, Starnes, whoever she is, she's one lucky woman." The phone went dead. The black bird disappeared.

A cold nose shoved at his thigh, and Starnes scrubbed the big dog behind the ears. Lindsay's message faded like the early morning fog. "She's come home, Bubba-Boy." The dog whined in pleasure and tilted into the stroking hand.

Starnes tried to bring a vision of Gen to mind, the grownup who had jumped into the chute, the sweaty, white-faced Gen in the backseat of the car, the clean slicked-down Gen in the hotel lobby, even the Gen he had seen on the TV the night before as she ran through the gauntlet of reporters, and on a rare *People* magazine cover over the years. But the vision that leapt into his head was the memory of *Ginny* in eighth grade. Sitting near the heater one cold winter day in Mrs. . . . What was her name? Mrs. Latham. In Mrs. Latham's English class.

Jeez. He could still remember the teacher's name. He had to be nuts.

She had been shivering, her coat forgotten at home, and he could tell she was miserable, her arms crossed, shoulders hunched. He had wanted to get up, cross the room, and offer her his jacket, but he was too scared. And then the sun came out, falling on her head, lighting her hair like a halo. God. She was beautiful, even then. And he had loved her with a pierced, aching schoolboy heart.

The music in Serena's room changed mid-tune. A raucous rock-and-roll riff blared, nasty guitar like a burr in the air. The tune and words were lost in the insulation that kept their lives apart, however superficially. But he didn't have to hear the words. Rock-and-roll meant a change in his sister's mental state. He should check on her.

"*Co-dependent,*" L'ron's careful voice spoke inside his head. "*Co-dependent, you.*" The cop had been serious. Careful, cautious about Starnes' feelings, but deadly serious. Starnes gripped the sink edge.

Gen was back home today. And she was alone. Single.

Once upon a time he had let her get away, climb the steps of a Greyhound bus and take off for New York alone. He had only been a kid, had let fear keep him from following her.

And then there had been college, and Serena to consider. To

take care of. Serena who wanted none of his help, none of his care. Serena, who was into self-destruction and wild-living and drugs and men and who had lost all self-control years ago. Serena, who lived under a dark cloud, in a state of emotional misery he could have prevented, had he been there for her that first time. . . . Guilt wrapped around his mind like a snake around a thick tree, writhed like a serpent in his chest.

Starnes stood, chilled by the AC blowing up his jeans legs. Feeling hollow, he remembered L'ron's words, *"Co-dependent, you."* He turned and went to his room, dressed for the day.

He didn't go check on Serena.

He was going to see Gen.

But first, he had chores. And therapy.

◆   ◆   ◆

Accustoming her body to the rhythm of the slowly walking mare, Gen and horse moved down the unpaved roadway into the breaking day. She had no route planned, no special intentions, but somehow she found herself on a familiar path through the woods. Ahead was a view of Bayou Incendie she remembered from her childhood. The name meant burning bayou, and wasn't the proper name of the sinuous strip of water. Bayou Incendie was the name given to it by the locals after an oil well ruptured in the sixties, spilling into the water. Burning crude exploded down the length of the bayou, the fire raging, igniting foliage along the curving banks and threatening homes and businesses for over a mile. A drenching rain from the gulf put it out after three days and nights. Today such a spill and fire would be called an ecological disaster and would have made worldwide news. Back then it was just a great fire, a good excuse for a party, and something to talk about. Something different. The media never showed.

Shawnee stepped from the path onto a manicured strip of lawn and paused. The view had changed. Instead of a decrepit fishing pier lying in half-ruin and a shack falling to rot, Gen found built-up land like an artificial hill, with a sprawling ranch house perched on top. The deck was only a few years old, made of green dyed planks attached to massive treated tree trunks that had been shaped and then driven into the silt of the bayou. It was beautiful.

And it owned the best view of bayou in the parish.

Gen stayed only a moment. There was a "Beware of Dog" sign on a post at the back of the house and she didn't fancy hanging onto the back of a terrified horse as they raced away from a Doberman or a Pit Bull. Instead she pulled the mare back onto the path and made her way upstream to the old Pershone house.

Here, there was little more than a freestanding chimney and a few vine-enshrouded, half-rotted six-by-sixes. The Pershones had left town when Gen was a child, taking their six dogs and four kids and the fortune bestowed on them by Shell Oil for the oil rights on their back sixty acres. Leaving behind everything to start a new life in Baton Rouge, they hadn't even bothered to turn off the power or the phone, and area kids had made it a party house for weeks afterward until the police shut it down. She had heard Beverly Hillbillies-type jokes about the Pershones for years.

Now the old place was wild and beautiful and overgrown with some type of hardy flowering vine. Gen wondered if the Pershones had ever come back to see the old place and if the sight of it made them as melancholy as it did her.

She shifted in the saddle, lifted her left foot from the stirrup and straightened her leg to relieve the pressure on her knee. She was going to be sore, no doubt about it. And not a single masseuse in sight. Sweat prickled down her back and under her arms as the fast-rising sun brought heat in steamy waves. Mosquitoes were beginning to swarm in the low foliage, promising the blood hunt to come.

Opening the camera bag, Gen loaded a roll of Kodak 400 film, and took several shots, hoping to capture the pensive pathos of the place. The angle of the sun was too high, though, and she had few illusions about the quality of the shots.

Following the path, she made her way past the fallen house, through a small wood, and came on a mobile home perched on a bluff overlooking Bayou Incendie. It was a fairly new home, a singlewide with a screened back porch and a wide front stoop, both visible from the side. On even higher ground, there was a four-room-shack overlooking the surrounding land. It was Mrs. Landry's house, the board siding clearly unpainted for decades, half-rotted, yet lived in. Frilly white cotton curtains hung at every window, pulled back with ties, and a new rocker sat at rest on the rotting porch. Mrs. Landry had been Gen's French teacher in high school.

At that thought, Gen closed her eyes. What was she doing? Taking a trip down memory lane? "God, I've been brainwashed." Her mount flicked back an ear. "It's a case of Stockholm Syndrome. Got to be."

Shawnee snorted in agreement and, without taking a single photograph, Gen turned her mount back toward Deveraux Estates, touching heels to flanks in the hope of a bit of speed. Shawnee broke into a slow trot that Gen could not sit through. It had been too many years since she sat a trot in true Western tradition. Instead she posted, rising up and down in her stirrups, knee protesting.

The estate wasn't far, as the crow flies, but following the bayou's winding curves took much longer, and Gen was beginning to feel real hunger, and a few blisters on the insides of her knees, by the time she moved onto Deveraux land again. So fixated on the breakfast she was certain to be missing, Gen almost rode past the overgrown path forking off to the right, away from the water and up a small bluff. The path was just a blur of sandy white in the gloom of overgrowth, so narrow she had missed it on the way out.

It was a path she knew well, even after twenty-nine years. She pulled Shawnee up shortly, and the mare jangled her bridle in displeasure. "Sorry sweetheart," Gen said softly as Shawnee stamped her hoof and looked off toward home and the barn and the treat she knew would be hers after a ride. But the mare was well trained, and stood, awaiting Gen's pleasure.

Geneva sat and stared at the old path, the pain in her knee fading in the face of a new sensation. Cold seeped into her bones, drying the sweat that clung to her skin. It was silent here in the woods, and lonely. Far from the world and people and laughter. Off in the distance, a branch fell, the sound echoing. Shawnee stamped again, making her disapproval clear. Gen shook herself and turned the mare onto the path. With a blowing sigh, the sneaky kind used to loosen a saddle girth for a planned getaway, Shawnee followed her lead.

The narrow trail hadn't been recently traveled. It was overgrown in places and Gen had to compel Shawnee to step over fallen trees, once dismounting to pull tangled vines away from the path to clear it. Though there was a twinge from her left knee, Gen was surprised how easily she remounted from a fallen log. There were some things it seemed she had not forgotten.

Shawnee was not happy with the course, kept trying to turn her head for home and her barn, but Gen forced her in the direction of the clearing at the end of the path. It was apparent that no one had been this way in years. Mosquitoes were out, attacking horse and rider in a buzzing swarm. Shawnee shook her head and looked back at Gen in disgust. In the growing heat, Gen pushed on.

Only now did Geneva realize that she had been subconsciously looking for this path for the last two hours. This was where she had meant to come, had known she would come. Flicking the reins, Gen encouraged Shawnee down the path. Slowly, the mare stepped toward the clearing.

At the edge of the trees, Gen pulled her to a halt. The graves were snarled in weeds, the low crypt yellowed and chipped with age, sunken into the ground with time. The angels that guarded the site had been defaced, the smaller stone cupid lying on its back. The head of the larger stone angel had been knocked off by vandals, its once beautiful form now pitted and scarred by acid rain and teenagers' hands. His wings were spray painted blue and gold, the colors of the local high school, flecks of paint scattered the ground. Old beer cans littered the crypt cover and the angels' base—the six-inch-thick, poured-concrete slab the Old Man had set in place to keep the angels upright. The remains of an ancient fire on its surface were almost obliterated.

Gen slid again from Shawnee's back, her boots touching down on a can hidden in the weeds. She looped the reins over the saddle horn and pulled a length of nylon rope from a rawhide saddle-tie. Knotting one end to Shawnee's bridle, she tied the other end to a low limb before loosening the saddle girth, letting Shawnee graze. It would be hard chewing with the bit in her teeth, but Gen wouldn't be here long.

Leaving the camera bag securely tied to the saddle horn, she moved through the weeds, her boots breaking a new path. When she reached the graves, she paused, fingers on the rough marble. Gen traced wing feathers, followed the folds of angel garments, rested her palm on the jagged place where the head was once attached.

Tears gathered in her eyes, as yesterday's grief returned with a vengeance. To stop the tears, she bent and pulled at the old dry weeds. The brambles crackled in her hands, stems hollow and fragile as she pulled them away from the stone. A thorn tore her palm and she tossed the offending weed from her. Whatever the plants were, they had not sprouted in this year's summer heat.

The last of the weeds ripped free of the ground, and she stood in the sunlight, breath like a bellows, blinking back sweat that stung her eyes. Sucking on her bleeding hand, Geneva read the plaque that marked the graves on unhallowed ground.

HELENA A. DEVERAUX	MATTHEW C. DEVERAUX
1933 – 1962	1962, Age 6 Months
Beloved Wife and Mother	Beloved Son

Her fingers traced the words on her mother's grave, and Gen finally understood why she had come home. There were things from the past that were unsettled, unresolved. Issues that needed closure, as her friend Marcy would say, Marcy who had been in therapy for over ten years.

Helena Deveraux was buried on unhallowed ground, the only burial permitted a Roman Catholic who died by her own hand, even in those forward-thinking years. Most Catholics still believed that suicide was the unforgivable sin, and so her mother had been banished, unfairly, unrightfully, to unhallowed ground.

Gen had never understood why Matthew was buried here. He was an innocent who died due to no fault of his own.

Gen clenched her fists and stepped back from the broken angel. An idea blossomed, born fully developed in an instant.

If possible, while she was here, Gen would see to her mother's and brother's removal to a more fitting place. She would right a wrong buried for nearly four decades. And she would bury the Old Man and his effect on her life once and for all.

5

THINK BACK HARD, GIRL and DON'T WHINE

Gen rode slowly back to the barn, letting Shawnee choose the path, giving the mare time to cool off and taking time for her own sorrow to fade. An anger was growing inside her, rising and spreading its wings, anger like a dark angel, trapped for decades in a dusty tomb, suddenly set free and resolved on vengeance.

There were too many secrets buried here, on the land of her youth, too many wrongs needing to be righted, and Gen was determined to expose the truth. If it destroyed her in the process, so be it. She had run from it long enough.

When the barn came into sight, its white-painted walls advertising home and feed and rest, Shawnee picked up speed and cantered slowly back. Gen let her have her head, and the mare's shod feet clopped against the earth in a satisfying rhythm. She would be sore from the morning's ride, but it was worth every moment of blisters and stiff muscles.

Out in front of the barn where Gen dismounted, appeared a wizened old man, his face shadowed by the brim of a sweat-crusted western hat. Gen nodded to him and turned to her horse. Shawnee was blowing contentedly and nuzzled Gen when she pulled the saddle, with its camera bag accessory, off, her head pulling against the tie rope. "I have a carrot for you girl, just let me get you—"

"Got no call taking a horse when I ain't here and runnin' her into the ground."

Gen's chin shot up and she turned to the man, both brows raised. "I beg your pardon?"

"I said—"

"I *heard* what you said. I was simply questioning your right to say it."

The man started forward, his hands fisted. Surprised, Gen

backed into Shawnee. The mare darted quickly against her tie-rope, front hooves rising from the ground in a half-lunge. Gen tripped, the saddle in her arms throwing her balance off.

The man's black eyes sparkled with malevolence. An arm drew back. Loathing etched his worn face. Confused, Gen tried to back-step, but twisted her ankle and fell, booted feet trapped in the fallen girth. She landed beneath Shawnee whose ironclad hooves danced dangerously as the mare tried to move away from the human writhing under her belly.

"Grandpa, *no!*"

The man stopped, Olivia at his side, her small hands reaching for the threatening arm. "Grandpa, this is Miss Geneva, home from New York. She has a right to ride any horse on the estate."

"I know who she is." He spat into the dust at Geneva's side. "I know she and her white-trash sister left the Old Man to die in his own misery and grief. I know they ain't never called nor come home to see him in near thirty year. Now he's dying and here they come like buzzards circling, throwing their weight around like they got some special rights. They ain't been responsible for nothing and here they are taking over like *family*. They ain't family!" he roared. "You river rats, you girls, and I don't have to let you near my barn." He spat again, the rust-brown spew of tobacco.

As he shouted, Geneva rolled away from Shawnee's feet to safety near a Jeep that hadn't been parked there when she left. She lifted herself to her feet and tossed the saddle onto the Jeep's hood. The padded camera bag made a hollow, clumping sound.

Gen's breath came fast. *Fight or flight.* Fear required her to strike out. Blood rushed to her extremities. With a jab of pain, her left knee warned her that it was a liability—stiffening, injured from the protracted ride and the fall.

The man didn't attack, as she expected. When he spoke again, it was softly, though he glared at Gen through curling white brows very much like the Old Man's. "Barn privileges is for family."

She sucked in a ragged breath. "I don't know who you are, old man, but you know absolutely nothing about John Deveraux. And nothing about me."

He drew his shriveled body up, and Gen had a clue how big

this man had once been. In that moment, she almost recognized him, a faint haze of memory.

"I'm Asa Rogers and I'm the manager here. Have been for over fifty year. You think back hard, girl, you remember me," he stated. "And I know what I know 'bout you and your white-trash sister."

Suddenly, Gen did remember Asa Rogers, a tall, muscular, white-haired man who had taken care of nearly everything on the estate, answering only to John, the Old Man. He had been one of the few on the estate who tried to restrain John Deveraux, and the only one who ever had any measure of success.

Asa had changed. He had gotten old and mean, just like his boss.

The Jeep engine was ticking with heat in the silence left by his pronouncement. The vehicle could have used a new coat of paint and new tires to replace the bald ones she had landed against. She remembered the bald tread from the instant when she lay in the dust. Odd what details one notices when in danger. . . . Gen's breath slowly returned to normal as she swept her eyes back and forth between Asa and his mortified granddaughter.

Fleetingly, she considered that she should indeed have asked to use the horse. Asa was right, she wasn't family by her own preference and practice. Instead she had waltzed in and taken one. . . . As if she belonged. But she was not about to tell him that.

She focused on Olivia, whose dust-streaked face was white with embarrassment. She still held her grandfather's arm, fingers curled around his fist. Gen stood carefully upright, testing the strength of the banged-up knee. "I'll leave you and Mr. Rogers here to brush down my horse. And I suggest you remember this, Olivia. I don't care who your father is, or was, around here. If he threatens me again, I'll see him put behind bars. Understood?"

"Understood," she said softly. Asa jerked his arm away, pulled his hat from his head, using it to slap his thigh in anger. Without another word, he walked off, moving with the tale-tell rounded gait of the life-long horse handler. He spat again, his disgust crystal-clear. "I'm sorry," Olivia said.

Gen pressed the puncture site on her palm. It had come open again during the scuffle and dripped blood. "Just keep him away from me. He doesn't know whatever it is he thinks he knows. He only knows what the Old Man told him, same as everyone else around here. And that means he knows nothing."

"I'm sorry," Olivia said again.

Without another word, Gen turned, grabbed her omnipresent camera bag, and headed for the guesthouse and the shower she needed. As she moved, tears again filled her eyes. "This is ridiculous," she murmured. "Downright ridiculous. I have no reason to cry. No reason at all."

But suddenly she remembered her words. *If he threatens me again, I'll see him put behind bars. Understood?* They were the words and tone she would have used when she was Miss Geneva Deveraux, pampered plantation-owner's-daughter, belle-of-the-ball, with nothing too good for her. Miss High and Mighty she had been called. *By Starnes. . . .* Heat washed thorough her at the thought. Ridiculous heat. She shook the thought of Starnes away.

Her threat to Asa Rogers had been haughty and contemptuous, clear evidence of a class distinction she had hated in her father and rejected in herself. Something she thought she had left behind when she left the estate. Abruptly, Gen was ashamed.

◆　◆　◆

Starnes, dressed in old jeans and worn work-shirt, tossed busted bricks and half-rotten timbers from the pile that had once been an old well-house. The bricks he would clean and keep. The timbers would be hauled off when he was done. He had long envisioned a barbecue pit at the back of the house, just off the deck and at an angle to the barn, and using the old brick would tie it to the house architecturally. Doing most of the work himself would be exercise and therapy. Breath bellowed through tight lips as he worked, steady and even, breathing through the agony.

When he stood, the old injury zinged through his body like razor-wire, when he bent, the pain was more like a hot iron, and when he tossed the heavy debris, shifting his body with the weight into the transfer, the ache was like an old bruise. He had once measured his life by the pain. Now it was simply an unchanging part of living, something to be ignored if possible, worked through all other times. It would never go away; he had accepted that. It was something he would have to live with until the pain put him in a wheelchair permanently or until medical researchers found a surgical procedure to re-wire the nerves in his hip. Until then, he lived with it, day in and day out, and seldom thought about it anymore in any substantive way. *Live with it,* and, *Don't whine.* About the only words of his father's that he lived by today.

The sun beat down on him, darkening his clothes with sweat, sticking his shirt to his chest. His fingers were slightly blistered in the leather work gloves and the uneven place in his boot sole was getting worse. He'd have to shop for another pair soon, or have these resoled. Lindsay had offered to take them into town to the shoe shop on Thurston Street, but he had refused. Refused most of her offers of kindness during the months they had been engaged, perhaps knowing all along that he wouldn't marry her. *Don't let her get too close. Don't let her love him too much, because when he pushed her away, her hurt would be even greater.* Bastard. It was what he was to women, and he knew it. He had been told so often enough.

Oddly, Serena had actually liked Lindsay, approved of his marrying this one, and even spent time with her shopping in New Orleans. His sister hadn't been the one to ruin this particular relationship, he had.

"*Ça va bien.* Got you some goo' lookin' old brick there, bo."

Starnes paused and swiped sweat from his brow with a damp sleeve. "Useable, you think?"

The pile of rubbish had been reduced to standing weeds and bare earth, a few roly-polys waddling across the soil. The two piles he had made were neater looking than the original haphazard, overgrown mess, and, by evening, would be reduced to one, the brick piled beneath the shade of the old dogwood tree's sinuous limbs, ready for cleaning. Herman Potts bent and lifted a brick, scrapping his gloved thumb across the rough red surface.

"*Ils sont vieu.* Recycle, they call using old stuff now." Herman shrugged. "Goo' enough, I think, yeah," he said, his Cajun accent thick as Louisiana bayou mud. "Make you a nice cookstove outside for sure."

Starnes grinned at the intended insult. In Herman's mind, cooking of any kind was woman's work, and he had voiced his objections to the barbecue idea on several occasions.

"I be cartin' off the rotted timber before dusk. Mebe bush hog the back five acres, too. Got you some saplin' comin' up. 'Less you, big time lawyer-man, want do some real man work. . . ."

Starnes laughed, catching his breath and adjusting his hat. "No. Might damage my pinkies and we lawyers need them in court." He held a gloved little finger up for inspection and Herman huffed in indignation. The law was beneath him, too, not a real man's job like breaking horses, fishing, hunting, and building a good strong barn.

The opinionated, gruff old man was living on Social Security and his veteran's disability check; the extra cash he earned doing odd jobs helped keep him in groceries and liquor. It also gave Starnes a handyman who could do anything, and who lived behind the barn in a small mobile home, always available for chores or errands.

Herman had taught Starnes how to set pavers into sand and level them so that they would drain. Had taught him how to build a corral, setting the posts deep in the soil and smoothing off the tops so that delicate horseflesh wouldn't be rubbed raw, how to lay a dry-stack stone wall so it would stand for centuries, how to wrap a horse's leg when inflammation set in, and most importantly, had taught him how to live with pain.

Herman had lost a leg in the early years of Vietnam. The government-issued prosthetic had left him in agony, and no subsequent prosthetic had ever been pain-free, yet, the man worked as a hired laborer from dawn to dusk in half-hour increments as his pain allowed.

"I'm done here, Herman," Starnes said, lifting the sledge-hammer he had used to break up larger lumps of mortared brick. "Got an errand to run or two. Pick you up anything while I'm in town? Beer?"

"Six-pack a that Coors be a nice li'l charity to an old man, yeah."

"I'll bring one by the trailer later," Starnes said, baiting his friend.

"Mobile home, they call now, bo. 'Member that," he said sternly. "And tell Lindsay I say 'lo." His green eyes twinkled. "That gir' too goo' for the like a you."

Starnes thought about telling Herman that he wouldn't be seeing Lindsay anymore, but the words died hard. The older man had a soft spot for her, and the two had spent many hours together when Starnes was out on the bayou, painting. With the older man's help, Lindsay had even overcome her fear of horses and learn to ride.

But Serena was acting up again, and Lindsay was gone and it wouldn't have worked out anyway. If he was honest with himself, he would have added that he was tired of playing daddy to the younger woman's fears. He was tired of being depended on and being dependable. One clingy, needy woman in his life was enough.

"I'll bring the Coors by."

On the porch behind him, the screen door opened and Bubba-Boy jumped out, long legs bouncing up and down in excitement. Serena followed the dog out, her limbs moving with medication-induced lethargy. She sent Herman a slit-eyed smile, watching as the old man blushed a deep shade of crimson.

Serena had a way with men. A way of making them think of sex. Hot, wild, forbidden sex. She smiled slowly, her nostrils widening as if in anticipation, her long hair swinging across her shoulders. Herman turned away, muttering in French beneath his breath.

"Serena!" Starnes barked. Without missing a beat, she turned the smoldering gaze to him. His hands clenched on the sledge. "Stop that!"

"Why?" She purred, dropping forward across the deck railing, her upper arms making a tight V of her small breasts beneath her T-shirt. "Half the parish thinks Daddy and I used to have an incestuous relationship." She smiled sleepily. "And the other half thinks you and I do."

The words were glacial, freezing him into silence, as she always intended when she got like this. Shocked, not wanting Serena to see his reaction, Starnes dropped his hands and turned away, the sledgehammer pulling at his shoulders. He had heard the comments and speculation about his father for years. So far as he had ever been able to determine, it wasn't true, but truth had never silenced a gossip, especially in this parish.

He hadn't realized that the gossip had begun to include him. If it actually did. With Serena, truth was selective. She manufactured intricate, multi-layered lies quicker than anyone else could speak the truth. She'd have been a great fiction writer, the way she plotted out the details. Half the time, she believed the lies she wove.

Shrugging, as if to rid himself of a too heavy load, Starnes tossed the weighty hammer into the back of his truck and walked up the steps and into the house, leaving Serena and the dog on the porch. Bubba-Boy was utterly loyal to Serena, staring at her adoringly whenever she was present, resting a long-eared head against her leg, or lying draped across her feet. Bubba-Boy might be his dog, but Serena was Bubba's baby. The big dog looked after Serena as if she were a puppy. In many ways she was just that. A child, never grown up.

In the shower, standing beneath an icy spray, his clothes lying in a heap on the floor, Starnes remembered Serena's comments. Sick. Sick comments from a sick brain. *"Bon à rien,"* he muttered as cold water ran into his mouth. "The whole damn lot of us."

6

MIND YOUR MANNERS, GIRL

Gen found a plaid shirt hanging in the closet of the guesthouse. It was clean, though musty, and she pulled it over her shower-damp body. She slipped into her last pair of clean panties, leaving dirty underwear and her T-shirt soaking in the sink with a dollop of shampoo in lieu of detergent. Her jeans stank of horse sweat, the smell had not improved when she shook them outside, though barn dirt and horse hair went flying. She might be clean, but unless her luggage arrived today, she would have to resort to borrowing Lily's clothes, which would hang on her like ill-fitting hand-me-downs. Gen grimaced sourly, inspected the too-big boots for bugs and minute specks of horse manure, pulled them on, and headed to the estate house. She was starving.

Breakfast was long over and the kitchen empty, but Gen raided a fruit bowl for an apple, a pear, and a banana, which she peeled, diced into a bowl and ate with skim milk from the Big House's new stainless steel fridge. She fixed herself a cup of green tea; it was tasteless stuff but it gave her a needed lift. She was sitting at the long breakfast table sipping the tea when a woman entered.

"Hi, hon, is there any coffee around here? I'm Mary Anne, the Old Man's day nurse. *Love* your hair. I wish I could wear mine bobbed at the chin like that. It must be *so easy* to take care of. Not like my new perm. *Hate* this one," she patted her stiff blonde mass. "Makes me look like a poodle-dog at a fancy dog show, you know? You must be Geneva, John's oldest daughter," she said as she poured herself a mug of coffee.

Before she could speak, the woman continued in what Gen assumed was a characteristic non-stop chatter.

"Are there any of those doughnuts left?" Mary Anne asked as she rummaged through a basket beside the stove. "I know I don't need anything else sweet, but I *do love* a Krispy Kreme jelly-filled, you know? *Blueberry's* my favorite. I already had two for breakfast with John and Lily—and let me tell you, hon, I *really* like your sister. She's *class*, you can just tell. Have you seen that *diamond* she wears? Oh my God, it is *fab!* Anyway, since I started this job I've put on nearly *six pounds*," she paused to take a bite of jelly doughnut but went on while she chewed, one hand providing some cover from flying pastry as powdered sugar fell and dusted the front of her pink uniform, "*all* of it in my butt. Don't you just hate that?"

She took another quick bite and washed it down with coffee. Half of the doughnut was gone, dark blue filling bulging from the bitten hole. "When I came here I was a size twelve, but I just *know* I'm up to a fourteen, you know? I mean, not that *you* would ever know something like that. What are you, a size eight? Six?"

Gen nodded.

"I would sell my body on a street corner if it meant I could have a little skinny butt like yours." Mary Anne popped the last bite of jelly doughnut into her mouth. "Well, back to the old salt mines. It's about time for John's bath. He likes to be called the Old Man. Isn't that weird?

"Oh. I saw you on the cover of the *Enquirer* with that *gorgeous* young thing! I never knew anyone on the cover of a national magazine," she said as if Gen should be honored to be a tabloid scandal.

"Anyway, that man is *so fine!* I don't blame you one bit for dumping the old guy for fresh meat. You go girl." Quickly, Mary Anne slurped down the last of her coffee and put the mug in the sink. "See ya, hon."

Mary Anne retreated from the room on a wave of Tabu perfume, her fingers fluttering in a "tootle-loo" wave. Gen sat still, listening to Mary Anne's rubber-soled shoes as she took the stairs to the second story. She was surprised that the nurse could remain quiet for the seconds it took to find another unfortunate listening ear. She could hear the perky voice as she reached the Old Man's bedroom, and then the door shut, leaving Gen in silence. She hadn't had to say a word.

Fresh meat? An unexpected smile tugged at her lips. *Were people really dumb enough to think that about her?* For an instant she wanted to laugh, but the urge fell short.

Gen sipped, enjoying the returned quiet, not thinking about Barry and the paparazzi and the foolish, gullible people out there. She heard Lily's distinctive footsteps as her sister glided down the stairs, her hips swaying slowly side-to-side in a sensual rhythm Gen could never hope to match. Lily was earthy and sensuous, in counterpoint to Gen's polished elegance. An elegance she had cultivated and groomed, and then discovered not to be enough for her husband. . . . *Fresh meat.* . . . Lily entered the kitchen carrying a tray that held dirty breakfast dishes.

"Mary Anne called you classy," Gen said, to distract her own mind.

"Mary Anne thinks money equals class. Mary Anne thinks divorce and remarriage are fine if you move up financially in the world with husbands two and three. Mary Anne thinks that the *X-Files* was real and that the government had used the show to prepare the American people for the day when the aliens land on the White House lawn. And Mary Anne thinks she should *dye her hair black like mine* and asked *what brand of hair color I use,*" Lily said in a 'can-you-believe-it' tone. She slid the tray onto the counter, dishes clinking.

"Well, isn't that what you did? Move up financially with husband two and three?" Gen smiled into her tea. Lily had not a strand of gray on her head and was unabashedly vain about the natural glossy mane. Any fool suggesting she dyed her hair wouldn't be suffered for long. Her marriages were of less concern to her than that the world note her beauty for its perfection.

"I do *not* dye my hair," Lily fumed as she poured herself a cup of coffee and stirred in a package of sweetener. "The little twit has the manners of a barn dog.

"And, yes, I moved up financially, but it wasn't as if I divorced and remarried for profit. I left Jason because he preferred Johnny Walker Red to me, and I divorced Mason because he hit me one time too many, and we both know that one time is too many. And no rhyming sarcasm about Jason and Mason, please. I am quite sick to death of them from the Old Man." Lily settled at the table and blew on her coffee.

"So, how is marriage to number three?"

Lily smiled like a cream-fed cat and smoothed her hair back, checking her flawless chignon or displaying her diamond ring. Her *fab* diamond ring. "Profitable *and* satisfying. You were right to marry an older man, sister-mine. Hollis does work extra hard at . . . shall we say *satisfying* . . . a younger wife." And then Lily's eyes opened wide. "Oh, Gen. I didn't mean—"

"No offence taken," Gen said easily, her tone belying the painful flutter of her heart. "Barry is a good name to rhyme with. What has the Old Man said about my situation. Something like 'Barry, Barry, quite contrary?' Or has he become more sophisticated in the last twenty-nine years?"

"He hasn't said anything about it," Lily said, drinking her coffee. "Only asked me what I knew about why you were leaving him," Lily's brows lifted suggestively and Gen repressed a sigh, "to which I answered truthfully that I didn't know, which he did not believe, as he knows we talk about everything."

Gen steeled herself for the next comment and, true to form, Lily didn't disappoint her. Her sister asked for the hundredth time, "So. When are you going to tell me what's going on with you two? You've been little lovebirds for more years than I've been married if you combined all my three. When I saw you last April it was disgusting to be around you, all kissy-cooing and loving smiles. Even the tabloids got bored with you because there was never any good gossip. And suddenly you up and leave him? The man is rich and head-over-heels in love with you," Lily said, typically putting rich and love in the order that seemed most appropriate to her.

"Was," Gen said, surprising herself.

"Was what?"

"Was in love with me. Things change."

"Sister-mine, Barry Stone is solid as a rock."

"Old joke. Poor taste under the circumstances. And I have no intention of discussing my situation. Not with you, not with a shrink, not with a minister, and not with a gal-pal. So stop suggesting it."

Lily wisely noted the tone and changed the subject. "It's time for the Old Man's snack."

"I thought it was time for his bath," Gen said, feeling contrary herself.

"He eats and then gets his bath."

"I thought cancer victims typically lost their appetites."

"The Old Man will be hungry at the gates of hell, sister-mine. And likely take a bite out of the devil himself if he isn't fed on time."

Gen managed a small smile at the image.

"He wants a plate of leftover cold boiled shrimp and hot sauce with crackers and a glass of wine. And he wants it now."

"Are you going to let him drink wine? Isn't he on painkillers?"

"Yes, and yes. Maybe he'll have a drug interaction and die sooner rather than later."

Gen chuckled into her tea cup. "We should be so lucky. I think God doesn't want him dead. He might join forces with Lucifer when he gets there and start an unholy war on heaven."

"Well, that's better than the martyred tone you've been using for weeks."

Gen looked up, not certain if she should be insulted or amused at another ploy to wrest information about her break-up. "I have not been sounding like a martyr."

"Yes, you have. And if you're not going to share the details then you can't pout."

Unwillingly, Gen's smile spread. "It is so good to see you again. Even if it has to be here and not some place with better memories."

Lily lifted her mug in a toast. "To putting the past behind us and moving forward."

Gen lifted her cup. "To correcting old evils."

Lily looked mildly bewildered. "Is that what we're doing?"

"Why not. We—"

"I just praise the Lord to know my babies together in my kitchen once again, yes I do," the old voice came from the stairway. "And I gives Him the *glory* for finally answering the prayer of an old woman, I do, I do," Della said, the breath wheezing in her throat as she rounded the corner to the kitchen. "Now you girls be nice. We got us enough problems living without dragging the past back from the dead. The past is the past. It gone forever."

Gen had been so intense that she hadn't heard Della's slow footsteps on the stairs. She wondered how much the housekeeper-cum-surrogate-mother had heard and how much her praising the Lord had to do with stopping conflict and conversation before it took a direction she disapproved. Della had always been one to avoid conflict where she could and ignore it the rest of the time. She had single-handedly prevented discussion of family problems when the sisters were children, and it seemed she had no intention of allowing it to raise its ugly head now.

Gen remembered weed-covered graves and sipped cold green tea to mask her reaction to the interruption. With a last cryptic look at Gen, Lily rose from the table and began removing delectables from the fridge. Silent, she arranged the shrimp on a plate and added some of Della's ketchup-based hot cocktail sauce. She put a bunch of grapes to the side for color, as they all knew that the Old Man wouldn't eat the stuff. If it wasn't meat, potatoes, seafood, or deep-fat-fried in a crisp crust, he wouldn't touch it. With his diet he should have croaked long ago, Gen thought unkindly.

Della put a wine bottle on the tray and stretched up to remove a crystal goblet from the overhead cupboard. "Come on now, Geneva, girl. It time you say hello to your daddy. Now you here, you can't keep puttin' it off."

Feeling that something important had been snatched away, Gen stood, her boots scraping the floor. Della looked over at the sound, affronted that anyone would wear barn attire in her house. "I can wear the boots or go barefoot," Gen said. "My luggage still hasn't arrived."

Della sniffed. "You make well and sure you don't got any that horse stuff on them boots, little girl. And no mud neither. Took me close to twenty year, but I trained the Old Man to leave it outside and I don't be intending to clean up after another one of you Deveraux. I got me a staff three days a week for the mopping and vacuuming and the heavy lifting, but that don't mean I lets them clean up after you like you a queen. We got rules in this house, and you expected to abide by them same as always."

"Yes ma'am," Gen said meekly, and inspected her boots to make certain that they were still free of "horse stuff" and mud. And this time she followed silently when Della led the way to the back stairs and up to the master bedroom where John Deveraux lay dying.

There was no cold sweat or clenched jaw as she climbed the

stairs to the family wing. No chills or fevered memories. No great dread. But a dark despondency settled on her—what Della would have called a "shameful funk". Gen was breaking a lifelong vow. She was going to see the Old Man before he was in his coffin. She was finally home.

John Deveraux, the Old Man of Deveraux Estates, the last male of his direct line, lay in a cheerful suite, walls painted bright yellow below the chair railing and papered with pale yellow tone-on-tone wallpaper above. Floral linens covered the massive bed, with striped bed skirt and matching striped chairs in the corner, angled beside the oak rope-leg drop-leaf table. The room was essentially unchanged from the time of her mother's death so long ago. Though it had been repainted and re-papered numerous times when Gen and Lily lived here, it had always been redone in the same shades, the wallpaper matched as closely as possible to the original picked out by their mother. The height of hypocrisy. Gen pursed her lips. The Old Man was still the Old Man even after all these years, and dying a slow death.

Boots clomping on the ancient cypress floor, Gen crossed the room behind Della and paused at the foot of the bed. She studied her father as he studied her. Twenty-nine years had not been kind to him. The Old Man had deep furrows in his cheeks, drooping lower lids exposing the red lining of his black eyes, and age-spotted skin. Of the black hair he had worn with such élan, only a sparse frothing of white remained, brushed in a parody of his old style, over the dull dome of his skull. He didn't look like he was dying until Gen noted the yellow of his eyes and the way his hands shook to make room for the tray Della placed across his lap. But his voice was sonorous and judgmental as always.

"So. You're here."

"I'm here."

He stuffed a pink shrimp into his mouth, hot sauce dotting his lips, his dark eyes keen on her, as if evaluating a peculiar fish in the bottom of his net as he chewed. "You look good."

"You look like hell."

John laughed, the sound raspy in his chest. "I'm dying. Getting ready to meet the devil. So it's appropriate to look like hell, isn't it?" He ate another shrimp, his strong teeth crunching the crackers. "I saw you land yesterday. Good entrance."

Gen fought a smile, determined to resist being drawn in to the Old Man's web. "Thank you."

"You're wearing barn attire. Airport still hasn't brought your luggage?"

"No," Gen said, knowing what was coming next. "And I can take care of it myself."

"Course you can. Always been independent and stubborn. Like me."

Gen's chin came up and she glared at her father, which was exactly what he wanted, a rise out of her. And she stupidly had given him his desire. Her eyes narrowed and he laughed.

"How long has the doctor given you before you croak?" she asked.

"Geneva! You mind your manners, girl," Della said.

But The Old Man just chortled, the sound thick with clotted mucous in his cancer-filled lungs. "Too damn long," he said finally. "Too damn long," and he broke into a terrible cough, sounding like ripping flesh, harsh and vicious.

Gen just watched him. "I'll be here," she said. "To watch the end."

Without speaking, he lay his head back and closed his eyes, exhausted by the coughing and the disease that permeated his body. Gen turned from the room, unwilling to see Della wipe his mouth and help him settle into the pillows.

Stepping into the hallway she kept her eyes down. There was an old Persian runner down the length of the hall, the real thing, probably created in some Iranian village, made to order for the Old Man by a hundred adolescent girls knotting until their fingers bled. But to her it was new. The morning sun made bright rectangles at each open doorway and turned the carpet into burnished persimmon and a green so pure that the hooked vine flowing along the border might have been living. It was gorgeous, like everything else in the house, except her memories.

The doorway three down and across the hall beckoned, though it was closed. And though she didn't know why she bothered, Gen walked straight to the door and opened it. The scent of fresh paint hit her, not so strong she wanted to pass out, but new enough, a few weeks old. It was a guestroom done up in shades of yellow so pale they looked like melted butter and cream with a slice of mango tossed in. Florals and stripes and a little ottoman in dotted Swiss made up the décor. Familiar and not familiar.

The room had new linens and drapes, and without asking, Gen knew it was the room she had been expected to stay in before she took over the guesthouse. Of course. Put her back in the room she had grown up in, just as if nothing had changed, though the room certainly had. No maudlin, overly sentimental treasury to remember her by.

"It right pretty ain't it?"

Gen turned, wondering when Della had started moving like a cat. She remembered her footsteps sounding like a drum when Gen was a kid, hiding from the sharp eyes and quick tongue. She and Lily would hear Della coming for a mile. Plenty of time to stop improprieties before they got caught. And then she realized—the new/old carpet muffled her steps.

"Yes. It's pretty."

"It been done up twice since you left, both times in these colors you like. Las' time the Old Man got right difficult with the decorator cause she wanted to change the colors, said them colors wasn't in style, and didn't he want to do it up in turquoise and teal and white. Showed him a book with pretty rooms in it. He say 'No, I want it done like I tol' you.' And she tell him 'them colors be hard as sin to find this season.' And he give her a look. You know the one I mean."

"I know the one you mean."

"And she found the color he wanted and did it up nice. But this time it even better. Your colors mus' be popular again."

Gen said, "Must be." After a moment she asked, "You were going to put me in here, weren't you?"

"Umhum, I was. It got its own bath, and a closet big enough to hold a few things. Seem right to put you here."

"I'm staying in the guesthouse."

Della sighed and turned, moving down the hallway toward the kitchen stairs. "I got a girl coming out here today to clean it up a bit. Air it out. Put out a few mouse traps just in case."

"Thank you."

"Stubborn. All you Deveraux folk stubborn as old mules."

Gen stepped into the room and looked out the window. The old live oak that had obscured the view when she was a child was gone, hit by lightning or killed by disease. The Old Man would never have had it removed had it been savable. It was part of the history of the house, like the live oaks planted all around, like the grove of pecans that grew just down the road near an old sharecropper's cabin. Now there was a new live oak less than twenty years old in its place, and Gen could see the front forty acres across the road. It was more like the front eighty-seven, but it had always been referred to as the front forty. The acreage was planted in soy instead of cotton or hay or sugarcane, but it was still planted. The Old Man ran a working farm at the estate, settling for the tax benefits when the profits on the product weren't enough to make it worthwhile to farm. That, too, was history.

The roots of the place ran deep, soaked into the ground like blood. Blood spilled by her family on the backs of others for centuries. Some of that blood had been spilled by the Old Man and no one had ever done a thing to bring him to justice.

"Ma'am?"

Gen turned, seeing a Hispanic girl in her late teens framed in the doorway, but her eyes barely registered the girl. To the side of the door was an antique highboy polished to a high luster. And in a lean line beside it were two rectangular photographic prints.

"Are you Miss Geneva? Miss Della said you'd be in here."

Gen nodded absently, her eyes on the prints.

"You have a call in the study. Miss Della said it was New York. *Wochy*-something."

"I'll be right there," she said, distracted. The girl left, her passage silent on the Persian. Gen walked toward the prints, put out a hand to touch them, and stopped. They were numbered prints, each number one of one-hundred. And they had been hand signed by her.

It was some of her early work, when she was still trying to break in to the business. A scene of Central Park before they cleaned it up, trash lying in a gutter, a wino sleeping wrapped in newspapers, one filth-encrusted hand on the dirt beside him, and crocuses about three inches tall blooming right out of the thawing winter ground. It looked as if the man was reaching for the frail buds, trying to grasp some moment of beauty in his gray world.

The second photo was of a young girl sitting on the steps of a brownstone wearing a flapper's beaded dress, rings that were too large, ropes of fake pearls and satin shoes with pointy toes. She was playing dress-up, waiting for her father. A chance shot, back when one could take shots of strangers, even children, without facing an irate and protective parent or a lawsuit. Gen still had the negatives somewhere.

Number ten, of the first one-hundred prints of the little girl, hung over the fireplace in her master suit. Barry's master suit. The old wino hung in Barry's business office, above his desk. She hadn't taken the photographs with her when she left her husband, though the prints were among her first sales from her first showings. And these . . . these had sold to the anonymous admirer who acted as patron for her early work. He had purchased several numbered photographs, all number one in the first series.

They were hanging in the original frames, just the way she had shown them. She had no idea how they came to be here, but a slightly sick feeling was growing in the pit of her stomach.

"Miss?"

The girl was back and Gen summoned a smile. "Yes. I'm coming."

7

TABLOIDS, BUZZARDS, AND A MAN IN SHADOW

When she picked up the phone in her father's study, Joachim's voice was muffled, as if he held his hand over the phone to engage in another discussion. Rather than waiting, Gen said, "Jo. I'm here. Problems?"

He grunted to indicate he had heard her, and returned to his muffled conversation. Jo, the nickname pronounced Yo, sounded angry and Gen's mind flew through the job details she had left for him to handle. There shouldn't have been anything to cause a crisis.

She sat on the huge table her father used as a desk, swinging a leg. The room was dark, the drapes pulled to keep out the sun on the south side of the house, and it appeared the room was unchanged. With one hand, she pushed back the drapes a bit, allowing in a shaft of light. The old brown leather sofa was the same, the bookcases seemed to hold the same books, all slightly musty from the mold that loved leather best. The rug was an old braided oval in faded shades of brown, blue and a muddy cream, the braids a bit looser and torn in spots, but the same rug. Those things lasted forever, and why not. They were ugly and ugly always seemed to be immortal.

Jo came back on the line. "Oh, Geneva. I am so sorry. So sor—" His voice faded quickly as if he handed the phone off to someone else. Or it was taken away by force. Gen sat up straight, sliding off the desk into a standing position.

"Gen, why the hell are you in Louisiana? Is it your father? Is it Della?"

A snake-like fury whipped through her, so sharp it cut. "Barry." Her voice had an edge to it she didn't like. Unsteady. Out of control. "Put Jo back on."

"Joachim has nothing to do with this. I didn't give him much of a choice about calling you." The voice was a deep baritone, so rich it sounded as if he had trained for years to achieve the musical quality. It was an asset that none of his competitors in any area of life could hope to match. Just the sound started a curious heat in her midsection and some emotion that prickled at her eyes. This tendency to cry was getting ridiculous. "Is it your father? Did he pass on?"

Gen took a slow breath to force the quaking from her vocal cords before she answered. "My father is dying. Lung cancer."

The silence on the far end was reassuring; it meant that she had surprised Barry. He was extremely difficult to silence. Gen waited him out.

"And you went back to Louisiana for *that?* You broke your vow of not returning until he was dead," he accused.

"I changed my mind. People do that. You should know." Her tone was stable now. Without inflection. Even the taunt at the end was indifferent, as if she said the words out of force of habit and not the raging heat of anger or pain.

"You have no right to interfere with Jo or my business. You do it again, and I'll get a restraining order. The tabloids will love that, and I'll make sure they all hear about it. Now let me speak to my assistant."

"Gen. I. . . . They called me. I wouldn't have seen it except for that." His voice was hoarse suddenly, as if he, too, was holding back tears, an event so rare that Gen wasn't sure if she was interpreting correctly. "I saw you land. I was frantic."

"I'm fine. Let me speak to Jo." It wasn't a request; she would never again make a request of Barry Stone. It was a demand. Her fingers tightened around the phone.

Barry ignored her, still speaking. "The only time I appreciated a call from one of the buzzards. And I turned on the television in my office and there you were, jumping out of a plane. And walking barefoot through the terminal. Gen—"

"Someone from the press called you?" Now it was her turn to be surprised, and the surprise fueled her anger. "And you took the call? What? Did they want to see what you thought of me walking barefoot in public?" Her voice was rising. She was loosing her fragile control.

"I—"

"Well, we all break vows and we all do stupid things, don't we Bare. In fact, you're getting pretty good at it. I landed. I'm fine." Her voice roughened, ready to break. "Don't call again. Go home to your little Jamaican lady-friend and leave me alone, and if the press calls you again, why don't you try telling them the truth. That you screwed around on me and I left you for it." Her voice broke. "And Barry, I'm serous about the restraining order. Stay away from Jo."

She slammed the phone down in the cradle. She would make it a point to refuse all calls while she was here. Messages only from now on. And she wouldn't talk to Barry again. Ever.

The tears she had been holding suddenly burst free, sliding down her face. A single sob escaped. Beneath her hand, the phone rang again. Gen stared at it, listening to its ring. The sound seemed to go on forever though it was only six rings until the answering machine picked up. The Old Man's voice spoke, strong and assured, followed by a click as the caller hung up.

Gen took a deep breath, her chest feeling like it had a case of early rigor-mortis. Wiping her face with the musty borrowed shirt, she stood, waiting out the episode. Finally the tears subsided and she heard her own voice whispering in the darkened room. "I will not cry. I will not be afraid. I will not."

Gen clasped her arms; the cold of this room was the extreme cold of the born-and-bred Louisiana native. Icy indoor temps was a southern tradition she had not recalled until her landing in the 727, but the cold helped now as she fought for control and won. The anger Barry had brought to the surface subsided and Gen found her breath returning to normal, her fingers unclenching from her upper arms.

She turned and moved away from the phone. But as she moved, her attention was caught by the framed photos hanging above the desk. Gen stopped, staring at the photographs. Like the two upstairs in her old room, these were hers. Two were from her first showing, two were from her second.

Gen understood what their appearance in this house meant. Perhaps she had understood from the instant she saw the two upstairs, and the knowledge was like a living thing uncoiling inside her. Her father had not let go when she left the estate in a towering rage at age eighteen. Somehow, he had tracked her down. Kept an eye on her. Now she understood that her vaunted independence, her ability to make her own way in New York City as a young photographer in the seventies had been bankrolled by the Old Man.

She tried to walk away from the photos, but the truth that they represented held her there against her will. Her throat closed up as more sobbing threatened and Gen fought for breath. When it came at last, it tore through the silence of the room like a hoarse scream.

Her father was the anonymous benefactor and admirer who underwrote her first two showings and bought so many of her works. Her father was the man who arranged the meeting with *Mademoiselle* magazine when they were looking for a staff photographer in seventy-six, the interview that gave her an entrée into a different world of photography, the world of high fashion. Her father had done that.

The rage that scourged her during her talk with Barry returned with such fury that she panted with it. She wanted to scream. Weep. Wail. Beat her fists against the photographs until she ground them into dust. Instead, she groaned, the sound echoing in the silent room.

Her father had never let her go. He had made her the success that she had become. Her autonomy was a sham. And she hated him for it. Gen whirled to leave.

A man was leaning against the doorframe, his face and body in shadow with only the tips of his boots catching a stray beam of sunlight. He looked relaxed, almost negligent, his thumbs in the front pockets of his jeans. Wearing work clothes and a two-day beard, he was clearly one of the farmhands. Behind him in the hallway, resting on a hunt-table was a dirt-streaked, sweat-stained hat.

The man looked as if he had been there a while. Watching. Listening. Gen sucked in a furious breath. He was a perfectly framed photograph, and even as her anger found a new target, Gen itched for her camera. Her hands clenched into claws.

He tilted his head slowly.

And instantly she knew him. The posture, that slow gesture, was unforgettable.

Without a word, Gen moved for the door. He didn't shift,

didn't slide to the side to make it easier for her to pass. Didn't take his hands from his pockets. Her boots clomped off the edge of the braided rug and past him, their arms brushing. The contact created a shock of heat in the intensely cold room, a piercing blade of ardor so strong it shocked her to her core.

Suddenly Gen was outdoors beneath the blistering sun, racing for the guesthouse. Soft cries of anguish escaped her as the control she had worn like armor stripped away. Her world was shattering, fracturing into a million pieces. Nothing was as it appeared. Nothing. Tears streamed down her face blurring the vision of the house, trucks and the white Lincoln parked on a concrete pad, barn and horses trotting through the wet waves of misery with Keri and Destan atop, their voices calling. She had no connection to this world of heat and suffering, and suddenly New York was a deception as well. A lie.

The guesthouse door was open, the inside like a furnace, a girl vacuuming the floor beneath the bed. Gen raced for the bathroom, slammed the door and slumped onto the toilet lid, sobbing into the sink. She hated this. Hated this agony, this horror that her life had become. Hated the smell of her clothes, the smell of her own body drenched in a hot sweat. Hated the blister that was forming on her big toe in the boots that were not hers.

Gen drew a shuddering breath and met her reflection in the mirror above the sink. The laughter that bubbled up was hysterical. She was a mess. Red welts ran in tracks down her face, snot ran from her nose.

Raking a hand through her hair, she stood and turned on the tap, flushing her face repeatedly with cool well-water, washing away the signs of her anguish, soothing her irritated skin. Finding a bit of calm in the process of purging her misery. When she looked up, her skin was paler, smoother. If her eyes hadn't been red she might have looked okay. Might have.

Behind her on the shower rod were the things she had left soaking. Her silk outer-wear hung beside them, clean and damp. She would have to tip the cleaning girl. Gen laughed again, the sound still half-sob. Her life was royally screwed up.

And she had to change it. She didn't have to live like this. There was no way she could survive this house, this impending death, this divorce, like this. And so she wouldn't.

Body quivering as if she had run for miles, Gen stood erect and dried her face on a freshly laundered towel, dragging the thick terry across her tender skin. New makeup went on with a shaking hand, and she combed and brushed her hair until it shone and her reflection was more controlled, more like her usual unruffled self. By the time she was presentable, the shakes had passed.

Gen studied herself in the mirror and squared her shoulders. "In the face of my feminist leanings," she said to her image, "I'm going shopping."

◆　◆　◆

Starnes pursed his lips as the sound of her boots dwindled. "Hummm," he murmured. "That went well."

He had meant to speak as soon as he saw her standing in front of the photographs. Had meant to say something suave and smooth and. . . . She had been silent, clenching her hands, gripping her upper arms. The sunlight from the open drape caught her, turning her golden, just like his earliest memory of her. She was still trim, tall, and oddly enough, dressed just the way she had been the day he let her get on a bus for New York and leave him forever. Now she was back and unchanged. Was that an omen?

He rested himself against the doorframe for a moment. Just a moment to watch her. To know that she was really here.

And then she had made a sound and he realized that she was crying and he was intruding. And it was too late to get away. And now she was royally pissed. Starnes sighed, turned, and picked up his hat. He might as well check in on the Old Man while he was here, and bill a few hours. At least he had thought to bring his briefcase.

"I take it things didn't go like what you 'spected."

Della was standing at the end of the hallway, watching Gen cross the yard, and he joined her just as Gen entered the guesthouse. "She staying there?"

"Yes. She staying there. And my baby hurting. She hurting bad." Della looked up at him and lifted a brow. "And I'm wanting to know what you intending to do about it, Mr. Lawyer man. I send you to pick her up at the airport, give you a whole hour to talk to the girl on the way back, and Destan tell me you put her in the back seat and let her go to sleep."

Starnes looked at her, surprised. She had? "Ma'am?"

"Oh, don't you be acting all innocent and upright with me, Mr. Starnes Templer. I know you got eyes for my Geneva, even after all these years. Can't tell me different."

"Only because I know I never stood a chance with you, Della."

Della laughed and shook her head. "Well, I reckon you can go on up to the Old Man, and do whatever it was you planned to do if my Geneva wouldn't have nothing to do with you today."

Starnes smiled down into her face. "I'm that transparent, am I?" he asked wryly.

"Like crystal glass," Della said, patting his arm, amusement in her warm, dark eyes. "But you can stay for supper if you mind your manners. I got on a pot roast and them little red potatoes you like so much. Fried squash and a pot of lima beans, too. And a spinach salad with some raw vegetables and stinky goat cheese for Keri. She a vegetarian, you know."

"I had heard." He wanted to ask about Geneva. Wanted to find out what Della knew about the high profile divorce that had hit the papers. Is that what Gen had been crying about? But Della moved toward the kitchen like a ship under full sail, and he knew that his chance to learn about Gen and Barry Stone was gone, if it had ever existed in the first place.

Gathering his briefcase, he lifted a hand to Della on the way up. The Old Man was awake and still had about a hundred things he wanted to put right before he died. It was proving to be a pain in the neck to be John Deveraux's lawyer, especially as estate planning was not his area of specialization. But he owed the Old Man. And if this was the way he got to see Geneva, then he would take all the Old Man could dish out. And more.

◆　◆　◆

Down below, Della smiled knowingly, stirring the lima beans, tasting, and moving on. She knew her men. And she knew that Starnes Templer was just what the doctor ordered for her baby Geneva.

◆　◆　◆

Gen shopped for four hours, changing out of the smelly jeans in the dressing room of Dillards, trading them for a pair of boot-flared Levi's that were washed to a comfortable softness and a pale indigo shade. The odorous jeans went into a plastic bag that she hoped would mask the horse scent while she shopped. She bought silk underwear and a silk nightgown—the first silk anything she had purchased since leaving Barry—and a dozen pair of cotton panties for riding, She bought two new pair of sandals, a pair of running shoes, and new boots in the same store, appreciating for the first time the convenience of a mall—everything you need under one roof.

She found a dozen T-shirts at Wal-Mart to complement the two rayon skirts that caught her eye, and tossed in a pair of shorts that looked as if they might keep her cool. J.C. Penney had bathing suits on sale and she tried on half a dozen, buying a one-piece maillot with turquoise flowers on a black background because it came with a wide-brimmed hat she liked.

From the mall she drove uptown. There were dresses on sale in Saks Fifth Avenue on Canal Street, and in a wild splurge of multiple-platinum-card-buying she decided on two by B. Michael and one by Renee DuMarr. A red suit created by Karon Lorrance caught her eye, and was added to the pile. She could wear it to her father's funeral with red Rangoni spike heels that seemed made to match.

Red for a funeral. Perfect. There would be no false impression of mourning when the Old Man died. Nothing black. If she was feeling feisty, she might even wear a red rose in her hair.

Somewhere in the buying spree, Geneva found herself again. She smiled and joked with the salesgirls, had a cup of cappuccino and a high-fat po-boy sandwich for lunch, while having her nails clipped short and manicured, had a fresh pedicure, bought some jewelry, some perfume, and enjoyed herself immensely. Barry would have approved the sybaritic pleasure, and so she let him pay for the whole day. The credit cards were his.

Weighed down with packages after hours of shopping, Gen returned to the muffler-less truck she had taken from the estate. It wouldn't have been her first choice for transportation, but it had been the only vehicle with keys in the ignition. It made an awful noise when running, smoked and vibrated like a blender on overload, but the air-conditioner worked. Sort of. Enough to make driving bearable. She just hoped it was an estate truck and not a visitor's truck.

Keys dangling, she remembered the man leaning against the doorframe. Starnes' truck? Not this truck, though it reminded her of his old junker from high school. But he became a doctor or something. Surely he could afford better.

For a moment, she remembered the lazy posture, the hard lean length of him. The man-smell of horse and something like mint. . . . A flare of anger lit her. He had been listening. *Men.*

She layered her packages in the passenger seat and floor, and when the largest package simply wouldn't fit, Gen put it in the truck bed and wedged it in with the spare tire and a plastic gasoline container. "That should do it," she said, slapping the gas-can with an open palm. It was close to rush hour when she finally left New Orleans. The sun a hot golden ball in the west, hitting her eyes with enough glare to blind. Though she hadn't driven the distance in years, she had found her way to the city easily, and the way home seemed like it was tattooed on her eyelids. Some things you never forget.

As she drove, she catalogued her purchases, deciding what she would wear to dinner tonight. She had been forced to wear the jeans last night, and a pair of bedroom slippers borrowed from Keri. Not exactly proper attire for dinner at the Deveraux Estate. Tonight she would make a different kind of impression. If not New York chic, at least not poor-white-trash-come-a-visitin'.

Gen turned on the radio and, amazingly, it worked, blasting a volume of sound she had not expected. The owner of the truck must have put all his upkeep money into a really good sound system. When she couldn't find Public Radio, she settled on a country station playing a retrospective and sang along with Clint, Reba, and the Dixie Chicks as she drove.

Barry had hated country music, and it had remained her secret passion until she left him, at which time she started playing country while she worked. The models she photographed for several high-fashion magazines had been amused. Gen knew all the words. They soothed her. With the music blasting, her mind was free to work, to create. And now it was free to remember the man in the hallway . . . *Starnes.*

He had looked good. Both times she had seen him. Of course, the light had been poor in the study and she had been startled in the terminal. But he had looked . . . better than good. He certainly hadn't been fat. And there had been no indication of the injury that had nearly taken his life. She remembered that, remembered reading about it in numerous letters from Della.

There had been a Lexus parked in the drive. His?

He had gone to med school, gotten a prestigious job—or was it something else? And then she remembered the lawsuits. Civil cases, big settlements. So, he was a lawyer. What had he been doing at the estate? Gen recalled the heat of the accidental touch. She didn't need another man in her life right now. Maybe not ever.

A thought occurred and Gen gripped the steering wheel. *Lily.* If Lily had sent him to her, had planned the whole thing with Starnes to get her over Barry. . . . Gen laughed. "I'll get you sister-mine, if you planned this. I'll get you back. . . ." Relaxing, she drove into the dazzling sun.

8

TRAINED FRENCH RAT TO PERK HER UP

"You can't just admit to murder and expect me to forget it," Starnes said, slamming papers into his briefcase. He had known this job would be difficult, but it was worse than he ever expected. "At least not this lawyer. Damn it, John—"

"Why not?" the Old Man said, sitting up angrily, his arms braced back against the pillows. "I'm telling you," he panted, "to take it to the sheriff. He'll have to re-open an investigation closed nearly thirty years, but that's his damn job. It's what the taxpayers . . ." he gasped, ". . . pay him to do." The Old Man's flesh had taken on an alarming hue, the mottled purple of rage and oxygen deprivation.

Starnes turned from the sickbed to the window, not seeing the garden below. Not seeing anything except the crater the Old Man had dug for him. The headache he had been fighting for the last hour was growing into a monster and if it hadn't been ethical suicide, he'd have pummeled his client senseless.

"Damn your Frenchy eyes, face me when I'm talking to you!" Slowly Starnes turned and met the angry black eyes of John Deveraux. The Old Man had been the most powerful man in the parish for nearly fifty years, the boss man who hired and fired field laborers, who put politicians, judges, and sheriffs into office, determined which businesses and which newspapers were going to find success, and which were doomed to failure. He ran the parish as if it were his own personal fiefdom. He had bought and sold power for decades, and now he was dying, his hands still around the throats of the people he had bought. And Starnes was one of them.

"It'll take time to find witnesses, question people, most of whom are probably dead anyway," the Old Man said with a wheeze. "By the time he has enough to charge me, *I'll be dead.*"

Deveraux laughed hoarsely and coughed into a tissue, cleaning away bloody spittle that clung to his lips in long strings. He fought for breath that refused to fill his diseased lungs, his face gray and exhausted as he fell back on the pillows. The huge tabby cat that sat on his lap stared hard at him, her tail twitching nervously.

The cat was a fairly new addition to the sickroom, and Starnes had to admit surprise at seeing it. As a kid, he had once seen the Old Man shoot a cat just for kicks. He had been trying out his new handgun, and the cat made a good moving target. John and cats had always hated each other, but this feline seemed to like the Old Man, a traitor to its species.

Starnes looked down at the papers in his briefcase and smoothed out several he had crushed in his anger, waiting out the attack, hoping this one wasn't the one that killed John Deveraux. It was hard to stay angry at a man on his deathbed, even if the man was a certified pain in the butt.

"And if by some miracle I *am* still alive," John finally wheezed again, "he'll have to find money . . . in the parish budget . . . to pay for the chemo I'll suddenly decide I need. . . . So put it in writing . . . and stop being such a wuss."

Starnes shook his head. "Wuss?"

"Destan taught me," the Old Man said, gasping like a fish pulled to shore. "Smart kid, my grandson. He thinks it comes from a combination of wienie and p—"

"I know the word."

"Good word. So?"

"Tell me about it. The . . . killing."

"You gonna take notes like a real lawyer, or you gonna stand there like a *gou-gut?*"

Starnes clicked a pen open, fighting amusement. "What do you know about *des gou-gut?* That's Cajun talk, there, Old Man." When John answered him with a glare, Starnes sat and slowly pulled a legal pad towards him. "I reckon I'm going to take notes. Sir."

The Old Man rested, ignoring the tone of his legal council, breathing shallowly for a long moment. And then he started speaking, talking for an hour until his voice was little more than a rasp and his breath was completely gone. His eyes stared out the window, distracted, seeing nothing except for the ancient pictures in his mind. He shared details as they came, random remnants of blood and anger nearly four decades old.

It was the kind of tale that couldn't be faked. Starnes knew that if it was a made-up thing, a concocted story, then the details would have been expressed in an orderly way so the mind could remember what it wanted to say. Could remember the falsehood for future repetition. But this was grisly and random, and had no rhyme or reason behind it. It was just rage and violence, and as the Old Man talked, Starnes knew that this story could ruin any legacy the Old Man had hoped to leave. It was a story that could destroy his daughters, hurt Della. This was a disaster.

Starnes sat silently throughout, taking the requested notes. Finally the Old Man stopped, his breathing so ragged and thick it sounded like he was breathing pond scum.

"If you can find any heirs after I'm gone—a brother or sister still living—they get the money, the restitution in the will," he whispered. "And do whatever you think best about going to the sheriff, now or after I'm dead. I couldn't care less at this point. But don't mention this to the girls, you understand? Not until the sheriff opens an investigation and it becomes public." The Old Man's eyes flared a brief black fire beneath bushy brows that time hadn't thinned. "This is privileged information," he said fiercely, "client to lawyer."

"I know my ethics," Starnes said mildly, closing the pad he used for notes and putting it away.

"That's why I picked you as my estate lawyer. Honest Abe. Your reputation preceded you." The Old Man rested his head against the pillows and closed his eyes. He was gasping, his face gray, and Starnes knew he needed the oxygen he had removed during his recitation. Stubborn old man. The cat rose and walked up John's chest until she was nose-to-nose with him, purring.

"And the fact that I was the only lawyer within a hundred miles who would agree to work for you might have figured into your thinking a bit."

The Old Man laughed silently and shook his head against the cotton shams. "Cheeky bastard," he said, his voice roughened by coughing. "Should have turned you over to the police when I caught you pilfering that sweet-feed."

"But you didn't. Instead you sent me to law school."

"I figured I might need a trained rat one day," he breathed. "Trained French rat."

Starnes laughed then, and the Old Man opened an eye. He grinned back and closed his lid, one hand smoothing the cat's coat, settling her back to his lap. "I'm not going to last much longer. You don't have much time."

"I'd have been finished tonight if you hadn't thrown in this monkey wrench," Starnes said as he snapped his briefcase shut.

"Just . . . do it." The Old Man waved him away with a weak hand. His nail-beds were a deep shade of purple. "See you . . . tomorrow."

"I'll be here."

Starnes crossed the hallway, inhaling the mouthwatering smell of pot roast. Hungry, having worked through lunch, his stomach growled. He stuck his head in the equipment room and greeted the night nurse. "Howdy beautiful. The Old Man took off his oxygen."

"So what color is he this time?" Beckah asked.

"Somewhere between gray and purple."

"Stubborn old coot," she said, squinting at him above her reading glasses.

Starnes said. "He is that." *And a murderer, if what he said was true.*

Starnes was too tired to be angry with the Old Man. John Deveraux had given him permission to call the sheriff. Had practically ordered him to call. Starnes knew Sheriff Pritchard pretty well. Maybe he could talk to him about the confession, and together they could keep an investigation unofficial. At least for a while.

"Oh well, it's time for a breathing treatment anyway," Beckah said, pulling herself out of a desk chair and turning to an array of blue plastic equipment. "He always gets worse at night, just to spite me. And I mean he gets harder to work with at night as much as he gets sicker at night."

"That's why they pay you the big bucks, Beckah," Starnes teased.

"So marry me, handsome," she said in her thick west Texas drawl, "and let me take you away from all this. With my millions I can support you in the style to which you're accustomed."

"Howie would pin my ears back if I even tried. And I kinda

like my ears the way they are."

Beckah snorted with pleasure. Starnes had known Beckah since he was a kid fresh out of law school. She had been the private nurse of his first client, and he had recommended her to other clients since. She was loyal and knew her business—and she was particularly good with recalcitrant patients. Howie, her husband, was retired now and the two traveled to whatever city the private nursing business took her. They lived in a big silver travel-home for as long as a job lasted, and then pulled up roots and moved the R.V. on to the next locale. They were good people. And Starnes bet that Beckah would never ruin *her* lawyer's day by confessing murder.

◆　◆　◆

Gen dressed for dinner in one of the new rayon skirts and a loose T-shirt, both in shades of pale butter. While she was shopping, a window unit air-conditioner had been installed in the living room of the guesthouse, and with the place clean and deodorized, it was rather homey, and certainly cooler. Her clothes didn't stick to her skin the moment they touched her.

However, with her needs met and her body clean and relaxed, there were no distractions for her mind. Nothing to stop her from dealing with the truth. Gen brushed her hair, remembering the afternoon for the first time. While in New Orleans, she had managed to put it all from her. She hadn't thought about the Old Man finding her, paying her way in New York when she left home. She hadn't thought about the photographs hanging on the walls of the house. Hadn't thought about her vaunted independence—an independence that was a lie.

Gen sighed. She had to admit that she had wondered about the financier who backed her first two shows. But the thought that it might, possibly, be the Old Man had never occurred to her. After all, how could he have found her? She left no clues and it was years before she wrote home to Della. Knowing the Old Man, if he had found her, he would have brought her home, not left her in a strange Yankee city. And he certainly would not have supported her.

She could hear her own lie. Gen put down the brush and closed her eyes. Her father had supported her financially for years, until her photography became successful. Could she accept that? More importantly, could she deny it any longer?

Gen moved through the small guesthouse, touching a vase on the mantle, adjusting a curtain. Feeling the new reality settle into her. It was truth, she finally decided. Truth with a capital T, and therefore not to be ignored. She had always been good at handling the truth, even painful truth, like Barry with another woman. She could handle this, too. She pulled the pair of new gold sandals out of the box and slipped them on her feet. "Perfect."

A knock sounded at the door, but before she could respond, Lily opened it and came in, dropped on the couch in a melodramatic faint, closed her eyes, and sighed. She looked wilted. "God, he is such a pain in the tush."

"Still alive and kicking, I take it."

"Not kicking exactly, but making demands like I'm his servant. With Della waiting on him hand and foot, which seriously ticks me off."

"Della always did wait on him hand and foot."

"He put her kids through college. She was grateful."

When Gen didn't respond Lily opened her eyes and surveyed the room. "Barry must have called. You went shopping without me."

Gen laughed at her sister's tone and sat on the edge of the bed. "I was angry. He forced Jo to call the Estate. And then he made a smart comment about going barefoot after the plane landed."

Lily paused a moment. "I *said*, 'You–went–*shopping*–without–*me*.' "

"Oh. Okay. I'm sorry. I know better."

"Forgiven." Lily leaned her head back. "You look good. All you need is some jewelry and you'll look like a million dollars."

Gen ignored the jewelry comment for the moment, and asked the question uppermost in her mind. "Did the Old Man support me while I was in New York?"

Lily lifted a brow, her feline body suddenly, oddly motionless. "You saw the photographs."

Gen watched a change come over her sister as she spoke. Watchful. Wary. Vaguely defensive. Speaking to that change, she said softly, "I saw them. . . . And you were the only person I wrote to when I first left. Through Starnes Templar." Lily grew still as Gen spoke, pale marble, waiting. "Was it you or Starnes who told him where I was?" Gen asked.

Lily sat up stiffly, her eyes hooded, guarded. After a long moment she said, "I told him."

When Gen didn't move, Lily continued, speaking slowly, as if Gen were a wild animal needing to be gentled, as if she might attack or fly away. Gen watched her sister, feeling dissociated, strangely detached from the conversation.

"He had Della search my room until she found the letters. And when she did . . . he turned me over his knee and beat me until I told him everything he wanted to know about you," Lily said.

Gen blinked, watching her sister's face, ashen in the lamplight.

"That was the night I left home and moved in with Jason. We took off for California two weeks later and didn't look back."

Gen looked down at her hands. Subconsciously she had expected something like that. She had hoped that no one would get hurt when she left. She should have known better. "I'm sorry you were hurt because of me," she said softly. "I'm sorry you left home and didn't finish high school and went through hell with Jason because of me."

Lily smiled slowly and shrugged. "Water under the bridge, sister-mine." And then she changed the subject as Lily often did when things became too personal or too painful to discuss. "I still think you need some jewelry. I have a pair of gold hoops—"

"What are you up to?" Gen asked, smiling, glad of the reprieve.

"Me? I'm up to nothing sister-mine. I'm too tired to be up to anything."

"So why all the sudden interest in my looking good. Does it have something to do with Starnes Templer picking me up at the airport and dropping by the house today? I told you I am not interested in being fixed up."

Lily straightened. "Starnes is the Old Man's estate lawyer. He comes about three or four days a week. But now that you mention it, an old lover might be just the thing to perk you up."

"I do not need an old lover to perk me up."

"You went shopping without me. Have you been shopping

since you left Barry? At all?"

Gen rolled her eyes.

"Um-hummm. You haven't been shopping at all until now, have you."

"Starnes had nothing to do with it."

Lily just grinned. "Good. Because Della invited him to dinner. And you look ravishing."

9

COON-ASS FOR DE TRUTH and THE BOSS MAN

Gen was half-sitting, her camera in her lap, when Starnes stepped down from the master suite. Her back was turned, her attention directed to Destan, who slumped on the loveseat beside the fireplace, one leg over the arm, foot swinging. Starnes stood in the shadows and watched.

"I was too mad to go riding this afternoon, Destan. Your Uncle Barry is a—well a problem, and he had me steaming. Besides, *I* went riding while you were still sound asleep this morning. While it was cool?" Gen said, as if to point out that he never got out of bed until noon.

Destan grinned at her comment, unrepentant. Gen snapped the shot of the impudent smile. Starnes leaned against the doorjamb and watched.

"I haven't been on horseback since I was your age," Gen continued. "My knees and backside have to be broken in slowly, not at a hard gallop with you two. As it is, I'm stiff as a board." She extended a leg, stretching the knee joint to its fullest extension. Gold sandals caught the light and Starnes stared, mesmerized at the length of calf revealed by the motion.

"How come I have a feeling you meant something about Uncle Barry besides 'problem'? Watching your mouth in front of the kiddies, Aunt Gen?" Destan teased.

"Exactly." Gen said. "Your Uncle Barry is not a topic for polite conversation. Let me take another shot. No don't move. I like the pose." She rose and crossed the room, stepped behind a serving table and focused on Destan. He smiled up at her, his expression cocky, unembarrassed at being photographed. As if he was accustomed to the camera when his Aunt Gen was around.

"Head tilted a bit. No, the other way. Good." The shutter clicked several times, the handheld flash throwing shadows.

"Now, close your eyes halfway and lay your head back, like you're sleepy. Perfect," she said, taking several more shots. "Hand at your waist, tuck it into your pants. No, fingers in, thumb out. Yes, good.

"I wish we had better light. Keri, would you open the shutters? I think. . . ." She paused as the girl moved to the windows and opened the wooden shutters allowing in the last rays of pink sunset that softened the room and Destan's face into something approaching angelic.

"Oh, yes. I like that." She adjusted the camera and took a half dozen more shots, adjusted again and took the rest of the roll before changing for a new one.

Destan looked amused and relaxed. Starnes knew it would be a great photograph, one a model would take to an agent, or a mother would proudly frame. He had a few of himself in his house, photographs Gen had made as a teen. He hadn't looked at them in years, but even then she had shown promise, the instinctive ability to capture a subject and work with light.

Keri came over and slipped an arm around Starnes' waist, her eyes on Gen. "I want to be just like her someday," she whispered. "You know?"

"I know. You want to live in Noow York City," he said, in a broad Oklahoma accent, "go to parties, eat that there *paté*—did you know that stuff is made with gizzards and livers and such?— hang out with the rich and famous."

"No!" Keri punched his arm, her voice still low enough to leave photographer and subject undisturbed. "I want to be able to see things like she does. Know how to take a scene and make it better, adjust for light and shadow. She sees things differently from most people. Purer maybe, like she sees things the way they are supposed to be instead of the way they are. You know?"

Gen moved Destan's foot to the front of the sofa, pulled off his shoe and took two quick steps back as if the foot stank. Destan laughed at her as she re-focused the shot while making stinky-foot faces. She was oblivious to everything in the world right now except Destan, and even he was little more than a subject to be cajoled into the correct position for the perfect shot.

Starnes stared, feeling an ache he hadn't known existed. "She always did see things differently from the rest of us," he said.

"She always had something . . . special."

"Mom says you had a thing for her once." Keri looked up at him, her expression knowing and arch. Far too mature for her age. "And she says you're Cajun. That's like French, right?"

Starnes grinned and pinched her cheek. "Your mom talking about me, huh?"

"So, are you? Did you? Have a thing for Aunt Gen?"

"*Oui, mamselle*, a French-man, me," he said, watching her eyes sparkle with delight. "Coon-ass for de truth. And yes, *me sha*, I had a thing for your Aunt Gen," he said, and the words felt heavy and thick in his mouth, clogged with the residue of years.

"Hmmm. I thought so. Come on, she's done. I want her to take your picture now. So I can have a copy to take back to South Carolina with me."

"Why?" Starnes asked, as Keri pulled him across the room. And then *Ginny* looked at him and the answer to his question fell on deaf ears, if Keri even bothered to respond at all.

"Starnes." Gen put out a hand, took his and drew him into a polished New York hug, her cheek brushing his just long enough for his bristles to scratch her skin, long enough to catch a whiff of her cologne, something spicy and smoky, before she drew away. Fine laugh lines etched her eyes as she smiled. He could see the powder on her cheeks, lipstick a pale pink on her mouth.

She wasn't what he expected, and a rush of something primal and shocking went through him. She was not the girl who walked away from him when she was eighteen. She wasn't some memory pieced together from bits and fragments. She was the woman she had become by living in New York, taking photographs for fashion magazines and political campaigns. She was the woman who counted couture designers and Fortune 500 magnates as friends, who attended parties and hosted charity functions on the arm of Barry Stone. She wasn't his little Gen anymore. And he didn't know her at all.

"You're still as beautiful as ever, *Ginny*," he heard himself say.

She laughed and blushed. "Thank you, Starnes." No simpering declarations of false modesty.

"Aunt Gen, take his picture. He's gorgeous for an old guy," Keri said.

And Gen laughed again, sharing a look with him that said, '*Old* guy? That dates us!'

"I took many a picture of Starnes when we were in our teens. Mind?"

Starnes shook his head and shrugged. At the moment he would have let her carve him up and serve him as appetizers at one of her parties if it made her happy.

No. She wasn't what he expected. She didn't smell of horse and barn and clean sweat; she smelled of that exotic scent, one so lightly applied that he found himself bending to catch and identify it, even as she bullied him into the hallway outside the Old Man's office to take his photograph, placing his hands in his pockets, his old hat on the hunt-board in the hallway. And when Della called that dinner was served, and Keri and Destan took off, leaving them alone, she smiled up at him.

"I'm sorry for running off earlier today." She took the shot at that moment, catching his face in whatever emotion her words drew out of him. "I had a difficult phone call and you caught me at bad moment."

She took another shot, as he tried to master his expression. Somehow it was more difficult to find control with Gen and her camera watching than it had ever been with a judge and twelve jurors. He wasn't accustomed to feeling off-base with women, except with Serena, and that was a different situation entirely. "I didn't mean to intrude." He exhaled, trying to force out tension, knowing he was reacting like the teenager he had been, the last time he was alone with Gen.

"No problem. No. Don't talk. Just stand there." She took several shots, then came close and reached up, tilting his face into shadow, avoiding his eyes. Her fingers were cool, sliding over his rough beard like silk. "I like the two-day beard. It's perfect with this poor light. Now. Hold that pose."

Several shots later, she handed him his hat and turned off the office light. "Put it on. I want to see. . . . No, pull it down, so the brim covers your eyes. Great. I love this. You are just lean and rough enough to make this work. Put your thumbs in your pockets, let your hands . . . Yes. I like that. Long lean fingers, the hands of an artist on the body of a roughneck. So sexy," she breathed.

That strange something sped through him again at her words,

though he knew she might have spoken them to any model who pleased her.

"Perfect," she said, sighing as she took several shots, stopping to adjust the F-stops and shutter speed before taking more.

Starnes was acutely aware of the shadows, Gen's nearness, the touch of her hands as she moved his finger a fraction of an inch to the left, shoved his toe back and crossed one ankle over the other, moving her hands over him with effortless proficiency. If he didn't stop this, she would have no doubt about his reaction to her. Or maybe this wasn't the time to stop anything.

"Gen. I'm hungry," he said, his lips moving under the brim of his hat. She grunted and moved close again, tilting his head to suit her. Moving him as if he were one of her models. He smiled. "No, I mean I'm really hungry. I haven't eaten since morning." Ignoring him, she took several more shots before coming close again.

With a single quick motion, Starnes took her arm in his hand and bent close. Startling her. "Let me eat, woman, or pay the consequences."

"Con...Consequences?" she said. And her voice was suddenly breathless, the professional tone dissolved. "What kind of. . . ."

Starnes smiled slowly, moving his thumb across her skin. It was like expensive silk. That real shiny stuff. Charmeuse. She shivered and his smile widened. He bent his head, bringing his lips close to her mouth. "Feed me, *mamselle* or I might die. Right here at your feet—"

"You two comin' or I got to go ring the big brass dinner bell out on the deck," Della said. "I got me a good meal going to waste. Now come on. You can court later."

She bustled them into the kitchen and sat them down across from one another, serving up huge portions of pot roast and vegetables and potatoes, just as she had promised. And Starnes ate like the roughneck he had just been called, satisfied to catch Gen looking at him with a puzzled look in her eyes. Twice.

Della had used the word *court*. Starnes thought that might be just the right word to express what had happened in the hallway. Finally, after all these years, he was courting Gen. Though she wasn't what he remembered or expected, there was still something there, something. . . .

She didn't sit down to table in jeans or a '70's peasant dress; she floated into the room wearing some filmy linen thing that caught the light and looked like a million dollars. She didn't sit quietly while others spoke at the dinner table; she led in conversation, she pulled everyone into it, even him, made certain that each person played a part in the discussions. She steered all talk away from anything remotely unpleasant. Paris hotels, fast horses, and New York fashions were acceptable subjects for conversation, as was the Washington political scene. The Middle East, local politics, and religion were not. She sparkled. It was a battle to keep his eyes off her.

He wanted her. Twenty-nine years had passed and neither of them were the same. Both of them had led full lives and had established professional reputations. Neither of them were simply the children of their parents anymore, looking for something new and exciting and self-defining. They were grown, and actually *old*, if Keri was to be believed. And he still wanted her. He would have wanted her even if this had been the first time he ever set eyes on her.

Starnes wasn't a particularly religious man. Raised Catholic, then attending an evangelical Church of God with his father, after one of the drunken old sot's many religious rebirths—a conversion that actually lasted beyond the need of the next bottle—Starnes had seen too much to believe in anyone else's God. There were too many of them, all called the same thing, or all evolved from the same pattern. God-of-love who offered an unreasoned, injudicious un-analytical love and expected that to be enough. God-the-opposite who was hellfire and brimstone and judgmental and vicious. God-Allah, Jesus, God-Jehovah, the Holy Spirit. . . . Too much and too little, and all likely contained something of God, yet Starnes believed that God was something more and better than any one version of Him—It—Her?

But something about Gen made him question his previous cynicism. Just sitting across from him, she was evidence of something beyond his understanding. Kismet? Predestination? Providence? Something. Because he belonged with this woman. The knowledge was crystal and sunlight, sparkling together inside him. He wanted her like an ancient ache in his soul. His body cried out for her with the acute need of a teenager, his pulse and breathing too fast. She was his, and he was hers. And she didn't know it.

And if the Old Man didn't live long enough for him to have a chance, then Starnes might have to travel to New York to court her. But court her he would. Starnes smiled at Gen across the table and she smiled back, her expression quizzical.

Beckah's voice sounded down the stairway, interrupting his thoughts. "Starnes! Della!" she shouted, her tone restrained panic.

In an instant, Starnes was up and climbing two steps at a time, pain he ignored shooting through his leg and hip like wildfire, his boots resounding throughout the house. He could hear Della pushing past the rest of the family, no longer as fast on her feet as they, she used her bulk to make a passage through them. By the time he entered the Old Man's room, Della was just behind him, shutting the door in the family's faces.

The Old Man was a deep purple shade, his eyes glassy and half open, his mouth hanging to the side. Starnes glanced at Beckah and lifted John's head, following her unspoken command. The movement opened John's airway, but there was no instant intake of breath. Beckah placed an ambu bag over John's mouth and began to compress the bag, forcing breath into the Old Man's lungs.

Della checked his pulse, counting aloud, comparing the numbers to her watch until she reached a satisfactory 107 at 60 seconds. "A little too fast, but it's real regular, Beckah. An' strong." Lifting his lids, she said, "His pupils is fine, but maybe a little too tiny. Dat medicine you and the doctor got him on make it hard to tell much 'bout them."

But, pulse rate notwithstanding, the Old Man didn't come around. His color deepened, his limbs slack, limp.

"Another minute and I'm calling nine-one-one," Beckah said.

A moment later, John Deveraux groaned and lifted a hand as if to push them away, or argue with Beckah's statement.

"He coming around," Della said. "Stubborn ol' coot."

John took several shallow breaths, coughed and gagged, trying to clear his airway. Beckah removed the ambu bag, allowing him room to breathe. She wrapped the nasal cannula around his ears, tucked the ends into his nostrils, and tightened the plastic tubes in place.

The Old Man pushed at her hands, and Beckah said, "Sorry John. You need this oxygen and I don't care whether you like it or not. Take it off again, and I'll suture it on."

"Old Man, you take that ox'gen and don't let me see you saying no. I slap you up both sides you head you give Beckah trouble."

"Della," he whispered. "Bossy old . . . woman."

"Uh huh. Dat me. And you know I means it, too."

John laughed breathlessly. "I'll be good."

"Dat'll be the day."

Starnes sat back on the small upholstered chair and stretched out his legs, drained. The pain that started on his rush up the stairs wasn't fading. He had pulled something, and the agony was a bright heat in his foot, his knee, his hip. He stared at the Old Man, watching his color slowly turn less gray, though not a healthy pink.

This wasn't the first time the Old Man had crashed when he was on the premises, and now Starnes had assisted both times to keep him alive, once even pumping the ambu bag to feed his client oxygen. It wasn't an activity usually covered in an attorney's billable hours, but there were extenuating circumstances with this client.

John had signed a complicated living will designating Starnes as his legal representative for as long as he was clinically alive. Starnes had resisted the legal stratagem, not wanting the responsibility, but the Old Man had insisted. Should his lungs give out too soon, John wanted extended life-support until the will and estate papers were completed and filed. Then he would be ready to go, and Starnes would be responsible for whatever legal maneuvers were necessary to have life-support removed.

John Deveraux had no intention of vegetating on a respirator, he wanted to be in charge of how long he stayed around to torment the rest of the world. It looked as if Starnes had avoided that life-and-death responsibility for the moment. His hands were shaking, however, and he glared at John. "You took off the oxygen again, didn't you?"

"Dries out my nose. Can't stand it."

"I'll be forced to tape the O-two to your face and around your head. Or call the hospital and tell them to come get you," Beckah said, standing and moving to where the Old Man could view her unimpeded. "I won't be responsible for your expiring due to lack of oxygen. This is the last time, understand Mr. Deveraux? If you take off the O-two again, I will tender my resignation."

Starnes looked up in surprise. He had never heard Beckah threaten a patient before. He knew the Old Man was a sneaky pain in the butt, but Beckah could handle anything. Yet, she stood there, all five feet two inches of her, arms akimbo, face flushed from dealing with the crisis, clearly angry. In fact, furious.

"Do you understand me, John Deveraux?"

The old man cocked his head. "So quit," he managed in a hoarse whisper.

Starnes began to smile, caught himself and looked down at his hands. He had a feeling. . . .

"And if I quit, my last official act will be to find a judge and tell him that you are no longer in control of your faculties, not competent to make the decision to accept home care."

The Old Man gave a weak version of his patented glare, but it slid right off Beckah's shield of righteous anger.

"I'll insist you be moved to a hospital immediately. By calling it a life-and-death situation, there won't be time for the usual court rigmarole. You'll go directly to the hospital to be evaluated by competent specialists, and put on a ventilator for the rest of your un-natural days. I'll see to that."

John lifted his head a fraction. "Starnes?" he whispered.

Starnes continued to look at his hands, lacing his fingers in that lawyerly fashion that suggested deep thought, but really giving himself something to look at so that John Deveraux couldn't see into his eyes. "I guess Beckah is concerned that her license could be threatened should you die for lack of oxygen. This sounds like a move designed to protect herself as well as you." Starnes nodded slowly as if thinking. "I think she might go through with it."

"And?" he whispered.

"And a judge might listen. She's been your nurse. She could call me incompetent to be your legal representative, imply I might benefit somehow from your early death. A judge might take over, make you a ward of the court—"

"Bullshit." He lay his head back to the pillow. "What's that line

. . . about dazzle 'em with bullshit? . . . Both of you. . . . And, young man . . . I'll hold you responsible if this . . . ogre-in-white attempts anything . . . legal." He had seen through the ploy. But he was smiling. Sort of.

Starnes shook his head. "Are you going to keep the oxygen on, John? Beckah may really have a problem if you died without it just because you're a stubborn old bastard. And I like her too much to let that happen."

"I'll keep it on," he said, waving them off. "Go away. Want to go to sleep."

Beckah looked at Starnes and gave him a half smile. "For a lawyer, you don't lie too well."

"A little warning might have helped."

"Go on. Get out of here. It's about time for his breathing treatment and then I have to get him on the bedpan."

"No privacy," the Old Man whispered. "And no dignity."

"Oh, cry me a river," Della said, opening the door.

"How is he?" Lily asked.

Starnes was surprised to see the whole crowd in the hallway, Lily and Gen trying not to look anxious, Destan and Keri looking worried, as much for their mother and aunt as for the old man they had never met until this week. Ignoring Della's attempt to shoo them off, they all crowded into the sickroom.

The Old Man looked up, saw them standing there with sober faces, and he sat up in the bed, his face a thundercloud. "Out! All of you."

"I see you survived," Gen said, dryly.

"Out. You want to stand around and gawk, go to the zoo. And you can go back to New York where you belong."

"I intend to. As soon as you die. I came here to see you dead and no one is going to deprive me of the pleasure. Remember?"

"Ginny!" Della said severely. "Shame—"

John Deveraux started laughing and lay deeper in his pillows. His color continued to improve as he chuckled, pinkening up nicely. Starnes looked at Beckah who shrugged, but didn't insist they all leave. "Just as feisty as your mother," the Old Man said, "and just as pretty."

Gen's eyes narrowed at the mention of her mother.

"Go home, girl."

"Or what? You'll haul me out to the barn and whip me unconscious? Like you did that black stablehand who didn't rub down your horse to suit you?"

The Old Man's eyes widened and the amusement slipped from his face.

Starnes lifted his head, scenting trouble. But Gen turned on her heel and left the room. Lily sighed and said goodnight, following her sister, the kids close behind.

"Whipped a stablehand, John?" Starnes said softly. "This something else you intended to tell me someday soon?"

The Old Man turned his face away, his expression stony.

"And felt right shamed of it afterward," Della said after a moment. "Brung in the white doctor and had kep' that boy in the guesthouse for three week, till he well enough to go, and him a black Cajun, too. Tell him, Old Man." When John turned his head further, divorcing himself from the conversation, she continued. "Sent that boy to medical school, he did. Got him a practice in Detroit, now. Rich man. All because of the Old Man."

"And all he had to do to win a college education is get whipped like a field slave. Right John? *Quoi t'as dit?* Boss man say you git whipped, then you git whipped!" Starnes anger built. The Old Man kept his face to the wall. "And you think it's all right, what he did?"

"No. It ain't all right," Della half shouted. "It was wrong and I tol' him so then, to his face. He tried to make up for it when the sheriff come. Told him what he done. But the sheriff askt 'round, listen to all the stories Asa and me had to tell, and the other hands who was there. Say he *'can't charge no white man for disciplining no nigger Cajun, worthless trash, all of 'em.'*"

Starnes turned to her, his anger dissolving into something less hard, something impotent and paralyzed. He had heard such talk himself when he was young, talk directed at his father and mother, himself, his friends, though his skin was olive and French, not black and French.

Della's face was stony, wounded. "That the way it was back then," she said, stating fact, but not excusing it. "I don't say it right. It dead wrong. Lot wrong with the world then, and still a lot to change now, but that the way it was. So the Old Man make up for losing his temper bes' way he know. Make Adam Wellspointe well, he did, support his mother and the rest of her chilrens while he in school, and pay for the school. Not a loan, mind you. Just *pay* for it. *Outright!*"

Sick at the story, and even more sick at Della who seemed to accept it with equanimity, Starnes pressed his fist to the hollow of his belly where acid boiled and burned away whatever was left of his stomach lining. It was a case of the Big Boss complex, something left over from slavery and the days of sharecropping. The days when the white land-owner was *king*, the Boss Man. Lord of his land and his people, whether they were slave or sharecropper or employee, the white male had the power of life and death over those who worked land they didn't own. Della, watching his face, stomped from the room, her wide skirts swinging, swishing displeasure.

Starnes' own people had been sharecroppers, poor Cajun drunkards who were treated as the young black man had been. People who had no power, no rights under the law, and even if the law itself offered protection, the elected officials who were paid to uphold that law refused to do so. It was part of the reason Starnes had gone into law, back when he was idealistic, young and foolish, to protect the powerless. Thinking that, even if Deveraux's money did pay his tuition, he could stay free of Deveraux taint, the shackles of being bought and paid for. And here he was, working to make John Deveraux's last wishes possible. No wiser than any of the legions who had taken the Old Man's gold for services rendered.

"Starnes. . . . Come here."

The Old Man's raspy voice brought him back, demanding as always. John sat upright in the bed, supported by pillows, the oxygen cannula in his nose as Beckah attached an IV to the heparin lock in his left hand for nighttime painkillers. The nurse ignored them both as attorney and client stared across the room. Finally Starnes moved, slowly, unwillingly, to the foot of the bed, and John's eyes shone with fierce amusement.

Between harsh, shallow breaths, he said, "Don't think we're done . . . with my will, Frenchy-boy. . . . We got lots to cover yet. According to the good . . . Father Tony, I have lots to atone for . . . and you are the one going to see . . . that atonement through."

"A religious conversion, Old Man? Don't sound like you

somehow."

A wet-sounding laugh came from the cancerous lungs. "Okay. So I got a few forest fires to put out . . . before I let the Devil have me. However you want it, long as you handle them for me," He grinned, the smile managing to appear lascivious, even beneath the oxygen lines.

10
LITTLE MISS HIGH AND MIGHTY DEVERAUX

Gen sat on the swing on her little guesthouse porch, gold slippers to the side, her bare feet sliding on the smooth boards, the slight breeze created by her passage sweeping her long skirt back and forth. The night was balmy, the buzz of insects muted off in the distance, the silence of the night broken only by bullfrogs croaking in the bayou and the horse pond.

She heard the crunch of booted feet and instantly knew it was Starnes, the slight limp that was not visible to the naked eye a faint irregularity of sound. On some level, she had been waiting for him, expecting him. She wasn't exactly comfortable with the thought that she had been sitting in the moonlight waiting for Starnes Templar, and she smiled ruefully in the darkness as a mild case of guilt assailed her. Barry Stone's specter wasn't easy to dismiss; he may as well have been sitting in the swing beside her. And then she remembered the woman in his office that day only a few weeks past, and her guilt shriveled.

"Out for a stroll, counselor?"

"Nice night for it." He stopped just beyond the porch, propped one boot on the second step and crossed his arms. His skin gleamed in the darkness, his black hair seeming to catch the moonlight and throw back dark reflections. She remembered that moment in the hallway and closed her eyes.

"Your father's going to last the night, looks like."

"Ummm."

"He's a stubborn old man. Should have been dead months ago." When she didn't reply, he said, "Want to tell me about it?"

"Tell you about what?"

"Whatever you're thinking about so hard."

Gen had no intention of telling him that she had been thinking about his thumb on her arm this evening, or about the memory that was suddenly so vibrant in her mind. The remembrance of the young Starnes, his long fingers playing the piano in the church basement. Like watching them dance across the keys. He had played by ear, eyes closed, a smile on his lips, fingers stroking the keys. A small pulse of warmth had shimmered through her at the sight, and the memory of his hands had stayed forever fresh.

"My father is a sorrysonabitch," she said slowly. "And I am just as ashamed of him today as when I was a kid."

"That why you never told me about the stablehand he whipped?"

The memory of the long fingers withered. After a moment she said, "I never told because I played a part in it." Gen looked up at him standing in the moonlight and shadow. "I brought a mare in all sweaty and lathered that day, and left her with the head groom. That was when I was younger and a bit too big for my britches."

"Little Miss High and Mighty Deveraux."

Gen laughed. "I haven't been called that in years." After a moment she went on, not certain why she told him this now, after all these years. "Anyway, I dropped off the mare and took the shortcut through the barn. I could hear someone crying."

Gen paused, and Starnes stepped to the porch, propped on the railing and stared at her. She could feel his eyes on her in the darkness, warm and probing. Another memory surfaced, of his mouth on hers in his old pickup. A hard shiver took her and she gripped her arms in the night.

"The whip cracked and he screamed. It was a broken sound, like an animal. I put my eye to door and saw him hanging by his hands from a chain looped around the rafter. He was stripped naked and blood ran down him like sweat. And my father was splattered with the blood, wielding the whip, his arm rising and falling. Shouting. Raving. Asa stood just beyond, watching, smoking a cigarette. And that poor young boy. . . ." She swallowed, mouth dry.

"I ran to the house and told Della. She took off for the barn and I didn't know what to do. So I called the sheriff." Gen looked up at Starnes again, his eyes like mystic holes in the darkness. "The dispatcher laughed at me. But she said she'd send a car around. I called the sheriff to tell them my father was killing a man and they laughed at me." Gen shook her head, the memory abruptly pungent and ripe. She could almost smell the sweat and the ammoniac scent of urine and fear that had wafted beneath the door from the man hanging from the rafter.

"When the car came, about half an hour later, Della already had the boy down, treating his back, smearing on some kind of salve, wrapping strips of gauze around his chest. I went down there, to see what would happen, see if the deputy would arrest my father. And the two of them were leaning against the new rail fence, watching Della work, drinking beers with Asa. I knew then that my father was above the law. Always had been, always would be."

She shook her head. "So. What's it like being his lawyer?"

"I haven't been bullwhipped yet, but he is a royal pain-in-the-butt."

Gen laughed, the sound lost in the silence of the night. "You've lost your accent," she said, suddenly realizing what seemed different about him. What had kept her off base all night as he spoke and moved and brought back memories she had forgotten long ago. "The wonderful Cajun lilt that made all the girls crazy."

After a long moment he said slowly, "Cajun accents weren't exactly welcome in the best homes back in the seventies. Coon-ass and Frenchy-boys and swamp-rats were stopped at the door." His voice changed, dropping into the lilt, the rhythms of French-Cajun. "*Mais oui*, I can talk still dat broken English-Cajun talk. Boy I was then, still me, yes. Coon-ass, Frenchy-bo."

Gen couldn't interpret his tone, and looked down, remembering her father calling some of her friends those hurtful names, and the way their expressions would change, harden with anger and pain. The Old Man had run Cajun kids off the estate in her youth, and only after she was in her teens had she understood their pain and fought back, demanding her friends be allowed to attend a party. Was it her fourteenth birthday party? She remembered welts from the Old Man's leather belt when he beat her for insolence. She wasn't surprised Starnes had lost his Cajun accent.

"Why didn't you ever tell me about this?" he asked.

Gen looked up surprised.

"About the stablehand and the beating," he clarified.

Gen shrugged. "That was the last straw. I turned eighteen two weeks later and left. I was too angry to tell anyone. And too afraid. The Old Man let it be known that when he found the person who called the police, he intended to give them the same treatment. I think he figured it was one of the other stablehands. But I knew my father. If he had known I called, he would have kept his word, whipped me just like he whipped that kid."

"So," he said, his voice rough. "Now I learn it, after all these years." At her quizzical look he said, "Why you took off for New York. You were afraid. And I let you get on that bus never knowing why you were running. I'm sorry, *Ginny.*"

She shrugged. "You never had a reason to be sorry, Starnes. I can't even remember his name after all these years. I wonder what happened to him? I never found out if he lived or died."

"According to Della, your father repented of his anger, put the kid in the guesthouse, nursed him back to health—or had Della do it—and sent him to medical school. Paid the way, supported his family while he was in school."

Gen sighed. "Big Boss Man takes care of *his* people. After beating them nearly to death first."

Starnes said. "I guess I need to look into the statute of limitations on hate crimes."

Gen tilted her head in the moonlight, found his eyes on hers, cool and warm at the same time. "If you could get the man to testify after all these years. A professional man, a doctor? Might refuse. And if you discovered something else about my father, something worse than a thirty-year-old beating, what then?"

"Like. . . ." Starnes let the word drag out slowly.

"Like something worse." She didn't want to say what might be worse. It was the secret she and Lily had carried for so long. But after a moment Starnes went on, and Gen didn't have to say the word that had haunted her and her sister for over thirty years.

"I'm an officer of the court, *me sha*," he said, pronouncing the old French endearment in the Cajun manner. *My love* . . . words spoken to young children or pets or a lover equally. "If there was any evidence to point to the truth, or a confession, and if the statute of limitations hadn't run out, I could be forced to bring it to the attention of the court. Or my client might ask me to bring it to the attention of the sheriff."

"Turn the Old Man over to the law?" She laughed, still hearing the "*me sha*" on the night breeze. "That would be rich. A little late, but rich."

Starnes said, "So, are we going to waste the moonlight talking about your father, or would you like to go for a walk." He smiled down at her, suddenly so close the swing bumped his legs and came to a stop.

Their eyes met and something in Gen fluttered again, this time internally, where it didn't show. "I think we should take that walk, though I have to tell you, my left knee is stiffening up. I haven't been on horseback in too many years to count, and I'm paying the price for riding today."

"I could offer to rub it for you," he said solemnly. "I've been told I have great hands."

Gen laughed, not sure of the tone or the look in his eyes. "I think the walk will be enough, thank you, kind sir."

And then the breeze kicked up or the moonlight ducked behind a cloud or someone walked over her grave, because she remembered the last time she said those words, "kind sir," to Starnes Templar. The memory snaked through her with strange warmth.

It was only minutes before she climbed on the bus that was taking her out of Louisiana, and she had asked Starnes to come with her, escape to a new kind of freedom. He hadn't even considered it. Instead, Starnes had offered to marry her, giving her a way to stay in town without living at the estate. New York and independence weren't lures for him. She had turned him down, certain he was being foolish, noble, and not very bright to contemplate thumbing his nose at John Deveraux by marrying his daughter and taking her to a life of poverty. Her father would have crushed him like a roach beneath his boot heel for the affront.

She had wanted Starnes to come with her, wanted his presence beside her on that bus so badly she ached inside. For the first time in twenty-nine years, Gen wondered if Starnes had ached at her leaving, at her refusing his proposal. He had loved this town, this parish, this way of life, even back then, yet, after all this time, she wondered why he had refused her. He'd had nothing keeping him here.

Starnes took her hand as they walked, and their fingers fit together now just as they had when they were teens. The air was warm, but the breeze off the bayou was cool and the sound of their footsteps on the shell paths took them back to another time far better than any softly spoken words.

The silence wasn't enough, however, had never been enough even when they were kids, and they started talking after a time, catching up on the last twenty-nine years, stories of successes, failures, loves, battles lost and won. The only thing they didn't talk about was the impending divorce. The pain was still too raw and Gen was thankful that Starnes chose not to pry.

They meandered to the bayou, along the back of the barn, and through the flower garden, little tended but full of blooming perennials that filled the air with sweet scent. And after an hour, Starnes brought her back to the cottage. His fingers tightening on hers, shoulders brushing. He didn't kiss her. But they both thought about it—that kiss that didn't happen. And he left her there, on the porch, and drove off, the sound of his truck engine purring into the darkness.

11

LAISSEZ LE BON TEMP ROULER, OUI? and GATORS

Long before Starnes entered the backdoor, he knew Serena was home. Led Zepplin was blasting through the house and every light was on, the scent of cigarette smoke and old liquor hanging on the air, the sound of voices shouting over the music. Music was Serena's security blanket, the more earsplitting and raucous the better. In fact, he could scarcely remember a time when Serena hadn't surrounded herself with music. The louder the music, the faster his sister ran from the voices in her head, from the memories of the event that shaped her.

He wondered if the music had been off the night she bit off Deon Hoffpauir's penis. In 1988 Serena had not yet been diagnosed with any of her many mental conditions. If the music had been off, back when Deon attacked her and forced her to perform oral sex on him, the silence might have pushed her to snap. Would things have been different had Deon loved loud, raucous music? Would Deon still have the last three inches of his penis, and would Serena still be with him, undiagnosed and dangerous? Or would things be even worse? Would his sister be dead?

His father had been a cruel, violent, vicious man, taunting and slapping Starnes just for kicks, kicking and beating when the need for jollies increased. When he was drinking, which was always, simply passing in the hall was a danger. The old bastard had been similarly cruel to their mother; her bruises had been as dark and painful as her son's.

The same cruelty had been directed at Serena from the time she was a tiny baby. Even as a kid, Starnes had known it and tried to protect the little sister, the diminutive body so much smaller, so much younger than he. He had watched out for her, taking their father's anger and fists onto himself whenever he could.

Protecting both of the women in the house. But it hadn't been enough. His father's violence and brutality had driven Serena into a lifestyle of wild partying and too many men.

Crazy, drunken laughter screamed from the house. Starnes paused at the entrance and lowered his head to the jamb for a moment as old anger rose, choking and insistent. *Damn* her. It was *his* house. . . . The wood was cool and smooth and the sharp edge bit into his skin. *Serena. If ever a child had been misnamed.* Breathing deeply of the smoky air, he reined in the useless emotions, the squandered energy, forced calm into his spare frame. Pressed his face harder into the pain of the sharp edge, the discomfort pulling at him, separating him from wasted reactions. Pain always did that for him, its elegant simplicity a primitive lever for his mind. At the thought, Starnes backed away from the doorjamb. He was getting as crazy as his sister.

He shouldn't have been surprised at the party going on inside. It wasn't like this was the first time or would be the last. Not for Serena, not for him. And if his face mirrored a momentary grief at the knowledge, it wouldn't be seen by anyone who mattered. For an instant the image of Gen flickered in his memory.

Starnes stepped through the door. There was no need to be stealthy. The music was vibrating the house on its foundations.

There was a couple necking in his den, most of their clothes off, but at least they hadn't been into his desk or tried to turn on his computer. One of Serena's recent parties had made him the proud owner of memberships to over a dozen porno sites. The addition of a password to his system had stymied any more such endeavors, but drunks could be amazingly persistent.

Starnes had no qualms about tossing the shirts and jeans piled at his door over the embracing pair and escorting them out of the house. They were too drunk to offer more than token protest, and he wasn't about to allow drunken coupling on his leather couch. He finally had the leather to a perfect level of softness, body-oils, dirt, and wear, and cleaning it now might damage the finish. The amorous couple scarcely noticed the intrusion, simply sank to the dew-wet grass and picked up where they left off.

Through the house, Starnes spotted several couples dancing in the living room, arms entangled and hips grinding. Led Z. wasn't his personal choice for romantic music, but he figured the dancers weren't listening with a discerning ear. Sounds to the side made him pause.

Serena was in the kitchen with three men, all of them stoned on something and looking for trouble. His sister was on the dough station, her legs around a man's waist, his hands inside her shirt, their mouths locked together. The others were looking on as if knowing their time would come. One man was drinking Starnes' best scotch straight from the bottle, the other was tossing his Bowie knife up into the air and watching its point skewer into Starnes' custom-made cutting board. That was a quick three-hundred-dollar-loss for the night.

Starnes might have stepped in and ordered all of them off his property, except for the expert manner the knife wielder. Even drunk as six cats at a country still, his hand was steady and sure. And the man attached to it looked like he wouldn't take kindly to interference in his future love life. Maybe it was the intensity of his gaze on Serena's half-exposed breast, or maybe it was the fanged-snake tattoo crawling down his arm, but either way, Starnes knew he was likely overmatched.

Without being seen, Starnes stepped back to his office, opened the locked desk drawer, and took out the old .45. His daddy's gun, big as death and heavy as sin, fully loaded with slugs. Starnes considered the weapon, the men in the kitchen with Serena, and the gun once again.

His daddy had used the .45 several times in Starnes' own youth to run partying kids off the property, the barrel pointed into the air, the shots sounding like cannons as they echoed down the bayou, his daddy drunk and raving, vomit on his shirt, his boxers hanging on bony hips, belly like a keg out front, hair standing out in wisps. Starnes' hand trembled as he remembered the time his daddy had nearly shot his best friend—Remmie, stoned on weed and too far gone to realize the danger. It had been a party a lot like this one. Remmie. . . . Until Gen said his name, it had been years since Starnes thought of him. Wonder what had become of Remmie Walker?

Still holding his daddy's gun, Starnes sat at his desk and called L'ron, who was off duty and sleeping, but as usual, agreeable to helping. That was what friends were for. Starnes had helped L'ron when a Rebardi cousin had a bit of trouble with the law in

Vacherie a few years back, did a little legal work with the local Fraternity Of Police, and helped out with the occasional carpentry or repair job at the Rebardi Place. In return, L'ron helped out with Serena and her scrapes. Starnes didn't fool himself that L'ron got the best part of the bargain. While he waited, Starnes replaced the gun in the locked drawer.

Hair standing up in the shape of a pillow on the left, but dressed in his uniform with weapon and badge in the proper places, the sergeant arrived in less than ten minutes, parked his black Jeep Wagoneer and stepped over the lovers in the yard. "Fine show," he offered Starnes by way of sympathy as he entered the house. "Get you video camera and make you'self movie for de internet."

Starnes snorted at the humor and stepped aside for the cop.

"Dis better be worth mah time, Templar. I spend de day wid a forensics pathologist looking at old bones and listening to him prattle he doctor-speak. Trouble, I gots already."

"You sound frustrated, L'ron."

The cop halted just inside the door. His jaw had a heavy stubble with pillow folds pressed into his skin, and he smelled of soap and linseed oil, as if he had cleaned his gun just before bed. "Frustrated as hell, bo."

The comment about the bones sank into Starnes' conscious mind. "Why are you doing an investigator's work?"

L'ron looked back through the screen door, not meeting Starnes' eyes. "Sheriff Pritchard idea. Something special he got he claws into." A second later, he added, "And I find dem bone. My investigation." With those cryptic comments, L'ron stepped past Starnes and into the house.

The cop paused again at the entrance to the kitchen, just watching. Starnes stood back, seeing the muscle in his jaw bunch and jump at the sight of the man's hands under Serena's shirt. L'ron's hands fisted uncontrollably for a moment, as if he had the man's throat in them. But whatever his personal inclinations, the guy with the knife stood between them, and not even a case of frustration could cause L'ron to leave a knife at his back.

The cop reached over and lifted the knife-tosser by the scruff of the neck, shaking him slightly, like a dog with a new toy. Smiling down into the man's face, L'ron said softly, "Joubert

Boutte, *ça va*, bro? You still on probation, brozzer? You know, for that plastic surgery you perform on your girl . . . eh . . . what her name, uh? Sylvie?"

The hand holding the knife tightened. L'ron smiled, showing big horse teeth and eyes that begged a challenge. The hand hesitated a long moment. Then, gently, Joubert turned the knife, holding it hilt-first to the cop. "Not mine, bo," he said in a wheezing voice, air fighting past the fist on his windpipe. "Sssswear it. Found it on de cabinet. Right here. Swear, bo," Joubert said, sounding less than sober, face a deep red, edging to purple. His eyes bulged. "You know me, bo. I ain't going to do nothin' that send me back. I got kids, bo. Swear."

Still holding the smaller man by the throat, L'ron moved slowly out of the kitchen, allowing Joubert's toes to touch the tile as he moved. The other man, the one nuzzling Serena, ignored the quiet voices at his back. Perhaps he thought that a queue was forming for Serena's attentions.

"So, you want to give the man his knife back, Joubert? And go home to the chi'rens? Umm?"

"M-man?"

"Dat man," L'ron said, softly still, turning Joubert toward Starnes. "You say you fin' dat knife, you give it back, *oui*? An' I no tell Jarrett Hotard you touch it. He you parole officer, *oui*?"

Joubert swallowed, his eyes moving quickly from the blade resting in L'ron's hand to the cop's eyes. "That knife cost lotta money, L'ron."

"Yes? So?"

Sluggishly, his expression weighing possible actions and consequences, L'ron spun the knife and offered it to Starnes, pearl handle with sterling hardware first. The knife was heavy as Starnes checked the balance and heft, holding the blade to the light. Razor-sharp. Evil-looking. It was an expensive knife, resting beautifully in the palm of his hand. Selling it might make up for the damage to his solid-oak cutting board, or he could keep it for his treks down the bayou.

Joubert looked longingly at the knife as L'ron guided him from the room and out into the yard, but he didn't protest. Starnes could hear the cop's pleasant voice. "Get you'self gone, Joubert, and don' let me hear 'bout you doin' nothin' rest a this night, or I suddenly remember this knife you lef' at my friend house. Yes?"

L'ron didn't even have to raise his voice to clear out the other two men. The look on his face was enough of a goad. Serena pouted at their expulsion, sitting on the cabinet, her plaid western shirt gaping open, revealing the upper curve of her breasts.

"Come on, L'ron, baby. *Quoi tu veux, eh?* Don' you go and spoil mah fun," she laughed, her voice made sultry by cigarettes and hard liquor, her mouth bruised from kissing. "*Laissez le bon temp rouler, oui?*" *Let the good times roll,* the state motto and Serena's personal credo.

L'ron's fists bunched again in reaction to the words. He uttered a low growl, and Serena smiled as if the sound pleased her.

Starnes' stomach burbled acid, as it always did at the sight of Serena trying to prove to the world that she was indeed a tramp. Trying to prove Gerald Templar's accusations correct even after all these years, and doing a pretty good job of it, too. The anger seared through him for a moment, out of control, and Starnes was glad he had put away the gun or he might have shot something, accidentally.

The thought of his anger fighting free, the old gun blasting away in the night, the thought of possibly shooting Serena waited just below the surface of his mind, half-seen like a fish in murky water. Taunting. Questioning. And then the thought was gone, his love for his sister ripping through him like a fierce wind. Tears stung his eyes. He could never hurt her. Hurt her? He couldn't even help her. And that was the essence of his problem.

Co-dependent, you . . . The words were a soft echo in his memory.

L'ron stepped to Serena and jerked her blouse together, his hands steady now, but strained as he buttoned it up the front. "No goo' time tonight, Serena. Just me and you brozzer."

"Spoilsports, both you," she slurred.

L'ron sighed, lifted her from the cabinet, and shoved her gently toward her apartment at the far side of the house. "Turn off dat music, Serena. I got de headache. Party over."

She sulked but moved off, hips swaying in time to the beat. Shortly the sound died, to be replaced a moment later with Jewel moaning something whiney. To the sound of the singer's voice,

L'ron cleared the dancing couples out, tossing shoes and purses and even a pair of panties out onto the lawn after them. His movements were controlled violence, a leashed savagery. Starnes watched, letting L'ron do the work as he had numerous times in the past. He was glad he hadn't resorted to the .45; Joubert might have been less cooperative at the sight of the gun, and a knife in the hands of a skilled man was deadly.

As L'ron worked the crowd, Starnes opened the windows and turned on the attic fan to air the smoke out of the house. Near the porch he stepped over a pool of vomit and stopped, staring at the mess on the expensive rug. The anger that had hidden just out of sight burbled up. Gripping the window, he stared at the floor, breathing shallowly until he had it under control. Unlike Gerald Templar of the drunken binges and the brutal belt, Starnes never lost his temper, he reminded himself yet again. Never. Instead, he returned to the kitchen for paper towels and white vinegar to clean up the mess. It seemed as if Serena's long interval of good behavior was over.

The two women entwined on Starnes' screened porch swing were less amenable to being tossed out on their ears, using drunkenness as an excuse to resist. L'ron sternly offered them the choice of leaving or a ride to the pokey for the night. Literally, he called it "the pokey."

Starnes, bent over the last of the pizza-beer-stomach-content-mixture, shook his head at the word. Pokey. Made jail sound a lot less threatening. Even so, the two women didn't want to leave. He could hear them whining—along with Jewel—at the unfairness of life. And he found himself on the floor helpless with sudden, silent laughter. The pokey was unfair, he had to agree. So was vomit on his rug and knife nicks in his cutting-board. Sitting on the floor, smelling the stink of a stranger's vomit and laughing helplessly, he watched the uninvited guests and L'ron.

His old friend got the two lady lovebirds out the door, saying again and again that the party was over. Starnes watched through the long front windows as they staggered into the back of the truck driven by Joubert's pal. A six-pack of drunks in the pick-up truck—three in the cab, three in the bed—all in various states of undress, taking the party elsewhere.

"Think you should let them drive?" he asked L'ron, as tires

skidded in the loose gravel at the edge of the road, sending the truck fishtailing into the street, lights bouncing off scrub growing beside the ditch. A second truck followed it, the couple from the den and the yard cuddling in the cab, other bodies visible in the bed. Starnes didn't get a good look at their activities, and didn't want to.

The cop shrugged and went inside, the two men bumping shoulders in the doorway. At the refrigerator, L'ron popped the top on a Coors and drank deeply, tossing Starnes one only after he had slaked his thirst. "Dey sober enough," he said finally. "And I don' feel like goin' back to the station tonight." He shot a swift glance at Starnes. "I might wan' to git at least one hour a *do-do* sometime tonight so I can work tomorrow. If dat all right wid you."

"I thought sleeping on duty was part of the job description, L'ron. Pulled up near an intersection in a cruiser, sacked out for nappy-time, a box Krispy Kremes open on your belly."

L'ron grinned but the grin slid away when Serena moved into the room. She had showered and changed into a white cotton gown, a faint scent of perfume wafting from her. Standing barefoot in the doorway, she brushed her midnight hair and watched the two men, the ivory-handled brush sliding through her hair almost idly. Only a few strands of silver appeared in the black hair, a trait brother and sister shared, passed down from some Choctaw ancestor or another. In the simple gown, her hair shining, Serena looked virginal and innocent and somehow lonely, like a child left behind when her parents went to a party without her.

L'ron drank the rest of the beer and turned to go as Starnes caught a glimpse of his face. The cop's expression reflected a lifetime of pain. *L'ron loved Serena.* But he wasn't a fool. She wasn't the innocent she appeared, never had been, never would be. "Night," L'ron said shortly, voice tight. "Thanks for de beer and entertainment."

"L'ron?" Serena asked softly.

He froze at the tone. So did Starnes. Serena sounded as lonely as she looked. And more than a little bit lost, yet her face was smiling, contemplative, dreamy.

"Will you take me fishing *demain*, L'ron? In the morning? I want to go fishing." The brush slid slowly, so slowly, through the dark hair. She swayed to Jewel's minor chords, her white gown drifting at her ankles. "Fishing befor' de sun, she even t'ink to shine. Fishing out at . . ." she paused as if drawing upon some ancient memory, a half smile on her face. "At Bayou *Je Vas Jamais Oublier.* Will you take me?"

Bayou *I Will Never Forget.* There was no such bayou, not that Starnes knew, and he knew them all. But L'ron's hands unclenched, his shoulders slumped as if suddenly free of burdens, and he settled his eyes on Serena as though the name had some intimate meaning just for the two of them. *I will never forget.* . . . He smiled a worn, forlorn smile full of hurt and care and too many years. "I take a sick day *demain, me sha.* Pick you up a *cinq heure.*"

Serena gave him a winsome smile and turned back to her rooms. "I'll be ready."

Without explanation, L'ron left the house, turning on his heel and closing the door silently. It was only then that Starnes noticed the cop was not wearing regulation black, spit-shined shoes. He had come to the rescue in his bedroom slippers.

◆   ◆   ◆

The kids were still in bed when Gen joined Lily and Della at the kitchen table and heaped egg casserole and melon onto her plate, with grits to the side. Sunday breakfast was no longer the huge morning ritual of her childhood with three meats, eggs, pancakes, drop biscuits, and juices. Della had made the egg casserole with sausage and cheese, grits were in a pot on the stove, coffee was fresh and hot, water for tea sat nearby, and fresh fruit for the newly vegetarian or health conscious was in a frosted bowl on the table. The casserole was on a warmer and steamed the kitchen with fragrance. Gen tucked into the meal as if starving and managed to control her blush when Lily asked what time Starnes had left the Estate the night before.

"Don't know. No clock in the cottage." Hearing the way that sounded and seeing the knowing look Della and Lily shared, Gen said casually, "Besides, I stayed on the porch after he left and listened to the night. Frogs and crickets aren't exactly a replacement for New York traffic and sirens. I couldn't sleep." She added, "This is good Della. You ever decide to come to New

York, I know this little place near the park that would snap you up in a skinny minute."

Della harumped and mock shuddered, the action sending waves of motion through her heavy body. "Too cold, too loud, too many peoples. Esmee say the place stink like exhaust and you got mens sleeping in doorways and eating outta garbage cans. Here, if a man need a place to sleep, he can bed down in a barn or a hay shed or sleep in the woods if he be of a mind. And he can hunt to feed hisself or fish or crab and most folks willing to feed a man if they's askt. When the last time you fed a hungry man in that New York City? Huh?"

Della was working up a head of steam and Gen would have felt a little ashamed if she hadn't been trying to take the focus from Starnes and the midnight walk. "Can't say, Della. Feeding men in the city can be dangerous. Bare and I—" She stopped, surprised by the shaft of pain that slicked through her. "*I* give to support a soup kitchen every month."

Della harumped again, stood, and poured them all steaming coffee from the carafe on the table. The hint of chicory in the Community Coffee wafted to her and Gen sighed, warming her hands on the cup. Della sat back down with a sound like a small earthquake.

"Supportin' ain't the same as assisting. You ever gone down and helped?" she asked. "Get your hands dirty?"

Gen's pain was buried under a wider blade of guilt as she shook her head. Leave it to Della to slice straight to the core of the matter. Lily carefully did not contribute to the conversation but concentrated on her meal. Coward.

"No. You ain't never. I 'member me the time your poor mama tried to start up a soup kitchen for the wetbacks coming up from Mexico. They be entire families with little chil'ren and old womens. . . ."

Gen and Lily shared a startled glance. Their mother? Helena Deveraux, the woman known for partying and her lack of responsibility and for killing herself—surely an act of selfishness if ever there was one, or so said the town gossips—had tried to start a soup kitchen?

"This before you born, o' course, and she took sick. My little Helena sent out a letter to all the church women's missionary

groups and called them to a meeting in the town hall. Served up
hot tea and them little white-icing-cakes, whachyoucallem, petit-
fours? And she present the idea of a soup kitchen for the
'*transients*', she called 'em. There was such a ruckus you never done
believe it. Them old white-glove, gray-haired women in the
church with they girdles and they little hats just fussed and would
a cussed if they was men-folk, but being as they was polite and all,
they just chattered and nattered on about it and found fault 'til
they killed the idea."

Della twinkled as she passed around the sugar and cream.
"And then they had all them wetback folk a coming to they *houses*
looking for work and handouts instead a to a central location.
And they all knowed they should a listened to my little Helena,
but o' course by then they couldn't admit they was wrong and ask
her to start her soup kitchen." Della shook her head ponderously
and shoveled a portion of casserole into her mouth, chewed, and
swallowed before continuing.

"Now, they all got green cards and jobs doing work the white
mens wouldn't *never* do and the black mens is too good for now.
Shame the way them Mexicans is treated sometimes. Near 'bout
as bad as the black man was not so long ago." Della shook her
head. "Always gots to be one color on top and all the others
underneath. Our Lord in Heaven must be right shamed of us."
Della took a sip of the coffee, tasting, and then drank half a cup
in delight.

"I aint never tol' you that story 'bout your mama?"

The sisters shook their heads and Gen remembered to eat a
few more bites of her now-cool breakfast.

"I reckon that because the Old Man couldn't bear to hear her
name spoke. Couldn't bear it at all. Poor man." She shook her
head sadly and freshened all the coffee cups again, ignoring, as
always, the tension in the room as she talked about their father.

Gen was surprised to see that her own cup was half empty,
and she passed around the cream and sugar again as they all
attended to the coffee ritual. "I remember Mama passing around
the coffee when I was little," Gen said. "Just like this. But she
used the silver coffee set."

"Silver don't keep the coffee warm like my carafe do. Coffee
was always cold by the end of breakfast," Della complained.

"Ain't nothing worse than cold coffee. Now, my new carafe keep it warm and tasting fresh all day."

"Iced coffee is all the rage in New York," Gen said, hiding a smile behind her steaming cup.

"Like I said, that ain't no place for civilized folk. Though your mama did go there one spring with the Old Man."

"To New York?" Gen asked. "When was this?"

"I reckon it was, oh, the spring after you was born. Helena done got a little sick by then, like she had the blues, was what your daddy say. So he buy the tickets to New York on the sleeper train, and they take off. I gots to take care of you, and you the sweetest thing in the world. A good baby. Not like your sister who cry and cry and scream till you want to pull out your hair. Collicky she was. But you just fine. Quiet, like you was looking around and taking the world in. They gone for over two week, and when Helena come back she like a new woman, like her old self again. 'Course she pregnant with Lily pretty soon after, but she seem fine. They brung back pictures, must be near six dozen a them. They up in the attic most likely."

"Pictures? I didn't think there *were* any pictures of Mama," Lily said. Gen felt a spurt of excitement as she met Lily's eyes. "Except the little one we had."

"The Old Man took 'em all down and stored them in town for over twenty year. They back upstairs now, but still not in the house on the walls, like they supposed to be. Now, Geneva. Back to the important things. You ain't answered the question yet," Della said, laughter lurking in her dark eyes.

"Question?"

"What did you and Starnes do last night?" Lily asked, lifting a brow.

"That was not the question," Gen said, this time losing the battle to the blush. "I thought the question was, 'What time did he leave?' "

"And?"

Gen sighed and put down her coffee cup. "Starnes stayed about an hour after he left the Big House. We walked around the property, and then he left."

"And did he kiss you?" Lily teased, her eyes alight.

"No. He did not kiss me," Gen said with what dignity she

could muster as Della chuckled into her cup. It was like being eighteen again, having the two women question her about Starnes Templar. And just as hard to handle the intrusion into her privacy now as it was then.

"Did you want him to?"

Gen fought a smile. Intrusion or not, it was good to be with Della and Lily. Irrepressible Lily. She picked up her cup again. Sipped. Shrugged slightly. "It crossed my mind."

This time Della laughed and asked, "Did he hold your hand like a young man come a courtin' ?"

"He did," Gen said, finally laughing with them. "But he was the soul of propriety."

"Della, we have got to talk to that boy," Lily said. "He needs some courting lessons."

"I say so. He got the moonlight, the dark, the owls hooting and the fish jumping and he don't kiss the girl? Crying shame is what that is." Della whooped with laughter. "A crying shame." She slapped the table and laughed at the expression on Gen's face. "You think after all the women's that man done been engaged to he would'a learned a *little something* 'bout courting. Yes, you would." Della had broken out in a sweat from her laughter, the beads of moisture like tiger-eye stones across her forehead.

Gen leaned away from the table, the remains of her meal forgotten in the shared laughter. She knew she shouldn't ask but did anyway. "Starnes has been engaged a lot of times?"

"Near twelve times."

"Only eight," Lily corrected.

"Too many times, anyway you look at it. He a one woman man," Della chuckled, wiping her face with the drying towel she used as a napkin. "Lots a women, but only one at a time. Most problem wid' dem women come from dat sister a his, o'course. Serena a peck a trouble any way you look at it."

Lily leaned over, an avid, have-I-got-a-story-to-tell-you look on her face. "Did I tell you about the time Starnes' sister bit off most of the . . ." she cast a quick look at Della and amended whatever she had been about to say, ". . . private parts of Deon Hoffpauir? That boy grew up mean as a snake. Had a list of arrests a yard long, most of them drunken brawls or abusing women. Somehow Serena fell in with him, and one night he had a gallon too much to drink and he beat Serena to within an inch of her life." Looking around to make certain that her children were nowhere in sight she finished, "He stuck his privates in her mouth and she bit it off!"

Gen grinned at the look on Della's face, half-amused, half-censorious. She had clearly heard the story many times and had never decided just how a Christian woman should respond to the incident. "Served him right," Gen said, and saw a flare of amusement in Della's dark gaze.

"But it's nothing to what I heard in town." Lily said gleefully. "Some say Starnes never got over a broken heart when he was a kid. Some woman he fell in love with left him. . . ?" She let the half-question hang in the air.

"Some folk say she went to New York City and never came back. Sad, *sad* story," Della added in cheerful harassment. "Ever'body done heard that story."

"Of course some say it wasn't the girl who left him for New York, but that girl he was married to when he went to college in New Orleans. Eloped, or so I hear, with a hue and cry from her rich daddy that rang across the state and back."

"That one got pregnant," Della said, "and then got dead. Now that *was* sad. For real sad. His baby dead, too."

"Baby?" Gen said, her amusement dying away.

"The girl was pregnant. 'Bout three month, way I hears it. Which was the only reason her mama and daddy allowed her to stay with Starnes. Too late for an annulment, them being Catholics and all. The pope frown on some things, and I gots to say I agrees with him on this one. Folk make them a baby, they should get married and stay that way. Her kin was some big fancy New Orleans folk. The cousins of that white-lace Irish family the Masseys, I think it was. Lord that a long time ago."

"A city garbage truck ran a red light and drove them down in an intersection. Practically cut the car in two. Killed the girl instantly," Lily said.

"Nearly killed Starnes, too. He come back to town to mend. Stayed in the guesthouse you in now. Lord, I done forgot that part, 'cause that the summer my cousin Delana had that first baby—only three pound it was, and so tiny I could hold it in my cupped hands—and I was gone a good bit, helping her. He took all summer to mend, had to learn to walk again. The doctor say he always be in pain for the rest of his life. Yes, sir. I forgot that part, I did. In pain forever. But he learned to live with it I reckon, because he went back to school the nex' fall, leaning on his cane and all, and he graduate with honors pretty quick after that, he did."

The silence after the last remark was interrupted only by silver clinking and coffee being poured as the three women considered the situation of Starnes Templar and the age-old gossip. Gen stared at her plate, the eggs congealed and the cheese hardened. The grits were still warm and she lifted the bowl, held it close to her chin, slipping a spoon under the scummy grits' top. Melted butter slid into the depression and swirled. She ate a small bite, the forgotten taste like a gift, another of the few good things from the past.

Starnes had lost a child. Something else they shared. Another tie she had not known, another shared hurt. Putting down the bowl, Gen pressed a hand into the flatness of her stomach, remembering the feeling of fullness from the one time a baby had taken root there. Six months she had cradled that long-awaited child. And then lost it, never to know that feeling again.

"So," Lily finally said, breaking the silence. "What else is in the attic we never saw before?"

♦ ♦ ♦

Starnes' pirogue sat dead-in-the-water, a shallow-draft, slat-board canoe with pointed ends. His feet were braced to either side to minimize potential sway. The small boat was tied to a stump sticking out of the water bent like a small hook. The larger johnboat was beached upstream.

Starnes' prey, a blue heron, watched him with suspicious eyes, scarcely visible in the dead cattails and couch-grass and dried mud of the shore where she had hidden her nest. Because he had drifted with the faint current instead of using the long pole, and because he kept his movements slow as the water beneath him, she didn't move, uncertain if he was a threat. If Starnes shifted his brush too quickly or bumped the side of the boat with an errant toe, she would frighten and be gone in a limp-legged run followed by a thrashing of wings as she took off.

Even in the heat, he moved with slow motion care, his brush painting in the browns and greens and the bird's black, unblinking eyes, making the most of every stoke, every dab onto the palette. Her feathers were the most difficult part for him, requiring a generous dab of black and blue mixed with a hint of brown to create just the right shade. She was a beauty, long of neck and delicate of beak. White water lilies bloomed upstream, and if he transported the heron into that scene, she would be perfect.

His hip began to twinge just as he got the eyes right, and he moved the brush faster, ignoring the inevitable pain, tilting his head as the current dragged the pirogue around. The sun moved from behind clouds and he painted in shadows, streaks of dark color to be filled in later. His pain began to increase, little jabs at first, then stronger and longer, growing like living things through his hip and buttocks where they rested against the wooden slat seat, and finally moved down his thigh like liquid heat. Painting furiously, he raced the pain, his brush flying, and when his movements began to alarm the heron, he tossed the brush and palette down, scooping up the 35mm camera. Fingers flashing, he took a dozen shots of her growing fear and her concluding rush to flight.

Adrenaline pumping, he managed to see every shot as it clicked off, the bird's twisting head, limping run, and spread-winged take-off, feathers alight. And then she was gone and he groaned, rolled to the pirogue bottom and dropped the Nikon beside him. He grabbed his hip with shaking hands. Even through the denim he could feel the scar tissue and poorly healed muscle beneath, bunched and angry. Face grinding into the bottom of the pirogue, he massaged the hip until he could stand the pain again.

The only consolation for the agony was the near completed painting and the film of the heron in first flight. He could paint that later. Much later.

As always when the pain took him, he could see Sally. Blood spreading through her blond hair, frothy spittle at her lips as she fought for breath and failed. Died in his arms inside the twisted car, her pale blue eyes on his and her hands clutching at her belly and the new life planted there. His baby. *His baby.*

He had made sure that there had never been another.

Minutes later, as the pain eased, Starnes felt the bottom of the pirogue scrape across something hard and then slide into slick mud. Easing himself from the rounded hull, he glanced where the hooked stump had been. His tie-off had slipped its moorings, allowing the pirogue to float free. Now, he faced into a low bluff, tree roots dangling toward the water, the slim, twisted nether-boughs hosting a gathering of blacksnakes hiding from the heat. There must have been two dozen, the smallest a foot long and slender, the longest over five feet. The inky granddaddy opened rounded, obsidian eyes and watched the watcher, lazy, in the heat and unconcerned. A bulge the size of a small nutria or large squirrel marked a recent dinner just behind its head.

Heavy ferns fell in lacy curtains from above and ebony water trickled quietly below. Diffuse shadows tinted the eroded bayou bank even darker, creating a cave mouth where none existed. Starnes lifted against the dregs of pain and found his mama's box-camera with fingers that still shook. He adjusted the light-meter on the old camera for heavy shadows and clicked off several shots of the nesting site using black-and-white film, pushing the pirogue against the current for different angles, some dense with ferns, some with none. It would make for a somber, almost menacing painting if he decided to work it up. Perhaps a better medium might be charcoal or pen and India ink on heavy parchment.

In the water the snout of a *congo* broke the surface, the water-moccasin coming up for air and a look-see. The black snakes ignored the deadly cousin as they ignored him.

Something brushed the bottom of the pirogue again, and this time Starnes recognized the scaly bump for alligator. The water swirled ten feet from the pirogue, leaving Starnes wondering just how big this gator was. The eyes that rose, dripping, staring from the water, left no doubt that it was a monster. And he had no shotgun. It was upstream with the johnboat, tied off near the patch of water lilies he wanted to incorporate into the heron painting. He had been to this site several times with no gator sightings and had let safety precautions go.

"Howdy, Mama," he said to the unblinking gator eyes. "I am not a tasty meal. Too scarred-up, too old and stringy, too big to be delectable. I'd be difficult to chop into small enough pieces to digest, even with your teeth. Easier eating might be a nest of nutria or even a small doe. Maybe a garfish, even. And let me assure you, I'd fight it out. I may not have my shotgun handy, but I do have a bush knife in my boot. A particularly fine one, according to Joubert Boutte. Sharp as sin, according to the scars in my cutting-board. And then there's that pretty blond woman waiting for me back at the Deveraux Estate. So, you see, I *would* fight."

The gator blinked and water swirled again twelve feet from the eyes. Then again, a few feet further on. "You a big mother gator, ain't you?" Starnes said as his fingers inched his jeans' leg up and squirmed into the boot after the sheathed knife.

The pirogue bottom was rounded, making the little boat easy to maneuver at the best of times, and easy to flip over at the worst of times. A hungry fifteen-foot alligator could be considered the worst of times.

The gator head rose from the water, exposing snout and nostrils much closer to the pirogue than Starnes expected. The gator blew, showering him with fine droplets, the stench of old death, the rotten stink of fetid breath, and then sucked in air, only to slip beneath the surface.

Starnes stayed perfectly still, his palm sweaty on the pearl knife hilt, the pain in his hip forgotten. Listening. Watching the water for tale-tell swirls. Waiting. Gators were opportunistic hunters. They took what was offered by the unwary and the foolish, but they seldom chased anything down as land carnivores did.

Minutes passed before Starnes decided he was not going to be dinner, and he stood, pushing the pirogue off from the bank and weeds it was tangled in. But he didn't let go of the hunting knife, the vicious blade looking small and puny against the threat of gator-teeth he hadn't seen but could imagine. Gator that old would have a hide so tough even the softer underside would be like a suit of mail. It made Starnes want to sharpen Joubert's knife just thinking about it.

One-handed, he unlocked his pole and guided the pirogue upstream, keeping close to the bank and his eyes peeled for gator. He saw nothing, no sign of the huge reptile. And no sign of the blue heron near her eggs. Starnes regained the johnboat and his shotgun as the sun was setting. Stepping into the larger, flat-bottomed craft, he instantly broke the .20 gauge open to check the shot. "Still there. *Cher pacan*, Starnes-bo," he whispered. "*Pas tout là.*" He called himself several kinds of stupid fool as hot sweat broke out on his body and he sat deeper in the johnboat.

The stink of hours in the sun was much worse when mixed with the reek of fear, and he grinned as he sniffed himself. "Gator may done got a whiff a you," he said in his native Cajun patois, "and decide him fresher meat was call for. *Pooyie,* you stink. And now, *tout d'ein coup,* you talking to yourself," he added as he stowed his canvas and his gear for the trip downstream to home.

He'd have to pass the gator's resting place again, and wasn't particularly happy at the prospect. Gator that big would have to move around a bit to stay fed. Likely to clean a bayou out of game if she stayed too long in one place. And she wasn't likely to move just because he was inconvenienced.

Moving with economical grace, he couldn't stop himself from watching the water as he lowered the little propeller into the bayou and cranked the motor. It was a good three miles home and the sun would be below the horizon before he docked. Black as pitch. His grin still firmly in place, Starnes wondered how fast a gator could swim three miles.

Picking up his cell phone, he dialed the Deveraux Estate, hoping for Gen, but speaking to Della when she answered. "Hey there, *petit mamselle.* There a *fais-do-do* at the Carscaden Place *ce soir.* Let's us go dance."

"Starnes? That you? Stop that Frenchy-talk and speak like I can understand," Della demanded.

"How long since you danced a jig, Della-love?"

"You been drinking, Starnes?" she asked with a laugh. " 'Cause the last time you askt me to go dancing, you was still using that cane and I was a good two-stone lighter."

"And we made a pretty pair that night, didn't we? A big beautiful black woman and a gimpy, skinny, little white fella." He felt in the dark for running lights and flipped the switch that lit up the bow and stern. Wet wind blew in his face and he suddenly wanted Gen to be here with him in this boat, speeding along the flat, black water. "Gave me my confidence back, you did. Did I ever thank you for that, Della-love?"

"Oh, we made a pair alright. Talk of the parish for weeks, and me having to listen to the tongues wag. Good thing my man wasn't the green-eyed type, or you'd been gut-shot and left for dead, stuff he had to listen to."

"But it was fun. Can't deny that, Della-love."

She laughed and wheezed and said, "Stop flirting with me, boy. One night on the town with you is enough for a lifetime. My knees can't take dancing no more. But if you is really ready to party, I'll tell my Geneva to put on a party dress and be ready in a half hour. Now, *that* girl is in dire need of dancing, I tell you true."

"Why's that? Della-love?"

"She talk to that man in New York City is why. I know 'cause I was listening at the door to the Old Man's office."

"Eavesdropping, Della? For shame," he teased.

"I did, and I ain't shamed in the least. He done her wrong. Bad wrong. And *somebody* got to look after my baby."

"What did he do to her, Della?" The words were low-pitched, a growl in the back of his throat.

"Ain't my place to be telling you, 'cept to say that he on the cover of *People* magazine with some young blonde *thang* on his arm. They was at a party together, one of them fancy charity things rich folk go to. Only my place to tell you she need some attention from a good looking man, one got her best interest at heart, and one who remember she vulnerable right now. One who know better than to take advantage of her in her current *condition.* You understand what I'm *sayin,* Starnes Templar?"

The misery around his heart eased. "Oh, I think I understand, Della. You're warning me not to take her to bed until she's healed," he said laughing, imagining the look on Della's face.

"Watch your mouth, Starnes Jasper Templar, or I'll maybe ask one of the Pennison boys to take her dancing tonight 'stead a you." Starnes laughed and promised several times to be good before she would continue. "I'm looking for a man who know how to dance and make her forget another man hurt her. Make her remember that she young and beautiful and still got life ahead a her. And your former comment to the contrary, I think you *might* be that man."

"Give me an hour, Della. I'm on Bayou Incendie and about twenty minutes from home. And I really do need a shower."

"I'll tell her you taking her to the party, and send Lily to help her get ready. That way she don't change her mind or chicken-out. And you remember what I said about taking care of my baby's heart, or I'll skin you alive, Starnes-boy, you hear me?"

"I hear you, Della. I'll be there in an hour."

"Uh-huh." And the connection broke.

The gator forgotten, Starnes raced through the night. He had seen the distinctive cover of *People* in a stack of magazines delivered that morning. Maybe he didn't need Della to tell him what Barry Stone had done to Gen. Maybe he could figure it out all by himself.

12
DANCE LIKE A WHITE GIRL

It was easy to see that Gen didn't want to go dancing, or go anywhere for that matter. She looked over the truck he had driven with something akin to revulsion and tossed her camera bag onto the floorboard at her feet with defiance, as if daring him to comment on its presence. Her eyes were red and puffy, and her makeup looked as if it had been applied by someone else, someone with a heavier hand than her own. Lily's trademark-red lipstick she wiped off with a tissue as soon as she slid onto the white leather bench-seat. She slipped off the earrings, too, dropping them into a shirt pocket. Starnes watched the rebellious actions with amusement as he rounded the back of the 55 GMC.

He eased into the truck, his left hip still a bit stiff from the earlier cramp. She stared through the windshield, mouth in a tight line, her body radiating hostility in vibrant waves. He pulled the heavy steel door shut with a solid thunk. Reaching across her, Starnes pulled the retrofited seat belt out in a long loop and hooked her in. To her credit, she didn't flinch.

"I–*don't*–want–*to–be–here*," she said through lips that barely moved.

"I don' particularly want you here either, *me sha*," Starnes said mildly in return, watching the shocked reaction vibrate through her hands and arms at the insult of the words and the sound of his old Cajun accent. "I ask Della *pour le bal, ce soir.* Instead, she stick me with you."

Gen's eyelids flickered as she absorbed that bit of information.

He turned the key in the ignition, the big engine roaring to life. Starnes still used a Cajun accent when it pleased him or when it seemed prudent, or when he was with kinfolk, and he didn't mind using it now with Gen. In a courtroom he played with his accent as with a furtive weapon, turning it on and off as the argument, the jurors, and the judge seemed to demand, winning a rapport with the down-home in the crowd. He always won in a courtroom, and this night seemed little different. He had something to win here, too. "And it my guess you dance like *chockay* white girl, still, yeah?"

An unwilling smile touched the corner of her lips. "You asked *Della?*"

"Della on dance floor is like," he draped his hands across the steering wheel, staring into the night, "an active volcano . . . smothered in silk. She smoke, yes? She bump and grind, she—"

"I get the picture." Her lips twitched. "And I may still dance like a white girl, though not a drunk one. *Chockay* white girl my rear-end," she muttered before continuing. "Ba—" she started over. "*I* learned how to swing, Mambo, and tango, and I can waddle through a creditable Rumba, too. If *you* can."

"Hum" he said thoughtfully, eyes still on the black sky beyond the windshield. "I 'member you twitchin' and flailin' you arm in gym at . . . ah, was it Rosemont Junior High to . . ." he threw a glance at her, his face serious, " 'Mony, Mony', I think it be. You try Monkey, maybe? Or Jerk? You arms slap up and down and you hair flyin' all 'round in front you face."

Gen snorted and looked away, fighting not to laugh as he put the truck in gear and pulled on to the road, the old engine throbbing with power. The night was heavy with moisture, and a swarm of flying bugs blasted into the windshield leaving green splats. Compensating, Starnes hit buttons and soapy water and wipers flushed the remains away.

"Nice hair, you got. . . . But you look like you have the tetanus." When Gen didn't respond, he questioned gingerly, "Maybe you dance Watusi?"

"Okay, okay. Point made. Now that you've charmed me out of my funk—"

"Is that what I doing, *me sha?*"

Gen punched his arm.

"Ow! What that for?"

"Not sure. But it made me feel better." She pulled the earrings back out of her pocket and slipped the slender hoops into the holes in her lobes, watching him from the corner of an eye as she worked. "So where are we going, and who's playing?"

Putting away the broken English of his childhood for a moment, he told her about the Carscaden Place. Two bachelor brothers in their forties had moved into the parish in the late seventies and opened a little music/beer/food joint catering to Zydeco and traditional Cajun musicians. It was now located on a bayou near Napoleonville. "Word of mout' advertizsin'," he said, the accent back, heavy as a Cajun TV chef, "great food, and they own brewery out back." He smacked his lips. "And I mean *great* beer, *sha, saloprie*, yeah! You get *chockay* wid it in no time! Dey got dis little dance floor in a screened house and t'ree band each night dat take to de stage and share billing." He glanced at her, dropping the accent. "I don't know how the Latin dancing will work with Zydeco, but you *could* try the Watusi again."

◆ ◆ ◆

Gen settled against the warm leather upholstery and sighed, her fingers working at the soft rolls and pleats. Maybe she did need to get out a bit. Seeing the article about Barry had left her worn and exhausted, and the Old Man was hanging on longer than expected. She needed to get back to New York, to Joachim and the shoot that was scheduled two weekends from now. Supplies were needed for an extended stay on Maui, bulk film that may not be readily available on the island, a generator for her lights in case the remote site had no power, and a hundred other things she needed to pick up, pack up, and send on ahead. She also needed a facial. Badly.

And then there was the court appointment. Barry and she were scheduled to meet before a judge about the property settlement, not that she intended to accept diddly from Barry. Not a thing. Especially not after—

"You want to talk about it?"

Gen twitched slightly, startled from her thoughts. She looked up at Starnes, his profile slightly green in the dash lights. He was staring ahead, his attention on the road. She could see the tension in his jaw, the muscle bunched tight. Dread washed through her. "Talk about what?"

"About why you're jumpy as a spider on hot tin." He reached over and uncurled her fingers from the death-hold they had on the delicate leather. They immediately twisted together in her lap.

"About why you're wearing Lily's makeup, although I like the look. About why you've been crying. About Barry Stone escorting the 'daughter of prominent socialite Joycelyn MacAdams' to a charity function 'Geneva Stone helped plan and promote and yet did not attend'," he quoted from the magazine.

Gen clutched her upper arms in unexpected fury. "You've been reading gossip magazines?"

"*People.* It came today. Barry Stone is on front. Kinda hard to miss, though the details are a bit sketchy. And then Della tells me I have to take you dancing and won't say why. Kinda adds up to you having more than just a bad day. So talk, *sha.*"

A bat flew at the GMC, highlighted for an instant in the headlights, catching bugs. Gen fought for control. Seconds passed as she breathed deeply and resisted the urge to scratch out Starnes' eyes or jump from the moving vehicle.

"I can't have children." The words burst from her mouth and she sucked air at the sound. "I tried. God knows, I tried, but I'm barren, like a desert where even weeds can't grow. Like all those women in the Bible. And I'm staring down the barrel at turning fifty, and it's too late."

A laugh burbled on the edge of her tongue, and she knew if she gave way to it, she would never find control again. But the words themselves she couldn't seem to stop. "I can't cook, sew, paint, or grow roses, any of the things my mother wanted me to do. My husband . . . *ex*-husband . . ." she was shaking, and gripped her arms tighter, "wants a younger woman, a *trophy* on his arm, and he can have her, though she isn't the same woman he's been sleeping with," her voice broke, and tears ran down her cheeks, "because I've seen her *up close and personal* and she isn't blond. She's Jamaican and a whole lot more beautiful than Amanda MacAdams or I will ever be or have ever been." Gen slashed at her face with her palms, slicking away the tears, hating the sticky, salty flavor of them.

"I have a job I'm good at, a professional reputation to uphold, and a father who won't just go ahead and die so I can get the hell out of this *god*forsaken place and go back to New York."

Starnes passed her a box of tissues and she wiped her face, smearing the makeup Lily had applied.

"I hate the heat and the moisture and the smell of the Big

House. I hate that my left knee is swollen and sore and hurts when I bend, and my upper arms wiggle more than they should even though I exercise with weights every day. I hate the way Della bows and serves the Old Man as if he were her master and she his slave. Is that *talk* enough for you?" She could have added, *I hate the way Lily's kids buzz around, and the music they play, and the fact that they'll never be mine. Pitiful, aren't I?* But she didn't. She kept that much of her dignity intact.

Yet the laugh finally broke through, the tone out-of-control, betrayed and needy, shattered and worthless. She laughed hysterically, turned away from Starnes as she cried into the tissues, the sound of her sobs broken and hollow. She blew her nose with abandon, not caring if her nose was all red and swollen and Lily's makeup job ruined, and suddenly not caring that she had ripped her heart open and displayed all the flawed and damaged contents. She just didn't care.

Gen sucked up air, glad of the coolness blasting from the AC, glad that Starnes hadn't turned on music, glad that the tires sounded so soothing on the smooth roadway. She sighed and wiped away the last tear. "I'm always doing this, aren't I?"

"What's that?"

"Crying on your shoulder."

"Actually you haven't done that in twenty-nine years. Right now you're crying in my truck, and I'm driving. We're lyrics to a bad country song."

Gen hiccuped with a last spurt of laughter and stole a glimpse of Starnes. His face was cool and unemotional in the dim light. She may have wanted comfort, but she was grateful for the practicality. He glanced at her, reading her face, and made a sudden left turn across traffic, as if deciding at the last possible moment.

"And right now I'm taking you to my house, not dancing."

A strange heat passed through her at his words. "Why? I look that bad?"

Starnes ignored her and turned off the secondary road onto an unpaved, two-rut trail through the trees. They splashed down through a crick, a drainage canal leading to a bayou, and up the other side to flat land, half in pasture. Horses danced in the shadows along a fence. Gen clutched the box of tissue she still held. She had forgotten the back way to Starnes' parents' house, yet the memory of it came back from long ago. They had parked here once, drinking a bottle of aged Cabernet stolen from her father's wine cabinet and necked. It was the closest she had come to losing her virginity until she met Barry in New York a year later. Suddenly she remembered the feel of Starnes' thumb along her arm, the heat from his body, the warm musky scent of him as he stood in the doorway to her father's study.

"I didn't know you lived at the old homeplace."

He said nothing, and the raw sense of the past grew in her soul. In the beam of the headlights she recognized the old live oak at the side of the road, though it had lost a huge branch sometime in the past and stood now like a man with only one arm, a shoulder lost fighting in some distant war. She remembered the old pigpen that once fouled the world with the stench of pig poop. The little shed where the pigs escaped bad weather had long since fallen to the earth, its fencing a vine-coiled heap lying on the ground. She recalled the old sycamore tree, it's branches spreading out over the water of the little cove where the teenaged kids used to swim, a bedraggled old rope still hung from the highest strong branch, a tire tied onto the end. She remembered the little beach of white sand and the time Becky Ryan got drunk on Boone's Farm Strawberry Wine and went skinny dipping with the entire football team.

Starnes' headlights turned onto the drive and Gen noted the carefully manicured lawn, the heavy foliage of verbena and azaleas, with gladiola standing against the house, the barn stark white in the distant security light. The house was brick now, larger and finer than it had ever been when the family lived here and Starnes' daddy ran things. She leaned forward, wanting to see the house and walk barefoot among the flowers, across the lawn that was mostly garden. And she wanted it when the air was cool with the hint of winter night, not hot and muggy with the summer.

Before she could examine that thought too closely, Starnes pulled into a parking area big enough for six cars and cut the engine. Still wordless, he stepped from the truck and came around to her door. Silent herself, now, Gen took his hand and let him help her from the high seat to the ground, the distance of the step nostalgic and familiar. She realized that the restored truck could be the same one they had necked in so long ago. That was a 55 GMC, wasn't it? With ratty old seats, no AC, a pitiful little radio and a rattle that jarred to the bone.

Starnes kept her hand as he led her up the steps to the deck and in through the back door. His hand was cool and dry, and held hers with an ancient intimacy. Inside, he guided her through the mudroom to the kitchen and paused, propped a hip on a low countertop clearly meant for bread-making, and indicated that she could look around. Her hand felt strangely empty as she stepped away and moved into the house.

Nothing of the past was left in the thoroughly modernized home. There was hardwood on all the floors, hand-cut silk Chinese rugs beneath the furniture, and white woodwork on the pale walls. Lots of old leather gleamed in the darkness of the study off the kitchen where his father used to sit and drink and watch baseball on the tube, until he was converted. The kitchen that had been a little hole-in-the-wall the last time she saw it, was now huge, boasting a central stainless cook-top, two refrigerators and two ovens, and a brick hearth in the corner for baking bread. It looked little used but it was beautiful. The bayou beyond the house was visible through large windows whose white shutters were thrown open for the view.

Expensive artwork hung on the walls, most acrylic but a few watercolors with that washed look so popular in the early nineties. A few bayou scenes stood out from the rest for their intricate detail and vivid colors. They were signed Starnes Templar. She paused and studied one, a doe, standing in several inches of water drinking, her reflection moving with the rings her delicate lips made.

A wet snout pushed into her hand and Gen jumped, squeaking. The dog's tongue tasted her hand once before it—he? she?—sat at Gen's feet, waiting. It was a big dog, a red-coated, long-haired setter with soulful brown eyes. Favoring her knee, Gen squatted and let the dog sniff her again before she offered her hand to scratch behind the smooth ears and under the floppy chin.

"Meet Bubba-Boy."

"He's beautiful."

"She. I just like the name. Actually, she's only the last in a long line of Bubba-Boys, but the only one that ever had a pedigree. A client gave her to me as a pup in lieu of partial payment. I figure I got the best part of the deal."

"She's sweet." Gen looked up at Starnes, his eyes dark as bayou water in moonlight, and just as unreadable. "Why did you bring me here?"

Face expressionless, he held up the camera bag she had not noticed. "You still carry girl-stuff in this thing? Makeup, comb?"

"Yes."

"Go make yourself up. Serena's out, so we'll have a glass of wine on the deck, prop our feet up for a while, and then we're still going dancing. If you don't take too long in the bathroom, we can make the last two sets. The bands play long on weekends."

"Everything is different here," Gen said.

"Things change." He placed the camera bag on the counter beside him and shifted his body as if uncomfortable.

Her eyes still locked to his, she said, "I'm changed. You are . . . different. Educated. An artist. In control of your life, instead of . . . floundering."

He smiled, a little sadly it seemed. "I'm not the nineteen-year-old-kid who let you get on a bus alone and go off into another world. I've lived a life. So have you. Had my share of successes and survived my share of tragedies. And yet . . ." Starnes tilted his head, a smile playing for an instant on his lips, then gone, "you are still as beautiful as you ever were. As beautiful as I remember in my dreams."

The dog's hair was soft as silk under her hands. She slid them along the coat as she watched Starnes' eyes. "Do you dream about me?"

He nodded slowly. "And I don't care if you can't have babies or have firm arms or cry like a four-year-old with snot in your tears. I don't care if you are a photographer or a bad cook or have a knee that hurts, though I wish it didn't because it might make you dance worse than I remember."

She smiled at that comment, but his face remained grave.

"I'm just glad you're here in my kitchen. I'm glad you like Bubba-Boy. I'm glad you came home, even if it was only for a little while. Because even though twenty-nine years have gone by and circumstances are changed, different, there are still a lot of unsettled things between us." He paused, reading her face, the dark and empty places in her soul. Seeing her just as he had when they were young and had their whole lives before them. "And I want the chance to settle them."

After a moment, Gen stood. "Point me to the powder room."

He did, and she left him there, sitting on the counter, Bubba-Boy curling up on the floor at his feet.

◆ ◆ ◆

Starnes stayed where she left him, still smelling her perfume, Bubba-Boy scratching contentedly. Gen's eyes had looked a deep ice-gray in the poor light, wounded and frightened and trusting him. He didn't want to be trusted. He wanted to strangle Barry Stone for hurting her, and simultaneously shake his hand, thanking him for being so stupid and leaving Gen for him. Barry Stone was a fool and he was glad of it. He wanted to take Gen in his arms and make her forget she had been hurt. He wanted all the things he had never allowed himself when he was a frightened nineteen-year-old and had nothing to offer her except a little room in the house of a sermonizing reformed drunk, a kid sister, and a mousy little mother who had never made an impact on anyone.

The pain in his hip was growing and to prevent a spasm, Starnes pushed off from the counter, picked a bottle of wine at random, gathered a corkscrew and two glasses and walked into the great room. The view of the bayou was bright tonight, the water almost silver with black eddies where it passed over a sunken log. Silver and dark, like Gen's eyes. The water lilies on the far side were bright in reflected moonlight. A fish jumping sent black rings through the water. Is that what he was about to do with Gen's life? Send dark rings through it like a tossed stone?

Mechanically, he moved through the exercises that worked his hip, moving slowly, without thought. Balancing on his good leg, the left extended in front, he opened the wine, poured it into the glasses, not bothering with the silly, outmoded wine tasting ritual. The making of wine was no longer just an art, but a science, and bottles simply didn't go bad these days. Who had told him that? Blanche, maybe. She had been knowledgeable about such things. She was married now, with two teenaged sons. Perhaps she had forgiven him for not marrying her. Perhaps.

Gen was suddenly beside him, watching his movements. He held out a glass, holding her eyes as his leg rotated to the side, heel pointed, toes to the front. "I was starting to get stiff. I'll likely be a crippled old man, in a wheelchair by the time I'm seventy. Dancing is therapy. So is this."

Gen took the wine, held the glass up, brows raised, waiting for a toast. He dropped his leg.

"To rings on the water," he said and tapped her glass with his. Unsmiling, Gen lifted her glass in salute and tasted.

Sitting in the weathered deck chairs on the screened porch, they talked for half an hour, a vagrant mosquito buzzing at their ears in spite of the Deet-based repellent he offered. Time moved slowly as they talked, and because Gen seemed unwilling to discuss Barry Stone after her outburst, Starnes talked. He told her first about his father's death, the bare bones of the story. He told her about Serena and her problems, then about Sally and the accident and the baby, thinking that Gen had probably heard the story, though not as he told it, because he never had. Not to anyone. And now, as he spoke, the words were rigid and pedantic, lacking the extremes of emotion that had once lain there, smoldering like the heat in ashen coals.

She listened with wide eyes, listened with her soul and not just her ears, if such a thing was possible. Despite his unemotional voice, he knew she heard the aged pain as he told about the baby and the woman he had married and lost. He could feel his pain meshing with hers, like old leaves settling to the bottom of a still pond. Silence finally enveloped them.

In a voice low and murmuring, she told him about her attempts to have a child, all of which ended in failure until she and Barry had finally given up. They had talked of adoption years ago, and opted not to. Not just now. And the right time had never come. He heard the misery that decision now gifted her. She regretted not adopting. Regretted not holding a child, changing diapers, potty-training.

And yet, he felt that there was something she was not telling him. Something she held back, like an injured hand cupped to the chest. But because he wanted her to come to him freely, of her own choosing, he didn't pursue it. Didn't corner her and demand that she tell him everything, now, this instant.

"And now I'm too old," she concluded. "Or so the state adoption agency said. I called after I left Barry, just to check. Just to see. We waited too long. Having a child of my own would have been worth any hardship, and I let the possibility slip away."

Starnes understood. "Children are important. The most important thing of all." And then, deciding that they had been somber long enough, he stood and took her glass, leading the way through the house back to the truck and the drive to the Carscaden Place, the scent of fried foods and the strains of music reaching them long before the source was in sight.

13

CARMELITA and FAIS-DO-DO

Gen climbed from the high seat without waiting for Starnes to assist her. Vivid colors, whirling bodies, and mouthwatering smells lured her and she grabbed her camera, automatically checking the F-stops, the light meter, and dangling the flash from a thong on her wrist. By instinct, she skirted the outbuildings where food was cooked and served, following a tall cowboy in peacock-tinted boots toward the music in a screened building in the center of the compound.

Starnes didn't suggest that she leave the camera, as Barry might have done, didn't reprimand her for always thinking work when this was time for other things. Starnes simply grinned, tucked his hands into this pockets and followed her through the throng, standing aside when there was a shot to be taken, acting as a blockade when the crowd would have pushed her beyond the place where she stood. Exactly as he had done so long ago when they were kids and she had just discovered the joy of the camera and the microcosm of the world she could capture with it.

A Cajun band was playing a wailing tune with guitars, a mandolin and an old hand-organ, stomping feet on the dilapidated boards beneath them the drums. The dancing crowd was mostly Caucasian, decked out in checked Western attire and cowboy hats, the men in jeans and boots, the women in long denim skirts, petticoats flashing, all whooping and shouting, red-cheeked with exertion. But a second crowd waited just beyond, of African origins, hair in dreadlocks and beads, men in batik. Lycra was the fabric of choice for the women, moving with panther grace in spike-heeled shoes, bracelets jingling, hats and hairpieces adorned with feathers and bangles.

Not even in New York would she have expected to see both young and old, black and white, together in one place. Not that they were dancing together, or even eating together, being drawn into distinct groups, one with pale skin, the other with dark. But they were in the same place, listening with appreciation to the music of the other, laughing and talking, with some small groups spilling over, as if old yarn of different shades were being woven into one new cloth.

Sudden excitement drew her like an undertow as she raised the camera and played with possible shots. Great faces. She had never seen anything like this.

"Starnes, *bébé*. Give me kiss, *mon*."

Gen turned and got a shot of Starnes kissing a woman on the mouth, her dark skin like ebony against his, her mouth cerise red, her hair in a colorful turban. Her fingers slid through his hair, his arm around her waist, the contact like a dance step too quickly ended.

"Save all you dance *pour moi, oui?*"

"Anything for you, most of the time, Carmelita. But I brought a date tonight. I'll be forced to dance with her at least a bit."

Carmelita pouted and Gen snapped a shot, caught the look, so sensual an expression she was certain it blasted its way onto the film. "She white. She dance like a white chick, I bet."

Gen laughed behind the camera. "I've been told I dance like I have tetanus. But I'm willing to learn. Kiss him again. I may have missed the shot. That's it. Hold it. Starnes lift your hand a few inches. Perfect. If only she tangoed. . . ."

Carmelita lifted an arched brow and dropped the island accent. "Listen, honey chile. If they play music, I can dance to it. They got Ricky Martin on the jukebox. When this set over, I'll show you a tango. And while we talkin', if that shot come out, I want me a copy. It looked hot."

Gen laughed again and moved away, overhearing Carmelita's last words on the subject. "I like the chick, Starnes, baby, but she's a little old for your taste, ain't she?"

The dancers ended the set with a flourish, feet banging onto the boards, skirts tossed high in the air, "Yeehaw"'s all around. Gen caught a dozen shots, changing film as the musicians and dancers filed out and another group moved into the screened house. These musicians held a jug, a washboard, a battered banjo, and a trombone polished so often it was silver in spots. They all wore locks, the twisted hair long and tattered, torn jeans, marijuana leaves embroidered on the seats like vintage clothing. Several of the dancers smoked hand-rolled, marijuana-laced cigars, even the women, and the scent of the weed and harsh tobacco hung like a pall over them.

The jukebox kicked in and true to her word, Carmelita pulled Starnes into a Ricky Martin number, her hips grinding into his, a wild, untamed version of the tango, its roots in sex and the rumba. The crowd shouted and whistled, other couples dashing onto the floor in competition.

Calls of, "Do it, Starnes!" and, "Show the white boy how to move, mama!" created a storm of catcalls and cheers and more couples poured onto the floor, two-thirds of the number white and Hispanic, the rest black, all young and full of sass. Gen ran through four rolls of film during two Martin numbers, the Latin flavor striking in the Zydeco and Cajun crowd.

She hoped for a round dozen *really* good shots; was certain of at least two, bodies flashing, grinding, whirling. And then someone pulled the plug on the jukebox for the next set. From the groans in the crowd, Gen bet her camera that the Carscaden Brothers would soon be adding a Latin band to the eclectic musical mix.

Sweating, breathless with laughter and exertion, Starnes joined her, pulled her to him and kissed her soundly. His lips were firm and salty and she nearly dropped the Nikon in surprise. But before she could react, he was pushing her away from the dancing to an outbuilding that smelled like heaven—if heaven meant roasted pig. Steam spat and fat sizzled; the meat he bought them was so hot it burned her hand through the paper tray.

In the next building they picked up bottled beers with voodoo queens on the labels, fried boudin balls, fried onion rings, hush puppies with jalapeños, and hot dipping sauce. And there was a bucket of bright scarlet crawfish, boiled in beer, butter for dipping. The fat content alone would give her five pounds, but it tasted so good she didn't care. Spices she had never tasted as a child stunned her and brought a fine sheen of sweat to her nose, for the Deveraux girls had never been allowed near a party like this, food like this, people like this.

She drank beer and pulled tails off crawfish, eating the hot,

spiced meat, laughing as Starnes sucked the heads, catching all the
boiled juices in his mouth and swallowing them down. And all the
while she remembered the feel of his mouth on hers.

The music started again while they were eating, and it was
music she had never heard. A hard fusion of country, blues' and
African, yet nothing like any of them, Zydeco existed alone, and
people danced to the syncopated beat with an abandon she hadn't
seen since Woodstock footage.

Barry had been at Woodstock. Barry would have loved this
music.

The thought of her husband, her cheating husband, her lying
husband, brought her to her feet, pulling Starnes to the screened
building, leaving behind the food, the beer, her camera bag. She
heard Starnes shouting to Carmelita to watch their "stuff" and she
kicked off the gold sandals she had worn, pulling the dark-eyed
man into the center of the crowd and against her.

Much later, her body hot and sweat-slick, they left the dance
floor to younger people with more endurance and found their
belongings as they had left them. Someone, likely Carmelita, had
covered the open spouts of beer to keep out bugs. Dehydrated,
they downed the warm beer in long draughts, throats extended,
bottles in the air. Geneva felt more alive than she had in months,
perhaps in years. This was a Louisiana she had never known,
sparkling and vigorous, alive and joyful. A Louisiana she could
have grown to love under different circumstances.

She tossed a limp onion ring into her mouth, tasting the oil,
the salt, the spicy clear-cooked onion, aware of the heat of
Starnes' thigh pressed against hers, both familiar and something
else, something almost pungent and foreign. And while she
chewed, she took random shots of the thinning crowd, finally
focusing on a man in black. He looked like a priest. She pulled
back from the viewfinder to be certain, but the unrestricted view
was the same. A priest talking to a young black man, one of the
musicians from the last set, his washboard by his side.

Carefully adjusting the shutter speeds, double-checking her
light meter, she took several shots without flash, hoping the
mercury vapor lights scattered about the compound might be
enough to capture the setting. Behind the incongruous pair,
Christmas tree lights winked in the desultory breeze. A bug light

zapped beetles, moths, anything but the mosquitoes they were intended for. The two men drank beer from sweating bottles, engaged in animated conversation, oblivious to the people passing by. With the shutter speed slowed, any actions they made would appear as swishes of light against the black water beyond.

"Father Anthony," Starnes supplied.

Gen grunted and took another shot, balancing the camera on the tabletop in lieu of a tripod.

"Grew up here on the wrong side of town. He's done a pretty good job of bringing the young black males back into the church. Opened a game room for them on South Broad Street. Teaches Bible lessons in the back. Even arranged for local industry and the technical school to provide loans for improving their education."

Gen grunted again. "Good for him. Now if he'd just hold the beer steady."

"He's your father's confessor."

Gen raised up from the camera, seeing the man in black clearly. He was no older than the kid he was talking to, fresh-faced, bright-eyed. And *he* was the Old Man's confessor? "The Old Man ever call him a whipper-snapper?"

"Calls him Kid."

The young man the priest was talking to laughed long and loudly, slapping the father on the back and walking away. Starnes raised his arm to attract the priest's attention, and Father Anthony walked over, a big smile on his open, Black-Irish face. He wasn't handsome, but there was something in this man, something clean and vigorous and honest, that transcended standards of beauty. He made you glad to be near him just with a smile. If she could find a priest like this in New York, she'd attend mass every week.

"Call me Tony," he said when introduced. "I know your father. How is he?"

"Dying," Gen said baldly.

"He's known for some time," Tony agreed. "I'm glad you came. It gives him the chance to put things right."

Gen looked at the earnest young man and wanted to say, *My father can't make right what he did to Lily and me.* Or, *My father never repented of anything in his life.* Instead she said, "My mother and baby brother are buried on a bayou. I want them moved to hallowed ground. What chance do I have of that?"

Father Anthony opened his mouth then clamped it quickly shut as if he had been about to speak and realized he couldn't. The mantle of the confessional, Gen wondered? Had her father confessed to killing her mother? How heavy a burden would that be for a young man to carry? It had been awfully heavy for two little girls.

"It could be arranged," he said.

Gen smiled wryly. "Church politics?"

Tony looked at her, hearing the edge in her voice. "Church compassion. Rome has come a long way in recognizing mental illness and its consequences."

"And if she wasn't really a suicide, but a murder victim, how far does the Holy Mother Church go in repairing the wrong done to her?"

Starnes pulled in air, startled. Father Tony blinked.

"And how about allowing a murderer to be buried in hallowed ground? Does the Holy Father in Rome think that's okay?"

Confusion flickered in the young priest's eyes, and something darker. Instantly Gen understood the Old Man really had confessed to Father Anthony, the man called Kid. This man knew the truth. But he answered calmly, his eyes now giving away nothing. "If a true confession has been made, and the penitent is judged truly repentant, then he may receive absolution."

"And be buried in hallowed ground."

"Yes." He smiled at her, almost sadly, seemed about to speak before again changing his mind. "I am available, if you want to talk. Della has my number. Call anytime. And I hope . . . you will join your father and me in prayer when I come next. This family is wounded and needs a lot of healing. Perhaps it could start with you."

Gen smiled politely. "Some wounds are impossible to heal Father. Some wounds actually bring the sufferer death."

◆   ◆   ◆

Starnes walked slowly back to the truck, his mind on Gen's words. How much did she know of the murder her father had confessed to? Did she really believe, as it sounded, that John Deveraux had killed his wife? The road was a long black blur beneath them, the powerful engine thrumming against the night.

He took her hand; it was cool, dry, and clasped his tightly though she didn't turn to him. He asked her. "Do you want to tell me about it?"

" 'Bout what, this time, Starnes Templar?"

"About your mother's death."

14

BOXES IN THE ATTIC *and* BLOODY LACE

It was dawn when laughter, quickly stifled, came through her bedroom window. It had been cool when she came in, with a wet breeze blowing off the distant gulf, and Gen had left the windows open to the rain and wind that stormed through in the night. Now, she wished she had used the AC, as the giggles had her awake and wide-eyed.

She rolled off the sweat-damp sheets, bare feet hitting the floor with a soft thump, her left knee twinging with warning. Dancing had not been good for it. Gray light, dark enough to make walking difficult, suffused the guesthouse, and she moved by feel to the bath. Without putting on the light, she brushed her teeth, splashed water over her face and neck and down her body, dried, and dressed. Jeans and sandals, a T-shirt, her hair in a ponytail. She was ready for the dawn. Decades since dressing had been so simple.

Keri and Destan were on the bayou dock, black forms in the fog that wisped off the dark water. A bucket, a large-mouthed fishing net, and the scent of rotting meat informed her what they were up to this early. Crabbing. Blue-shelled crabs would eat anything rotten, at anytime, but seemed to like dusk and dawn best. Kids didn't need sleep as she did, she thought as she stepped onto the smooth boards, yawning a "Good morning."

"Aunt Gen!" Keri's arms slipped around her in a fierce hug, the girl's black eyes sparkling. "You ever crabbed?"

Gen smiled faintly and settled herself gingerly on a deck stool whose surface was sun-damaged to the point of splinters. "I managed to sneak away once or twice to crab when I was a kid." She stared into the cloud-streaked sky, the eastern haze showing tints of gold. "The Old Man didn't believe that his daughters should participate in anything so *lowly*, but Lily and I did contrive *some* fun with local kids. I have to admit, though, that I preferred to ride." If she hadn't argued with Asa, she might be there now, mucking out stalls, feeding horses.

A rare longing pierced her for the feel of the wind in her face, the massive beast beneath her, saddle creaking. Keri, her face intent, finished webbing the smelly chunk of meat into a makeshift net of twine, tied the last knot and lowered the meat into the water. Longings of another kind touched Gen. She had not thought about children in a long time. Now they were all she could think about. It was all Barry's fault, too. Keri laughed softly as something in the deeps tugged on the twine, her young face alight.

If she had stayed in Moisson, married Starnes when he had asked her, would she now have a bevy of children around her? Children as endearing as Keri and Destan? Gen's mouth twisted wryly. Starnes would never have gone to law school and she would never have made a name for herself in the fashion industry if she had stayed in town. And any children they raised would probably have turned out as gang members or terrorists, not bright and charming kids like these.

Last night Starnes had spoken of taking her riding this morning before he had to go into the office, but after their talk, had not mentioned it. He might not ever want to talk to her again, not after what she told him. It couldn't be easy being the recipient of skeletons in the Deveraux closet. After three hundred years there had to be an awful lot of them clanking around in there.

Instead of riding, Gen rinsed the stiff fishing net in the bayou to soften the strings and helped Keri retrieve the two crabs that had attached themselves to her chunk of rotting beef. One of the crustaceans was a monster, a huge, shelled brute with an attitude, it's stalked eyes rotating, one fore-claw gripping the meat, the other snapping at Keri, who squealed in delighted terror. It felt good to rescue the girl, knocking the crab off the bait with the net and into the bucket of water.

They crabbed for an hour as the sun slowly rose, attacking the mist with its heat, burning off the night's cool. With seven large crabs in the bucket, they trooped to the house for breakfast. Della and Lily had eaten, and so had Mary Anne, the morning nurse, if the traces of powdered sugar and donut crumbs could be believed. There wasn't a single blueberry donut left among the jelly-filled in the Krispy Kreme box.

Geneva poured hot water into a cup, added a lemon-ginger teabag, and peeled a banana, eating it as she climbed the back stairs, leaving Keri and Destan eating their way through the picked-over remnants of the donuts. The kids had left the bucket of crabs unheeded in the sink, claws clicking against the metal, while they played a rousing game of checkers on an oversized, hand-loomed cloth "board". Neither noticed her departure.

The Old Man was asleep, his jaw slack against the pillow, upper teeth exposed and dry. But the green cannula carrying oxygen was in place beneath his nose, so perhaps he was cooperating today. His color looked good. Gen slipped away before Mary Anne, busy at some chore in the nurses' room across the hall, could spot her and start talking. Gen simply wasn't in the mood.

There were voices in the far reaches of the house, muffled and garbled, but Gen didn't think it was a television. She followed the sound down the hall from the sickroom, around a corner and through an open door. The attic stairs were beyond, and the voices resolved themselves into Lily's and Della's. Something scraped across the attic floor and thumped heavily. Gen remembered Della's comment about her mother's things being brought back from storage and she started up, stuffing the last of the banana into her cheek and chewing quickly.

The attic was surprisingly clean. Gen remembered it from the days of her youth, when she and Lily would climb the steps to bring down the Christmas lights and boxes of ornaments. The place had been dusty back then, the eaves open to the weather on the sides and back at each gable. Squirrels had often gotten in and made nests, rooting in anything not protected. Now the attic walls and ceiling were lined with wallboard, enclosing the rafters and insulation, and air-conditioning vents kept it cool in the summer, warm in the winter. It was neater as well, with trunks stacked against the low walls, cards on the front of each, declaring its contents.

Lily and Della were around the corner, an overhead light bulb hanging from a wire above them. Her sister sat on a pillow surrounded by piles of clothes. A jewelry box lay open by her side, something silver gleaming softly. Della sat in an old rocker, the wicker broken out on the back where her massive shoulder shoved through. Della held a photograph album. Hurt reared itself in Gen's chest at the sight of the tableau from which she had been excluded. A trunk and two boxes had been pulled from the walls and were open, contents piled and draped at random. Gen saw a pair of shorts, wrinkled with age and brown along one side, recognizing them as her mother's. A warped wooden tennis racket in its frame. A porcelain doll she had not seen before. Excitement rippled along her skin, shadowed by the faint sense of betrayal. Lily had started without her. Maybe this was the way Lily felt when left behind on a shopping trip, but somehow, Gen felt her hurt was the greater. These were her mother's things.

Gen slurped down the cooling tea, the sound attracting Della who swiveled her head and scowled. "I done taught you better than that. You sips your tea like a lady."

"Yes ma'am." She looked at her sister, surrounded by her mother's things. "Why didn't you call me?"

Something in her voice must have alerted Lily because she stood instantly and stepped over the clothing to slip an arm around Gen's waist. "Ohhhh. . . . You're right. I'm sorry, sister-mine. Della mentioned the attic and we started up, just to see if we could even get to Mama's things and then I opened one trunk and. . . ." She looked around the attic at the clutter. "Oh, d— heck," she amended with a quick glance at Della. "I guess I got carried away, didn't I?" She put her forehead against Gen's, black eyes chagrined. "I'm sorry. I didn't think. I couldn't stop. I should have sent Keri or one of Della's housekeepers to get you. Forgive me? Please?"

Gen took a deep breath. She could stay hurt and spoil the rest of the morning, or she could finish her tea and join Della and Lily in the search through her mother's belongings. Though making a scene was the more attractive option, Gen trammeled her own hurt into the corner of her heart where all the misery was collecting, hugged Lily, and jutted her chin toward the center of the attic space. "Got room for me?"

"Not only that, got two boxes I haven't opened. They're both yours. And I really am sorry, sister-mine. If it had been you and Della, and you had started up here without me. . . ."

"You would a raised the roof and carried on like we'd done cut out your heart," Della said, her tone acerbic. "Your sister got better sense, and better manners for that matter, even if she do slurp her tea. Come over here, girl, give old Della a hug and then fine you a pillow to sit on. We got us some memories to cherish."

Gen found an old divan that had been her mother's, a long, sleek looking ottoman with faded olive upholstery and moth-eaten fringe all around, and pulled it to the center of the room.

"I remember that," Lily said, pointing. "It used to be in the bathroom, and Mama sat on it to put on her makeup. But look at this hat. You remember when Mama used to wear it to mass? All this little netting beaded with black onyx stones."

"Paid a frightful fortune for that hat, too," Della said. "Made the Old Man so mad I thought sure he'd be hopping. But she put it on and modeled it for him, turning around in circles and smiling. He just shut up and give her a hug, and that was that. My little Helena must a wore that hat for two year every Saturday night to de church. Likely got some shoes in there somewhere, too, what matches it."

Gen opened a pasteboard box, peeled back the tissue paper layered on top, and lifted out an evening gown. It was a peach silk sheath with beaded, black gauze overlay, and Lily sighed behind her. It was beautiful, or once had been, the silk now faded to yellow in the creases, the black gauze stiff with dry-rot.

"I don't remember Mama wearing that," Lily said.

"I do. One summer. To the governor's mansion, was it Della? A ball for the Kennedys, I think. She was so excited." Gen refolded the dress before sticking her head back into the box, careful of the delicate gauze crinkling into a fine black powder as she set it aside.

Seeing what was still inside she lifted her head and grinned, sly. "Lily, you are going to be *green* that you left this box for me, but I'm not sharing so stay there," she added as Lily started to rise. Della laughed at the expression on Lily's face; Gen ignored it. "I think this one has Mama's ball gowns. Look." She lifted out a velvet, winter gown in celery green, the arms long and slender, coming to points at the wrists. It was fitted, the fabric supple. Gen held it up to herself.

"Sister-mine, I think it'll fit you," Lily said, excited, her pique forgotten. "Try it on!"

Gen paused, eyes startled, refusal on the tip of her tongue. But . . . she did want to try the dress. She did. Her hands slid down the velvet, ruffling the nap of the cloth. It was silk velvet, and must have cost a fortune. She lifted the sleeve and noted the tiny hand-stitched seams, the pearl button and loop at the cuff.

Lily smiled gently, tears in her eyes. "Put it on," she whispered. "I want to see it like she might have worn it. You look like her, you know, and I was always so jealous of that. I want to see her in that dress."

Gen's mercurial sister was crying now, tears in a slow, graceful glide down her cheeks. Lily had always been able to cry without turning all red and swollen. She called it an art. Said men fell for it every time, tripping all over their own feet apologizing when they had done her wrong—or when she thought they had. Gen slid her hand across the rich fabric once more, then gave Lily the dress, pulling her T-shirt over her head and slipping out of the jeans.

The dress fit like it had been made for her. The hem fell to the tops of her arches, the sleeves cupped her wrists above the palm, the points falling to the first knuckle of her middle fingers where a real pearl dangled on each. Lily stepped back, sniffed and wiped a hand across her nose. "You look just like her. I never realized how much.

"I saw some green shoes in this trunk." Lily turned and bent over the humped trunk, rounded bottom in the air. "This one had shoes, some pictures, and the costume jewelry box," she said, her voice deadened by the trunk. She lifted out several pairs until she found the spike-heeled, dyed-satin shoes. They matched the dress perfectly.

Gen slid a foot into one, or tried to. "Mama had little feet. I mean *little*. What was she, a five?" she asked, lifting the shoe. There were no size marks on it. Gen had really wanted to wear the entire outfit. Tears pricked again, tears she was growing to hate. To stave them off, she held the offending shoe in the air. "How can I play dress-up if I have bigger feet than Mama?"

"I can wear them," Lily said, slipping on the miniscule shoes. "My feet are the only thing about me that's little. The rest is luscious, rounded, and meant for loving," she laughed what was almost a giggle and went to find a mirror, the little heels tap-tapping on the tongue-and-groove attic flooring. There was a dirty Cheval mirror with beveled edges in a corner behind a kitchen hutch. With a little rearranging of stacked furniture, Lily pulled it out, dusted it off, and turned it so Gen could see herself.

It was like looking into the past. Gen remembered this dress, her mother slipping little dangling pearls onto her lobes, hair swept up in a French-twist, gray eyes sparkling, her lips coral. *"This is just the shade that Sophia Loren wears,"* she had said. *"And your daddy thinks it looks better on me than it does on her."* Her father had come into the room, bent over her mother and kissed her mouth. Not a little quick peck, but a real kiss. Lingering. And their lips had pulled apart slowly as if neither one wanted the kiss to end.

"Aunt Gen, you look hot!"

Gen blinked the memory away.

Keri stood at the corner, eyes wide and a bit awed, Destan behind her peering in. "Can we come watch?" her niece asked.

"Help me out of this, Lily," she said, bustling in the small space as the bittersweet moment passed. "I don't want to damage it. Of course you can come in. These were your grandmother's things."

Loud scuffling ensued as a dressing room was created for Gen so she could change without Destan's presence being a problem, and model the clothing. They spent two hours going through the boxes, Gen trying on the well-made, vintage evening clothing. What didn't fit Gen, seemed perfect for Keri, or would in a few years.

Keri would be the toast of her prom in a full-skirted lavender dress with a matching amethyst necklace in its silver filigreed setting, and they found a fuchsia sheath that could be altered if needed for a coming-out party. The style was a little mature, but it was striking with the girl's dark coloring.

Of the everyday dresses, many styled after Jackie Kennedy with fitted shapes and capped sleeves, some were still usable. Gen selected a few that she might wear, and the rest, unsuitable to the era or showing signs of disintegration, Helena's daughters put aside. They could decide later what to donate to charity, what to discard as worthless.

The cotton sports clothing was in poor condition, sweat stains permanently darkening the arm-holes of tennis outfits, creases frayed, pleated skirts folded wrong, riding breeches falling apart as they were lifted. Nothing from that box was salvageable except a few cotton blouses meant for gardening or riding which Keri claimed, and two good pair of riding boots, which Lily snapped up though she had no intention to ride.

Bored, Destan said he was going to the stables and left the attic. A teenaged boy could only watch a group of women play dress-up for just so long before making his excuses. He lasted longer than Gen expected.

The silk underclothes Lily had found earlier were in better shape, each piece individually wrapped in tissue paper as the evening clothing had been, the fabric still smooth and scented with their mother's favorite gardenia sachet, the fragrance barely detectable. Gen lifted a gown and breathed deeply, remembering the scent of Helena fresh from a bath, her skin so smooth it rivaled the finest silk she might wear.

The bras had been custom made to fit Helena's small chest, and were uncomfortable by today's standards, but the panties, edged with fine silk lace and delicate embroidery were perfect. Lily looked enviously as her sister and daughter separated them into two piles, but accepted four bed-jackets that Helena had worn when pregnant, and two robes, lose enough to fit her own hips.

In the last carton were the dresses so necessary to a woman of society in the sixties. Dresses for bridge club, for book club, for garden club and music club. Dresses for mass, for working in the garden, for visiting the sick. Dresses for every occasion. And lying on top was a photo album of Helena, with shots of her in many of the clothes, posing like a pin-up girl, one toe pointing to show off a length of calf, others, candid shots at the meetings that had been held at the estate, white gloves and wide brimmed hat for outside, white gloves and pillbox hat for indoors.

In the photographs, their mama wore many of the boxed dresses, and the visions of her and the touch of the clothes she had worn brought her alive again as they plundered. Each of them claimed something once belonging to the woman in the photos, new memories for tomorrow.

Near the bottom of the big box was a lace-collared, beige linen dress with long slender sleeves. The lace was stained and tattered, and when Gen held the dress up to herself, inspecting the odd stains, Della gasped, her eyes wide with shock.

"What that dress doing there? You put that dress down, Geneva, you hear me? *Put it down!*" she thundered when Gen didn't move. Gen dropped the dress, backing away. Della moved like a landslide, shoving all the piles of clothing aside with her girth, reached the dress and snapped it up, stuffing it behind her back, eyes flinging sparks at the two sisters.

She whirled, bunching the dress into one hand, pointing the other at the door. "Keri, you gets yourself downstairs, right this minute. *Go!*"

The young girl ran, snatching up her pile of finery from the floor, casting a frightened glance at her mother and aunt. As if suddenly realizing that she was retreating and leaving them behind, she paused at the top of the stairs, just out of sight. "Mama?" Her voice quivered.

"It's alright, sweetheart," Lily said calmly, her dark eyes on Della. "I'll handle it."

"Go on," Gen said. "Your mama will be fine. I promise."

After a moment Keri's sneakers pattered down the stairs. A strained silence filled the attic. Della crushed the dress in both hands now, balling it tightly. Her eyes darted from Gen to Lily to the doorway downstairs as if seeking escape. Slowly, Gen stepped forward and took Della's arm.

"Give me the dress, Della."

The old woman held the dress close to her chest, protecting it, hiding it. Tears filled and overflowed in an instant, and she buried her face in the old cloth, a stained bit of lace brushing her cheek.

"Give me the dress," Gen said again, gently.

Della moaned. And Gen understood, suddenly.

"It's blood, isn't it Della?"

Della sobbed, the sound brokenhearted and anguished, but she released the dress when Geneva tugged on the garment. Boneless, she allowed herself to be persuaded back into the rocking chair. It groaned in misery with her weight, the sound a harsh counterpoint as Della cried, lifting her apron to catch the tears. "My baby. My precious little baby," she moaned.

Gen held the dress out, inspecting it. "It's blood," she said

softly, looking at Lily. "All over the sleeves. Splattered on the
bodice. Some under the knees, as if she knelt in the blood."

Lily moved, her limbs stiff and unnatural in shock. She put a
hand on Della's shoulder patting her. "Okay. It's blood," she said
hesitantly. "But whose blood? Who is the precious little baby?
Mama, or Matthew?"

Gen jerked. It was her mother's, wasn't it? Defensive blood
patterns? From the night her mother died? Wasn't it? Matthew
had lived for three days after Helena died. It *had* to be Helena's
blood. . . .

15

LOW-LIFE LAWYERS and LEGAL RECORDS

Sheriff Pritchard leaned back in his old leather chair, the wheels and springs beneath groaning like creaking bones. "You learned about this over the weekend and waited until now to talk to me?" he asked caustically, turning through the three legal pad pages of notes. "I suppose you fancy-pants lawyers don't believe in *billing hours* through the weekend." In disgust he tossed the pad to the desktop. "That's just for cops and blue-collar types who have to *work* for a living."

Starnes shrugged, a professional smile firmly in place. "I'm here now, Sheriff, and you have a full report. And if I recall correctly, the last time I was in here, you called me a low-life Cajun, and my sister, Serena, a loony little witch." Moving his jean-clad legs a bit wider, bending forward with his elbows on the chair arms, he asked casually, "Now I'm fancy? What'd I do to move up in the world?"

Pritchard's arms settled across his belly, big fingers playing with a pencil, rotating it slowly. He ignored Starnes' rejoinder and questions as if they had never been spoken. "Way you take your time, I might think you was trying to obstruct justice or something—did I not know you and your . . ." he paused as if he had a bad taste in his mouth, "*lawyer-ly ethics* so well."

Starnes lifted a brow and sat back in his chair, stretched out his legs and relaxed, his posture a faint imitation of the sheriff's but showing no subordination to the other man's authority. Rather, a subtle amusement, which the sheriff noted with pursed lips. It was part of the game they played whenever Starnes came to Pritchard's office.

Pritchard didn't like lawyers, preachers, women, drunks, gays, Cajuns, Amerindians, Jews, Asians, Hispanics, or blacks, and still managed to get elected to public office in a parish with a preponderance of all the above except Jewish and Asian. Starnes, being part Indian, mostly Cajun, a lawyer, the son of a drunken preacher and brother to Serena fell flat on several levels. Pritchard didn't like him on principle and never bothered to hide the fact, but in fairness, Starnes had to admit that the sheriff treated him no worse than any other lawyer in the parish.

It had taken Starnes a few visits after the man was elected sheriff to discover and understand the baiting game Jim Pritchard played with lawyers, and especially lawyers with *problem* family members, like Serena, or lawyers with ethnic backgrounds. Once Starnes understood the game and how it was played, he subjugated his natural reactions to unsubtle insults and used the sheriff's prejudice against him. Sometimes it worked, sometimes it didn't. Now, the two men dallied back and forth as a natural part of every encounter and Starnes had the feeling Pritchard actually enjoyed the mutual hostility.

"Well, we could play the obstruction game awhile if you want, Jim," he said, using Pritchard's given name as if they were equals or friends, "but we both know I didn't have to come in here and tell you anything. Client confidentiality still counts for *something* in the courts, though the conservative faction at the federal level tries its best to steal our Constitutional rights."

"Good thing, or the lily-livered, ethnic-loving, homo-butt-lovers, and bleeding heart liberals would have the nation run by the criminals and dykes and the rest of us would loose everything it used to mean about being an American."

"Oh, yeah. *That* America," Starnes said, as if in sudden understanding. "You mean the America of your childhood, where civil rights were only for the white male. Where a man could beat his wife and children if he had a bad day at work or if he got drunk and unruly or if he just felt like it. Where the government routinely poisoned, infected, or radiated its citizens and military as a part of science experiments. Where—"

"You ain't never married, have you? You a homo? A Cajun, Indian, lawyer, homo. Damn, your daddy must be proud. Oh, that's right. Your preacher daddy was too sotted to know what was going on with his boy."

Starnes smiled and it must not have been a pretty thing to see. Pritchard sat back in his chair. "My wife and baby *died*, Pritchard.

A long time a ago." Starnes' voice was a silky-soft. "You can call my old man anything you want, but if you ever mention my family again, I'll find a way to get one of your typical conversations on the local airwaves just so I can watch you crash and burn with the voters. Got that?"

Pritchard narrowed his eyes and the rotating pencil stilled. In the last campaign, he had kept his prejudice from the voters, kissing babies of all ethnic backgrounds and speaking to the League of Women Voters and the Baptist Women's Missionary Union as often as to firefighters, law-enforcement and the VFW. He liked his job, its power and perks, and he wanted to keep it. Usually he trod a careful line even with Starnes, but a crafty reporter could edit enough out of a casual conversation to do damage to his career. He seldom crossed the line, but he balanced on it with great care and Starnes watched as Pritchard reconsidered his argument.

"Now, I'm not saying things was perfect in the past, my boy, but they sure ain't good now, not from a crime prevention standpoint. You a lawyer." The pencil resumed its figure eight rolls in the Sheriff's big fingers. "You know how easy it is for criminals to get back on the streets."

"Lots of innocent men in jail," Starnes said pleasantly, playing his part in the little dialogue.

"Lots of guilty ones roaming free, psychopaths and sociopaths and serial killers and such. Con-artists, whores, baby killers, murderers and thieves. Take the man or men what killed these two." The sheriff pushed a box toward Starnes with a booted foot, a grin on his face, half amusement, half challenge.

Starnes lowered one hand and opened the flap, peering into the box. Careful to keep his face blank, he let the flap drop and lifted a single brow in question. "You always keep skeletons and skulls in boxes underneath your desk?"

Pritchard pursed his lips in disappointment at Starnes' mild response. "Some murderer running around free for decades. Killed and buried these boys and so far got off scot-free. But he made a mistake or two. Enough for me to identify him, I get half a chance. I intend to see the murderer in jail where he belongs."

"Murderer? Like John Deveraux?"

Pritchard's face fell. He had quickly gotten so tied up in the game that he had forgotten the Old Man's part in it.

Starnes just laughed. "He spent a lot of money putting you in office, didn't he? And now you have to investigate him for murder. A deathbed confession." Starnes shook his head. "Wonder what the constituents will say?"

The sheriff pondered a moment, the pencil still turning lazy somersaults in his hands. Pritchard had huge hands, linebacker hands, meat cleaver hands, yet they turned the pencil with graceful dexterity.

And then he smiled, a purposeful baring of slightly uneven teeth behind stretched lips. "They'll say I'm the kind of man not blinded by money, nor position. The kind of man who treats all men equally under the law whether they be rich or poor, white or black or Spic or Coon-ass." His smile spread slowly. "If I play my cards right, I can parley this incident with John Deveraux into a landslide election in two years. A triumph for Law and Order and the American way."

"Even if you find proof that he killed his wife and his infant son?"

Pritchard's breath blew out slowly, his eyes widening. "I don't believe it. Not John Deveraux. He's mourned that woman for nearly forty years. Coulda had most any woman in three parishes as mistress or wife, and so far as I know, never did neither."

"That mean you intend to ignore the possibility that he killed her, simply because he never remarried?"

Lips again pursed as he thought it over. Finally Sheriff Pritchard sat up in his chair, pulled the yellow pad back toward him. Putting the pencil to paper, he said, "I want the details."

His eyes on the man who was both politician and cop, Starnes complied.

It was late when he arrived at the estate, his old truck throbbing powerfully at a restrained pace down the road out front. To one side of the estate road were pecan groves and acres of soy, cotton, and even a section of feed-corn, the house and grounds glimpsed between tree trunks and rows of crops. Shadows stretched long legs across the lawn, streaking the immaculate turf with black tiger stripes. To the other side of the road were hayfields, recently mown, huge rolled bales dotting the landscape like a giant's toys, tossed and forgotten. Gen was on horseback, cantering slowly across the cut grass, the horse beneath her, muscles rippling.

Starnes braked, matching his speed to that of the horse, keeping Gen ahead of him, watching her ride, himself unnoticed. Lowering his window, he heard her laugh, the sound thrown back by the stand of trees beyond the field. A mellow warmth filled him as he watched, listening, and some of the day's tension slipped away, absorbed by her freedom and grace.

A dark sheen of sweat slicked the horse's flanks, bleeding out from beneath the blanket and western saddle with its wide girth. Sweat lathered the horse's neck where the single reins rubbed, guiding the horse. Gen was dressed as he remembered from his youth, in jeans and boots topped with T-shirt and cowboy hat. Her hair was in a ponytail pulled through the hole in the back of the hat, flouncing with the horse's motion up and down.

Keri and Destan rode in front, bodies bent forward for speed, their mounts racing. Gen called to them, the words lost, only the notes carrying to him. Delicate. Lilting.

The kids reached some predetermined finish line and slowed, turning their horses in large circles and trotting back to Gen, who slowed to meet them. Together, they veered toward the barn, now moving at a walk, the horses' heads bobbing in the still-humid heat. The head groom stepped from the barn and shouted, her words lost in the distance.

Starnes made the turn into the estate drive and parked. Taking his briefcase and the box of police records from thirty years ago, he went to the house. The Old Man was sitting up, breathing harshly, his face slightly gray. The cat sat on his lap, her eyes intent on his. Deveraux's black orbs met Starnes' eyes across the room as the lawyer shut the door to the hallway, crossed the room, and put his burdens on the table by the window.

"So," the Old Man said, finding breath for words. "What did Pritchard have to say?"

Starnes stood, one hand still on the faded record box, its ancient tape curling along the seams that gaped open, freshly cut. "He saw a judge this afternoon."

The Old Man waited, knowing there was more.

"Wants to bring in a backhoe and the state crime lab. Start the process of finding the. . . ."

"Bones," he gasped, concluding for Starnes. "If there are any left."

"Yes. And. . . ." Starnes paused before plunging ahead. "He gave me a box of old records. He gave me permission to look through them. Discuss them with you."

"Records?" The word grated out, sounding like rusted machinery turning beneath deep water.

"Of your wife's death. And Matthew's. There have been . . . certain charges leveled."

John Deveraux's eyes slit, looking like the cat's narrow gaze, which turned now to Starnes, too. Deveraux tried to speak, his lips moving, but no sound escaped. His color darkened, the breath sounds slowing as the Old Man struggled to inhale. Panic and rage burned together in the dark depths of his eyes. The cat sprang to the floor, hissing.

Starnes stepped forward and stopped, knowing he was unable to deal with the medical emergency that was taking place. He shouted for Mary Anne and Beckah, who rushed into the room so quickly that he knew they must have been standing in the hallway. In the rush to clear the Old man's airway, suction out the clogging mucous and fluid that suffocated him, Starnes was useless, watching the Old Man's face as he began to breathe once again. Over the nurses' heads his client's black eyes met his in fury and something more. A command to tell all that he knew. And a promise of vengeance.

Starnes stepped back as the violence in the bloodshot eyes leapt out at him. It was clear that if the Old Man had been able, he would have throttled Starnes at that moment.

Tell me! the eyes commanded. *Tell me who!*

Knowing he shouldn't do it, not right now, but unable to ignore the demand in the angry eyes, the lawyer leaned forward, catching a whiff of something foul and decaying—the Old Man's body dying even while he still inhabited it. Speaking softly, so that Mary Anne and Beckah couldn't hear, he said into Deveraux's ear, "Your daughter tells me that you killed them."

The dark eyes widened in horror. And sudden understanding. And then, grief. John Deveraux looked away, out the window that overlooked his vast estate. His shoulders slowly slumped; he settled into the mattress like a pile of old leaves in a damp breeze, eyelids drooping, revealing moist, deep-red inner-lids. The Old Man seemed to give in, for the first time, to the disease that had stalked him for years.

16

GOOD LITTLE WIFE and UNCOOPERATIVE HUSBANDS

The Old man was breathing again, the ambulance and emergency techs standing waiting for a trip to a New Orleans' hospital that wouldn't take place. Dr. Boulanger had arrived ahead of them and administered a sedative, a huge dose of Lasix, and a stronger breathing treatment. Once again, John Deveraux had cheated death and the drugs and machines that could keep him alive for a few months longer. A few months. And that was only if he would allow the doctor to administer the chemotherapy he needed, or put him on a ventilator. John Deveraux had refused repeatedly, not wanting to die weak and sick and at the mercy of machines.

Starnes knew he had contributed to the Old Man's attack. He had caused it when he told what Geneva knew about her mother's and brother's deaths. John Deveraux would make certain that he didn't ever forget it, too. Starnes sighed as he stared up at the patch of black sky above him. The air was too moist and the live oaks too numerous to offer a glimpse of many stars, but Venus shone brightly between one set of branches and Orion's belt lined up neatly between others.

Behind him, the EMTs pulled away, grumbling about dinners missed and wasted calls. True, and his fault. Starnes had already offered to pay for the missed meals, but the men had declined. Ethics or parish rules or just a way to make him feel even more guilty, Starnes didn't know. Either way, he didn't turn and watch as they drove from the estate.

Instead, he slid the incriminating record box into the truck bed and gathered the now-cold paper boxes of Chinese he had brought for Gen's dinner. He knew his way around the Deveraux kitchen almost as well as Della, and quickly heated the food, heaped it into bowls which he set on a tray with utensils and freshly starched napkins. For the second time in his life, he lifted a bottle of wine from the Old Man's wine cabinet, added two glasses and walked out of the Big House, all without disturbing Della in her rooms off the kitchen, that is, assuming that she wasn't still dancing attendance on the Old Man as she had done all these years. Starnes finally understood her devotion, but that didn't make it any easier to watch. John Deveraux had never once said "Thank you" to her.

With his foot, Starnes tapped on the screen door of the guesthouse. Moments later Gen opened the inner door, her head swathed in a towel, her body in a fluffy white robe. On the floor just beyond her were two dark gray Givenchy suitcases, zippered open, contents spilling in disarray. On hangers over the back of the closet door were a black dress and a red suit, as if the two were being compared and considered. Prospective funeral attire?

"He still alive?" she asked, her face without emotion.

The faint scent of her perfume wafted out to him on a draft of cold air. A droplet of water slid from beneath the turbaned towel, down her long throat, and melded with the terry collar. Starnes' insides clenched. He nodded, then tilted his head in the direction of the dresses. "For the Old Man's funeral?"

Ignoring his question, Gen sniffed. "Is that Chinese?"

"If I feed you do I get to pick out which dress you wear?" he countered.

One hand on each jamb, she considered, a stern frown on her face, but her stomach rumbled, spoiling the effect. "I'll be willing to listen to your opinion," she conceded loftily.

"I guess I could force the issue, but you sound hungry, and I'm a gentleman."

Gen snorted delicately and stood aside, allowing him access to the guesthouse. It had never been intended for visitors to eat here, only in the Big House, but there was a small table and two mismatched chairs, which Gen swept clean of lacy under-things, and silk gowns, and pantyhose in little packets. She disappeared while he laid out the meal and returned moments later dressed in a yellow T-shirt and a wrap-around skirt that looked like it had last been worn in the sixties.

When she leaned across the table to lift a green snow-pea into her mouth, he fancied that he could see a sheen of silk beneath the T-shirt, perhaps the camisole with yellow daisies that had lain over the back of one dining chair while he stood on the porch. The thought of Gen in the camisole and nothing else did things to his body he wasn't planning on, and he turned his attention to the spicy Szechwan dishes, rice, and spring rolls. Gen opened the wine and poured it, the Chardonnay the same color as her damp hair. It was room temp, but she pronounced it luscious. He liked that word. Luscious. Like Gen.

To keep himself from touching her, he pulled out her chair and intoned, "Milady's dinner is served," and sat himself quickly opposite her.

Gen dipped her chopsticks into the pork with an expertise he couldn't match, and he watched her eat with refined little bites, lifting the rice bowl to her mouth to scoop the rice between her lips. He contented himself with the fork, having given up on chopsticks in law school.

They ate in silence for a while, the only sound the clink of his silver and an occasional low moan of pleasure from Gen. He had forgotten she used to do that, make little groans while she ate something particularly delicious. She had made the same sounds when he kissed the back of her neck, he recalled from ancient necking sessions in his old truck. With the thought, the image of Gen in the silk under-things took him again. He wanted to groan, himself. They finished the meal, Starnes distinctly uncomfortable, and afterward, he couldn't remember exactly what he ate.

"I wish I could offer you some coffee," she said later, sitting back from the table. "But even without it, this was wonderful." She smiled. "Thank you."

Her hair had dried in the cold air blowing from the air-conditioning unit by the bed, and little ringlets had formed around her face. Her skin was porcelain in the light from the bed-side lamp, shadows forming in the hollows of her cheeks. Even barefoot and without makeup she was elegant, as beautiful as ever, but now with character and strength. She looked up, caught his stare, and smiled, a darkening of gray eyes into deepest charcoal, a slow widening of lips.

Starnes had a sudden memory of Gen, stretched out in the bench-seat of his truck, her T-shirt pushed up to her shoulders, breasts gleaming in the moonlight. He made a fist to keep from touching her across the table. "I see your luggage arrived." The words came from nowhere, rescuing him from the images in his mind.

"And are you going to lecture me about the red suit I bought to wear to the funeral? Barry would have a conniption fit if he knew I was going to wear it."

Barry. . . . Her husband. The thought helped the images to recede. "Barry is the proper one in the family? And you're the rebel. I should have figured that."

Gen shrugged. "Was. The divorce will be final in a few weeks," her voice hardened with the words, then lightened. "And I don't intend to let anyone tell me which dress to wear ever again." She tilted her head saucily and toasted him with the stolen wine. "So, don't think you can dissuade me from wearing red just because you brought me supper. I am my own woman now." A dangerous grin finished the sentence, sparkling and sassy. He remembered that grin from decades ago, the grin that issued a challenge and asked a question all at once.

Though the smile was not intended to be erotic, it had that effect on him. The words, however, gave him an outlet for the pressure that had been building inside since she answered the door in the robe. The robe he wished he had pushed from her shoulders. . . . "Did I ever tell you about the *fais-do-do* your mother went to during some senatorial campaign? My mother was there, and I suppose my father, too, though he was likely passed out drunk in a corner somewhere."

Gen shook her head, her eyes glowing in anticipation and from the effect of the Chardonnay. She poured the last half-glass from the bottle holding it upside down, letting the final drops descend into the waiting wine. And then she drank, a bit recklessly, eyes laughing. "Tell me," she commanded.

"Helena was a party girl, always had been," he said, trying to settle into the story. "When she married the staid, respectable John Deveraux, it was expected that she would settle down, start having babies, become domestic and matronly. But your mother had other ideas."

"I don't blame her one little bit," Gen said with a quick, wicked grin, instantly gone.

Starnes insides tightened again and he took a quick breath, suppressing the urge to pull her to him across the table. This was getting out of hand; he really should leave. Gen sipped the wine, the tip of her tongue visible for a moment. The thought of leaving vanished like candle smoke. From somewhere, the thread of the story wove itself into his thoughts. "This was before you were born, of course. I was maybe a few weeks old."

Gen's eyes were rapt, traces of a strange, sensual smile visible in her eyes. Or maybe it was just the wine. He had wanted her, alone like this, from the moment he saw her jumping from the 727, and he was reading too much into her expressions. He shifted uncomfortably in his hard chair.

"Anyway, the party was a barbecue out on some bayou, with state dignitaries and the governor and a couple of hundred parish citizens and your father and a band of Cajun musicians and a *lot* of beer kegs. Your mother wanted to dance, and was waiting for your father to find time for her, but he was involved with discussions about some law he wanted to see passed and he ignored her. It wasn't the wisest thing he ever did."

"What did she do?" Gen drank the last of the wine, holding the glass up as she had held the bottle.

Starnes watched the curve of her neck as she swallowed. The image would have been ill-mannered, almost rude, but for a glint of challenge in her eyes as she lifted the glass. He knew instantly that Barry would have commented on the action, calling her down, calling her to heel.

Starnes grinned as she sat the glass back on the table, laughing. And for an instant, as the laughter died, he saw a glimpse of something else in the gray depths, a memory, a hunger quickly shielded. He knew then that she was remembering their past, just as he was. Remembering was dangerous. She was a married woman. . . . Almost divorced. Only *almost*, he told himself. The most important word.

When he spoke, his voice was rough, dry. "What would you have done?"

Gen laughed and turned the empty glass on the bare table. It made a scritchy sound, hollow. "I'd have found me someone else to dance with and would have made a spectacle of myself. I'd have gotten his attention."

The words were sobering. Was that what she was doing? Getting Barry Stone's attention? But Barry wasn't here. And she wasn't Helena. And Starnes wanted her enough to read desire into an expression when it perhaps wasn't there.

Her face clouded over. "At least that's what I would have done when I was young. Until he had me made over into the kind of woman who was respectable and responsible and *boring*. And then I would have *waited* until he found *time* for me. Like a *good little wife.*"

Though lightly spoken, Starnes heard the bitterness beneath and knew she was no longer speaking about her mother's marriage, but her own. He looked down, moved his wineglass a fraction of an inch, then drank his own last two sips, placing the goblet back on the small table. The clink was loud in the room.

"Well, your mother followed the first course. She started a bunny hop around the grounds, which was still respectable, sort of, until she pulled all the wives into the dance, including some prospective senator's very fat, very tipsy—and until that night, very imposing—wife."

"No! She didn't!"

"And when that didn't get your father's attention, she set up a limbo stick. Your father found her and the proposed senator's wife, both half drunk, boobs in the air, vying for the championship."

Gen laughed, eyes mischievous, no doubt seeing herself in the role of Helena. The wicked smile was back in place, resting at the corners of her lips.

"The wannabe-senator's wife won, by the way. And your mother got what she wanted. The Old Man drug her off and the two didn't leave the house for weeks. You were born roughly nine months later. Or so my mother told me."

◆　◆　◆

The picture Gen had of her mother, young, happy, defiant, alive in every way, shriveled and died. Just as her mother had. Gen looked at her empty glass, at the plates with smears of grease and flecks of rice and little else on them. And she met Starnes' eyes, black as night, so dark the pupils were lost in the irises except in the brightest daylight. The wine was singing in her veins, a rich threnody, sensual and forlorn both. Gen swallowed, her throat dry.

"If I had married you . . . and stayed in Moisson . . . and I danced the limbo. . . ."

Starnes' eyes widened fractionally. "I would never have left you alone long enough to dance a bunny hop or start a limbo," he said softly, "and if you had, well . . ." Starnes didn't move, didn't alter in any way, yet the room was suddenly warmer, smaller. "I once was pretty good at limbo," he smiled slowly, exposing white teeth, his eyes intense. "So, I'd have joined in." The smile vanished, leaving his face fierce, fixed. He was speaking of limbo, but his eyes were saying something else, something more, speaking some promise she had never recognized, never comprehended. Something that had been there so many years ago, and been overlooked, abandoned before it had been tasted. After a long moment, he finished, his voice so low she could barely hear, "I never did get over loving you, *Ginny* Deveraux. I never did."

Looking into his eyes, Gen shivered, her skin raising into tight gooseflesh along her arms and up her back. The moment lengthened. Outside, a whippoorwill sang its lonesome call. Starnes never looked away, his eyes blazing, dark pools. Waiting.

Gen stood slowly, hands braced beside her plate. Without pulling her gaze from his, she stepped around the table, and after what seemed like eons, into his arms. His hands touched her as if making certain she was real, and slid slowly across the curve of hip, up her spine as she bent to him, and into her damp hair, tangling in her curls. He pulled her mouth down and his lips touched hers, awkward, eyes still uncertain. He stood slowly, as if she might bolt. She sighed into his mouth, a sound that was half groan, half memory.

His kiss was tentative, gentle, his eyes boring into hers, questioning for an instant, and then hardening, mouth slanting across hers as he pulled her closer. She could feel his arousal, his sudden need, possessive. Demanding. His hands found hers, gripped them behind her back, his mouth brutal. Teeth clacked against hers with the force of the kiss. Gen wrenched her hands free and wrapped her arms around him, rising on her toes. Grinding against him. He laughed into her throat, the sound feral and savage. Mouth bruising hers.

Gen whimpered with need. Misunderstanding, hearing the

sound as pain, Starnes checked himself, gentled his mouth. Gen remembered to breathe, pulled him back hard. And still she stared into his eyes. He laughed again, and Gen laughed with him, the twin vibrations rich with promise and urgency.

They danced, thigh-to-thigh across the cool floor, mouths now barely touching, yet the tension between them rising. She could see the want, the desire. He never closed his eyes, and she stared into him as he touched her, his mouth smiling as his lips moved.

She was burning, her skin alive and scorching, his hands cold to the touch, yet stoking the heat, tracing the shape of her beneath her clothes. Wordlessly, breath fast and loud in her ears, she pressed herself into him, her fingertips remembering shoulders, corded arms—hardened strands of muscle like individual bands of steel, solid stomach, his eyes smoldering coals, tightly banked.

Her skin was a flame as the icy air brushed her, her shirts and skirt dropping to the floor beneath her feet. The cool of the mattress pressed against her back, and she pushed him away, pulling at his clothes, pushing his shirt over his head until she could touch him as he touched her.

His teeth sank into the soft tissue of her shoulder. Tongue stroked her throat, hot and then cold as the chilled air hit moist, bare flesh. His mouth slid down, landing hungrily over her. She gasped. Pulled him closer, fingers of one hand fumbling at his belt. Fine hairs startled her, soft against her fingers. Gen laughed again, their eyes meeting.

She felt him reach over, turn off the air-conditioning unit. The air instantly warmed. His buckle came free and Gen pulled the belt through, tossing it to land with a slither and clatter.

From somewhere, far off, Gen heard the sound of a car engine through the thin walls. Bumping down the estate drive. Then silence. And Starnes was naked beside her. Later, distant footsteps, a pause, and Destan's voice.

"She's staying at the guest cabin, Uncle Barry. You can see the light."

Gen jerked away. "No. . . ." She twisted herself and shoved at Starnes' shoulders. "Starnes. Starnes!" Panic filled her as black eyes lifted from her body, befuddled and confused. And then the fury hit her. *How* dare *he come here! How* dare *he!* She sobbed, shoving at the man over her.

"What?" Reason entered his eyes and Starnes paused, alert, his face inches from hers, his breath ragged. "What, *sha?*"

"Barry," she said, thickly. "Bare is here."

"Here?" Starnes' face slammed shut as he heard the sound of footsteps. "I thought you were divorcing him." Betrayal, anger in the tone. And something more. Accusation . . . ?

"I am," she said, wriggling away from him and slipping to the floor. "He just isn't being very cooperative."

"Did you . . ." Starnes raised up on his elbows, the sheet twisted through his legs, a line of dark hair trailing down his body. "Did you know he was coming?"

Ah. . . . So that was it. Rigid with fury, angry with Barry and Starnes both, and with men in general, Gen pulled on the T-shirt and tied the skirt, swept the panties under the bed with a jerky kick, and tossed Starnes his clothing. "Right," she hissed. "I arranged for you to bring Chinese and feed me and then I seduced you. . . ." She stopped and laughed, dragging a shaky hand through her hair. "Okay, so I made the first move. You want me to regret that?"

Starnes grinned crookedly, his expression wry. "Sorry. I didn't mean that. I know you better." He pulled his shirt over his head and scooped up the rest of his clothing, escaping to the bath just as a knock sounded on the door. "I never met the man but I don't like him or his timing one bit." The door closed, the sound of water running in the sink.

"Neither do I," Gen whispered, raking a hand through her hair and tossing the covers over the bed. She felt ridiculous. And guilty, which was stupid. Anger surged through her. How dare he come here and—

Barry knocked again. "Gen?" Rich voice, staggering, even through the door.

Gen closed her eyes against the sound. "Just a minute." The bed looked only unmade, instead of recently rolled in. She tossed Starnes' shoes into the corner, bent and looked at the image of herself in the cottage's single small mirror by the door. Her hair was a fright, lips swollen. She looked just-kissed. The guilt that had germinated moments earlier sprouted and grew.

And then she remembered the woman in his office the last

time she saw him . . . that terrible day. Oralee, Barry's secretary, had tried to stop her, but she had been so excited she had just burst into his office. And seen *her.* Tall, willowy, legs up to her neck. Dark, smooth skin like hot-chocolate and vivid green eyes beneath high cheekbones. Hair upswept with snaky tendrils down her neck. Utterly beautiful. And at least eight months pregnant. In Barry's arms.

"Gen!" Louder. Demanding as always.

Suddenly she didn't care how she looked or what he thought. Throwing open the door, Gen shouted, "What, damn it!" The door crashed into the wall and bounced back, hitting her elbow. Pain shot through her arm, tears sprang to her eyes. Barry stood there.

He was beautiful. God, she hated the way he always made her feel. Small and delicate and sometimes downright ugly. Certainly unsophisticated.

"Gen?" He sounded uncertain.

She hesitated. Barry Stone had never been uncertain one day in his life. Not one moment. Her nascent tears dried. The light from the cottage lamps threw strange shadows across his face, leaving only a shock of silver hair and his eyes clearly visible through the screen door. Blue. Electric blue, midnight blue, crystal blue. She had given up years ago trying to pin a name on the blue of his eyes, though the tabloids still tried.

Barry started to smile. The light caught a glint of perfect, white teeth, eyes crinkled at the corners. Gen wondered if his new woman had successfully found a word to describe the color. The thought broke the spell that seeing him had woven.

"I can't believe that you actually had the gall to come here."

The smile vanished. He reached for the door and Gen slammed the little latch home. The motion caused her elbow to ache, but the tears didn't come again, which pleased her immensely.

"Get out of here. Go back to New York, Barry. Go back to your little Jasmine and your baby."

"Gen, you don't underst—"

"No. I don't. I don't understand. And I won't share. You knew how I felt about marriage when we met. You knew."

"But you have to let me explain—"

"Explain!" she exploded. "*Explain?* I know perfectly well how to pull down a zipper. *I know how it's done!*" she screamed. "I know how to *fuck!*" Gen sucked a painful breath, watching the shock enter and fade from his eyes, a special shade of blue, anguish-blue. In a calmer tone she said, "And I don't need you and your ivy-league education and your fine ambassadorial upbringing to tell me how it's done! Now get away from me or I'll have my lawyer—"

Barry roared. The screen door slammed against the outside wall. The small latch ricocheted into the cottage, pinging. Barry was in the room. Eyes fury-blue. Insane-blue. Gen ducked as if to run.

He gripped her arms and shook her, his rage a wordless bellow.

"It no wonder she lef' you, bo."

The words stopped Barry. His face lifted from Gen's to the cottage, focused and refocused as he took in the room, the unmade bed, the clothing piled and hung around, the dishes for two on the small table. One chair on its side that Gen hadn't noticed when he knocked. A pair of men's shoes. And Starnes. Oh God, Starnes.

◆ ◆ ◆

He knew he couldn't best the man in a fair fight. The size difference alone was overwhelming, not to mention the handicap of his hip. Now if he had his daddy's old .45 with the pearl-handled grip, he might have a fighting chance, if he could run fast enough and long enough to allow a full six rounds to do their dirty work and bring the big man down. But Starnes knew his limitations. His hip ached and he hadn't even started to move. So he settled on audacity. Standing with legs crossed at the ankles, bare feet on the wood flooring, leaning against the wall with arms crossed, he put an insolent go-to-hell look on his face, letting the expression and body language constitute his weapons of choice. They had worked well enough in high school when the resident bully wanted to pick a fight.

"Me? I'd a lef' you, too, de way you ak. You treat yo woman like dat at home, brozzer? Big ol' *fonchock* lak you is, shakin' daylights outta *petite fille* lak *Ginny*." His voice lowered, menacing.

"Bruisin' her arm, both. Scare her lak to death, *je vas t' parier.*"

Barry dropped Gen's arms as if they burned him, stepped back.

"Yep. Bruise her, you did. Just lak I thought in my head." He nodded, as if his worst predictions had come true, and Starnes' voice dropped even lower, becoming little more than a deep rumble bouncing off the walls of the tiny cabin. "Look a dat. *Ça c'est de la couillonnade.* Shape *des mains*, you hands."

The accent disappeared. "A good photographer and a deposition could make life a bit difficult for you back in New York. Now, *Ginny's* a photographer," he said thoughtfully. "I reckon she could take a few self portraits. Course she'd need a witness. And a lawyer. Be even better if they were the same person. Wonder where I can find one of those around here?"

Barry Stone made a sound so close to a growl that Starnes had to fight the urge to react. His choices were hit Barry and die, run like hell, or talk his way through this.

"Oh, yeah," he said as if just remembering, "*I'm* a lawyer." He smiled the fierce, vicious smile he reserved for the petty career criminals he was forced to represent when first out of law school. And saw reason begin to return to Stone's eyes. "*And* a witness."

Rage was swept away as understanding dawned in the blue eyes and the man recognized the signs of his wife's—soon-to-be ex-wife's—tryst. His fists balled. Barry Stone had *big* fists.

"Of course if you were to ball up a fist and hit her—or me—I'd have to intervene or fight back, and then I'd have to call the sheriff. Who happens to be a good fishin' buddy of mine." Starnes smiled, showing teeth, lying through them with impunity. "You is in good-ol'-boy territory now, Stone," Starnes said with a thick southern accent. "You lookin' to spend the night in the pokey?"

Barry Stone's fists slowly opened. He closed his famous blue eyes and took a breath, then a deeper one. Moments passed, Gen uncoiling a bit from her protective posture. The rich color of high blood pressure and wrath slowly drained from Barry's face. His shoulders drooped.

Geneva, her body poised for pain or flight, uncurled fully. Her eyes were wild, the gray of broken clouds ripe with rain and storm. She glanced at Starnes and back at Stone, wary. She was afraid, but it wasn't the fear of the beaten woman. Starnes had seen enough of them in his early years of practice to recognize the defeated stare, the look of perpetual fear and degradation. Gen wasn't one of those. Perhaps this physical . . . *intimidation* . . . was a first. Perhaps it wasn't.

Pushing away from the wall, Starnes said calmly, "Okay. I suggest that you take yourself off to a hotel, get a cold shower, a hot meal, and a good night's sleep. Then catch the first flight back to New York in the morning. Deal with *Ginny* through proper channels."

Barry shook his head, turning the full wattage of his gaze on Starnes, speaking to him as if Gen were not in the room. The voice that addressed Congress and the President and the press with such sonorous poise turned to him alone. "I'm not going anywhere until I speak with my wife." At Gen's weary, pained reaction to the word *wife*, he said, "I'll stay in a hotel tonight, but I have to talk to her. Witnessed, if you like, but she has to hear what I have to say."

"You have nothing to say that I want to hear, Barry," she said, her voice sounding exhausted. "Nothing." She closed her eyes, swaying slightly. Starnes put out a hand and steadied her, drawing the fierce, possessive glare of her husband. *Her husband.* Starnes forced himself to remember that. He had almost gone to bed with a married woman. Still wanted to, if he were honest with himself. Even now.

There was no doubt that Barry understood Starnes wanted Gen. The signs were glaring in the room, in his own posture, in Gen's expression of defiance and guilt. The man was too smart to be fooled even if Starnes had wanted to do so. And though Starnes felt a bit like a teenager fighting over a girl in school, he knew that Barry now considered him a rival, was measuring his new opponent, judging the alternatives with a keen mind. Abruptly, Starnes felt like prey beneath the piercing blue eyes. Barry stood straight and smiled slightly, calm, controlled, now that anger had been replaced with competition. Competition was something the man understood.

Starnes went on alert again, this time still and vigilant. He knew that on some level, he was still in danger. If reports were true, Barry Stone never lost a battle, once he turned his mind to a match of wills.

"If she listens to me, I'll go back to New York and leave her in peace. She can decide what she wants without any interference from me. And I'll abide by her decision."

Dirty pool, thought Starnes. The man was speaking to him as if he was her lawyer, rationally, calmly, suggesting a compromise a judge might grant. And against his will, Starnes was reacting like a lawyer. As Barry Stone had known he would. The memory of the photograph on the cover of *People* magazine popped into his mind. Barry Stone was brilliant, dangerous. And a fool.

"A judge would recommend a conversation if he phrased it like that," Starnes said to Gen, his eyes still on Stone. "We can get a judge to allow you privacy in chambers if you like, if you're afraid he might hurt you. Send a letter to your divorce lawyer if needed to prove that due consideration had been made to the possibility of reconciliation."

Gen looked at him, eyes wounded. He had betrayed her, too, Starnes could see it in her expression. He dropped her arm.

"I'm a lawyer, *Ginny*, I'm not your conscience. I'm not recommending anything. I'm just telling you what might happen anyway, when you go before a judge."

Gen looked back at Barry. "He's never . . . hit me." Their gazes met and held a moment, Barry's with an electric intensity, Gen's with pain. Dropping her head so that the curls fell over her face, she stepped to the overturned chair and righted it, the wooden legs scrapping on the floor with a high squeak. She stacked the dishes one inside another. Thinking, busying her hands.

"You think a judge will force me to . . . ?"

"It's a possibility. Maybe New York judges have too much going on to take the time, but I know of a few around here who would insist."

She sighed. "Tomorrow morning. Late. He can come here. I'll see him in the Old Man's office." She smiled slightly. "You don't have to be here, Starnes. Della will be around. And I defy anyone to hurt her babies while she's on guard."

Barry's eyes were still on Starnes. "I'll be here at eleven." He seemed about to say more, his eyes darting to the bed, the piled clothes, the luggage, Starnes' bare feet. He clamped his mouth shut, turned and walked from the guesthouse. They could hear his footsteps on the path as he made his way back to the car. Controlled. Decisive. Leaving his wife with another man. Strategists on the field of battle won more often than tacticians. Strategists saw the long-view and planned toward a specific end, minimizing anything they could not control or destroy. Starnes knew he had been effectively minimized. Gen busied herself with the dirty dishes again and couldn't meet his eyes. Embarrassed? Shamed? He sighed, lifted his shoes from the corner and tucked them under his arm, took the tray of dishes from her hands and went out the door. The door hung on by only one hinge.

"Gen?"

"Starnes?"

They both spoke at once and the words broke the tension between them. Gen smiled. "It was a good dinner. And it would have been a great dessert."

Startled, Starnes laughed, a single bark of surprise.

She leaned over the tray of dishes and kissed him, gently. "Thank you. I know. . . ." She lost the train of her words.

He leaned in and kissed her back. "I know, too. I forgot something tonight, *Ginny*," he said, the French syllables soft. "I'm not interested in sleeping with a married woman. Never have been. Unless she's married to me." Gen's eyes widened at the deliberate implication. "Call me tomorrow, will you? When he leaves? Let me know what you decide?"

"I know what I'll decide."

"No. You don't. Not until you hear what he has to say."

Starnes forced a smile, turned, and took the dirty dishes back to Della's kitchen, putting them in the dishwasher. If he had left them out Della would have had a few things to say about his upbringing and his parentage, and since most of them would be true, he didn't need to hear them again. When he drove off later, the lights were off in *Ginny's* cottage.

17

OLD LEATHER COUCHES, LAVA LAMPS and LIMOS

The Old Man's office was cold, frigid air blasting through the vents. Gen shoved open the drapes, allowing in bright light, before bending to slide the little metal knob on the floor, closing one air vent. She couldn't control the air flow in the rest of the house, but she could control the fierce cold in this one room. The whole house was icy today, chilled down by doctor's orders to help the Old Man breathe. It felt like a morgue. Cold shook through her and Gen turned off another vent, opened another drape. The room likely hadn't seen pure daylight in years. She couldn't remember seeing the drapes pushed back since her mother died.

The office looked old and shabby, the rug tattered, frayed threads sticking up, the sofa's leather upholstery cracked, about to separate at the seams. But it was clean, the wooden table-desk gleaming with furniture polish, the floor at the edges of the old rug picking up the unaccustomed daylight and throwing it back. The state-of-the-art computer in its specially built cabinet was dark and dead-looking. She hadn't noticed it the last time she was in the room. The Old Man had entered the modern world, it seemed. Just in time to die in it.

Della had set a plate of cookies and a pitcher of iced tea on a tray. Two of her mother's best crystal glasses sat side-by-side, each with a twisted mint leaf in the bottom. Starched napkins lay fanned out. Like a little tea-party instead of the unpleasant face-to-face she expected.

Gen sighed and poured herself a glass of the tea, the mint leaf swirling in the bottom. The tea was sweet, full of calories. She drank it anyway, dissatisfied, uneasy, jittery. Something was wrong or maybe everything was wrong, but she couldn't put her finger on what all wasn't right.

She had changed clothes three times this morning, ending up in the old pair of jeans she had ridden in yesterday, T-shirt and sneakers. She smelled of horse and didn't care. Her hair was curly and defiant, pulling itself out of the rubber band that secured most of it at her nape. Her eyes were circled with dark bruises from lack of sleep and she hadn't bothered to cover the blue smudges with makeup.

She didn't want Barry Stone. She didn't want this meeting. It wasn't a date, it was a command performance. And she wasn't about to get prettied up for it.

Gen ate a cookie, crumbs landing on her T-shirt. She brushed them off, not caring where they landed. For the thousandth time she checked her watch. Eight minutes till. Barry would be exactly on time, not a second early, not a second late. Eight minutes of apprehension and then however many minutes of meeting. . . .

Why had she told Starnes not to come? She remembered the feel of his arms beneath her hands last night. Corded steel, well defined.

She ate another cookie, the vanilla flavor and the mint in the tea settling her nervous stomach. She hadn't been able to eat breakfast and ominous rumbles warned her that she should have forced something down. Barry's stomach never grumbled with hunger. Barry would have eaten and would have made certain that she had eaten. And so what? She plopped down on the Old Man's sofa, plumped a pillow for her head, stretched out, and put her sneakers on the leather arm. She ate another cookie, the sugar surging into her bloodstream, more crumbs landing on her shirt, ignored. Setting the glass of tea on the rug beside her, she closed her eyes, exhaustion making her limbs heavy.

Pot lids clanked softly, cutlery jangled, china clinked as Della moved ponderously in the kitchen. Della on watch, looking over her. Gen smiled, breathed out deeply, and unexpectedly, she slept.

"Do you remember our first apartment?" he asked softly. "We had a leather couch we picked up from a thrift store. It was in such bad shape we kept it covered with a Mexican blanket, one I had from my father's stint in Mexico City."

She could hear the smile in his voice. "I remember the first time we made love on that blanket, it nearly flayed all the skin from my knees."

Gen smiled and turned on her side, curling her legs up. She loved it when Barry talked like this, his voice soft, little more than a burr of sound for her alone.

"And the little table, do you remember? Made from a crate we covered with about thirty layers of paint and shellac. You put that awful lava lamp on it, the one that glowed purple with tides of red blobs. Ugly thing. Where did you pick that up?"

"Kids love them nowadays," she murmured. The sound of her own voice woke her. Instantly she knew where she was, *when* she was. She sat up, furious with herself for falling asleep, and with *him* for catching her at it. *Had her mouth been open. . . ?* He was grinning at her, amused. Probably, yes, and droopy, too, teeth showing. At least she hadn't been asleep long enough to drool. Yawning without covering her mouth, in defiance of Barry, Gen rubbed her eyes, and narrowed them at her husband.

Barry was dressed in jeans, a denim shirt tucked in, boots gleaming beneath the denim. *Barry in cowboy boots?* He'd gone shopping for his trip west. Gen almost smiled and drank her tea to cover the reaction, setting the glass back on the floor without offering him any, deliberately rude. His grin widened, and Gen felt like a teenager, testing the boundaries of a grownup's authority. She sighed, pointed to the tea-tray with her chin. "Help yourself. Della made the sugar cookies."

He settled a napkin across one knee, handling the glass and the pitcher smoothly. He bit into the cookie and closed his eyes in appreciation. Not a crumb fell, Gen noted sourly. Years ago, she had given up wondering how he did that. Raised by nannies and tutors in foreign countries while his father served in the diplomatic corps, he had the manners of a diplomat himself, urbane, cosmopolitan, polished. He had shared his knowledge with her, a tutor in languages, etiquette, the older man with his Galatea, but she had never come close to his social ease.

"Delicious," he murmured, his voice low, a baritone vibrato that jolted her to her bones. It was the tone, the intimate pitch, he used when they made love. Tingles started at the nape of her neck. *Bastard.*

"You can tell Della so on your way out. Maybe she'll give you the recipe to share with Jasmine."

Barry's eyes popped open.

Swinging her legs off the sofa, Gen stood, brushing the crumbs from her shirt to the rug. "You're here, Bare. I'm listening. Talk," she said, continuing the intentional discourtesy.

Barry looked away for a moment, set the tea glass back on the tray, folded his napkin and set it to the side. He was sitting in the leather wingback, the coffee table between them at an angle. Sitting forward, he interlaced his fingers, dropping them between his knees, and met her eyes. He took a breath. "I love you Gen. I hurt you. I'm sorry." He paused, watching her.

"How many affairs have you had over the years?" she asked conversationally.

Barry blinked, startled. *And a bit guilty? Or* afraid *perhaps?*

"I mean, all the time that you were swearing undying love for me, and fidelity, and faithful devotion, all that rubbish, how many women were you screwing on the side?"

His face twisted. He appeared appalled, at a loss for words. His eyes even filled with tears. *Nice touch.* Gen found herself curiously unmoved. He whispered, "None. Never. Gen, you have to believe me. You have to let me explain."

Gen stood and stretched, aware that his eyes followed her movement and settled for a moment on her breasts before looking away. "Never? So Jasmine got pregnant all by herself. How about that. Maybe I should notify the Vatican."

"Damn it, Gen!" he exploded. "I came here to explain! To tell you I love you." His voice gentled with great effort. "To . . . ask you to come home."

"I agreed to listen. That's all."

When Barry stood, Gen sat back down, pulling up her legs and settling Yogi-style into the padded leather. Barry walked to the window and looked out between the drapes, his face distracted, arms hanging limply, a cookie in his fingers. There was something lost about him, and Gen fought an involuntary desire to comfort him. It was the first real emotion she had felt toward him since he appeared on her doorstep. A bad habit. She picked up her glass and drank, poured more, and drank again, mouth dry. And wished he'd choke to death on that cookie.

He said slowly, "I made a mistake. One time in all the years we've been together. One time, Gen." He paused as if searching through memories, or perhaps he was trying to decide just how much he would tell her. Gen wasn't certain which, and the knowledge that he was holding back, hiding so much, stabbed her heart. Gen closed her eyes. Why in heaven's name had she agreed to this meeting? She was a fool to listen to what he said. A bigger fool if she believed it.

"Jasmine was on the same flight when I went to London last New Year's Eve. You had been on a shoot for weeks before that, we had missed Christmas together. I hadn't seen you in two months. I was lonely."

"Well, that explains it then," Gen said stiffly. Barry ignored her.

"I had too much to drink. So did she. We talked all the way across the Atlantic. And when we landed at Heathrow . . . we discovered we were staying at the same hotel. So we shared a limo." Barry dragged a hand through his hair, making the silver strands stand up straight. They caught the sunlight and shimmered as if they, too, felt the emotion he was trying to control. He turned and found her eyes, his beseeching.

"I don't know how it happened, Gen. But we ended up together in her room. . . ."

"You spent the night with her." Gen's voice was dead. She looked away, staring at the photographs she had made so long ago, hanging on the wall in the Old Man's study. "That night and how many more, Bare? The whole week?" When he didn't answer, she glanced at him.

His eyes were distracted, the blue indistinct as he looked back nine months. He swallowed, the motion coarse, as if his throat were too parched for speech. He whispered, "Yes."

Gen watched his face, wondering why he hadn't simply lied, told her "No, my dear, only one night, and she wasn't very good." Yet, some small part of Gen recognized his honesty, the truth he was sharing. Whatever he had felt at the time, now Barry was sorry about the affair. . . .

But not sorry about his child. . . . Of course not. Barry Stone. . . . *Daddy.*

This was Barry Stone. Frank, honorable, especially in the face of disaster. He was known for his complete and total candor in business and corporate matters. But this wasn't business.

He had spent the *week* with his . . . *lady-friend*. Gen examined her reaction to his confession, then turned her back on him. Light from the open windows caught a swirl of dust motes. Della clanked away in the kitchen. *A week*. He had stayed with her a week. Gen had known the affair had lasted longer than a single night. Pregnancy, while not impossible following a single encounter, wasn't as likely as it was following several. And, of course, they hadn't spent their time playing canasta.

"And after that week?" she heard herself ask. The sound was far away, distant. How often had he seen her since?

"She went her way. I came home," he murmured.

Home. To his wife. "Did you see your doctor?" she asked, her throat tight. "To see if you brought home any STDs? Because clearly you didn't practice safe sex."

"Yes," he said, the word barely audible. "I did. I was clean."

Gen's hands were folded in her lap, fingers laced calmly. She noticed there was dirt beneath one nail, and picked at it absently. "And after that?"

"She called several times. At the office. Oralee had specific orders to screen all calls from her. I was out of town, or in a meeting. I never called her back."

Typical masculine behavior, Gen thought. Do the lady and then vamoose. Have all the fun and accept none of the responsibility. Or, more likely, bury your head in the sand. Pretend like it never happened and it would all go away. That would have been in January and February.

Barry had bought her the diamond earrings then. And made a habit of bringing flowers home. In March, he had taken off a week from work and met her in Barbados for a rare tropical vacation after a shoot. All the signs of a guilty conscience . . . and she had been oblivious. *How stupid could she be?* "And you found out she was pregnant, how?"

"I. . . ." He took a breath, the sound rasping across the room. "The day she came to the office. Jasmine is French and Jamaican, but she decided to have the baby in the states. Better medical care." His voice was tortured. Hoarse. A parody of the rich baritone that touched her to the core.

Gen felt nothing. She had known all this, discovered it the day she left New York, courtesy of a few thousand dollars and a good detective. She had known it all. Perhaps that was why she felt nothing as he spoke the words. Until he finished.

"She had the baby on Friday."

Baby. Something cracked inside. Just a small snap. Inaudible to anyone but her. A breach in the wall she had built around herself. Grief began to trickle through in a thin, unmerciful stream, like water through cracks in a stone wall. It all made sense somehow. While she had been on a flight that nearly went down, nearly crashed and burned, his child was being born.

Though she didn't need to hear it, though she knew the answer in some dark place in her soul, Gen asked, "And did you see the labor through with her?" When she spoke her voice was so low she didn't think he would hear her. But he did. She could hear his sharp intake of breath. It wasn't a question he had expected.

"She called the office." The words seemed wrenched from him. "I. . . . Yes. I was there."

"Why are you here, Barry?," she asked. "Why aren't you with her?"

"I don't love her, Gen."

"Does she love you?"

The silence was long, and by it Gen knew that the answer wasn't a simple one. Of course not. It couldn't be.

Tears blurred the vision of her hands; a blink brought them back. She had cleaned out the offending dirt but the nail was ragged around one edge. With her other nails, Gen cut through and pulled the rough edge off. Ruined what was left of her manicure.

"No," he said finally. "And she doesn't want my son. . . . We. . . . We came to an arrangement."

Son. Gen lowered her head. The tear that dripped onto her ankle was hot. Scalding. She had never been able to give him a son.

"For a certain sum . . ." he paused as if to choose his wording, "to cover expenses . . . she has agreed to give up custody. She will retain visitation rights. Christmas. Four weeks in the summer, in France, with her. All spelled out in the custody papers." After a moment, when he realized she would not speak, he added softly,

"I signed them before I flew down to Louisiana." He pronounced it like a northerner. Lu-eez-ee-a-na. All wrong.

Gen wiped her eyes, pulled up her T-shirt and blew her nose on the hem. Gross, but she didn't care. She stared into the room she remembered from childhood chastenings, the occasional whupping with the Old Man's belt. She felt as if she had been beaten now, raw and wounded in her soul. Was that why she had chosen this room to hear this confession? Because it was already commingled in memory with pain?

"Gen?"

The honorable Barry Stone was here in Lu-eez-ee-a-na, accepting responsibility for his actions. A son. A baby to hold. Gen hated him suddenly, this baby that would, could, never be hers. And she hated his father even more. Yet, she couldn't help herself, couldn't stop herself from asking, "What have you named him?" Her voice was breathless.

"Stephan. Stephan Emmanuel Jonathan Stone." The silence hung between them a moment, and Gen could hear Della pad down the hallway, pause just beyond the door listening. When Barry spoke again, his voice was hoarse. "I named him the name we chose for *our* son, Gen, the name we always planned on, because I want him to *be* our son. Yours and mine"

She said nothing. Her heart was surely bleeding, grief pouring through the open wound in her defenses, filling up her soul as it might fill up a dark cavern in the earth. And still he spoke on.

"I want you to come home, Geneva. I want you to forgive me for being a fool. I want you to love me again. And . . . I want you to help me raise Stephan. He needs a mother."

"He *has* a mother!" A fiery flush ripped through her, blistering as acid, leaving behind pictures burned into her weeks ago. The memory of Jasmine in Barry's arms. The sight of his face when she opened his door and found them together, his arms around Jasmine's middle, one hand on her stomach. His eyes filled with elation that melted into horror when he saw her. *He had his child.* After all the barren years, he had his child.

And had lost his wife.

A photo fell into her lap. A Polaroid, of all things. Poorly centered. Worse lighting. Overexposed. It was a shot of a baby. A beautiful child. Gen felt her heart skip a beat.

Stephan was olive skinned with a fuzz of black hair, fisted hands, and wide-open blue eyes, just like Barry's. Gen hadn't known babies could open their eyes so wide. Another shot landed atop the first. Stephan sleeping. Better framing of this shot, but slightly out of focus. And the third, Stephan at a full breast, the skin of it creamy and dark, nearly translucent. Jasmine feeding Barry's son.

Abruptly, Gen shoved the pictures off her lap to the floor and laughed. Stood and walked from the room, still laughing, the sound becoming hysterical, ringing down the hallway. Della stepped aside, allowing her to pass from the house out the side door, stepping back, blocking Barry's passage after her. Still laughing, Gen heard soft words, Barry's voice, Della's, and then she was alone, running for the barn, breath hot and burning in her lungs.

Olivia had Shawnee saddled, her boots ready. Asa was nowhere in sight. Della must have called down to the barn, remembering from decades gone where Gen went when overcome with emotion. On horseback, into bayou country, alone.

Pulling on boots, Gen swung into the saddle as she had as a kid, slammed both feet into the stirrups and kicked Shawnee into a fast trot, sitting through the motion until the mare hit the softer grasses and could manage a canter. Away. Away from Barry Stone and the baby he wanted her to raise.

18

MINT LEAVES, MISTAKES, and A LEVEL PLAYING FIELD

Starnes watched her ride off, her face wild with grief, tears wetting the T-shirt she wore, the mare jittery beneath her. He gripped the steering wheel, the leather twisting beneath his hands. *Go after her? Or kill Barry Stone? Which would it be?* Without conscious thought, he punched off the AC, turned the key, and stepped down from the truck, ramming his battered, sweat-stained hat onto his head.

He hadn't been able to take his rage out on his sister after her latest antics, but Barry Stone was another matter entirely. The big man's image made an appealing target. Starnes slammed the heavy door and heard a rattle. His anger blossomed at the sound and he kicked the truck wheel. He thought he'd fixed it but here it was, back again, rattling every time he closed the driver's door.

Murderous rage must have shown on his face, because Della stepped from the Big House to the side porch Geneva had run from. Della raised a massive arm, calling him over. *Stone or Gen. He could still catch up with her. . . .*

When he paused, she shouted. "Starnes-boy, you come in this house right now. We gots to talk, you and me. 'Bout my baby. And you got a lot of listening to do from Mr. Barry."

Starnes' hands made fists. He had been a fool to let Stone off last night. He should have gone after his gun, killed the bastard, and been done with it. A man with a good story or a good hiding place could get away with murder in this parish. He knew that. After today, he had proof.

"He got a right to speak his peace. He a human being like us all. Make mistakes. Do penance, so to speak, to make up for what wrongs he do."

In the distance, Gen swung onto the side road following the bayou and took off. Too late for Gen. *But Barry Stone was still inside.*

Starnes tried to brush past Della, but she held her ground. So he simply took her upper arms in his hands, lifted her, and set her aside as if her bulk were insignificant. He ignored the startled expression on her face. It had clearly been years since she had been treated so lightly, in either of its meanings.

The house was cold, frigid, the air turned so low that Della had been wearing a light sweater, the temperature turned down to make life easier for the murdering bastard upstairs. Heat radiated off Starnes in waves braided with anger as he entered the house. He stopped inside the door, disregarding Della's pleas as his eyes adjusted to the darkness within.

He hadn't known John Deveraux when *Ginny* was young. He hadn't seemed any worse than his own father or the fathers of their peers. And so he hadn't protected her. Hadn't understood the depths of her fear and hatred for her father. But now he knew how bad the Old Man had been. And now he knew what Barry Stone had done to her, or near enough as not to matter.

Light poured from the Old Man's office where always before had been darkness. A noise came from the room, soft and odd-sounding. Barry Stone was still in the room. Starnes' booted feet rang on the wooden floor, the echo absorbed when he reached the soft carpeting. Black mud marked the floorboards and smeared the wool rug in his passage. Bayou mud, like the mud of his own past in footprints Della or one of the day maids would have to clean. And he didn't care.

Gripping the jambs, he stood in the doorway, braced for a fight. And saw Barry, Gen's husband, sitting on the floor beside the old couch, arms a nest for his head on the leather seat. Almost silently, he was sobbing. Starnes stopped. The sounds were soft, just at the edge of hearing. Broken sounds.

Instantly, he was an intruder. A meddler and trespasser, and a fool into the bargain. The heat that had been anger froze, chilled like the sweat on his body, and he gripped the doorframe to keep from barreling on into the room, into the man's pain.

Della appeared at his elbow, one hand drawing him toward the kitchen. Insistent. Obdurate. Starnes didn't resist. She led him to the long table and poured him a glass of tea. A mint leaf floated in the bottom. Starnes hated mint tea but he had never found the courage to tell Della. She was insistent about many things, one of them being the restorative powers of mint on a hot day. And it was hotter than blazes outside.

Starnes sat, pulled off his hat, put it on the table beside him, and drank, downing the entire glass in a single gulp. Della poured him another and set a plate of cookies by his side. Without tasting, he ate several, seeing in his mind Barry Stone on the floor, crying over his wife. Gen. Whom they both loved. The thought was a cold fist in his belly. Starnes loved her. Always had.

"You calmer now?"

Starnes looked up, abashed. "Yes, Ma'am."

Della sat across from him and ate one of her own cookies. Starnes had another. As always, they were wonderful.

"Your hip hurting? You pick me up like I was a small sack a potatoes and set me to the side." She smiled, her expression kind. "And I'm a bit more woman than the little things you always seem to be dancing around. You know, for your *therapy?* You dip a woman like me and you *know* you been dancing."

Starnes smiled wryly. "I'm fine Della. I'm sorry I manhandled you."

"That's good, Starnes-boy. Fine apology. Now I got a few things to say to you, and I want you to listen-up and listen-good. Because when Mr. Barry come in here, we going to be talking about the stock market or the LSU Tigers' latest acquisition. Not Gen. You hear?"

"I hear."

"Good. Mr. Barry made a *mi*stake. That happen with men, whether theys good looking and rich as Goldfinger or not. More often when they is, and Mr. Barry surely is. Women always be throwing theyselfs at him because he got power and money and that fine voice a his. Gen's Mr. Barry. He slipped. He got caught. Now he gots himself a son."

Starnes adjusted to this information, letting it settle somewhere deep inside him.

"He want the boy and he gots custody. I know because I stood in the doorway and I listened."

Starnes smiled to himself. Della always knew everything going on in the parish before anyone else. Her methods weren't always aboveboard.

"I ain't ashamed of it neither. My baby needed me, and I was there for her, holding her up in prayer. And I be here for her when she come back, all cried-out and wore-down from riding, just like I was here for her when she growing up all angry and hard-edged like a stone ax. It's what I do. What I promised her mother Helena when she lay dying."

Starnes looked up, surprised. *When Helena lay dying?* But he didn't have time to comment on that or question her. Della wasn't through. She bulldozed her way on to her point, not caring that in the same moment, she was reshaping his soul.

"Aside the fact that you gots problems a your own wid your sister Serena, and aside the fact you been chasing skirts in this parish for near thirty year, they's the fact that Geneva still married according to the law and the church. Mr. Barry want his wife to come back to him in New York and raise that boy." Della leaned closer to him across the table, her breasts plumping like huge pillows. "He done askt her forgiveness. He her *husband.* You understand? Before God and man, he her *husband.* And he got a child to raise. Ain't nothing more precious or important than a child, and his own mother don't want him. Mayhap, when she all cried-out, my Geneva do."

Ain't nothing more precious . . . than a child. . . . She was right of course. If his own child had lived. . . . Starnes looked away. He had grieved over his child for decades. Even after he had forgotten the mother's face, he had grieved for the lost child, envisioning in his mind, imagining its fingers curled around his thumb in total trust. In dreams he had sniffed the warm-baby smell and brushed his hand over the tender head, smoothing its silky hair. He understood the need for a child, and the sense of wounded loss when it was denied or stolen away.

"I'm not interested in taking Gen, from another man." Starnes said, his eyes steady, though his voice was rough. "I'm not interested in breaking up a marriage. If I had wanted that I'd have left for New York the day I heard she was getting married." Starnes looked down at the untasted sugar cookie, wondering if he really meant the words. "Maybe I should have, maybe I would have if. . . . But you're right. If she wants this child, and if she still wants Barry, then I'll. . . ."

The future opened up before him. No bleaker, no more empty than it had been before Gen had come home, yet somehow it was barren now, lifeless without her. Without her forever. He understood that. Somewhere deep inside he had waited twenty-nine years for her. Hoping. Foolishly, perhaps. Finding fault with woman after woman. None had ever measured up, not even Sally, though he had loved her with a deep and lasting passion.

Gen was home now, but if she left, she wouldn't be back. Not for him. Not ever. The thoughts left him raw inside, yet, when he spoke, his voice was calm, sounding almost convicted, almost convinced. "It has to be *her* choice, though Della. Her's alone, not Stone's, not mine. *And* . . . I won't let him hurt her again. No matter what, I won't let him hurt her."

Satisfied, Della reached across the table to pat his hand. Her palm was warm and moist. "I wanted her for you, Starnes-boy. And you for her. But things don't always work like we plan."

Della released his hand and stood, watching down the hallway. She had the best ears in the state, Della did, though she often complained of old-age deafness. Moments later, Starnes heard the crisp clomp of new boots on the hallway floor. Barry was coming.

Della walked to the sink and gathered up a roll of paper towels, a broom, and a dustpan. "No need to stand on ceremony, Starnes-boy. You done met the man. You go clean up that mess you made in my nice clean hall. And you mind the carpet. The vacuum-cleaner in the pantry.

"And you, Mr. Stone, you go right back in that room and bring the tea tray in here. You ain't in some fancy New York apartment now, with servants to pick up after you. While you be staying here, you picks up after yourself."

Starnes paused. Staying here? And then, with a half-smile, he understood. Della was leveling the playing field even more. And he could thank her for that later. At the same time he questioned the strange comment she had made.

When Helena lay dying. . . . But that was a question for another time, not now when Gen's husband was nearby.

The two men met in the hallway, Starnes with a vacuum in hand, Barry with a tea tray. The irony of the encounter-in-housekeeping was lost on neither. They paused, measured one another, and after a moment, Starnes held out his hand. Shifting the tray to his other hand, Barry Stone shook it.

19

Gen sat astride Shawnee in the shade of an overhanging limb, her mind numb, empty. The grave before her was open, the angel markers pushed off to the side, but still upright. The missing head had been carefully set beside the larger angel, near the fold of his gown. All around, the ground had been churned by heavy machinery, tracks of a backhoe grooved into the earth. Oversized truck wheels had crushed the smaller overgrowth, creating a road where none had been for decades. The stone crypt that had housed her mother and brother was gone, ripped from the earth, carted off. And she hadn't been here to oversee or say a prayer or. . . .

A fresh sob escaped her and she rubbed viciously at her face. The skin was raw from tears and sunburn but Gen just didn't care. Her mother had been dug up and taken off. And Starnes hadn't warned her. Hadn't told her. Her mother was gone. Gen sobbed again, sobbed as she hadn't since she was a child and her mother had just died. The desolation of the scene was total.

And yet, she couldn't blame Starnes, not completely. At least he had believed her tale. Had put credence in the memories of a child who saw her mother die at the hands of her father. Gen sucked in painful breaths and swallowed past a throat tortured by tears. She had been crying for over an hour as she rode, Shawnee at a slow walk, the Tennessee Walker's smooth gait the only thing keeping her in the saddle. And as always, she had ended up here, at her mother's grave.

But this time there was no comfort in the visit, the ground freshly opened, the graves desecrated. But *Starnes had believed her!* Della's silver lining. . . . Gen laughed shortly, wiped her face yet again, and studied the scene with aching eyes.

Machinery had lacerated the earth while digging out the old

sunken crypt that had housed the coffins. But something wasn't right about the scene. Gen tilted her head, suddenly alert as her eyes scanned the area again. She nudged Shawnee forward, closer to the opening.

The crater where the graves had lain was too large. Far too large. Gen had seen graves exhumed on the news, and this had been no simple exhumation. The ground beyond the graves had been disturbed, too. Much more thoroughly, in fact, than the area where the crypt had lain. And there had been no reason to move the slab were the angels stood. Not really. The slab had been added long after the burial, and had been set just beyond the crypt. Of course the ground could have shifted allowing the crypt to move, but not enough to account for the size of the hole, and the way the earth had been sifted. As if someone had been looking for something. . . . She swallowed again, this time the pain so severe that she massaged her throat gently.

Exhausted, too weary to speculate on the state of the graves, Gen reached back and opened the saddle bags that had been strapped to Shawnee's saddle. Inside one was a bottle of water and Gen blew out a long breath. Good old Della. She pulled it out, opened the screw top and drank, her head back. In the distance she heard hoof-beats, and Shawnee threw up her head, whinnying.

◆   ◆   ◆

It had been nearly an hour and Gen wasn't back. Starnes had stood Barry Stone's courteous banter for as long as he could. Did the man never get riled? If Starnes hadn't seen him rip the screen door off the guesthouse last night, he would think the man was without feelings at all. He had asked after Starnes' practice, shown an interest in the cases he had won, asked Della about her children, allowing her to preen over her kids' and grandkids' accomplishments, listening with an intense concentration Starnes envied. Likely, he now knew them and their histories well enough to quote it all back to her.

When Della took lunch upstairs, she told the Old Man that *Gen's husband* had come to Louisiana. The guest had instantly been commanded upstairs and introduced to John Deveraux, where he put the old bastard at ease at once, a feat Starnes had never seen before. The two had been chatting like old friends ever since, as if the younger man had not stolen Deveraux's daughter and kept her in New York for three decades. Starnes' couldn't decide which he hated more, the irascible, lying murderer, or the gracious, sophisticated interloper.

Downstairs, he paced the kitchen, watching the barn on each passage, boots clomping. He needed to talk to Gen and Lily, fill them in on all that had transpired during the morning. And eventually, he had to tell the Old Man the outcome of his deathbed confession and the results of Gen's revelations. He needed answers for Sheriff Pritchard and the coroner, and he needed solutions to the dilemmas that the morning had created.

Della made her slow way down the steps from the Old Man's room, carrying the lunch tray with its bottle of wine and spicy food. Doctor's orders to maintain a clear liquid diet had fallen on deaf ears. She made a whoooosh sound through pursed lips when she put the tray on the table and sat, smiling and satisfied. She undoubtedly thought she had done the right things, reuniting a family before it was too late, Starnes thought caustically. And silently cursed both men upstairs roundly.

"You waiting on Gen to come back, Starnes-boy, you may be waiting a right long time. When Gen go to her mother's grave for comforting, she tend to stay a while."

Starnes' head shot up. "What?"

Della looked at him peculiarly. "I said—"

"The part about Helena's grave," he demanded, reaching for his hat.

Della's brows raised. "My baby go to her mother's grave when she upset. Always did. You don't remember that?"

He did remember it. Remembered it vividly. The site where they had met when he was fourteen and raging both with hormones and anger against his father. He had taken a horse and ridden bareback into the brush, coming on the grave and the weeping girl. They met there often in the years following. It was where he knew to look for her when Gen wasn't home. . . .

He swore foully, ignoring the swat of Della's hand at his bad language. Stuffing his old hat on his head, Starnes was out the door and running for the barn. He didn't bother with a saddle, just slipped a hackamore over the head of a likely looking horse, mounted, and pounded after her, disregarding Asa's shouted questions. Gen was at her mother's grave and he hadn't told her about the exhumation order. Heart in his throat, he raced there.

Hooves pounding, he covered the distance in ten minutes, lathering the horse and himself, taking the shortcut through a bayou branch to speed his way. Covered in mud and sweat, splattered with sour water, he rounded the curve to the gravesite and reined in the horse. Gen, mounted on a horse, stood in the stirrups and lifted a hand at him.

She looked awful, her face red-streaked, her eyes swollen, hair bedraggled and hanging in damp strands, sweat, dirt, and tears mixing into a dirty gloss over her forehead. But she was smiling and his heart thumped painfully. Whatever she had thought when she saw the opened grave, she had obviously found a measure of peace. But then, she didn't know all of the story.

"Howdy, Templar."

Starnes nudged the heaving horse down the path, his hands shaking, his hip twitching with warning. He knew better than to ride like that. "Howdy Miss High and Mighty," he said. It was an old greeting, one they had created the day they met and Geneva Deveraux ordered him off her father's land. He slid from his mount's back to the ground, landing on his good leg, and quickly walked to her, leading the horse. He had to cool the animal down, and walking would—might—stop the pain in his hip before it got too bad.

Gen's smile widened. Even sweaty and dirty, she was blindingly beautiful to him. He smiled back, wanting her. Yet remembering Barry Stone back at the estate.

"You believed me," she said, looking down from the horse. "You got the graves exhumed."

He nodded as he reached her and took her hand in his. She squeezed his with more than casual warmth, a heat that was echoed in her eyes, remembered passion from the night before. He returned the pressure and the look. As if by mutual consent, they didn't speak of Barry or the interrupted scene.

"Sorry, *Ginny*," he said, gripping his hip. "Got to move."

As Gen dismounted, Starnes and his horse hobbled away, Starnes limping slightly, the horse moving hip-shot, as if worn to the bone. As man and horse circled the open grave, Starnes watched Gen loosen the girth of her saddle and tie off the mare to a low branch. She reached into the saddlebags and drew out two more bottles of water, using one to splash her face, washing away the traces of tears and streaks of dirt. When she was done, she brought the other to him, and he drank as he walked, Gen by his side, her hands clasped behind her back. When the water bottle was empty, he tossed it near her mount so that they would remember to take it with them.

The water she had poured over her face had damped her T-shirt, turning it transparent. She wasn't wearing a bra, only a lacy camisole, the one with daisies patterned on it that had been slung over the back of a chair the night before, also now transparent. The pain in his hip diminished as another pain grew in him.

"*Ginny?*" He took her hand, pulling her to a stop.

"There's more here than exhuming my mother's grave, isn't there?" She met his gaze and the rising passion he felt vanished.

"Yes. There is," he said slowly. "But I can't tell you about it just now."

"You found another grave here, didn't you?"

Part of the truth must have shown in his eyes, because she squeezed his hand. He wanted to take her in his arms, lay her down in the grasses as he had done so often years ago, and finally finish what they had started so many times in the past. However, he kept walking, circling the grave, the horse at his back and said, "Tell me about the night your mother died, Gen. And I need details, this time, *me sha*, everything you can remember."

She looked at him, surprise in her eyes. He had heard the story, but being a lawyer and an officer of the court, Starnes wanted to hear the tale repeated, perhaps numerous times, before he could process the information with assurance.

Gen moved closer, and despite the heat that hugged like a wet wool blanket, slipped her arm around his waist and breathed deeply, still smiling. "You smell of horse and sweat and man," she said softly. When he started to step away, she pulled him back, continuing, "acrid and musky and altogether wonderful."

Starnes laughed shortly. He could smell himself, too, and wonderful wasn't an adjective he'd have used to describe the scent, but then, Gen had always been an enigma. She pulled him closer still and Starnes' slid his arm around her. Her head dropped to his shoulder. "Now I can talk."

It was a simple statement, but one that slipped beneath his skin and hammered against his heart. He kissed her forehead, tasting the fresh water she had rinsed with and the salt-tang, wanting her.

The open earth was cool and damp, and they walked the edges of the clearing, beneath the trees. Insects buzzed around their heads and flew off, preferring the horse pacing behind for their lunch. Starnes waited as she ordered her thoughts. Sweat trickled down her temple onto her sunburn. Her clothes were damp with it, and dribbles slid down her back, the heat making her perfume intense and smoky. She kicked a clump of black dirt, sending it flying into the grave.

◆　◆　◆

"I was in bed. Asleep. I heard thumps and Della screaming." Gen stopped, surprised at the memory of Della's voice. That detail had not been there before, but she was certain that it was a real part of the memory, not something manufactured by a child's memory. She could even hear the words, and said them to Starnes, " 'My baby, my baby, what you done with my baby?' High pitched. Like a . . . keen, I guess you could call it. I never remembered that before! It must have been when she discovered the two of them and he was. . . ." Her eyes closed briefly before she went on.

"I crawled out of bed and ran across the hall to Lily's room. She was sitting up in bed, covers gripped to her neck in both fists. Scared silly. And I climbed in bed with her. The hallway light came on and someone closed her door, but the latch didn't quite catch, never did, still doesn't probably. It popped open again. We watched the hallway through that crack, as Della and the Old Man raced up and down, shouting and whispering. Della was crying, something like 'Fool, fool,' over and over.

"And after a while—"

"How long," he interrupted.

Gen shrugged, her shoulder moving beneath his arm. She turned and buried her face in the remembered scent of him. Warm and steady. Starnes, always here when she needed him to be. She stopped and he stopped with her, took her face in his hands and lifted it, kissing her mouth gently. And again. He tasted

of salt, his hands calloused and tender. She sighed into his mouth
and his lips moved into a smile beneath hers. Opening her eyes,
she met his, so black, so close, she couldn't focus on them clearly,
but she could see the laughter lurking there. His hands cupped her
face closer. When he spoke, his lips moved against hers, vibrating
with the sound of his words.

"You always do that. Sigh into my mouth. I remember that
from when we were kids."

"Oh," she whispered, sliding her arms tighter around his back.
His shirt was damp with sweat and it clung to her, as if it pulled
her to him. "And you always smile when you're kissing me. I
remember that." She breathed deeply of earth and maleness.
"You really do smell wonderful."

"I smell like sweat and horse."

"That's what I meant."

His smile widened, his tongue flashed out and touched her top
lip for an instant. Warmth shuddered through her. Then,
reluctantly, he released her and pulled her with him back into the
walk. Grasses caught at their legs and they plowed through them,
denim catching on the long serrated edges. Starnes was limping
slightly, but offered no comment, so, pretending not to notice,
Gen resumed her story, remembering his last question.

"I have no idea how long it went on. It seemed like forever,
but we were kids. It could have been five minutes or fifty, but
probably was closer to the five. I don't think we could have sat
still for much longer than that."

"You didn't stay in the bed?"

"No. I don't know whose idea it was, but I remember that we
were at the door, and there was no one in the hall. Lights poured
out of every room except for mine and Lily's. My door was shut,
too. I guess whoever shut it didn't bother to see if I was still in
the bed. Anyway, there was noise up the hallway, at the bathroom,
and we ran to that door."

Gen paused as memories surged through her, details she
hadn't thought about in decades. The muggy brightness of the day
paled, replaced by the darkness of so long ago. Her voice dropped
to a murmur. "It's strange. I can still remember the feel of the
wooden floor under my feet. This was before the Old Man put in
air-conditioning, and the attic fan was roaring overhead, pulling in

air from every open window. It must have been raining because it was almost cool and quite damp. Our nightgowns fluttered around our legs as we ran, our backs close to the hall wall. We stopped at the bathroom doorway. It was hanging open halfway, the light inside so bright it was blinding.

"Mama lay on the bathroom floor, blood everywhere. Della was holding Mama's hands and blood was dripping out between her fingers. Mama was wet and naked, as if she had been in the tub, and there was bright blood on her torso. About here," she showed, pointing to her chest at the sternum. "And water was running across the floor, all bloody and red. It was an old-fashioned bathroom, black-and-white tile floor with a drain in the center, and the floor slanted so that any water splashed there would flow to the drain. Her dress was on the floor in a corner." Gen breathed out slowly, remembering, "Ah. . . . I found that dress in the attic the other day. There were still bloodstains on it. Della took it."

She looked up at Starnes whose face was tight with pain. She realized he had stopped with her. *His hip.* . . . Gen started moving again.

"Mama was saying something. I couldn't hear what. And Della said 'I promise, sweetheart. I promise. But you got to tell me where . . .'" Gen stopped again, then started forward, moving faster for a moment. She broke away from Starnes and went to the edge of the crater where her mother had lain. Now there was only black earth and roots and a single old can that had fallen over the edge. *Budweiser.* The name was still legible in red, the color of her mother's blood.

She began to shudder. Chills raised up along her arms despite the heat, and she gripped herself as if to warm her skin, or perhaps to hold herself together. The past pulled at her, separating reality from memory. She blinked away the sights, but they stayed with her, bloody and piercing.

Starnes had continued moving, and she raised her voice to say the words. "I never understood this part, Starnes. But Della said something like, 'Matthew. You got to tell me where Matthew is. . . .' Never made sense. Not then, not now."

When he didn't respond, Gen continued, her voice coarsening. "The Old Man was standing over them, his boots in a puddle of blood. Splatters were all over his trousers and he was wet to the chest, covered with blood and water. And he said, 'Don't you comfort her, Della. She chose her own path and I hope she dies for it. *Damn her to hell* for taking him with her.'

"And Della said, 'She sick. She sick, I done tole you that, but you too stubborn to get her a head doctor.'

"And the Old Man said something like, 'Quacks and swindlers, the lot of them. I won't have them screwing with the minds of one of mine.' I always figured my mother needed psychiatric help and he wouldn't get it for her. At any rate, that was when he spotted us and he stormed out into the hallway. I have never seen him so angry. He picked us each up by a wrist, and threw us down the hall. He was screaming, incoherent. I hit the wall and bruised my arms. Lily hit and a picture fell off the wall. I remember that the glass broke and shattered all over the floor. I don't remember what the Old Man said, but he threw us both into our rooms and slammed the doors. He was raging. . . ." Her voice trailed off. "That's all I remember."

"Did your mother. . . . Do you remember how she was the last few months of her life? Was she normal? Did she have the same schedule?"

Gen watched Starnes as he moved slowly around the pit. The horse he led was cooler now, the foam on its coat dried to stiff peaks in spots, still damp in others. He needed a good currying. But still, Starnes led him, and Starnes' own limp was easing. He walked with almost his normal gait.

"She stayed in bed. I remember that. When she was pregnant with Matthew, she had to go to bed for months. We would have lunch on a tray in bed with her, and put our hands on her stomach to feel the baby kick. And then after he was born, she was up for a few days. Maybe a few weeks. And then she went back to bed. We didn't have lunch with her anymore, and she kept the drapes closed."

Gen searched her mind and a few bits and pieces came to her. "She cried a lot. We could hear her through the door. Matthew cried, too. Screamed really. Colic, I suppose. Della took care of him because Mama couldn't."

"Which bathroom?"

"It's not there anymore. It was a rear bath, added onto the

house in the early nineteen-hundreds. Two stories, built on from the outside, one upstairs and one down, right where the sun porch is now. The Old Man tore it off shortly after Mama died and added modern plumbing to the whole house."

When Starnes frowned, she said, "The Old Man took part of the room next to the master bedroom, which was a nanny's room, about the size of walk-in closet, and turned it into a modern master bath. Downstairs he had the bath and the half-bath installed, taking part of the butler's pantry, I think. Now there are baths in most of the rooms, or between them for sharing, taking some of the closet space."

Starnes tied off his horse next to Shawnee. Choosing a straight stick, he walked to a shady spot, knelt and laid the stick flat, scraping it across the black earth, creating a smooth spot. "Can you draw the layout of the bathroom for me, and show me where everyone was standing and lying?

Gen walked over and bent beside him. Taking the stick, she drew the bathroom, putting an X where the Old Man had stood, an O where Della had knelt, and drew a rough form that would have been her mother's body. Then she drew in a sink on one wall, and an oval tub against another. A toilet was on the wall with the door, offering a bit of privacy. "It was a claw-footed tub with a shower curtain on a metal ring above it. The curtain was pushed back."

"As if someone had been taking a bath?"

Gen nodded thoughtfully.

"*Ginny*, I want you to do something for me. I want you to lie down and show me exactly how Della was holding your mother's hands. Exactly. Can you do that for me?"

Rather than answering, Gen dropped to her back in the nearby grass and held her hands up, wrists close together. "Grip my hands. No lower down. Yeah," she considered. "That looks right. Mama probably had small hands, to match her feet. Mine take after the Old Man in size. But then, your hands are probably larger than Della's so it may all balance out."

"And the blood on her chest was where?"

"Directly under her hands. Here," Gen bumped her wrists onto her chest to show the location of the wound, "where he stabbed her."

Starnes pulled Gen to her feet. She wondered how he could do that so easily after the pain he felt, but the motion seemed effortless. His mind was far off, his hands still holding hers close. "Gen, I saw the photos of your mother's body taken at the morgue just after she died."

Gen stilled. A bird called off in the distance. From the bayou, something large jumped and landed in the water. It was a crisp sound, like a fish, not the slower, prolonged sound of an alligator slithering into the water.

"Morgue?" she said softly.

"Did you know that there was an inquest after your mother died?"

"No!" she pulled at her hands, but Starnes held her tight. "How could anyone have missed the—"

"The wound on her chest?"

"Yes! Starnes there was so much blood!"

"There was no wound on her chest, *Ginny*. I saw the photos. The only wounds were on her wrists. Not defensive wounds, *Ginny*." He took a deep breath. "Self inflicted wounds. And no bruising except for places on her arms where the Old Man pulled her from the tub. Nothing that couldn't have been explained by the existing evidence."

Gen stood, unmoving, sweat sliding down her sides. Her hair hung in hot tendrils around her face, pulled loose from the ponytail that had secured it. She felt as if she were choking when she sucked in the hot, wet air, almost too thick to breathe. "No. . . ."

"You *mère*, she kill herself, *me sha*," he said gently, dropping into a half-Cajun patois, the sound of the mellifluous syllables flowing like liquid comfort. "Your father, he din' kill her, no."

Her eyes pleaded with him, filling with tears when there was no denial in the dark depths. Only tenderness. Only compassion. "No. We saw him. . . ."

"You *mère*, she disappear that afternoon, *Ginny*, taking Matthew wid her. They was a search by sheriff deputy, all a them, and farmhand, too. Half the parish looking for dem by night-fall, *mais oui*. They was concern that she might a been kidnap." As if sensing her pain, one of Starnes' hands dropped hers, and caressed her face as he spoke. "No one really know where she be

all dat time or how she get herself off estate land, 'cept that two
horse was let out of de stableyar'. Only one was later recover in
nex' parish."

"How do you know all this?" she demanded, her voice
shuddering.

"I read results of parish inquest, *sha*. I still reading all dat
collected material. I'm sorry, *me sha. Ça me fait de la peine*. So sorry."

"But. . . ." Tears fell in hot streams down her face, landing on
her chest and his hand where it enfolded hers. "Tell me all of it,"
she whispered, her throat working against her tears.

The soft Cajun evaporated, though Starnes spoke gently, still.
"This is according to questions asked of Della and several others.
Signed statements, you understand?" At her nod, he went on.

"When she came home hours after the search started, your
maman, you *mère*, she was alone, without Matthew. Her face was
bruised, as if she had fallen or been hit, and there were blood
stains on her clothes. She fought with Della, refusing to answer
any questions. She was in a state, as Della said, and she stormed
upstairs. Della got on the phone, found the Old Man. Told him to
come home. According to the sheriff's report, he called off the
search and went straight home.

"Your mother was in the bath when he got there and he
stormed up the stairs. And he found her, pulled her from the tub.
She had slit her wrists, *Ginny*. Severed one of the main arteries to
her hands. Severed the tendons on one hand, too. Della held her
wrists, trying to stop the blood loss. That's what I think you and
Lily saw, just that small part. You stood in the hallway as Della
and your father questioned her about Matthew. And then she
died."

Gen shook her head, refusing the words. Starnes still held her
close, his voice calm and resolute as he told her the truth of her
mother's death, murmuring "*Oui Ginny. Oui. C'est tout.*" She could
see it in his eyes. He believed what he was saying.

He had seen the photographs.

Photographs she could believe. They caught the truth,
unchanging, even when it was ugly.

Her father had not killed her mother. She had killed herself. Killed
herself, just as the officials always claimed.

Gen's knees buckled, and Starnes eased her to the ground.

Releasing her hands, he went to Shawnee and brought back more water. Gently he bathed her face.

"There were no defensive wounds? None?" she whispered.

Starnes shook his head. "Nothing except for the bruise on her face, and that could have happened while she was missing. She could have fallen." Starnes shrugged. "And I saw photographs of her hands. They were perfect except for splinters on one palm and a couple of broken nails."

"Broken nails are defensive," Gen insisted. But already she believed. There were photographs. She couldn't argue with photographs. He lifted her hand and showed her the broken nail, the one she had ripped off during the awful conversation with Barry, eons ago.

The sob caught her by surprise and Starnes cradled her against his chest. She had thought there were no more tears to cry, that her deep well of misery was dry. She was wrong. Starnes held her for a long time, as she cried.

When Gen calmed enough, she asked, "So why did you exhume their bodies? If you knew already that she had killed herself."

"Even with the results of the old inquest, there were still a few questions unanswered. With your story, and with a few other things I . . . uncovered," he said uncomfortably, "in reading the files on the inquest and making out the Old Man's will, the sheriff thought that we should exhume both graves. Just to make sure."

"And Matthew's death?"

"That was one of the things we needed to make sure about. The photos of his body and the X-rays pointed to blunt trauma."

"I told you!"

"And we have only your father's word from thirty years ago, that Helena took Matthew. That she killed him. The story you told me of his death puts a different light on things. The sheriff wants to talk to you and Lily about the night Matthew died. And Sheriff Pritchard is very interested in hearing what Della has to say about several matters, though I imagine she'll never forgive me for that."

"Several matters?" When Starnes didn't respond, she said simply, "Della's loyal to my father, abnormally so, but she's got a long memory. We can work on her together." She lifted her hands from his and this time he let her pull away. She massaged her wrists with a small smile. "And the other thing? The other body you found here?"

"I never said I found a body here, Gen. You said that."

"I saw your eyes. You agreed with me."

"I can't talk about it just now. In a day or two. Then we'll see what I can say."

20

POLAROID, POLECAT, and PARSLEY

Gen stood beneath the shower for half an hour, the temperature
on cold, as sweat and filth sluiced down her body, turning the
water in the bottom of the old tub a dingy brown. The bathtub
hadn't been used in years and the drain was slow, unaccustomed
to the volume of water she used. She soaped her hair and adjusted
the spray to rinse it as she rested her head against the cool tile. It
was pink-and-white, not the black-and-white of the memories of
her mother's death on the old bathroom floor. This tile shouldn't
have brought old visions back to mind.

But the memories were so close now, resting just on the
surface of her gray matter. Every time she blinked or tried to rest
her eyes, the vision of her mother came rushing back. *She had
killed herself.* . . . She had deliberately taken her own life and left
her children to the pitiless attentions of the Old Man. How could
she? How could she have been so . . . so selfish?

All these years Gen had believed—had *known*—that Helena
had died by her father's hand. She had seen it.

And she had seen wrong.

A little girl, not even ten, and she had interpreted the sight of
her mother's blood as murder. She had been wrong. *And what else
might I be wrong about?*

Gen jerked back from the tile and shut off the water with an
angry yank. She wasn't wrong about Matthew. She had actually
seen the blows fall when her father beat him to death. She had
seen it with her own eyes, not come upon it later. *She knew!*

Drying off with the fluffy Estate towels, she stepped from the
tub. And her eyes alighted on the photos someone had placed
beside the sink. All motion stilled, as she took in the shock of
black hair, the caramel colored skin, and Barry's big blue eyes in
the face of an infant. Barry's son. Gen stood and took the top

Polaroid in one damp hand. She was dispassionate, almost cool as she studied the photograph.

He was lying in a crib, swaddled in blue, eyes wide and seemingly curious. He was beautiful. Utterly beautiful. And not hers. Gen set the photos facedown on the sink and dried off.

She had to talk to Lily about Helena's death. She had to be the one to tell her sister their memories of that awful night were wrong. Had always been wrong. While Starnes would need to talk to Della about the night Helena died, talking to Lily wasn't a task she could delegate.

◆   ◆   ◆

Starnes took Della's hands and pulled her to her feet. For a big woman, she rose easily, more easily than Gen had risen from the ground in the clearing earlier, though he would never tell *Ginny* so. But Della was much less complaisant than Gen. Already she had a mutinous glint in her eyes, one that promised retribution if Starnes crossed over the invisible lines she had drawn in their relationship. And, as he knew, he was soon to cross over them all.

"I got me a supper to cook, Starnes Jasper Templar. I got no time for any of your foolishness."

"It isn't foolishness, Della darlin'. It's deadly serious."

The flesh around her eyes tensed. "What you up to now, boy?"

Starnes took a deep breath and let it out, tucked Della's hand in the crook of his arm and led her to the screened porch, the porch that now occupied the same spot the double-decker bathrooms once had. He had invaded her kitchen while she was upstairs with the Old Man, poured two iced teas, without mint, and filled a plate with cookies. These now rested on the table with napkins and a sweating pitcher. He pulled out a chair and held it for her, waiting. Della frowned suspiciously and sat gingerly, leaving him in no doubt that she wasn't happy about this situation whatever it was.

"What you got to say to me, Starnes-boy? What be so '*deadly serious?*' "

Starnes sat across the table and took her hands. He seemed to be doing a lot of that today, taking women's hands. "Della. Did you know that the girls, that Lily and *Ginny*, believed that the Old Man . . ." Starnes looked into her eyes, ". . . had killed Helena and

Matthew?"

Della shoved his hands away and stood. Her chair rocked back, falling with a sound like a gunshot. Her eyes blazed as she leaned across and over him, lancing him with her gaze. "What kind of nonsense you talking about, boy?" she hissed.

Starnes stopped himself from pulling away, the instinct quick as an eye-blink, triggered by her stance. When he spoke, his voice was calm, almost gentle. "The girls. They came to me with a story about Matthew and Helena being murdered. By their father." Della threw back her head, her nostrils widening with alarm. "They said they had come to you several times after the . . . incidents . . . and you refused to discuss it with them."

When she didn't respond, he said gently, "Della, they came upon the Old Man and you in the bathroom, standing over Helena's body. She was bleeding. You were crying something about 'What have you done with my baby?' They thought he had killed her and you were mourning Helena's death. And that you protected him all these years."

Della closed her eyes as if absorbing a blow that took her breath. She swayed and Starnes leaped to catch her, pulling her to the glider in the corner. He sat her down and returned for the tea and cookies, placing the cookies and napkins on the little table to the side, the tea glass in her nerveless hands. Because she seemed incapable, he held the tea to her lips and helped her drink.

He hated himself for this. Della wasn't a young woman anymore, and here he was giving her the shock of her life . . . one of many to come, he feared.

She looked at him over the rim of the glass, wounded eyes filling with tears. When they flowed over her lids and coursed down her cheeks, Starnes pulled a chair closer, set the glass aside, and retook her hands. "I'm sorry Della. I didn't mean to upset you. Honestly, I didn't. But we have to talk about this. And we have to talk about it now." Apology in his eyes, Starnes offered the tea again.

Della shuddered, the motion rippling through her, but she drank the tea, finishing half a glass before pushing his hands away. "Lordy, boy," she whispered, "you 'bout brought on a heart attack in this ol' body. Turn on the overhead fan—would you mind?—move this heat around."

When Starnes got up, Della sniffed. "You ain't forgot how to bathe, has you boy? You smells of horse and what shorly mus' be polecat."

Starnes flipped on the fan and sat back down. If Della was insulting him, she was better. "I'm a working man, Della. And working men smell of sweat from time-to-time."

"You a lawyer. Lawyer's only break a sweat counting they money."

Starnes laughed and took a cookie, bit into it. Della drank more of her tea, staring at her glass. She didn't meet his eyes, but he could see the uncertainty swimming there. "You didn't know they thought the Old Man killed their mother?"

Della wiped her eyes with a napkin and sighed, the breath leaving her in monstrous waves. "They tried to talk to me . . . after. And I couldn't." She looked up at him, fresh tears spilling over. "I jus' couldn't talk about it. They was full of questions and I . . . I tol' them not to talk about it. Not to ever talk about it no more. And when enough time gone by that I *could* talk about it, they didn't askt me no questions no more. They seem to be over they mourning. I figure, why be asking for trouble? Why stir up a nest a hornets? So I didn't speak of it. Not ever again."

Starnes squeezed her hand.

Della sighed again. "Give me one a them cookies. I needs me a pick-me-up." She wiped her face once again with the napkin, ate a cookie and finished the tea.

Starnes stood and entered the darkened kitchen, returning to freshen her tea. When he sat back down, his own glass in his hand, the crisis seemed to have passed. The fan whirred overhead, just a bit off balance, making a sort of whirr-whirr-whirr sound. After a long time, Della spoke.

"I put extra vanilla in this batch. I do like my vanilla."

"Della," he said tiredly.

"I'm hearing you, Starnes-boy. I'm hearing you." She met his eyes again, hot misery on her face. "My Geneva tole you that? That she think John kilt my Helena and my Matthew?"

"Yes. She did. And I went to the sheriff."

Della's head shot up, her eyes wide.

"I went to him about other things, but I discussed this situation with him and he thought it should be looked into. We pulled the old records and went through them. We thought there were grounds enough to open, reopen rather, the investigation. Sheriff Pritchard wants to talk to you about the deaths, Della. And so do I, right now, if you can."

Della shook her head. "This hard. Hard thinking back on that time. Hard because of what happen. Hard because . . ." Della looked away and her voice broke, "because it seem I let my babies down. It seem that they had needs I didn't meet. And I be right ashamed that I didn't listen to them." She looked at him again, eyes questioning. "If I listened to them back then, all they years ago, this investigation be nothing now. Would it?"

Starnes shrugged. It wasn't his place to tell the Old Man's story. Not yet. Carefully, he said, "Tell me about the night Helena died."

◆　◆　◆

Lily was sitting on the porch, fanning herself when Geneva reached the house. Della bustled out as soon as she saw Gen, carrying three bowls piled high with salad greens, cheese, diced chicken breasts, and sliced tomatoes. "Lily skip her lunch, and I knows *you* hungry. Skip lunch, and breakfast, too, riding all over creation in the heat of the day. Sit down. You eat. I done made tea, fresh-baked rolls, and cookies for desert to fatten you up, Geneva, child. You is just fading away to skin and bones."

Gen sighed and pulled out a chair. It was true she hadn't eaten, and her stomach growled its protest, but she had hoped to speak to Lily alone before encountering Della. "Thank you, Della. I am hungry." In the distance, thunder rumbled, advertising a summer storm beginning to build.

Lily lifted a brow at her reply. "I take it *you* weren't summoned for a late lunch," Lily said. "You were expected?"

Gen questioned with her eyes, but Della busied herself pouring tea and passing the rolls. The smell of fresh bread and mint and whatever spicy dressing Della had applied to the greens made Gen realize she was hungry. If Della had become prescient in her old age, then Gen would deal with that later. Right now, the food was demanding, and she started into it immediately after Della prayed a blessing over it.

Outside of a four-star restaurant, Gen had never tasted greens

like the ones in the stoneware bowl. Some were spicy and others
were cool on the tongue. One was even a bit hairy and bitter, but
blended with the whole to create a wonderful treat. She ate in
silence, enjoying the flavors, as she listened to Lily and Della
prattle about the weather. The bright afternoon sunlight began to
dim and the sound of growling thunder moved closer. "What is
this, Della?" she asked, holding up a spicy leaf.

Della put down her fork and glared. "That be rocket, a salad
herb out of my garden. What?" she demanded when Gen looked
surprised. "You think a ol' black woman not smart enough to
grow and use herbs? That only you white, uppity-yuppity types in
New York City got them smarts? I been using herbs for more years
than you been alive. Sage, parsley, basil, lavender, I gots more
varieties than you can count," she said, her gaze withering. "Mints
Dandelion, jasmine, marigold, pennyroyal, cumin, purslane, rue,
chervil, savory, fennel, goat's rue, I gots them *all*," she said,
swiping at the air in front of her face. "My tarragon vinegar won
third place one year in the state fair. Would a been *first*, but a
judge was second cousin to the first *and* second place winners.
Should a been thrown out for doing what she done."

"Sorry," Gen said, stuffing the leaf into her mouth to hide a
smile. Lightning danced overhead and boomed almost instantly.

"And while I be fussing at you, what this I hear about you
telling Starnes Templar that the Old Man killed your mother?"

Lily dropped her fork. The heavy stainless clattered across the
brick floor, and lay glittering in a single shaft of sunlight that
paled and vanished as Gen watched. Lily's mouth opened in an O
of surprise before turning to Gen in accusation. Geneva sat back
and sighed, her appetite gone. To avoid the two pairs of irate eyes,
she picked at a roll, no longer hot, but glistening with honey-
butter on the smooth surface and full of holes inside. A sprightly
wind sprang up, misty and ozone-fresh.

"Gen?"

"I told Starnes about that night, Lily." She risked a peek at her
sister. The bottomless black eyes swam with tears. "I know I
should have told you, but things have been so crazy around here.
I told him several days ago and Starnes went to Sheriff Pritchard.
They pulled the old file on the deaths and the bodies were
exhumed today. I found out on my ride and was coming to tell

you. But Della beat me to it."

Lily laughed, a single yelp of sound, and covered her mouth as if to stop further outbursts. Her tears vanished, leaving the onyx orbs glistening with laughter and hope. "And?"

"And," Della said, "I reckon we three should have spoke about this long ago." She sat up straight and dropped her napkin into her lap. "Too much time done passed and me just now learning that you two be believing . . ." she paused searching for the words, "that awful *lie* for too many years. That nasty gossip what nearly kilt Mr. John."

"Lie?" Lily asked softly. "No. No *lie*. We saw it! We—"

Lightning and thunder shattered her denial. Rain, fierce and violent, slammed down against the earth. The sound on the house roof was like a snare drum on a loudspeaker, and the air was instantly wet, a slanting wind blowing a fine mist onto the porch through the screening. Everything on the porch was immediately covered with a damp sheen, the linens on the table, their clothing. The temperature dropped a fast ten degrees. Typical Louisiana summer storm. Neither the rain nor the cool would last very long.

Brusquely, Della motioned the girls to gather up the dishes and follow her inside. She didn't care much for lightning storms.

Gen lifted her salad bowl, the tea pitcher, and her glass. Raising her voice, she said, "Starnes has the report and photographs from the inquest." She paused as the three entered the house, braving the icy air that instantly chilled moist skin. "She. . . ." Gen dropped her voice, deposited the dishes on the long table and faced Lily reluctantly. "Mama . . . Mama really did kill herself, sister-mine." Lily shook her head in denial. "Starnes saw the pictures."

"That old bastard could have falsified the report. Paid off the coroner, or whatever person was in charge back then. The Old Man controlled every elected official in the parish, then and now! You know that! It's why we never went to the sheriff ourselves! No one—"

"Stop!" Della shouted. "You stop saying them crazy lies!" She slammed her bowl down on the table, cracking it in half. The separate pieces rolled apart, scattering salad greens and splattering dressing, the sound of her voice and the broken stoneware like the thunder outside, uncontrolled and frenzied. "*I was there! I fount* your mother the night she died, and your daddy was *nowhere* close by. He was out with the farmhands searching for Helena and Matthew!" Della speared them with furious eyes. "She kilt herself, you hear me? *She kilt herself dead!*"

Lily stepped back from Della's anger. Gen, on some level expecting the outburst, moved toward the old woman as if to take her hands, and when Della jerked away, touched her arm instead. "What we saw. . . . What we thought we saw—"

"*Was wrong!* And you both should be shamed, just pure-T-*shamed* to be thinking your daddy would kill Helena. He worshiped the ground that woman walked on, even after she got so sick in the head!" Della made fists and shook them both in frustration. "And to think you believed that *I* would cover up a murder—" Della's voice broke, and a peculiar look of horror crossed her face.

She sealed her lips together as panic crossed her face, and she whirled away, turned on water in the kitchen sink, the tap competing with the sound of the falling rain. Della was shaking as she stood at the sink, her back to the room, staring across the porch into the storm.

"Okay. Okay, Della," Gen said softly. She reached past Lily and gathered up the broken shards. Taking them into the kitchen, she rinsed them at the bar-sink and deposited them in the special box where Della put stoneware that had outlived its usefulness. She was surprised to remember the box that Della kept beneath the pantry's bottom shelf and raided whenever there was a gardening need. This bowl, she knew, would become filler in the bottom of a terracotta planter, making a space for water to gather before flowing out the hole in the bottom.

That done, Gen cleared the remaining dirty dishes, scraping the scraps into the old plastic bowl that held waste intended for Della's compost pile. The cleanup nearly done, Gen stopped. There was nothing else to busy her hands.

The three faced away from one another for long minutes, listening to the storm, and it was Lily who broke their silence. "I think. . . . I think you need to tell us what happened the night Mama died, Della. And the night Matthew died, too. We. . . ." Her voice lapsed away and Gen took over.

"We need to hear the truth, Della, love. We need to hear it

from you."

Della blew her nose and moved toward her favorite chair in the corner of the kitchen. It was placed so that she could relax, and yet see the stovetop and the long table, allowing her to monitor both.

It was an old rocker, pillows in the seat and back covered in bright yellow cloth twined with ivy leaves and grape clusters and peach-colored peonies. It looked handmade, the runners uneven on bottom from decades of use. Della sat heavily in the rocker, adjusting the pillows for comfort, and pulling her old crocheted afghan across her knees.

As if nearly thirty years had not elapsed since the last time they sat thus, the Deveraux daughters pulled folding chairs from the pantry and sat to either side, waiting. Lily took one hand, Ginny took the other. Eventually, Della began to speak.

"Did I ever tell you that my daddy made this rocking chair for me?"

"No," Lily murmured. Outside, lightning blasted close by. The silver and crystal in the glassed-in cabinets rattled overhead.

"I was pregnant with my first, working here in the big house. My man Ephram worked in the fields, driving a tractor for the *old* Old Man, your granddaddy. First man of color to drive a tractor in the parish," she said with a smile, her eyes far away. "Back then, black men was thought to be too *slow* to handle machinery what run on gasoline. Handle a pickax or hammer, saw or shovel, that fine, but drive a tractor? My man was proud as proud could be when Mr. John Senior hire him to drive that big Ford. Painted red it was. Purty as a piece of machinery can be.

"Mr. John Junior showed him the way it work, got him a book on internal combustion engines and how to take care of them and my man study all night and work in the field all day, to show his boss man, and the rest of the parish, too, that a black man was good for doing most anything a white man was. Made some of them white mens mighty unhappy to see a *nigra* on a machine, taking a job from a white man, taking food from a white baby's mouth. But the Misters John?" she questioned. "They jist went on with they business and my man Ephram went on plowing.

"And my belly went on getting bigger and bigger. I know it hard to believe but I was a little thing, and my feets swelled up something awful. I needed help to do the housework, and Mr. John Junior, your daddy, hired me two sharecropper girls to clean, so's I could concentrate on the kitchen.

"Back then, all the farmhands ate at the Big House for the noon meal everyday, and I might feed me half a dozen men at the table inside, and twice that many on the back lawn. The back lawn be where the black farm workers ate, so the white workers could eat at the table with the boss man." Her lips pursed at the reality of life for a black man in the forties and the fifties.

"My feets swelled up so bad it look like they might jist bust open any minute, and my daddy made me the rocker to sit in. Wasn't considered proper for a *nigra* woman to sit in the presence of a white. I suppose to wait as they ate, standing on my pore ol' feets. But the *old* Old Man, he say for me to sit. Put the rocker here *hisself*, he did. Say he call me iffen anything need be brought to the table. When I got close to being due, he even make them white farmhands get off they lazy butts and get they own seconds and such." She smiled, pleased at the memory.

"And I still sits in this rocker every day, remembering how different things was back then. How much better they is now. And how far the black man still gots to go before we is all one people in this country. Back then, your daddy and his daddy brought us a long way up from the bottom of the barrel. Caused quite a stir here 'round. Even put tables in the backyard beneath the oaks so the black farmhands could sit at a table in the shade and eat instead of sitting on the ground, which was something no other white landowner ever done before.

"And that why your daddy told the sheriff he found Helena in that bathtub, bleeding all over the place. But *I* fount her. I fount her and I was alone in the house when I fount her, the Old Man still out in the countryside, organizing the searchers to hunt for Matthew, and I hollered for Asa to go bring him back now. Right now. . . . If he had allowed as it was a black woman who fount a white woman dead, the law might a come after me for killing Helena, or being what they call *negligent* and letting her die. Lord knows, I tried to hold the blood in her veins. I squeezed so tight my hands hurt for days after. And then your mother die anyway."

The storm rocked the house, whistling wind tearing through the trees. A limb broke with a sharp crack and fell to the earth, a solid thump beside the back porch. The women sat, unmoving, silent, linked hands warm. After a time, the storm eased, the wind dying down into a soft susurration, and Lily spoke. "Mama was sick? Mentally ill, you mean? I don't remember that."

Della resumed rocking, the uneven runners whispering on the heart-of-pine floor. "They call it the blues, what she had. Now-a-days they call it post-partum depression. I done read about it in the *Ladies Home Journal.* But neither name say exactly what she was. Helena sit all day in the dark of her room, cryin' or staring into the dark, forgettin' her baby and her girls, neglecting her husband. Wouldn't eat. Wouldn't come out, 'cept to yell at me or the Old Man and throw dishes and break them. Couldn't sleep. She look like something the dogs dug up and drag to the door. Pitiful, she was. And the Old Man, he never was a patient man, no, not hardly. But the doctor say she come around if he lets her alone, and quits badgering her, so he did.

"And one day, she gets up, washes her pretty blonde hair and puts on her makeup and a fine yellow dress, and she walks down the stairs like she never was sick. Smiling, she was, I remember. Looking fancy. And everything back to normal it seem.

"Two days later, Matthew start crying with the colic. And your mama fell back to the blues." Della sighed. "She kilt herself, and I grieved and grieved, 'cause if I had stayed with her when she come back inside the day she disappear, she might not a cut herself. She might still be alive. But I was too mad at her, too filled with my own righteous anger, and, shamed as I am to say it, I was tired a taking care a her baby while she mope around. The baby and the house, too, and the farmhand lunches, and me without enough help that year because the crops didn't bring what the Old Man expected, and he be putting in a hunting preserve for his gov'ment friends. I be thinking of myself and mad at Helena. And she kilt herself while I was banging dishes 'round in the kitchen to let her know jist what I feeling.

"The Lord work on my soul for that one. For years, He talk to me about my hard heart. Teaching me tenderness, and how to put others first and not my own self."

Outside, the rain stilled, hard drips falling with steady plinks from the oaks to the porch roof.

"I remember Mama throwing things and screaming," Lily said

softly. "I remember the sound of breaking glass, and you shouting. And once, I came downstairs and saw the Old Man hitting her. I saw him do that, Della. I remember that fight especially, but others, too. We. . . . We believed that the Old Man killed Mama, because of all the other things we saw him do."

Della said, "Helena come after me one night with a kitchen knife 'cause I back-talked her. Your daddy tackled Helena and knock her to the floor. Send the knife spinning crazy. Sprung her wrist, he did, to protect me. And then carry her back upstairs and stay with her all night. I didn't know you was watching, child." Della shook her head. "All these year I jist know I was protecting you two from the ugly truth, and instead you be believing an uglier lie. The Lord working on my pride, still, I see."

Gen smiled and tightened her fingers through Della's warm ones. "Della, you raised us better than any mother could have. And raised your own brood at the same time. Sent them to college. You have a right to pride."

That brought an answering smile to Della's face. "Got my own young-uns to college and married off to fine folk, I did, thanks to the Old Man and his college fund, but not you two. You run to New York and live in sin with Mr. Barry, and Lily marry that good-for-nothing fool and then divorce him and take off for France. You two uneducated sinners. All because I didn't tell you the truth. I be right shamed a my own cowardice. Back then it seem too hard to talk about, and so I hid from the truth. I should have let the Lord lead me to the words and the courage."

"Well, Della, if you still have the courage to go on a bit more, now would be a good time to tell us about Matthew," Gen said. Della looked away. "You need to know that Lily and I heard the noise the afternoon he died. The banging and the thumping. We were coloring in my room. We ran down the hallway and stood in the doorway."

Della closed her eyes as a spasm of pain twisted her face. "Lordy, I didn't know you two babies was there. I didn't know it."

"We saw him beating Matthew," Lily said. "You were standing in the doorway and we looked past your skirts and saw the Old Man on the floor with Matthew, right beside you." Her voice dropped. "He was beating Matthew, Della. We saw it. We saw him kill Matthew. And you didn't do a thing to stop him."

21

BLUNT TRAUMA, SUPER-GLUE, and INFANTICIDE

Starnes waited in the uncomfortable chair for Sheriff Pritchard to end his phone conversation. Today, there had been none of the liberal-versus-conservative banter that Pritchard reserved for lawyers and democratic congressmen. He had waved Starnes in, indicated that Starnes should close the door, and then resumed his discussion. The lawyer followed the unspoken directions, sat, and listened with avid curiosity to the one-sided dialogue.

"Blunt trauma? You're sure of that? No chance that happened after he was in the ground? That slab weighed near on a ton, and it could have—" Pritchard paused as the person on the other end interrupted him.

"No chance, huh? How long has he been in the ground? Ummmm. That fits with the missing person report, give a year or two. And you're reasonably certain of the identification? Even without dental records?" Pritchard made squiggly little notes that looked like doodles, but may have been actual writing. The sheriff's personal code. Probably unbreakable even by the FBI.

"Sounds like a lot of supposition," Pritchard continued, "based on a single broken tooth his drunken brother told Sheriff Ulmer about."

Pritchard scratched his belly in the intervening silence. "Well, there is that, too, I reckon. Okay, so that's a positive ID. How about the boy?" Whatever the Medical Examiner said caused Pritchard's brows to rise and he turned an assessing glance at Starnes. "Just the same? You're sure?" Pritchard sighed. "Well, I reckon I better get over to the Estate and have a talk with the Old Man and Della and the Deveraux girls. Yep, from what I hear, they both came back to watch the Old Man die. Shameful for a family to be so full of hate, ain't it Doc? But maybe the Old Man deserved it after what we know now." He watched the effect his words had on Starnes.

"Yep. Folks'll be mighty surprised when all this comes to light. Well, thanks Doc. I can expect a written report, when? Yeah, fine. Later." Pritchard placed the black plastic receiver onto the hook. It was an old-time phone, perhaps the same phone used by Sheriff Ulmer in his tenure.

The sheriff crossed his big hands on his belly, the only part of his body to give up the fight to good southern cooking. Standing, it was little more than a rounded paunch. Sitting, it was a partially flattened beach ball straining against his buttons. Starnes waited patiently, seeing something happen behind Pritchard's eyes. Details of the investigation placed in some sort of order, and a decision reached.

"I may have to arrest your client."

"For?"

"The murder of one Billy Ray Spinella. I have a body, a cause of death, an estimated date of death, and a confession."

"And that cause of death is. . . ."

"Blunt trauma to the skull, broken ribs, one broken arm, couple broken fingers in a defensive pattern. Whoever killed him, beat him to death. And, according to you, your client has confessed."

"And Matthew Deveraux?"

"Well, there we have a problem. We have the statements from 1962 which point to Helena Deveraux as being the one who killed the kid and we have the record of the search the day she allegedly took the kid and disappeared—and the missing timeframe for the Old Man—and statements and investigative records, concluding that Helena came home and killed herself. But now, we have the Deveraux sisters saying the Old Man did it. And lastly, we have the body, buried beside the Spinella kid."

"And?"

"And the body, what there was left of it after all these years in the ground, points to blunt head trauma, same as Spinella. And I kinda get this little thought in the back of my mind that your client might not have been the daddy of Matthew Connor Deveraux. Maybe Spinella was. And maybe the Old Man found them during that hour, hour-and-a-half when the sheriff couldn't locate John Deveraux. Maybe he came on all three trying to get out of the parish, and killed them."

◆   ◆   ◆

Before Della could continue with her story, a muted scream
sounded from the kitchen stairs, followed by the pulse of running
feet. Outside, a car pulled into the drive and a trim, spry older
man ran to the side door, where Della met him. Without
speaking, he raced for the stairs and up them, an old-fashioned
black bag in one hand. Gen had an impression of white hair, jeans
and a work shirt, polished cowboy boots, and a rain slicker
thrown over one arm.

Further thumps vibrated through the house, concerned voices,
words lost, leaving only the tone. Instead of running up to the
sickroom like usual, Della went to the sink and began to load the
dishwasher as Gen and Lily climbed the stairs. Gen told herself
that she wasn't worried, that what she was feeling was more the
emotion that rubberneckers felt when passing a gruesome
accident. The need to know how another human fared. Yet, her
heart beat a bit erratically as she neared the second floor and the
emergency that was taking place in her father's room.

Destan and Keri stood just outside the sickroom door, Keri's
eye to a crack. "He's breathing again, I think," she whispered.
"The doctor took the ambu bag away."

"What's an ambu bag," Gen whispered.

Keri jumped guiltily and pulled away from the door. "Aunt
Gen!"

"Don't be embarrassed, Keri. Your mother and I spent most
of our youth listening at doors. So, what's an ambu?"

"It's one of those round bulbs attached to an oxygen-mask-
thingy and the nurse or doctor can force air through Grandpop's
mouth to his lungs with it." Deciding that she had adult
permission to eavesdrop again, Keri put her face back to the door.

"Yes, he's breathing again. He's cussing at the doctor." Keri
jerked back in surprise, then quickly bent back to the door. "The
doctor just cussed back at him. Wow! Dr. Boulanger just called
the Old Man a hardheaded idiot."

Keri jerked away again, this time leaning her back against the
wall, a look of innocence on her face as the door opened. Dr.
Boulanger stood there, back-lighted, incongruous in jeans and

boots, stethoscope around his neck. "Ya'll all can come in now. He's still alive, though how, beats hell out of me. He should be dead the last three times I came out here." He stood aside as the four stepped into the room. "He would be gone now, if I hadn't been down at the Magic Market getting milk for Sara. I just barely made it in time."

"For what I'm paying you . . . you should just . . . pull up a cot and . . . sleep here," the Old Man rasped. "Bleeding . . . blasted buzzards. . . . Quacks the lot of you."

Destan laughed, and smothered the sound at Lily's glare. Gen pulled herself into a corner of the room to watch, but Destan and Keri walked to the bed and sat down as if they belonged there. The sight surprised Gen. She and Lily had not been allowed near the bed once Helena died.

"Next time, we won't let you take off your oxygen," Keri said. "No matter what you say."

"What?" Lily asked.

"We were playing chess, me and Destan against him, and the Old Man said he couldn't sit up straight with the oxygen line pulling at his neck. So he took it off. He said he takes it off a lot."

"Destan and I," Lily corrected absently.

"Oh, he does that all-righty," Mary Anne said, "and then he crashes. This time he turned purple before I could get in here. Next time he tries to take it off, you call me. I'll super-glue it to his nostrils if I have to, to keep it on."

The Old Man harrumphed. "You're as bad as Beckah."

Mary Anne stood and glared down at him. "You think she's bad." She pulled a small metal tube from her pocket and held it to the Old Man's eyes. "You just watch, you old goat. I'll hogtie you and stick this on so fast you won't know what hit you."

The Old Man laughed, a wet, phlegmatic sound. "Always did admire feisty women."

"I'll feisty you, you old skunk."

Gen watched in frank amazement as the buxom nurse bullied the Old Man into a sitting position, administered a dose of something through the IV line in his arm, and called him worse names, all of which had her father laughing and his color returning. Alternately flirting and badgering him, she had him in the palm of her hand. She might eat donuts and complain about the size of her rear-end, but Mary Anne was good at her job.

Gen took a deep breath and was startled at the scent of gardenias. Gardenia perfume, her mother's scent. Perfume, bubble-bath, sachets for the drawers, hand cream. Everything Helena wore had been scented gardenia. And when the gardenia bushes in the garden were in bloom, the house had been full of vases of the white flowers and shiny dark-green leaves. In June, she remembered. The scent was still in this room, as fresh as if the sachets were frequently changed.

Dr. Boulanger picked up his bag and slicker. "Keep the oxygen on this time you old bastard, or I'll help Mary Anne glue it to your face. Your pardon, ladies," he added for his language.

Lily took his hand and smiled up into his face, thanking the doctor for his help and his quick arrival.

Gen followed him from the room and stopped him in the hallway with a touch on his arm. "Doctor?"

He turned, brows lifted in question.

"May I walk you out?"

"Of course," he said, indicating she should lead the way down the stairs. "I take it you want a private word."

"Yes," Gen said, leading him through the kitchen and into the Old Man's office. "Could I get you some tea?"

"Not necessary. I have milk in the car getting hot," he reminded.

"Then I'll get right to the point." Gen braced herself on the huge desk. "Were you my mother's doctor when she was alive?"

Boulanger's brows went up again. He set his bag and slicker on the desk and leaned against it. "I was."

"My mother was ill in the months before she died. And I want to know if she. . . . Was she—"

The doctor smiled sadly and said, "You want to know if she was mentally ill."

Gen wouldn't have put it so baldly, but she agreed and sat on the old couch, her hands clinging to one another in her lap.

"There is a problem of patient confidentiality, but I think Helena would want her daughters to know about her mental state, now that they're grown. She loved you both, you know."

Tears sprang to Gen's eyes, but she batted them away, not trusting her voice to speak.

"I think if Helena were alive today, and displayed the symptoms she did thirty years ago, she would be diagnosed with bi-polar disorder. Do you know what I mean when I—"

"Manic depressive?"

"Yes. She would spend months on a high, dragging John to every party they could find, dancing and living it up. She was, literally, the life of the party at those times, the best guest a hostess could find, and in great demand with hostesses all over the state. You could count on Helena to be laughing, encouraging the wallflowers to the dance floor, making sure everyone had a good time, even if she wasn't the host."

He smiled. "My wife assured me once that having Helena Deveraux on hand for a shindig freed up the lady of the house to check on food and servants and such, knowing that she left the guests in capable hands. She was a beautiful woman, your mother.

"And then. . . ." Dr. Boulanger's eyes softened, the deep brown of his irises darkening. "Then, suddenly, your mother would change, would begin to refuse invitations, start to stay in, nights. And finally she would take to her bed. Stay there for days. Today, I would have put her on Prozac or some similar medication, to help stabilize her brain chemistries. Help balance out her emotional swings. In those days there was only Lithium for people with Helena's problem, and Helena didn't handle it well. I had to take her off of it after a few months, and there was nothing else on the market. No pharmaceuticals. Is that what you wanted to know?" he asked gently.

"I remember she would sometimes stay in her room, and Lily and I would have lunch on a tray with her, and she would. . . . She would wear the most beautiful bed-jackets and lace peignoirs. But when Matthew was born, all that changed. *She* changed."

"Helena developed post-partum depression, aggravated by her bi-polar condition," Boulanger added. "I called on her often at John's insistence. At the time, I suggested electro-shock therapy for her, which had shown limited success in such cases, but John refused. I can't say I blamed him. The side effects of it were often as bad as the condition it treated, though today's methods are markedly better." The doctor waved that thought away as of no importance.

"The offshoot of it all was that Helena spiraled deeper into depression. And then she killed herself." Gen flinched, but the doctor didn't notice, his eyes firmly in the past. "Sad that. I wish. . . . But that was then. I did the best I could with what I had at the time. Medicine has come a long way since then."

Dr. Boulanger smiled sadly and looked into her eyes as if searching for understanding. Or absolution. Gen understood that, on some level, he blamed himself for her mother's death. For not providing Helena with a medical miracle that would save her. She clasped his hand. Though her throat was tight with unshed tears, she said, "Thank you. I know you have to go, but, please, did you . . . were you called to the estate the night my mother died?"

Dr. Boulanger's eyes were shadowed. "I pronounced your mother."

Gen stifled her reaction to the statement. "And my brother?" she managed.

"When they found Matthew, I did what I could. . . ." He shook his head with remembered sorrow. "Such a beautiful boy. John's golden boy." Slipping his hand from hers, he stood. "I have to go now or my wife will be calling the morgue to see if I've had a wreck, I've been gone so long." He patted her shoulder when Gen would have asked yet another question. "I'm sorry, but I'm sure we'll be crossing paths again in the next few days. Perhaps we can talk again later."

"Few days?"

He looked at her quizzically. "John hasn't long. I thought you understood that."

"Oh," Gen said, remembering belatedly that the doctor was here to attend her father, not to answer her questions about a decades-old death. She shook her head and stood. "Of course. Thank you, Dr. Boulanger. For taking the time to—" but he was gone, his boots ringing in the hallway.

Gen had wanted to ask him what he meant by "when they found him . . ." When who found him? And where? There were so many things she and Lily had not known about their mother and how she died. Were there also things they didn't know about Matthew's death?

Moving slowly, Gen walked back through the spotless kitchen, her fingers trailing over the surface of the old table. Della was nowhere to be seen, the door to her room shut tight. Gen climbed the stairs to the private floor, her feet dragging as if afraid. But she had to see. . . . Had to remember.

The hall light was off, the doors on each side all closed in the heat of the day, to prison the heat in the south-facing rooms, isolating them from the rest of the house. In the days before central heat and air, it was a smart move, allowing at least some rooms to remain bearably cool until the end of the day when the attic fan could be turned on and the day's hot air sucked from the house. Now it was just a habit that left the hallway murky, the carpet underfoot bleached of color.

Voices came from the Old Man's room, muted by the closed door. Two men's voices. Gen ignored them and stepped just beyond. To the nursery.

She paused, one hand on the knob. Overhead, a vent purred, dropping icy air across her exposed arms. A chill raced through her. She turned the knob, opened the door and stepped inside, closing the door behind her. Stifling heat enveloped her, shocking, and darkness. . . . *It was hot the night Matthew died.* . . . Her skin thrummed in the heat as that night so long ago began to crack open in her memory. A thin creeper of sweat trickled down her spine against the door.

The air vents were closed in the room. Why cool an unused room? Of course it would be hot. The air was close and humid. Dust rose from the floor with her arrival, prickling her nose. Her eyes adjusted gradually but breathing was difficult. Sweat began to pour down her face in little spider-leg-movements. Still, she didn't move into the room, but kept her back to the door.

The nursery appeared untouched by the hand of the decorators who had come and gone. The walls were still painted a once-cheery yellow, now stained and bleached, the rocker in the corner was still covered with plaid fabric, dull and split at the seams. The hand-painted mural of bunnies, chicks, and a rainbow graced the wall near the door, almost obscured by mildew stains. The shelves were empty of books and knick-knacks, the changing table and baby bed along one wall were free of pads and sheets and mattresses. The same and yet so different.

Gen blinked in the dimness. The drapery hanging over the windows was heavy mint-green silk, pulled shut in the heat of the day, dry-rotted. The rug that had once covered the floor wall-to-wall was gone. The antique French crib on its bent-wood hook-stand still graced the center of the room, throwing darker shadows, like the ribs of a long-dead horse, across the bare floor. Gen pushed back against the door, the wood warm on her shoulder-blades.

In the faint light of the child's night-light—the only illumination the little duck on the shelf beside the changing table—Matthew had lain on the rug in front of the crib. It had been swinging back and forth, throwing fuzzy, barred shadows around the room. The Old Man had been on the floor beside Matthew. Della, beside the door, partially blocking the room, had been standing guard. And the Old Man had raised his fist, his huge cruel fist, and slammed it down into Matthew's head. Again and again in the half-dark, the spokes of the bed dancing crazily as the fist raised and banged into the baby, the sound damped by the rug. Crying out that horrible cry. . . . "No! No, no, no! Noooooo!" Like the scream of a dying bird. . . .

That was what they had seen, clearly as possible in the dim light. The spokes of the crib dancing a twirling jig. The fist rising and falling. They had seen the Old Man kill Matthew.

Hadn't they?

22

FRENCH FRIED FELLAS and SPY-HOLES

Starnes stepped forward in the drive and shook the sheriff's hand. Pritchard had huge hands for his size. Standing only five-feet-seven, he nevertheless had the paws of a professional sports player and the grip to go with it. The bones in Starnes' hand ground together, Pritchard making the greeting a contest rather than a welcome. Starnes smiled in recognition of the ploy. Pritchard smiled back, showing tobacco-stained teeth that glimmered yellow beneath his hat-brim.

"That black maid here?" he gestured to the estate house behind him.

Starnes dropped both the hand and the smile. "*Della LaPointe* is inside," Starnes corrected coolly, nudging up the brim of his hat for better vision. He was really beginning to hate these mind games. It seemed every time Pritchard was around, Starnes was constantly keeping score, a grownup version of King-of-the-Hill.

"Of course. LaPointe. L-A-P-O-I-N-T-E," he spelled. "We'll need to have the spelling right on the arrest warrant."

"There'll be no arrest warrant for Della. The Old Man says she doesn't know what happened to the kid."

"We'll see." Pritchard bent into his marked car, lifted out a steno pad and a tape recorder.

"This is supposed to be a *casual* fact-finding interview," Starnes said, at the sight of the recording equipment.

"Of course," the sheriff said. "Fact finding. Casual. Nothing on record at this point." Pritchard grinned up at him, still baiting. "But if it turns into something more I need to be prepared."

"Leave it in the car, Pritchard," Starnes said, his voice low.

The sheriff paused and turned narrowed eyes on Starnes. "Say what? I'm the sheriff, here, Templar. I got a job to do."

"And I'm the lawyer. You follow our agreed-upon procedure

or I'll instruct my clients to refuse to speak, and John Deveraux will recant his confession before he can make it officially to you." Starnes smiled slowly. If he had to play the game, he was by-God going to win. "Or old Doc Boulanger may just decide that Deveraux's cancer has now metastasized to his brain, and he is out of his head. Raving mad. Your choice."

Pritchard's mouth twisted with distaste. "You think I—"

"Nope. I don't think," Starnes said pleasantly from beneath the rim of his favorite hat. "Take it or leave it."

"You and me got some other items to address when this casual fact-finding interview is over."

"About?"

"About your sister. And a couple a french-fried-fellas in a burned out car."

Starnes felt his hands and feet grow cold despite the heat. He had all but forgotten about the two bodies L'ron had told him about. The bodies and the boot prints that led away from the scene. Had Serena been there? Had her past once again caught up with her? Was that scene of violence what brought on the latest bout of craziness? He struggled to keep his features calm.

Pritchard grinned, dropped the tape recorder in the car seat and held up only the steno pad. "Okay if I take a few notes Mr. Templar?"

"Take as many notes as you please," Starnes said, his voice cool, composed, and very distant, "as long as you don't intend to ask my clients to sign anything while I'm out of the room."

"Would not dream of it, Mr. Templar."

"Glad to hear that, Sheriff Pritchard." Starnes mentally shook himself and tried to pull his thoughts from his sister to the matter at hand. "John Deveraux is expecting us."

The sheriff dropped the contentious attitude and glanced up at Starnes. "You really think he killed that kid?"

"Billy Ray Spinella didn't bash in his own head."

Pritchard followed Starnes into the chilled house, pausing with him at the entrance, allowing their eyes time to adjust to the relative darkness. Both men placed hats on the hooks by the door and ran hands through sweaty hair. In the quiet of the kitchen, Pritchard said, "I sent off for DNA analysis of Matthew and Billy Ray, to see if Spinella is really the baby's daddy."

"If Spinella was the kid's daddy, John would have said so when he confessed."

"Maybe so, maybe not. He still claiming Della didn't have any knowledge of the death?"

"That's the story I got. That's the story you're to follow. Remember? In order to clear a thirty-year-old missing person's report, you get all the details."

"I know the deal, though now that the report has been upgraded to murder, things might change," Pritchard said slyly. When Starnes didn't rise to the bait he added, sounding disappointed, "Prosecutor will go along with it. Unless I get a different story from Della. Now admit it. You told her I was coming."

Starnes sighed, put thoughts of his sister firmly behind him and gestured to the stairs. "No, sheriff. I didn't tell her you were coming. She has no idea the graves were opened, unless Geneva Deveraux told her, or that a third body was found beneath the angels' foundation slab. I kept my part of the bargain."

"What third body?" a voice boomed.

Pritchard jumped. Starnes managed not to react. Della materialized out of the deeper darkness beneath the stairs, hands on her hips, wide white apron like a sail before her. "What bargain that be? You saying you the one what dug up my Helena and little Matthew? Why in God's name you be doing something like that?"

Squinting slightly, she leaned in toward the two men. "I knows you," she accused, glaring at the sheriff. "You the little Pritchard boy. The one what pulled the plug in the baptistery in the First Baptist Church for a prank."

Starnes lost control of a grin and stepped aside, granting Della full access to the smaller man. Bending over the sheriff, she shook her finger at Pritchard's nose. "It was the Sunday they had the dedication of the new building, and they was planning a big baptismal service with some twenty or thirty new Christians. I 'member right, your daddy tore your backside up for that one, right there on the church grounds."

Della gripped the sheriff's arm and tugged him to the stronger light in the kitchen. Starnes pretended not to see the pained look Pritchard sent him as he lurched along after the older woman.

"Now, Miss Della—" he tried.

"Wasn't you also the one who sailed them paper airplanes tore from a nasty magazine into the girls' locker room at the old high school afore it was demolished?" Della raised her voice, overriding the sheriff's attempt to defend himself. "And if I remembers it rightly, you was the one who drilled them holes in the wall into the same room. *Spy* holes. Gots yourself suspended for a *week* for that little prank. *Shame on you.*" Della shook him by the arm like a rag doll, and Pritchard clamped his mouth shut, giving in to the inevitable.

Starnes sat his injured hip on the long table and watched, enjoying himself, but not fooled by Della's antics. Standing beneath the stairs, she had likely heard most every word spoken by the two men, and was establishing a pecking-order for the coming interview. She would be no cowed victim for Pritchard to badger.

"And, wasn't there that time you rolled your daddy's farm truck into old Mr. Rentrop's flower garden in the middle of the night, then tore it up more getting the truck out? And then denied it, too, I recall, till one of your friends told on you. Shame on you, boy. Pure shame what you put your mama through. And then gots yourself elected sheriff." She shook her head at the state of a world where such a man could be elected to public office.

"The Old Man done that for you, I reckon. Another one of John Deveraux's pet politicians. Well, if you think being some too-big-for-his-britches *e*-lected official is gonna help you, you can think again, if you been messing around in my Helena's grave. That poor woman and her boy deserve to rest in peace."

Pritchard yanked his arm away, stood to his tallest height, which was still several inches shorter than Della and a good three stone lighter. "What we discovered *Mrs. LaPointe*, was the body of Billy Ray Spinella."

Della jerked back, nostrils flaring, her eyes instantly wide, the whites showing all around. Starnes stilled himself. He hadn't expected Della to react to the name. The Old Man had said she knew nothing about the Spinella's death. Instincts on alert, he said, "Della you don't—"

"He died of blunt trauma to the head," Pritchard said loudly, watching her reaction. "You know anything about his death, Mrs. Della LaPointe?"

"Della, you don't have to say anything," Starnes cautioned, standing, searching for her gaze. "You don't—"

Della glared at him, silencing his warning. "Billy Ray done worked here, long time ago." Her eyes wrenched away and she moved quickly to the sink. When she spoke again, it was over her shoulder, her voice low. "A hand, he was, down to the barn, helping Asa." Back turned, Della picked up a towel and ran it over a bowl on the counter. Though it was already dry, she rolled the rag over the bottom of the bowl, around and around the inside as if buffing the stoneware to a high luster, her motions automatic. "He went missing," she said grudgingly.

Della stopped wiping the bowl, pulled it close to her chest, and stood there, staring out the window. A sense of panic filled Starnes. *Della knew something about Spinella's death.* The Old Man had indicated she would know nothing. Starnes understood instantly that he should have spoken to Della before he brought Pritchard into the picture. His oversight could—might—result in Della being charged as an accessory, if she knew something of substance and had kept quiet about it all these years. Starnes had screwed up. And he knew it.

He had to stop her, to end it now. But before he could reach for her, Della said vaguely, "The Old Man done gone and confessed to something, has he? Confessed to killing that boy?"

Starnes nodded though she was looking away, "Yes. He has."

Della placed the polished bowl on the counter, turned and went to the refrigerator, pulled out a pitcher of dark tea. And stood there, staring. "Well. Well, well, well," she said slowly into the lighted interior. "Bless my soul."

After a moment, she closed the refrigerator door, pulled four glasses from a cabinet and set them on a tray, adding ice, mint leaves, napkins, and pouring tea. She sighed heavily. "Well, I figure you is come to hear the Old Man's confession," Della said, picking up the tray. "Come on up then. I reckon I wants to hear it myself."

"Della—" the sheriff started.

"That's Mrs. LaPointe," she said with a withering look. "You may be the sheriff, but you is still Betty Corrine Pritchard's little boy, and 'less you want me calling your mama, you'll mind your manners in this house." Carrying the tray to the stairs, she started up them, her treads heavy.

"Jesus," Pritchard muttered, not looking at Starnes.

"And you watch your mouth, too. Your poor mama raised you better than to take the Lord's name in vain."

Giving up, Pritchard accompanied her up the steps that led to the Old Man's room. Starnes breathed deeply, searching for calm, and followed in the sheriff's wake. *What did Della know?* She avoided his eyes when she reached the top of the stairs, and kicked open the sickroom door. He had never seen Della abuse any surface in the Big House, and her action startled him. She entered the master bedroom, setting the tea tray on the table by the windows.

"John Deveraux," she said as she handed around glasses, "this here the sheriff. He done told me you confessed to killing Billy Ray Spinella." She fixed the Old Man with a piercing stare. Her chin quivered a moment, but when she spoke, her voice was steady. "Spit it out, Old Man. He dead? You *killed* that boy?"

The Old Man took the glass she offered. His hand shook with the weight of the glass. "Sheriff. Starnes." He toasted to his guests, gaze watchful.

"I done askt you a question," Della said, shoving her head forward on her neck. She fixed her fists on either hip, looking for all the world as if she would box her employer's ears if he balked at answering.

The pale head dipped in agreement, skin stretched tight across his skull. "Yes. I confessed to killing the kid."

"Humph," Della said. Settling her bulk onto a side chair, she met the Old Man's gaze. " 'Bout time we told the whole story, then."

"You got nothing to tell, Della. This is my business."

"I reckon if you got to tell this story, then it about time the *whole* story be told. And seeing as I happen to be a part of it, I intend to stay through the telling. Start talking Old Man."

23

CRYBABY, LIES and BLOOD STAINS

Gen sucked in a breath of hot air, the atmosphere in the closed room so moist it clogged her burning throat. Dashing tears from her eyes, she backed slowly toward the door. It opened behind her. Whirling, Gen retreated a step, blinking in the darkness. Her hip hit the rim of the suspended cradle and sent it spinning against her side and away.

Barry stood there, silhouetted in the doorway.

Though she couldn't see his features, he looked so broad, so calm, so ordinary, standing in the doorway of her brother's room. As if he belonged somehow.

"Gen?" When she didn't answer, he said, "I heard you crying." Still, she was silent, the only sound in the quiet room was the rough timbre of her breathing. Slowly, Barry held out his arms.

Mindless, Gen fell into him, into the remembered embrace, the remembered warmth, and his arms closed around her. With a foot, he pushed the door shut behind them, securing them in the hot, damp room, holding Gen while she cried.

"I hate this," she sniffled after a long moment. "I hate being a . . . a . . . a crybaby."

Barry laughed, the sound a mere rumble deep in his chest. His hand slid to her nape, lifted her hair from her moist skin. Fingers moving to an internal rhythm, he massaged her neck loosening her tensed muscles, the action easing her pain.

The denim shirt he still wore was soft beneath her cheek, an odd texture in Barry's button-down-linen world, but comforting. She snuffled and moved closer, his arms gathering her in. "It's hot as . . . as blue blazes in here, ma'am," he said, in a terrible attempt at a southern drawl.

Like the laugh, the words rumbled in his chest, solid vibrations. Gen once heard his voice described as "smoky Barry

White, stirred in chocolate liqueur and set on fire." And that was as close as anyone came to describing the texture, depth, and sheer power of his voice. Gen melted into him, not forgetting the baby, not forgetting the infidelity, but needing this comfort, this one moment. She curled her fingers into the fabric at his chest, clinging, feeling her misery slip away.

"I made a big mistake, Geneva," he said at last.

She stiffened.

"I should have shut us on the other side of the door where it's cool."

Gen shuddered with a giggle. And stifled it with a frown. She *hated* it when she giggled, almost as much as she hated being a crybaby. She could feel Barry smile above her head, knowing he knew her exact reaction to the silly laughter.

"I'm okay now," she said, pushing slightly away. "Thanks. I needed the hug."

Barry looked down at her, his arms stilled circling her back. "I have something to say before we go. Another apology. I've been stupid," his beautiful voice said.

"More so than screwing around on me?" Gen asked wryly, the words curiously pain-free.

His eyes twinkled for a moment in spite of her words, as if he understood her tone. The twinkle gradually vanished, his expression growing serious, cautious. "Matter of fact, yes. I shouldn't have named the baby the name we, you and I, picked out for our son."

Gen closed her eyes against the sudden shaft of pain, and Barry tightened his hold on her as if to stop her from running away. "It was thoughtless and cruel and. . . . I wanted him to be our baby so badly, that I didn't think. I just . . . didn't think."

When she didn't respond, he went on. "Gen, I called Isaac Mason in New York. He's handling the custody papers. It's not too late. I can change the name. Legally."

Eyes still shut, Gen pushed steadily at the arms holding her and they gave way, inch by inch. Letting her go. When she was free of the embrace, she moved around him to the door. Circled the knob with her hand. The metal was warm against her sweaty palm. She wanted to open the door, walk down the hall and away from her husband. Instead she spoke, as if her mouth and vocal cords had a will of their own. "What will you call him?" The sound stopped her forward motion and she paused, waiting for his answer.

"Deveraux Barron Stone. For your family, and after my grandfather."

Gen smiled, pleased in spite of herself. "Mouthful for a little kid." She tilted her head. "You can't call him Barry, that would be too confusing."

"Dev. I like Dev," he said, his resonant voice reaching out to her in the dim light, asking her to forgive him, asking her to come back to him. Asking her for more than she could give.

Gen nodded once, opened the door, and moved into the hallway. Frigid air swept away the heat and chilled her sweaty T-shirt. Barry followed her into the cool, watching as she moved away, waiting for her reaction to the name. She knew he was waiting. He knew she knew. They knew one another so very well. She could feel his understanding, his patient calm, as she let the name settle deep into her soul, considering.

When she was halfway down the back stairs she paused. Without turning, Gen said simply, "I like Dev, too, Barry. I really like it." And the strange thing was that she did like the name. It suited the beautiful child with the olive skin and Barry's blue eyes. When Barry didn't respond, Gen continued down into the kitchen and on out the side door into the blazing sun.

◆ ◆ ◆

Della sat almost passive as Sheriff Pritchard explained his intentions. "We're here for a simple fact-finding, Mrs. LaPointe, Mr. Deveraux. That's the purpose of this meeting, and I want you both to know that I understand that." Pritchard perched on the edge of a side-chair and pulled a small table close. On it he set his pen and steno pad, flipped open. As he spoke, he was writing the date, time, and names of all present. The pen scritched across the green paper.

"Though I'm here in an official capacity, I'll ask no questions until after you both have a chance to tell whatever story you choose to tell. Mr. Templar has my word that you are to be in charge of the first part of the meeting. I am only here to listen, though, if some point is unclear, I may interject a clarifying question."

Starnes head came up at that.

"Of course, I expect that you will defer to your attorney in any answer." Pritchard flashed him a quick smile. Starnes let it slide, and sipped the vile mint-flavored tea, hoping it would calm his stomach. He wondered if he should call a halt to this meeting. Or if Pritchard would even let him. Their agreement was the only thing keeping Pritchard from dragging both Della and John Deveraux down to the sheriff's office for questioning. Contrary to TV, lawyers only had just so much power once law enforcement became involved in a case. An attorney could suggest silence and offer advice, but couldn't speak for a client or overrule client's choices. Pritchard continued with the rules of the meeting, and Starnes listened with half an ear.

Della turned her head, ignoring the sheriff, ignoring them all. Starnes watched her, sick to his stomach as she pulled in on herself, retreating from the room, the men in it. She shivered in the cold and crossed one arm over her chest. The Old Man was a sorry bastard for this, whatever this was.

"Della," Starnes said when Pritchard stopped speaking. "I've talked to the Old Man. To John. I know what he has to say about Billy Ray Spinella. But he never said anything about. . . . About you. Della, you don't have to say anything today. In fact I would rather you say nothing until later, after we have a chance to talk."

Della shrugged and sipped her tea, eyes hooded, responses concealed. Whatever reaction she had experienced hearing Billy Ray Spinella's name, she now had herself in hand, emotions tamped down. The only sign of her feelings was the slight tapping of her foot in the carpet. When the Old Man agreed to the sheriff's terms and started talking, even that motion stilled.

"I don't remember the day exactly," Old Man Deveraux said, his words precise and slow, giving Pritchard time to take notes. "It was within a month after we buried Helena and Matthew in the clearing on the bluff above Bayou Incendie. I came into the house to hear sounds from Della's room beneath the stairs." His eyes swept to Della, to the Sheriff, and back to her. "You sure, Della? You could leave."

Della shook her head, the motion regal, somehow languorous. She didn't look around at all.

"Della was still living at her house then, raising her own kids, but she was spending more time here, looking after Gen and Lily, and so I cleared out the room beneath the stairs for her to put a few things in. For her convenience. They, the girls, needed a lot more than I could give them at the time. Maybe needed a lot more than I could ever give them."

John rested his head against the pillows, breathing shallowly, pulling in oxygen through the tubes in his nose. Even with the temperature turned down to the sixties, he was having trouble drawing breath. His eyes, a dull black, closed and remained shuttered as he continued speaking.

"I heard Della cry out. The sound of a fist hitting flesh. . . . That's a distinctive sound, different from any other sound I know."

Della turned her head and stared out the window, into the top of the oak tree. The glass of tea rested, forgotten, on her knee, a dark ring spreading across the white apron as condensation ran.

"I should have called out. I guess I might have misunderstood the sounds. But I just knew she was in trouble." The Old Man's quiver calmed, his shaking hands ceased their tremble as condensation gathered on his fingers in the ritual of afternoon tea, though he drank nothing. None of them did now. The glasses were little more than details to occupy restless hands, studio props that the actors had forgotten. A drop of water rolled across John's fingers, the skin beneath nearly transparent over bluish, knotty veins distended with age.

He had resisted the appearance of sickness for months, holding off the cancer that mutated and grew though his major organs. Refusing to give in to the pain. Even when he couldn't breathe, in the midst of an attack, he still looked hardy, hale, as if he would shake off the disease and rise from the bed, demanding his hat and boots and his farm manager, orders ready for the day's work. But for the first time, John Deveraux looked sick. Looked as if he was dying. Looked old and feeble and infirm.

The black eyes opened, blinked foggily, and he stared at Della. "I never asked. I just knew, assumed, he was attacking you."

Della inclined her head, the motion again stately, unhurried.

Starnes closed his eyes. He had never heard this part of the story. He *should* have heard it. He *should* have been told. And now he didn't know if he could protect Della from the fallout.

"I pulled him off of her. Threw him into the hall. I guess I hit him, I don't remember, though later I washed blood off my hands. Out of my shirt. But at the time," he shook his head, "I threw him into the hall and left him there, unconscious, bleeding. Then I went to Della."

Della smiled sadly, never taking her gaze from the view beyond the window, though the glare was so bright, it brought tears to Starnes' eyes. "Back then," she said, "no white man would ever pay for touching a colored woman. Being colored meant . . . a woman was ready for any man, anytime, to use as he saw fit." The smile stretched with effort and fell away. "Saying 'No' was not an option open to the colored peoples. But John Deveraux give me that right. That day, he say 'No' for me." Della smiled again, faintly. "He say it for me."

Pritchard started to speak, seemed to think better of it, and closed his mouth on the words.

"I covered her with a blanket," John said. "I don't know how bad she was hurt, but I called Doc Boulanger and told him to come by as soon as he could." Della smiled with those words, and the smile held. "I didn't want Della having to dress . . . go through the 'black's only' entrance into the colored waiting room, where people would start to talk. She deserved better than that."

"He drew me a bath in the downstairs tub, a white peoples own private tub," she said wonderingly. "Half carried me back there and put me in the water. I seen Billy Ray laying on the floor as we go past."

"Was he breathing?" Pritchard asked softly.

Della shrugged. "Didn't look to see. Didn't care then. Don't know now." Della turned and looked at the Old Man, her smile wide, tears tracing slow tracks down her cheeks. "Brung me a cup a hot tea, the Old Man did. Nasty stuff having to drink it hot. But he sloshed some of his best bourbon into the cup. I seen him do that. Made me drink it, and it warm me inside. I stay in that tub, I don't know how long, adding hot water till it so hot it scald me. Make me clean again. Wash away that man's touch. And when I come out, Billy Ray gone."

The Old Man opened his eyes and met Della's. He lifted his glass in a silent toast.

"He even clean away the blood that done splattered on the wall. I fount traces of it later, maybe it be weeks later. Brown stains somebody done scrubbed away, who didn't know about hydrogen peroxide." Della looked fondly at John. "I got me a bucket of paint and covered them stains up, I did."

Starnes glanced at Sheriff Pritchard. The man's eyes went hard at the words. Taken in the eyes of the law, Della's simple comment about covering up blood splatters could be construed as compliance, as accessory. Starnes set his tea glass down and leaned forward in his seat. "Della, are there any other things in a kitchen that might look like blood? Ketchup, for instance? Tomato paste? Something that someone else might have splattered, like mud?"

Della shrugged. "Old blood is brown. More like A1 Sauce. Or gravy."

"So you weren't one hundred percent certain the stains you painted over were blood?"

The Old Man looked hard at Della. "There were no blood stains left. None. I made sure."

Della, watching John Deveraux's eyes, nodded and said, "Could a been mos' anything in a kitchen. Most anything." But she smiled at her employer, gaze still tender.

"And you never asked about Billy Ray? Never asked if he lived or died?" Pritchard asked.

"Didn't have to," the Old Man said gruffly. "I came in just after Dr. Boulanger left. Told Della Billy Ray was gone. Left town. I had found a receipt in his pocket for Jessup Rooming House. Next morning, I went to the old Jessup Place and told Avanell Jessup I was hunting Billy Ray. Told her he hadn't come in to work. Got her to give me a key." John paused, his color bad. He was fighting to breathe, the motion of his chest fast and forced, but the sound of breath moving in and out was wet, as if he was breathing through soaked cotton pads.

"I cleaned out his room, put everything in a blanket and tossed it out the window onto the ground beneath a hedge. You remember how overgrown that house was after old man Jessup died." No one answered, but Deveraux continued as if they had agreed.

"I went back to Avanell and told her his stuff was missing, not that she listened, what with General Hospital on the tube. She just waved me off. Reckon she had a passel of folk coming and going in that rooming house of hers. Then I went outside, picked up the blanket of Billy Ray's belongings and drove back home. Buried the body that night, along with his stuff, poured the concrete foundation over his grave the next day and set the angels on it. No one thought it was odd. I heard about the missing person's report a couple weeks later."

"Mr. Deveraux," Pritchard said, considering.

John met his eyes and grinned with a hint of his usual bluster. "You want to know if Billy Ray was dead when I carried him from the house. No. He wasn't. He was unconscious but breathing." The Old Man's grin showed teeth. "But I made sure he was dead before I buried him. Damn sure."

24

PART ARABIAN, PART MOOSE

Gen stood in a patch of sunlight, its rays warming her. The Big House was miserable, a good forty degrees colder than the world outside. August in Louisiana was like a humid purgatory. Too wet to burn, but hot as Hades. Stepping slowly, Gen moved into the bedraggled garden surrounding the house, the garden her mother had loved. Most of Helena's roses had succumbed to black-spot, leaving only hardy varieties and climbing roses that had made their way up oak trees and along low branches. Thorny tendrils dangled down toward the ground. A single out-of-season pink bloom preened in the heat. Gen plucked the flower, careful of the hundreds of tiny barbs lining the stem. Scraping them off on a paving stone, she tucked the blossom behind her ear, shoved her hands into her jeans pockets, and meandered deeper into the garden, past beds of perennials that had escaped their borders and unruly beds of lilies, some in bloom.

Gen remembered Helena tending the garden, on her knees in the rich loam, and bent to sniff a daylily. It was deep pink with a ruby throat, as if it blushed. Pinching it off as well, she added the lily to the rose, the petals brushing her cheek as she walked.

Like her bedroom in the Big House, the playhouse where she and Lily hosted tea parties for parish friends in happier days had received a fresh coat of white paint, the Victorian moldings and carved wood door trimmed in shades of pink. The lace curtains in the windows looked new, stiff with starch even in the heat, and the window boxes were planted with wilted impatiens.

She wondered if the Old Man had ordered it cleaned up, or if Della handled such details now. How long had she been hoping the Old Man's daughters would come home? Tilting her head, Gen spotted the cupola, its galloping horse weathervane pointing into the faint breeze.

A shout echoed from the barn, answered with girlish laughter. Olivia? And then she remembered another sound from so long ago. The sound of her mother's voice, raised in anger and fear, screaming. Gen stopped. She and Lily had been playing in the little Victorian house, eating watermelon . . . spitting seeds out the opened window. . . . And they heard their mother scream through the opened windows of the Big House. Something shattered. The Old Man shouted at her. A bang of . . . furniture breaking? And then silence.

Helena in one of her manic phases?

The Old Man had never been able to tolerate anyone being sick. In her entire childhood, she never once remembered him visiting a sickbed. Not when she suffered with strep throat, not when she had the flu, not when Lily had chicken pox or had her tonsils removed. So it must have been beyond his tolerance level to have a wife who took to her bed and stayed there for days or weeks. Always a powerful man, he must have been beside himself at his wife's illness.

She remembered the sound of dishes breaking, waking her from an afternoon nap, her parent's voices raised in anger. The sound of Helena weeping at another time, the slam of a door as her father walked out. And she remembered the sound of her mother singing at full volume, off-key and laughing, a tune from Porgy and Bess, dancing around the house, pulling John Deveraux after her into a jitterbug. They both had laughed often, she recalled, the house filled with music. And the Old Man's face smiling. . . . The picture of her father happy was sharp, poignant. Totally out of keeping with harsher memories.

Gen remembered an incident when she was fifteen. She had defied the Old Man and slipped out of the house to go to Marie Lynn's party, and had come back in at nearly two in the morning, smelling of beer. The Old Man had been waiting up, the house reeking of cigar smoke. Furious, in a towering rage, he met her at the door, belt in hand. Face florid, ranting, he slapped the belt against his own leg and demanded that she take down her pants and bend over.

Blatantly defying him, Gen refused. Her father backhanded her across the face with one hand and swung the belt with the other. Della flew from her room at Gen's scream and stopped the

Old Man from beating his daughter. In a rage at both of them, Della sent them to their rooms and refereed a family conference the next morning when heads were cooler.

Though there were no more corporal punishments—not ever—Gen was on restriction for the rest of the summer for the sneaky excursion. As it was, Gen carried blue bruises on her arm where he grabbed her and a welt across her thighs for several days where the belt landed. The raised place on her face had been sore for weeks. The Old Man had packed a wallop.

The sound of car engines from the Big House drew Gen back to the present and she strained to see who was leaving. A glimpse of Starnes' truck pulling down the drive let her know that whatever had been going on in the sickroom had been brought to a conclusion. A breeze touched her cheek, surrounding her with the scent from the flowers behind her ear.

Drenched with sweat, Gen made her way slowly to the small guesthouse and into the cool. Frequent showers were the way to survive the summer heat, and Gen stood beneath the cool spray for several minutes before dressing in a fresh T-shirt and jeans. The flowers she had picked were a bit wilted, but she put them in an old Weller vase and stood it beside the bed. They might revive. The scent of the rose was still strong, and Gen wondered if the lily's bulb would flourish in a pot on the terrace of her studio in New York. She would dig up a few bulbs before she went back home; perhaps they would survive the trip in her bag and transplanting.

Dressed, cool, Gen checked the time. Dinner would be near dark, after eight P.M. and she had time for a ride in the relative cool of the day. She could take the camera and. . . . Gen didn't want the camera. For the first time in over thirty years, she didn't want the camera. Didn't want to record anything. . . . *Hide behind anything?* She stared at the camera bag, resting on the chair by the door. Restive, she pulled on her new riding boots and made her way to the barn.

Asa was nowhere to be seen and Olivia was letting the horses out to pasture when Gen arrived. Shawnee was already rolling in the dust, dark legs in the air. A big gelding, part Arabian, part God-knew-what—moose maybe?—was still in his stall, and Gen agreed to take him instead of Shawnee, and to groom him when she returned.

Olivia watched, chewing her lip as Gen saddled the animal, and Gen looked over her shoulder at the younger woman. "If you're trying to find a way to talk about Asa and our little incident, why don't we forget it?" Olivia shrugged and grinned in a, *what can a woman do about it?* gesture. "He's a man," Gen agreed. "An *old* man. Let's forget it?"

"Good by me," Olivia said, eyes brightening. "Thanks. Let me give you a leg up."

Straddling the big gelding, Gen said, "This horse reminds me of my first. Not the ponies I rode as a kid, but my first real horse, Rapunzel. She was a dainty bay Arabian with black stockings and black blaze and had a mane like long curly hair. Really beautiful horse. The first time I got on her I felt like I was ten feet off the ground. She was a gift from the Old Man."

As Olivia adjusted the stirrups, Gen thought about that horse, her heart still sore from the day the vet had been forced to put her down. Her father had been generous, stinting on nothing: dance lessons, piano, which she hated, cooking lessons, lessons in the social graces, clothing whenever she wanted it. She was one of the few teens she knew with charge accounts in Moisson at three different boutiques. And she had hated the man who made it all possible. He was heavy-handed and tough. He had killed her mother, killed her brother. Or so she had thought.

"Have fun," Olivia said, slapping the horse across his rump to move him from the barn. "Don't let him run. It's still too hot for that much activity, even for an eager beaver like Hoss."

"Good name for him," Gen said. "Thanks." Kneeing Hoss, Gen clicked her tongue, grabbing the saddle horn when the Arabian-moose took off at a fast trot and moved instantly into a slow lope. He obviously liked speed, urging against the tight hold she had on the reins. The big gelding was eager and as soon as he was sufficiently warmed up, Gen turned him along the bayou and gave him his head. It wasn't exactly a gallop, but wasn't any staid lope either, and Gen gripped the reins with one hand and the saddle horn with the other, moving her torso into the waltz that was horse and woman.

Cattails and marsh grass whipped by offering blurred visions of the bayou only feet away. Occasional scrub oak, hickory, and sweetgum tree, stunted by hurricanes' salt rains, hung on to banks of black sludge. Birds coming in to roost flew up from the shore, startled by the pounding hooves. Gen whooped and slapped Hoss' flanks with her boots, urging him to greater speed, the artificial breeze lifting her hair and his mane. He snorted and blew and stretched into the run.

It was like being a kid again. Laughing, Gen allowed the gallop to continue for long seconds before pulling Hoss to a fast walk, one manageable for an endurance ride. There had been days as a kid when Gen left the Big House at dawn and had not come back until near dark, in time to clean up and dress for dinner. Both she and Rapunzel had been winded and worn and caked with mud and sweat only half rinsed by bayou water from an impromptu swim.

At that thought, Gen turned Hoss, and he lifted his long legs over the bank, crashing into the placid water with a massive grunt. "Warm as spit," the neighboring kids had called bayou water, and it still was. Body temp and slimy with microscopic vegetation, it coated them both with sludge as Hoss crossed to the other side, half swimming, half stomping through deep mud.

Gen was wet to her thighs, her new boots full and her old saddle dripping. Both would need a good oiling when she got back to the barn tonight. In the meantime, she reined in and removed the boots, dumping the water out and tying them to the saddle to dry. As she perched atop the horse, Hoss shook himself free of water, nearly throwing her to the ground. She held on and patted him, receiving a happy glance back for her troubles. Hoss was contented with his little run, his swim, his new mistress, and it was all wonderful, even with the sour scent that was already emanating from her drying clothes and the wet saddle blanket.

Again, Gen remembered her camera. It had been days since she had snapped off a dozen shots. Days since she thought to lift it from the shelf in the small guesthouse. Even longer since she had been the old Geneva Deveraux, certain of her place in the world, of her own worth as a person, and of her father's ultimate guilt.

Sitting atop the huge horse, Gen tried her old smile, the one she had flashed at paparazzi and tabloid photographers, Fortune 500 magnates and movie stars. It felt strange on her mouth. False.

She let it slide away and turned her face to the sun, soaking up the waves of humid heat. No, she wasn't the old Geneva. But perhaps she was becoming something, someone, stronger. More real. . . . Along with the smile, she let the thought slide away, and patted Hoss' shoulder.

Gen rode for two hours, no destination in mind, as the sun began to set. Yet, she wasn't surprised when she found herself at the Templar Place. Starnes' family property. Shadows draped long arms across the land, throwing the world into grays, olive-greens and heavy browns.

Hoss moved at a comfortable walk, his head hanging low, his nostrils blowing. Tossing back companionable eyes, he turned into Starnes' drive, hooves clomping a steady rhythm.

The house, now that she could see it in better light, was brick with charcoal, gray, and white trim. A half-built barbecue and patio graced the side of the house, off the screened porch. Starnes' restored GMC truck, a rusty Jaguar that had been rolled once or twice and now sat wheel-less atop a flatbed truck, and a beat-up old work truck, the bed filled with debris, sat in the concrete parking space. Not the Templar place she remembered, but a remodeled showplace, grounds sculpted with flower beds and green lawn instead of the brown grass, balled-up rusted barbwire, old tires, and scattered beer cans of her memory. Hoss slowed, lifted his head.

Gen didn't have to call out, "Hello the house!" alerting the occupants to visitors. As Hoss moved up the drive, a door on the screened porch opened and Starnes stepped out. The big long-haired setter moved with him, and Bubba-Boy let out a bark, half welcome, half warning to his master. Starnes gentled the dog with a soft word and walked out on to the deck.

He was shirtless, his jeans unbuttoned, loose on his hips, feet bare beneath. Fresh from the shower, his hair stood out in black spikes around his head, rare silver strands at his temples bright in the low-lying sunlight, eyes black as midnight. God. . . . He was gorgeous.

Starnes' settled a hip against the railing and waited. His eyes met hers, his lips slightly quirked, familiar as her own hand. Dark hair across his chest trailed down in a sharp line and disappeared into the jeans. A slow warmth started in her midsection. Her lips parted, feeling heavy in the dying heat. Her bare toes gripped the stirrups, curling with reaction at the sight of him.

Hoss made his way toward the porch, big hooves moving slower, tired now, yet bringing them closer, and still neither of them spoke. The light made shadows across Starnes' stomach, flat and ripped with the muscles of a much younger man. His arms were strong, the deltoids and triceps sharp angles as he braced himself on the railing. When Hoss reached the deck, he stopped and sniffed the foliage, considering it as a possible snack. Gen stared into Starnes' eyes.

"Nice car. The Jaguar."

He looked at the car. "It will be. When I find time to restore it."

"I like the house," she said, knowing that her eyes were saying something else entirely. "I didn't get a good look at it earlier."

Starnes watched her, his eyes hooded and assessing. He wasn't going to make this easy on her.

"My father didn't kill my mother." she blurted. "I have a feeling he didn't kill Matthew either."

"I know." His voice wasn't Barry's, not rich and mellow and sensual, persuasive just by its timbre. Starnes' voice was grave, low, and steady, deep as the gulf only miles away. Clear and unambiguous. Just as it always had been.

"All my life I believed he killed them."

A drip of water fell from Starnes' hair and trailed across his shoulder, down his chest, and into the hair near his navel. Gen followed it with her eyes. And let them rest there. When she finally looked back at him, she could see the heat in his stare. Could feel the answering heat from her own. Her skin tightened all over with a scorching fever.

"If I come in now, I won't leave tonight," she whispered.

"If you come in now, I won't let you."

She started to slide from Hoss' back but stopped at his next words.

"But I'm not interested in an affair, *Ginny*. I'm not interested in a one-night fling." He smiled that little quirky smile again, holding her eyes with his, making certain she could see his longing. "I waited too long for that. Waited too long for you. Waited even when I didn't know I was waiting. For twenty-nine years."

Gen paused, wanting him. Remembering Barry's embrace this afternoon. The quiet laughter.

"No games, Miss High and Mighty." Starnes' hands gripped the railing. "No revenge, even if it's unconscious revenge, against Barry. You want that, you find someone else."

"I wouldn't—" The words clotted in her throat. *Revenge? Against Barry.* . . . "That's not—"

"Isn't it?" Starnes' smile slipped away. "I think you don't really know what you want yet. I think part of you still wants Barry and New York and the life you've lived there for nearly thirty years. I think only part of you wants me. And I want all of you, *Ginny.*" Soft Cajun cadence, *She-nay.* Passion in his tone. "Every cell, every fiber, every dream, every hope, all of you, all to myself." He tilted his head, said softly, "And I won't share."

Starnes' words echoed what she had said to Barry so long ago and again only recently. *I won't share.* Holding his eyes, Gen gathered up the reins in her hands. Watching her so closely he could have seen her skin breathe, Starnes smiled sadly.

Her hands tightened on the reins and Hoss tossed his head, snorting. Gen's torso moved with the huge animal instinctively and he settled beneath her. "Deep in my soul . . . where I keep my memories of joy and happiness . . ." Gen's throat tightened and tears stung her eyes, "where I keep my memories of my mother, the way she was when she was happy and well. Where I keep memories of Rapunzel and memories of church socials and memories of my first kiss . . ." she swallowed hard, blinking back the tears. "I've kept a place for you. A secret place," she whispered. "I've always loved you, Templar. Always."

"And I've always loved you, Miss High and Mighty Deveraux."

Gen laughed shakily. Hoss moved gently beneath her now, pawing the earth. "I'll be back when I know for sure."

"I'll be here. Just like always."

Gen turned Hoss and headed for home. She didn't look back, but she knew that Starnes stared after her. Watching. Waiting.

25

AIN'T NO TROUBLE TO FEED ONE MORE

Gen made it to the Big House for dinner with only seconds to spare. The meal, smelling of fresh baked bread, potatoes, and beef cooked to perfection, was on the table in steaming bowls, the tea already poured, as she slipped into her chair, still dripping from her latest shower. Hair wet, dragged back into a ponytail, skirt and T-shirt clinging to her damp body, she took a sip of tea while her eyes were still adjusting to the relative darkness of the kitchen. In her haste, she missed the fact that guests were sitting at the long table with Della, Lily, and her two kids.

Gen froze at the sound of Barry's voice. "I appreciate you letting me stay here Mrs. LaPointe, but I hate to put you out by feeding me, too."

"Ain't no trouble to feed one more, Mr. Stone. Always enough to feed family. Guests, too. And Starnes join us most every night now he looking after the Old Man's business. 'Sides, I love to see a big man eat, and you look like you gone make my heart proud. You say grace for us?"

Gen's eyes raked the table, widening at the sight of Barry on one side of Della and Starnes on the other. Starnes was amused at her expression, his mouth turned up at a corner; Barry looked startled by Della's request.

"Grace? Mrs. LaPointe, perhaps Geneva never told you, but I'm Jewish. My version of grace would be slightly . . . um, different."

"Gen done told me, long time gone," she said. "I reckon your God, Jehovah, be the same God what I talk to. He'll listen well enough to one His first chil'rens saying thank you." Della crossed her hands over her ample breasts, waiting. "You say grace," she commanded.

Barry shot Gen a pleading glance and she looked away,

amused but sympathetic. Would he even remember the words? It had been over twenty years. . . .

Lily kicked her beneath the table and the two shared a knowing look. Della had never been happy about one of her girls marrying a non-Christian, but she had accepted it, finally, absolving Gen in her letters for "being unequally yoked" years before. Yet, when Barry had stopped practicing his religion, she had been even more unhappy. It was clear that Della intended to see things put to rights where Barry and his God were concerned.

Gen and her sister had seen Della handle farmhands of every race and creed. She ran the Big House as if it were her personal fiefdom and they had never seen a man get the better of her, no matter how big, ornery, prejudiced, or drunk he was. Civilized, urbane, refined Barry Stone was hardly a challenge, and he seemed to know it.

As the uncomfortable silence continued around the table, Barry stood and unfolded two clean cloth napkins, one which he spread over his empty plate. "Keri, would you pass me the bread please," he asked.

Keri had never heard the Jewish prayers said over meals in the Stone household while on visits. Barry had stopped speaking the ritual grace years before she was born. Gen wasn't even sure Keri knew her Uncle Barry was Jewish. Wide-eyed, Keri placed the breadbasket with its fresh, uncut loaf before him.

Barry looked down the table at Gen and quickly away, seeming uncertain. Taking his water glass, he lifted it, stared at it a moment, and splashed water across his right hand three times from the wrist down, then repeated the splashing on his left hand. The water fell from his hands with tiny patters to the napkin he had prepared. Lifting the second napkin, he dried his wet hands, saying, "Blessed art Thou, oh Lord, our God, King of the Universe, Who has sanctified us by His commandments concerning the washing of the hands."

Taking the bread from its basket, Barry broke the loaf, the sonorous words flowing from his mouth, "*Baruch atah Adonai, Elohenu Melech Ha-olam, ha-motzi lechem min ha-aretz. . . .*" Barry paused a moment, as the Hebrew syllables resonated in the silence.

The ancient words sent tingles up Gen's arms and down

through the years, recalling the past, the marriage they had shared. It was the prayer Barry once prayed before each meal, back when he still practiced his religion, keeping Sabbath, and eating Kosher. He had wanted Gen to convert to Judaism but she had refused. It was the single point of contention in their early marriage.

In 1980, Barry's mother died of breast cancer. His father, grief-stricken, entered into ritual mourning and disappeared into the Torah, studying, praying, shutting out the world and his only son, never to emerge again as the vibrant man of Barry's youth. And then he, too, passed away, silently in the night. The death of his parents drove Barry away from his synagogue and his God. Della was forcing him back again.

After a moment, Barry began again in English, as Gen had expected him to. "Blessed art Thou, oh Lord our God . . ." he said slowly, the translation flowing like thick oil to the walls of the room and back in cumbrous waves.

Watching Della, Gen saw her smile, eyes closed serenely, agreeing with the prayer. Starnes was strangely still, watching Gen's husband, listening intently. Lily was smiling, too, sliding glances at Keri and Destan who attended to the strange sounding words with tilted heads, eyes wide.

". . . King of the Universe, Who brings forth bread from the earth," Barry finished softly.

The silence seemed almost to glow as his words ended. Barry stared down into the breadbasket for a long moment, his face curiously rapt. Pinching an olive-sized piece of Della's aromatic, home-baked bread, he ate it, then passed the breadbasket around the table. Following his example, each of them took a small piece and ate. The bread was one of Della's herbed loaves, the scent and taste exploding in Gen's mouth as she took the sacramental bite. Still damp, she quivered in the cold room, as a curious sense of peace twined, like a single sinuous bough, around her heart. Gen looked down at her empty plate, blinking back tears.

The ancient words were different from any the others would have spoken, the cant so foreign, the tone so melancholy, the supplication buttressed by four thousand years of history and suffering and survival. With their speaking, something odd had happened around the long table. Gen felt it. Saw it in the faces of the others, eyes open, but defenses down.

The Old Man was dying upstairs. Barry's prayer made that real.

As the words ended, Della raised her head and smiled widely. "Praise the Lord, but that was fine, Mr. Barry," she said gently, promoting him to a first-name relationship. "Real fine. That be a prayer the good Lord like to hear, I know that."

She nodded to each person down the table and said, "Now, Mr. Barry, you pass the meat, and Starnes, you pass the rice. We gots a lot a eating to do, to honor them words, yes sir. Lily, you start with the black-eyed peas. I be right hungry."

Food bowls were passed and Gen filled her plate, eating in uncharacteristic stillness, listening as the kids filled the adults' silence, telling about their afternoon with Asa. The three had spent the day at a high-tech horse-breeding farm, observing as an out of season mare was inseminated, and watching trainers and horse-handlers as they worked with million-dollar animals.

They had been privileged to sit with the horsemen over a late lunch of crawfish stew, home-brewed beer, and red beans-and-rice. Asa, it seemed, had insisted the kids drink Co-Cola, but each had managed to sneak a taste of beer. Destan manfully assured the other men at Della's table that it was good. Keri turned up her nose with a "Yucky stuff," comment.

The conversation flowed like eddies in a stream as the others responded to the teenagers' excitement. Ignoring them, Gen kept staring across the room at the stairs leading up to the sickroom and her dying father.

He had not killed her mother. He had not killed her mother. . . .

◆   ◆   ◆

Starnes watched as Barry Stone enacted the ritual that was as old as civilization itself, listened to the Hebrew words, and saw the effect that the old phrases had on the assembled. Especially Gen. He saw her face soften, her eyes trail again and again to her husband, and he felt his gut spasm at the look in her eyes. He wasn't sure what it meant, but the look was so tender, so yielding, it couldn't mean anything good. Not for him anyway.

He was losing her.

He had never had her. . . .

Moving mechanically, Starnes passed around dishes, filling his plate with whatever was in them. The teens were talking about their great day and horses and wanting to go to veterinary school so they could be large animal vets. He heard the chatter through a growing stupor.

He was losing her.

The meal was tasteless. It could have been ashes.

He had been a fool not to take Gen when he had the chance. A fool not to make her his. He remembered the look in her eyes an hour ago when she came to him, sitting astride the big horse, wanting him. But now Barry Stone was here, breaking the spell that had bewitched her.

Barry Stone offered her a lifetime, with all the history, memories, shared belongings, hopes and dreams. He had broken her heart with his infidelity, true, but he offered her reconciliation, a lifestyle of luxury she had grown accustomed to . . . and a son, if she could see past the woman who had born him. And—no small deed—he had left his business in New York City, flown to the backwaters of the world to reclaim her. That was powerful magic.

Though Starnes had money, his fortune paled by comparison to Stone's assets. When he looked critically at what he had to offer, Starnes had only his love and constancy and a lifetime of stored passion. It seemed he had waited twenty-nine years for *Ginny* Deveraux, only to lose her again to the same man. His mouth twisted wryly as he looked up and met Barry Stone's stare.

The famous electric-blue eyes held his, silently acknowledging the rivalry, the woman they both wanted, and, surprisingly, an emotion they shared. *Defeat?* Starnes put down his fork. *What had Barry Stone ever failed at?*

Somber, Barry lifted his tea glass and saluted Starnes, drank, and set the glass down, before excusing himself from the table. His plate was only half empty. Smiling easily at Della, he climbed the back stairs to the sickroom and John Deveraux.

Gen's eyes followed his progress across the floor, but she didn't rise to follow the man she had married. Instead, she turned to stare at Starnes, her face expressionless. Then, amazingly, she changed, her wide mouth slowly stretching, nostrils flaring, a smile resting in her eyes. Uncertain what the smile meant, he nevertheless smiled back, feeling his heart lighten.

"Now," Della said, interrupting the exchange, "Starnes and I gots something we got to say to all y'all. So you listen. Geneva, you tell Mr. Barry if you want to, but I think it right what Starnes and I got to say best be said with jist family here. Then, when we done talking, I got peach-berry cobbler and vanilla ice cream for dessert. Starnes?"

He blinked, meeting Della's eyes blankly. She tilted her head looking from him to Gen and back, pursing her lips. "About the sheriff? And tomorrow?" she prompted, amused.

Lily laughed, and Starnes felt himself flush. *Ginny's* smile grew wider, but she never took her eyes from him.

Standing, Starnes collected himself and braced his arms on the table, looking from face to face down the linen covered surface. "Sorry, Della. Sometimes I forget that I'm not just a friend, but the lawyer here."

"Family," Della corrected instantly. "You is family. Always has been."

Starnes grinned. "I stand corrected. But tonight, right now, I'm John Deveraux's and Della LaPointe's attorney of record. Tomorrow, Sheriff Pritchard and a few court officials are coming to the estate to take depositions from them both, and they wanted me to tell you why they're coming, ahead of time. Do you understand what a deposition is?" he asked the kids.

Keri's eyes grew wide at the word. Destan simply looked confused. "Sure," he said. "I know what it is, sorta. I saw it on TV. It's where a cop makes you talk on tape after you swear on a Bible. But what's that got to do with the Old Man and Della?" The faces of Deveraux's daughters mirrored hope and a fearful expectation.

"Quite a lot, I'm afraid," Starnes said. "There may be scandal over the depositions, but the Old Man wanted the story told before he died in order to protect Della from possible future prosecution at a time when he would not be here to defend her."

"Della?" Lily asked, surprised. "What has Della got to do with Mama and Matth—"

"This isn't about Helena, Lily. Not directly. It's about a man named Billy Ray Spinella," Starnes said.

"And this part of the story be mine to tell," Della said. Making certain that she had their attention, she indicated that Starnes should sit down. When he did, Della began a story that Starnes knew neither Gen nor Lily had ever heard. He had intended to tell it himself, but it was Della's tale. He settled himself to listen.

"Couple years before my Helena and my Matthew die, the Old Man come into insurance money from his uncle Maccabeus' death. Not much by today standards, but back then, fifty-thousand dollars be a lot of money. The Old Man use it to buy the old Spinella Place for a hunting preserve.

"Old Theodore Spinella done drank hisself to death, let his farm fall into a shamble, and two of his sons trying to follow in his footsteps. Rabble-rousers they was. They be wanting the money when they daddy die 'stead of the home place, so the Old Man buy it. One hundred acres of land, most swamp, wetlands, they calls it now. But good hunting in that parcel of land."

Her eyes were distant, seeing the past more clearly than the kitchen around her. "His brothers be good-for-nothing, but Billy Ray seem like a good boy. Studious-like. Pretty boy, too. Had Frenchy looking green eyes, the kind they call bedroom eyes, and curly black hair like coal. The Old Man take Billy Ray under his wing. Show him how farming suppose to be done. Teach him how to invest his money."

Della rose from her place at the table and walked slowly to her rocker. Sitting down, she sighed as if suddenly free from pain, began rocking, and picked up her narrative, the rhythm of the uneven runners punctuating her tale.

"Billy Ray work the fields, learn from my man how to run the tractor, learn how to rotate crops. Work close to Asa, learning barn management and how to take care of horses, break them to ride. Near on two, maybe three years he work here. And him and your mama start spending time together. Innocent it was at first. They happen to pass in the yard, or Helena happen to go by him working while she out riding her horse. Stop and speak, chat a while, like she done with all the hands. But she seem to chat a bit longer to Billy Ray. Bump into him more often.

"This a small town, and pretty soon people start talking. And finally the Old Man hear about it." Della shook her head sorrowfully.

"Helena been on a high for a long time then. Lily been born, and a hard laying-in and birthin' that was and my Helena come through it right fine, she did. And Doc Boulanger and the Old Man had hopes she be cured. Sometime that happen in cases of depression, like my Helena's.

"But the Old Man hear 'bout Billy Ray spending time with Helena. People talking 'bout the Old Man's wife, and he put a stop to Helena seeing Billy Ray. Put his foot down, though he knowed she love him alone. Knowed it right proper, too. Knowed she jist a friend to Billy Ray, but he shamed in the eyes of the town, he was.

"Now, the Old Man knowed better than to handle Helena like that." Della's head moved slowly side to side, her eyes moist. "You had to gentle her into a idea. Cajole, not order. John knew it, but he busy, too tied up with turning the old Spinella Place into a hunting preserve for his gov'ment friends to take the time. He jist tell her how it gonna be. How things gonna change.

"He say as how she can't leave the house, and as how Billy Ray gots to take his lunch with the colored mens in the yard from now own, 'stead of in the Big House with the white workers. Told me I was to keep him out the house. Keep an eye on Helena.

"When she fuss 'bout the changes, try to leave the estate and go ridin, he give charge over her to Hiram, one a the stablehands. Black Cajun boy he was and ugly as homemade sin. Say Hiram got to go with her when she take to riding. Say she can't ride out alone no more. Shame her in the eyes of the men-folk right there in the barn stableyard. Mistake that was. It all a fool mistake."

Della squeezed her eyes shut. Her rocking slowed. "I seen the look in her eye when John Deveraux lay down the law like that. I seen the flames sparking. But the words done been said, like a challenge they was, to Helena. Like a slap in the face in one them old movies. And she take up the gauntlet." Della sighed gustily, the air escaping like a hiss from a steam kettle just before it whistled. "Told the Old Man he could take his 'chastity-belt-Hiram' and . . . well, she wasn't very ladylike 'bout what she tole him to do with it."

Starnes watched as Lily and Gen exchanged a glance and rose as one. Crossing the room, Gen opened the pantry and lifted out two folding chairs. Placing them on either side of Della's rocker, they both sat, each taking a plump hand, as if this were their private ceremony. Della smiled at them with pride and a certain inexplicable sadness.

Starnes' heart thudded against his chest. He had heard the

story this afternoon, though without the personal details that made it a family tragedy. Just the bare bones of it as told by the Old Man, confirmed by Della. He could only see Gen's face now in profile, the classic lines clean and smiling, encouraging the storyteller. Mouth dry, he drank his tea and poured more, glad that no mint leaf floated in the bottom of his glass.

"Them two could fight, they could. Always hollering at each other and throwing things. Breaking dishes. Hot tempered. And the passion like flame 'tween them. Like Bayou Incendie when she burn, hot in the night. But now my Helena go cold and hard as a stone mountain. And the Old Man knew he done made him a mistake." Della looked between her girls, making certain that they understood what she was saying. The rocker thudded softly.

"He know he should say he sorry, take her on a trip to Paris or London like he been promising her. He know it 'cause I *tell* him so. But John Deveraux never say them words, 'I sorry.' Not *never* in his whole life. He jist close up tight, like a fist, start watching her, eyes like slits, accusing. This go on for weeks. Until one night, Helena don't come in from her riding."

Della shook her head. "She take the Old Man's horse that day, a big roan gelding, and rode into the bayou. Hiram horse turn up lame and he can't keep up. Lost her. Come back to the Big House, and the Old Man fire him on the spot. Take a horse and go after her hisself, he did. But he can't find her neither. Like a madman, he was. Crazy wild. Near killed that horse, riding him so hard."

Slow tears filled Della's eyes, sparkling in the overhead fluorescent light, brimming. "After ten that night it was, when she come riding in, horse all lathered up, Helena wet from a fall and all scraped up. Look like she been in a fight. And laughing at the Old Man from the top of his best horse." Della's moist eyes stared off into the distance, into a past only she could see. She squeezed the hands holding hers tightly, seeming to take comfort from the contact with her girls.

"The Old Man pull her from that horse and drag her upstairs. . . . I didn't see hide nor hair of either one for two day. Jist lef' they food outside they door and pick up the dirty dishes. When the Old Man come out, things was different 'tween them. Helena done changed. Took to her bed. And turn up pregnant later that month."

Della stopped rocking and stared into the eyes of her girls, making sure that they were paying attention. Her own eyes were dry and hard as she looked back-and-forth between them. "Your mama told the Old Man she couldn't be sure that baby she was carrying was his. A lie that was, but he didn't know that, and he didn't tell me what she be claiming. Not then. And I coulda tole him it be his. I coulda. I knowed my Helena womanhood cycles like I knowed my own. Matthew be the Old Man's. No question 'bout it. But he don't know it. He was burning up inside with the not knowing. Wondering.

"Fight something awful they did. And then stop talking at all." Della looked up at Starnes. He smiled encouragingly and sipped his tea, as nervous hearing her tale now as he had been earlier. The old saying that "God is in the details" was wrong this time. It was the devil who was in the details of this story. Gen's face was both rapt and distressed; Starnes wanted to hold her and couldn't. He drank more tea, to busy his hands.

"During that first month, she got the high blood press and start to spot. Doctor say she lose the baby if she move. Say she got to stay in bed. So, Helena take to her bed," Della repeated, her tone woeful.

"She shun the Old Man. Give attention to you two girls, have lunch in the bed, let you play in the bedroom, making tents and forts out of the bedclothes and drapes. Play baby-doll with you. But when the Old Man come home, she shut the door, pretend she asleep, turn her back to him. And the bigger she got with that baby, the more she turn from him.

"Billy Ray done gone from the estate. Don't know if the Old Man run him off or he hear the rumors 'bout that baby and take off all on his own, but he gone. And that jist make the Old Man believe Helena's lie all the more. Sad place this house be, all them months. *Sad* place. You girls didn't know nothing 'bout it. I keeps you happy. But 'tween them two, it not a home anymore. They marriage dying, I seen that clear as a bell, I did. I tole your mama to stop this foolishness, but she turn away from *me*, too.

"Lord knows I prayed over them and they marriage. But the good Lord can only work with willing hearts, not with angry hearts. And Helena and John Deveraux be angry. Soul deep angry.

"Now. What I gots to say ain't easy to hear, I knows it. Hard words I gots to say, all about the time your mama die. Things I didn't say last time we talk, 'cause ain't no reason to say ill of the dead. But I think it time you hear the truth in all it ugly self. You girls done say some awful things about your daddy, and if I had a listen to you back when your mama and Matthew die, you maybe live a different kind of life. I gots to live with that knowledge. I gots to live knowing I let you both believe a lie."

"You don't have a thing in the world to apologize for, Della-love," Lily said, holding onto Della, both hands gripping her left. "We should have come to you when we were older. We should have asked for the truth. We didn't. We let our hearts lead us wrong, too. Just like Mama and the Old Man."

Lily looked at Gen and shook her head. "Sister-mine, Della-love, my life is *mine*. And I wouldn't change a *thing* about it. If I had known we were wrong about the Old Man killing Mama, I might never have left town and married Jason, and if I hadn't married Jason, I would never have met and married Mason, who gave me my own two babies. And I wouldn't change a thing in the world about *that!* They're *mine!*

"So don't you spend time thinking about what wrongs might have been prevented. The past is in God's hands. All I have to be responsible for is the present and my choices today."

Gen nodded, agreeing as tears ran down her face, caught the light, quivered on her lips and dripped off her chin, ignored. Her hair, dry now, fell from a short ponytail in soft curling wisps, golden-yellow about her face. Her sunburned nose was peeling. Bending her head to Della's hand she rested there as if in prayer. All three women were crying silently. They held onto one another as if to lifelines, smiles strained and trembling, but open and real. Real in a way Starnes had never seen before.

He looked away from the tableau, his throat tight. Destan and Keri, sat at the table, still as death. Keri had Destan's hand, squeezing it, just as their mother squeezed Della's. As he watched, Destan lifted his other hand and patted Keri's shoulder. It was unthinking, unconscious, offering solace wholly without thought.

The simple gesture slammed through Starnes. *They were a family. . . .*

A keen shaft of pain pierced him, cold as frozen iron. *Family.*

Anguish welled up from some dark and forgotten place. *Serena. . . .*

Like a winding sheet from an ancient grave, the past enveloped him, suffocating. Tears burned in his eyes. Tears he recognized as a totally selfish loneliness. He inhaled past the pain, filling his lungs with an unsatisfying breath.

Could he have prevented Serena's misery, her emotional roller-coaster-ride through life and men? Could he have made a difference if he hadn't been co-dependent, as L'ron charged? Or was Serena like Lily, responsible for her own pain and misery. . . . The thought left a hollow place deep inside him. Serena. . . . *His* family.

"So. We together on this then?" Della asked.

"We're together," Gen whispered. "Always together."

"Well then, stop your crying. Sappy, the both of you," Della said, disengaging her hands and wiping her nose and eyes with her apron. Retaking their hands, she continued with her narrative.

"Matthew finally born. Look jist like the Old Man, he did. Same black eyes, same nose. Wasn't no question who the daddy was. But it be a hard birth, and Helena seem to spiral down. Dark circles under her eyes. Wouldn't wash her hair. I had to force her to move off the bed so's I could change the sheets.

"Doc Boulanger come and go, prescribe medicine for her. Don't do no good. Not a bit. Say he want to commit her. Again he talking 'bout 'lectric shock therapy on her brain. John read up on it again, but say it jist too dangerous. Say he won't allow it. I took his papers one night and I read 'em. More I read, more I was against it. I was glad he wouldn't shock her. Nasty business, that 'lectricity. I did ask him to send her to a head doctor, but he say no. Call 'em all quacks, he did.

"For months my Helena lay there. Cry and sleep 'bout all she done. Cry and sleep. And then she get a letter. . . . She say it from her sister in Atlanta. That be your Aunt Joelle what died back in seventy-two. But I know Joelle's writin', and that not Joelle's. Some other woman done addressed that letter. But I believe it then and I believe it now, that letter from Billy Ray.

"Nex' day, Helena up and moving 'bout the house, singing and making herself pretty again. Come down to supper and sit with the Old Man, eyes sparkling. Back to her old self, she was.

Teasing you girls, laughing at the Old Man. And he eat it up with a spoon. Think she fine, now. But I knew better. I knew it all about that letter she got. I even look for it, I admit I did. Snoop around while I was cleaning. But that letter gone.

"Three week later, she back to riding all over the bayou, alone, talking to the men-folk what be workin'. . . . Like as if Billy Ray Spinella never been in her life. Like as if she and the Old Man done never fought."

Della rose from the rocker and moved stiffly to the table. She stacked the dishes, scraping the plates into a single bowl. The spoon's quiet scraping sounded harsh in the kitchen. Starnes added his plate to the pile and discarded Barry's leftovers. Della tisked softly at the sight of the wasted food. "For a big man, Barry Stone don't eat enough to feed a bird," she murmured.

Keri grinned at the comment and lifted a second pile of dishes, carrying them to the sink. Starnes and Destan followed with serving bowls and salad plates.

Standing with her back to the room, Della loaded the dishwasher and resumed speaking, her bending and rising creating a tempo with her words, dishes softly clinking. "But one day, she come home late again from her riding. Claim her horse come up lame, though Asa say as how it be fine. And she take to her bed again.

"Depression hit her sudden-like, more so than usual, I think. And I be suspicious, pure-T-suspicious. Then, on about the third day I see in the back of her closet a little suitcase. *Valise*, she call it. Heavy it was, like it pack full. Ain't a suitcase I ever see before, and it got mud splatters on it. . . . Like it been out in the weather a bit, near bayou mud. Got a little lock on it and no key, because I done looked for it."

Della paused and turned back to Gen and Lily who were unmoving in their chairs, heads turned to follow Della's every move. "I think your mama was planning to run off with Billy Ray, but something happen. He didn't show up or she missed him. Jist my thinking. Got no proof. But things not what they was 'tween Helena and John, no matter what she pretend." Her eyes settled on Gen. "Some thing's get broke, ain't no fixing them. I knows that."

Gen's eyes smiled, her face softening. Starnes had a sudden

memory of her this afternoon, sitting astride the huge horse, toes curled around the wooden stirrups. There was the faint, familiar bayou stench coming from her horse, who tossed his head and sniffed at the dwarf nandina near his feet. Sweat-stains on Gen's T-shirt curled around her breasts and down to her waist, making the shirt translucent in the dying sunlight. She had gone riding without sunscreen and had reddened on neck, nose, forehead, arms. Her hair had been wildly curly, pulling itself out of its rubber band just as it had when she was a young girl. Innocent as a child.

But the woman on the horse had been no child. Her eyes had sparkled with a hunger that was fully woman, and when her hands tightened on the reins, he could feel their pressure on his body. When she shifted in the saddle, it brought a raw heat blazing through him. And he was three kinds a fool for not bringing her inside and claiming her for his own.

Della looked at him as if reading his thoughts. "Maybe you young folk should remember that," she said. "Sometime the past is jist the past, and there ain't no fixing it." Her dark gaze was full of both reproach and amusement.

Uneasily, Starnes shrugged, uncertain if it was his past with *Ginny* that was broken or Gen's past with Barry. Della was entirely too perceptive and he didn't particularly like being an open book, especially when he found Della so impossible to read.

"Matthew come down with the colic the nex' day. And Helena jist beside herself. Can't stand the screaming all day and all night. Can't sleep herself, up with insomnia. Had a problem with it all her life, but now it so bad, she can't get no rest at all. I make plans to move into the house for a few week to help her. Plan to move the baby down to the room beneath the stairs, get Matthew away from the master bedroom so's they can sleep upstairs. Got a Sholtz girl to come help with the housework so's I can take care of the baby. . . .

"And then Helena gone. One afternoon I finally gets the baby to take a nap upstairs in he crib and I lay me down, too. Slept hard in that little room." Della waved a limp hand to the small room she occupied fulltime now. "Slept too hard. When I wakes up it been near five hours and Matthew ain't slept that long a stretch in weeks. And I knew as soon as I wake up that things was gone bad. I run up the stairs and find Matthew gone. Helena gone. That little valise gone, too. I runs to the barn, meet Asa coming in with a horse trailer full of horses. He say as how he take off and been gone all day, but he look around and see two horses missing from the stableyard. *Two* horses.

"I calls the Old Man and he panic. He call the sheriff and get a search started. Half the men-folk in the parish be looking for my Helena and my Matthew. I gets my man Ephram to call up the Primitive Baptist Church minister. . . . I forgets his name right now, but he calls out the black mens and gets them looking, too. White and black, they all looking together. And then my Helena come home. Alone. No Matthew." Tears gathered in her eyes and Gen rose from her seat, crossing the room.

Taking Della's hand, she pulled the older woman back toward the rocker. "Sit down, Della-love. It wasn't your fault. Mama was a grown woman. It wasn't your—"

"Course it was my fault," Della said, trying to shake Gen's hands away. "I coulda took that little suitcase. I coulda give it to John. I coulda stayed *awake* and been there when she try to leave the house. But I sleep right through it all. *I was asleep!*", she cried.

"Let go a me, girl! I got to tell this story in my own way, and standing on my own two feets!"

Gen dropped Della's arm, stepping back in surprise.

Starnes started forward and stopped. They were a family. They had to deal with this shock, this trauma, in their own way. He was just the lawyer here. *Not family*, no matter what Della said. Starnes clenched his jaw tight and looked away thinking of his sister and his responsibility to her, unfulfilled and empty. *Co-dependent, you. . . .* The words rang in his memory. He should leave. He *should* do a lot of things. Instead, unable to help himself, he turned back to the scene.

"When Helena come in she be wearing a dress, not her riding clothes. She come from the bayou, walking, slow-like, dazed, she was. I seen her coming and I run to meet her.

"There be blood on her wrist lace and on her knees, and a bruise on her face. And no Matthew. *No Matthew!*"

Della seemed to crumple in on herself, growing smaller as Starnes watched. Her hands fisted in the wrinkled apron, pulling the fabric tightly down across her breasts. Rolling her head from side to side Della moaned softly. "She say as how the Old Man find her and Billy Ray at the bait shop after it close, Billy Ray holding Matthew, her with her valise, and a boat in the water at the dock, ready to take them three away.

"John hit her. Billy Ray fight him. Fight him while he holding my baby! And that boy, that Billy Ray, he drop my Matthew. Drop him on the dock. Break his head. Break his head open. . . ."

The room was so quiet that Starnes could hear them all breathe, a soft soughing like the wind across Matthew's grave, whistling past a gray headstone. He went and took Della in his arms, she swayed toward him, held him, moaning softly. She gripped his shirt and held him tightly bound. Her voice, when she spoke was muffled in his chest, the sound of her misery fluttering through him like bird wings beating against his ribs.

"Knock out the Old Man, Helena did. Knock him out cold with a boat oar. And then they two *sinners* picked up my Matthew and got theyselves into the boat and took off. Lef' him there. Lef' the Old Man there on the dock."

Della's quivering eased as she spoke. Wiping her face on Starnes' shirt, she turned and looked at Gen and Lily. An arm snaked around Starnes' waist for support as she leaned into him. Carefully he held her, certain she might break.

"When John come to, he break in to the bait shop and call me, ask me if I hear from Helena. . . . And by that time, she come home. The Old Man tell me to call the sheriff office and say she back. To call off the search, 'cept I tell him Helena without Matthew. He real quiet then, thinking. And Helena, she upstairs. Dying. Killing herself while I talk on the phone, banging dishes, mad at her. Dying while I do what John tell me to do. And when the Old Man come in, I done fount my Helena bleeding. . . . Bleedin' herself to death no matter how I try to hold in the blood.

"She look up at me while she dying and tell me Matthew be on a johnboat tied up at the old Spinella Place. Tell me the whole story. John took off and fount him. Call the doctor. . . . Too late. Matthew brain be at his ear, comin' out. Doc Boulanger say as how Matthew gonna die. Can die at the hospital or at die home. The Old Man look old then for real, jist like his daddy, that old. And he decide as how Matthew should die at home. Four day later my baby gone."

Della pushed away and stood tall once again, facing Gen and Lily on her own two feet, just as she had wanted. "What you two girls see when you come to the nursery door is the Old Man grievin', poundin' his fist into the floor beside Matthew head. Poundin' and poundin' with all he grief. Lost his only son and his wife. And didn't know it then, but lost his girls, too. All for a misunderstanding and old Della not being able to talk. I had a part in that. Knew it and didn't know it, too. And now John dying upstairs. And you girls know the truth."

"What I wants to know is—what is you gonna do to put things right 'tween you and the Old Man. . . . 'Tween you and your *daddy*. . . . Before he dies? What you gonna do?"

26

THE TRUTH BE A HARD PILL

Gen slowly stood, pulling her sister up with her. Lily was still holding her hand, long nails gouging Gen's skin. Hands together the sisters faced Starnes and Gen asked, "And what part of this story has to do with the deposition tomorrow?"

Della, angry eyes glittering, held up an imperious hand, stopping his reply. "I ain't say I done talking. I jist askt a question. You girls got an answer?"

"We have to talk about this," Lily said. Smoothing her impeccable chignon with a shaking hand, she released Gen. Diamonds flashed as she moved, the motion uncertain. "Gen and I spent our lives believing . . ." she faltered, ". . . a lie. It's . . . hard to digest, Della-love."

Della nodded reluctantly. "The truth be a hard pill sometime. But I ex-*spect* you both to swallow it. Learn from it. Things ain't always what they seem. The Old Man be a hard man, I knows that. But he love you two girls. Want the bes' for you. I *'spect* you to make things right with your daddy a'fore he die. *You hear me?*"

Lily smiled sadly and hugged Della, but Gen was rooted to the floor. Something wasn't right with what they had heard. Nothing in the story suggested a reason for a deposition in the morning unless the sheriff had reopened Helena's and Matthew's case. And Starnes had said nothing to that effect.

He was looking at her across the room, his face hard as he read her expression. The muscle in his jaw bunched.

"The reason for the deposition has to do with the third body in the grave, doesn't it?" she asked. Anger surged through her, tingling in her fingers.

Glancing at Lily, she said, "When Starnes and the sheriff exhumed the grave of Mama and Matthew, they found another grave. *A third body*. And that was the one you were *really* going after, all along, wasn't it, Starnes? Not Mama. That's what you were trying to tell me at the gravesite. Mama and Matthew were *incidental* to more of John Deveraux's *machinations.*"

Starnes' jaw knotted angrily. His eyes flashed black fire.

Heat poured over her. Another of the Old Man's little games. Shaking, she took a single step. "You were just playing me along, weren't you?" she demanded. "Making sure you got what you wanted while you *placated the little woman.*"

"I am not the one who betrayed you, *Ginny.*"

She flinched as if the words were a blow.

"I'm not Barry Stone. And I am not your father."

Stunned, Gen whirled away. Gripped her arms across her body. Held herself tautly.

"I looked into the story you told me," Starnes said, his voice tight. "I had the sheriff look over the old files, and at my insistence, he had the Forensic Pathologist reexamine the bodies. *For you, Ginny.* Just for you." Starnes' voice was closer now, moving toward her. "But there was no evidence of murder. The bodies matched the story you just heard *and I didn't tell it.* I didn't make anything up and I didn't *placate* you."

Gen could feel the heat of his body at her back. The cold of the room had seeped into her and she trembled, wanting to lean back and let him support her as he had Della only moments before. But she held herself stiffly erect. Isolated. Alone. After a moment, she said, "And the third body? The body in the grave with Mama?"

"Billy Ray Spinella," Della said.

Slowly, Gen turned back to the room. Starnes held his place, only inches from her, until she looked up and met his eyes. She flushed. Suddenly she remembered the old movie, *Love Story,* where the two characters had always said, "Love is never having to say you're sorry."

Gen had seen the show with Starnes, and afterwards he had said, "Bull. Sorry is sorry. Say it if it's due." The statement had been so . . . Starnes. Blunt, straightforward, immutable. His eyes spoke that truth to her now—*Sorry is sorry. Say it if it's due.*

"I'm sorry," she said softly. Starnes inclined his head, then carefully stepped away. Gen had wanted him to take her in his arms. Comfort her. Not hold her accountable.

"Billy Ray come back to town a few weeks after Helena die," Della said. "Get him a room and hide out. Don't know why he come back. Didn't care then or now. He should a known Sheriff Ulmer be looking for him, to charge him for Matthew' death. Gossip be saying that Helena kill her baby, but he knowed it wasn't so. And he knowed John know it. But he come back. Take to drinking hard like his brothers.

"One day, 'bout four o'clock, when John usually be coming by to check on the accounts and have a glass a tea, Billy Ray come by the Big House. I reckon to kill John as he had a knife and a gun on him. But that day, John running late, still out in the field, working."

Della looked back and forth between her girls, grinding her lips together. Some indefinable emotion marked her face, cutting deep grooves beside her mouth. Yet, when she spoke, her tone was steady, measured. "So he decide to get revenge on John bes' way he could. John not here . . . but I was."

The kitchen was silent and icy as a tomb, Della's eyes moving deliberately back and forth between Gen and Lily. Gen thought her heart might break at the expression on the older woman's face. "And Billy come busting in. And he rape me."

Gen's fingers covered her mouth, frigid against her lips.

"John Deveraux come in, in the middle of it. Didn't know it be Billy Ray. Didn't know who it be, but that it a white man and he *hurtin'* me. Pull Billy Ray off a me and beat him till he unconscious. I see his face when he knowed it Billy Ray. Shock. Happy. All sort of emotion cross his face then.

"But he drop Billy Ray in the hall and come back to me. Cover me. Take me to the bathroom and draw me a bath. Put me in it and give me whiskey and tea to drink. Take care of me, while the man who kill his child and take away his wife bleeding on the floor. Took care of *me!* A *colored woman. Hired help.* A *maid.* And when I safe and the doctor be called, *then* he take care of Billy Ray."

Gen looked up and found Starnes' eyes still on her. He took up the narrative, his eyes never wavering from hers. "John Deveraux called Dr. Boulanger to come by and see Della after work. And then he picked up Billy Ray Spinella and hauled him out to his truck, drove him to a shed on the Spinella Place. And beat him to death. Buried him that night beside Helena and Matthew. The next day he poured the foundation where the angels sat to cover it all up.

"But he always knew that he might have left evidence in the grave with Spinella. Evidence that a modern forensic team could possibly pick up—hair, fibers, something that might not decompose, something that might point back to Della. As long as he was alive, he could protect her, should the body ever be found. With him dying, he couldn't provide protection for her. And *that* is why the sheriff is coming tomorrow to take depositions."

Gen walked slowly to Della and took the older woman in her arms. Della stood stiffly for a moment, resisting the touch, the gentle solace. "I'm sorry Della-love. I'm so sorry you ever got hurt. Sorry you had to go through that. No man ever has a right to hurt a woman or a child . . . someone smaller and more helpless than he." Gen bent and rested her forehead on Della's shoulder, inhaling the accustomed scents of bread-dough, herbs, Roses Roses, and baby-powder.

"We were in the house that day when Billy Ray Spinella came by. Weren't we?" Gen whispered, her voice rustling though the silence.

Della grew even stiffer, if that were possible, a marble statue in her arms. Grew still as that same marble. Hard as rock and just as unyielding.

"Four o'clock was midway through our naps. And had Billy Ray known we were upstairs, he might have come after us instead. You took the pain he dished out, to protect us, didn't you? Just like you always did, you stood between us and the world and its dangers. Taking them on your shoulders." Tears fell from Gen's eyes.

"Oh, Della. I never said it before. But . . . thank you for all you suffered raising us. All the Old Man's hellish ways, and all our blindness, and selfishness, and. . . ." Gen's throat closed up on the litany of wrongs. "Thank you, Della-love. Thank you."

Slowly, Della's arms came up around her, enclosing Gen in the familiar embrace. Loving, tender, enduring as the world itself. Gen lay her cheek on Della's shoulder and rested there. For years she had avoided this place, the estate with all its memories—false memories as it now appeared. And the result was that she had lost decades with Della.

Gen understood, finally, as she rested her head against Della's bulk, that the old woman had been the only mother she had ever known. Helena, for all her beauty and vivacity, had been too ill, and perhaps too self-centered by nature, to be a mother to her children. It was to Della they had come with skinned-knees, and flower posies, and fired-clay ashtrays from girls' camp craft sessions. Not Helena. Not even when Helena was alive.

"Colored womens been looking after whitefolk chil'rens for centuries, this part of the world," Della said. "Offering love where no other love be. That old way of living be changing now, falling away. Seem like no one love anyone no more, these days." She sighed again, softly, and Gen felt her reach out, drawing Lily into the embrace. "And I do loves you, chil'ren. Like my own, I do. Like my very own."

"We'll be here for you tomorrow, Della-love," Lily said.

Tired, Della pushed them both away. "I gots to get my feets up. My legs be painin' me somethin' fierce." She speared them both with a blistering glance. "And you both be here tomorrow for the Old Man, too. You got some things to put right. You do all the thinking you want tonight. Tomorrow you be acting. Understand?"

"Yes, ma'am," they murmured in unison.

Lily picked up a rag and tossed it to Destan. "Wash up the table, son. Keri, get the broom and sweep beneath it. Time you two learned how to be Deverauxs. Here in the Big House, we all help out in the kitchen after a meal."

"And you stays out while the cooking being done. This my kitchen. Remember that," Della added sternly. To Lily she said, "That boy of yours say he want to learn how to cook. Keep coming in here getting underfoot. You want him to cook?" she demanded.

Lily looked at her son in surprise. Destan flushed and bent to the table, wiping assiduously. Keri grinned at her brother and poked him with the broom handle. "Des wants to be a chef *and* a veterinarian *and* a horse trainer *and*—"

"Shut up, Keri," Destan growled.

"I think it would be great if you taught him how to cook."

Destan looked up at his mother, startled, mouth half open.

"You do?"

"I do," Lily said. "Della starts her day at five forty-five. I'll make sure you're up then, too." Destan's face fell. "And Keri can hit the barn then and help Olivia out."

"Aw, mom."

"Don't '*aw, mom*' me. Are you finished with the floor? Never mind. Give me that broom. Get to bed, now. Both of you. Should have been in bed an hour ago." Lily took the broom from Keri and made little swishing motions in the air with the business end. "Go on up. And stop in and tell the Old Man goodnight, if he's awake."

"Can we get in a game of chess before we go to bed?" Destan asked eagerly.

"No. Tomorrow. It's late. Go on." She swished them again and they scampered up the stairs and out of sight. From above, Keri shrieked once, the sound tinny. And then there was silence.

"I don't know if they should have heard all of that," Gen said.

"No more secrets," Della stated severely. "Secrets done cause enough harm in this household. Enough pain."

Lily nodded as she finished sweeping beneath the table. "Kids grow up fast today. And Della's right. Deverauxs tend to keep things close to the chest, hidden away in secret, instead of dealing with them. We all do."

The words reminded Gen of the other man upstairs. Barry Stone. And the secrets in their lives. Secrets they had never dealt with. As Della padded ponderously to her room, Gen added the last of the dishes to the dishwasher, poured in soap, set the controls and turned the unit on. Secrets. Dark as the blackwater of a bayou.

◆　◆　◆

Tired beyond mere physical weariness, Starnes climbed from the GMC, slammed the heavy door, and moved up the steps to his house. Moonlight filtered through the trees overhead, throwing shadowy Valenciennes lace across the deck and lawn. Frogs croaked in the bayou shallows, crickets and katydids adding to the raucous chorus. He paused in the darkness. He loved the sound of bayou nights. In the distance some night bird called, the scream echoing down the slow-moving water.

No music boomed or wailed through the house. Serena wasn't home. He pictured her in a bar somewhere, some man's hands under her shirt. And then he remembered her in the white gown, brushing her hair, and he wondered how the fishing went at Bayou *Je Vas Jamais Oublier. I will never forget.* . . . Forget what? What had happened between L'ron and Serena on Bayou *Je Vas Jamais Oublier?*

Unlocking the door, he let Bubba-Boy out for a run and walked through the dark house, dress boots clomping on the hardwood. He retrieved a beer from the fridge, blocking the door wide with a gallon of milk he set on the floor. The milk was curdled, weeks old and never opened. Unused, like the rest of his house. Or mis-used like the wild party.

The kitchen felt lonely, almost desolate in the light from the open door.

In a long swallow, he drained the beer and set the empty on the counter. Pulling off his boots, he tossed them in the corner near Bubba-Boy's bed, pulled his T-shirt off over his head and dropped it on the low baking counter before claiming another beer.

The baking counter and the Italian stone oven had been Sheryl's idea. She had been a chef, running a successful catering business out of New Orleans. When they became engaged, she had remodeled this entire wing of the house, planning to move her business here, close enough to New Orleans to continue running her business until they had kids. Then she planned to be a stay-at-home mom. Full time.

A great planner, Sheryl. But she hadn't understood him, just as he hadn't bothered to understand her. Passion and a love of good food had been the only things they had shared. That engagement had died a slow death with Sheryl calling it quits during one of his big trials.

He had come home one night, exhausted, wanting only to crash and sleep for a month. The house had been empty. It was the next morning before he realized her things were gone. The note centered in the bread-oven he found a week later, by accident. That was the last time he let a woman live with him. He hadn't seen Sheryl in years, but he'd heard she had married and dropped out of sight. Most likely the stay-at-home mom she had always wanted to be.

The Coors in one hand, Starnes carried the milk to the sink, letting the door close behind him, enveloping him in darkness. Milk glugged from the plastic jug, filling the room with a sour stink. Turning on the house air filter, Starnes rinsed and tossed the carton in the recycle bin and opened the second beer. That one, too, he drank all at once before opening the third beer, taking his cordless phone from its base, and carrying both to the screened porch.

Bubba-Boy barked in the distance and he heard a splash as the dog leapt after an animal into the bayou. She'd stink something awful, unless Starnes pulled her into the shower with him and bathed her. Starnes fell onto the swing and pushed off, rocking slowly as the beer rushed through his veins. The oversized swing had been Lindsay's idea. Like him, she had loved sitting on the porch in the evenings, listening to the wildlife or rain falling, her head on his lap.

Lindsay had stopped calling sometime in the last few days. Starnes drank several sips and thought about her. Twenty-something years old, a lawyer fresh out of internship, she had been ready to combine her future with his, practicing law out of his office. Green-eyed. Blonde. Wore her hair like Gin—

Like Ginny. Starnes sat up in the swing, realizing that Lindsay looked a lot like a young *Ginny. Jeez.* His heart-rate accelerated in the darkness, his mouth dry. Blonde. Just like Evie, blonde and blue-eyed. Blonde like Rachael. And Sally. Of them all, only Rachael had brown eyes, or rather, hazel, the exact color of cedar heartwood. He remembered how she stared up at him while making love. She never once closed her eyes. He had loved her eyes. . . . They were so *different.* . . .

Different, because other than Rachael's eyes, each woman was a replica of *Ginny* Deveraux, Miss High and Mighty. . . . He hadn't even realized it before. He'd been blind to the resemblance. Blind to the obvious. . . . He'd told her he had been waiting on her for twenty-nine years. He'd simply not realized just how true that statement was.

He was a fool. Certifiable and demonstrable. A fool. Starnes' laughter cut through the night.

A ragged heat tore through him, inexplicable and undefined.

He broke out into a sour sweat. He could smell himself, rank with beer and something like revulsion.

Tossing off the last of the beer, Starnes ripped off his jeans, socks, and underwear in a single downward sweep. Night air swept his sweat-soaked body, raising a chill. He laughed again, the sound grating. Starnes bounded from screened porch, to lawn, to bayou, slamming into the warm water with an undignified belly-flop. It wasn't smart to swim at night when predators might be hunting, but tonight Starnes didn't care.

Fool. The word and the beer raced through his bloodstream. *Fool.* He swam strongly downstream to the old swimming hole, Bubba-Boy pacing him, barking on the shore, excited at this new game.

The swimming hole was a wide place in the bayou where the neighborhood kids swam in the summer, ignoring the No Trespassing sign, as this was the only place for miles, deep enough to dive. On the bank there was an old oak, seventy-five feet tall if it was an inch, with a rope hung from a branch fifty feet off the ground. Once each spring, a boy, braver or more foolhardy than the rest, would climb the tree and tie off a new rope. In the past, he had been that boy. Now someone else had that privilege and that danger and the accolades of his peers.

Starnes reached the swimming hole and swam its length before executing a swimmer's turn and heading back upstream, pulling against the mild current. He disregarded the pain in his hip brought on by exertion without a proper warm-up. Exercise would do it good. He swam hard, straining at the current, hearing the word with every stroke. *Fool. Fool. Fool.*

He'd always liked blondes. . . . That much he had known. That they had always looked like *Ginny* he hadn't realized. He *was* a fool. He could see Della's face in his memory the two times she had met one of his fiancées, knowing, amused, and a bit sad. Della had seen it clearly from the first. He had never bothered to look. Starnes crawled strongly through the tepid water feeling *things* slide along his body in the dark. Branches. Decaying vegetable matter. Fish. *Fool.*

He remembered the look on John Deveraux's face when the Old Man was introduced to Lindsay as Starnes' future wife and partner. *Recognition.* The Old Man had recognized *Ginny* in

Lindsay's face. The whole world had seen his foibles and understood. . . .

Bubba-Boy, tired of being alone on shore, dove into the water, joining him halfway back and swimming happily at his side, still making little half-barks that sounded more like squeaks of pleasure. The dog could swim almost as fast as he.

Fool. He was a *fool.*

And if he had been a fool about *Ginny*, had been blind to his feelings for her, what else might he have been blind to for his whole life? Instantly he saw Serena, sitting on the kitchen counter, the man's hands beneath her shirt, roaming.

Dragging himself from the water, Starnes trudged back to the house, naked, breathless, hip twinging with warning. The phone was still on the swing, and mindless of the sour water, he sat on the cushion and dialed L'ron. The cop answered on the first ring, sleepy and dry-mouthed.

"Brozzer," he said, instead of hello, "*quoi y'a?* It better be one motha big emergency you to calling me two time a week like this."

"When did you get caller ID?" Starnes asked, his breathing still heavy.

"What you want, bo," he growled.

"Serena still with you?"

Instead of an answer, Starnes could hear bedsprings move and the susurration of sheets and a soft feminine complaint. The almost silent sound of door hinges squeaking. So. Serena *was* still with L'ron.

"She here, bo," the cop said.

Starnes felt the wind pick up. A storm was building in the heated darkness, somewhere close by. "I need to know something." L'ron said nothing. Starnes licked his lips tasting bayou water. "I need to know about that night. The night I was . . . recuperating . . ." he couldn't actually say the words 'out dancing with Della,' "after my accident . . . and Serena had . . . Serena was. . . ." Starnes took a deep breath, fighting sudden terror. "The night of the homecoming game," he finally finished. In the distance, thunder rumbled gently.

"Den you need to talk to Serena, bo. Serena and me both. We be dere in half an hour."

27

HOMECOMING GAMES

"Serena?"

His sister rocked on the swing, one sandaled foot pushing off and swaying forward like a little girl. It was night, black as pitch, and Starnes had lit only a single citronella candle to discourage mosquitoes. The flame flitted in the rising wind, throwing shadows across her chiseled features as thunder rumbled out over the gulf. He had poured Coca-Cola and scooped bowls of vanilla ice cream for them all, and she sat, eating the pale frozen cream with a spoon as she rocked.

To the side sat L'ron, in jeans and black T-shirt, still and silent. He had clearly not told Serena what her brother wanted. The cop watched them in the blackness, bowl of ice cream melting on his knee. A Supremes CD played softly, "Baby Love" seeping around them.

Serena looked at Starnes, questioning. Her dark eyes moved through him like her music, washing every cell of his soul.

"Tell me about the night of the Homecoming Game. When you were attacked."

Her eyes shuttered instantly. She sat back, face hard, her ice cream spoon held like a club, cream dribbling slowly down the stem, pointed at the unmoving fan overhead.

"You tried to tell me once," he said. "I was. . . . I don't know. I was scared. Or something. Or I figured that you shouldn't think about it and then it would just go away. I wanted it to go away." She watched him and he had no idea what she saw. Had no idea how she felt about him, or felt about anything. "Serena? I want to listen. If you want to tell me."

In a voice as hard as her eyes, she asked, "You hear what happen? What dey *say* happen?"

"I heard. The next morning, the morning after the game,

Daddy came to the Deveraux Estate where I was recuperating. I heard what he said. His version of a party and you." *You as entertainment,* He didn't say aloud. "He'd been beaten up pretty badly, was still stinking of liquor. As he talked, I didn't think to question his story. Not then, not later, and I should have. But I want to hear the truth now. From you. If you want to tell me."

"All of it?"

Starnes said slowly. "All of it."

Serena shoveled ice cream, three quick bites, the spoon clinking against the glass dish, emptying it. Silently, he handed her his bowl, put hers on the table, sipped his drink, and waited as she stirred his melting ice cream, eating it in quick little bites.

In a tight voice, she started speaking. "It the Homecoming Game. We had won. Crowned de queen. Juliette Wiggans. I was fifteen, and no one had ask me to de game so I went alone, I did. I was Cajun-trash and skinny as a bean pole. Too tall for de boy my age and not round enough for older boy to date. Course dat didn't stop them from other things later dat night."

Starnes kept his face neutral and sipped again at his Coke. It was cold, though his fingers were even colder. L'ron was a statue to the side. The breeze seemed to whistle around him.

"There was celebration all over, little parties forming in de parking lot, on sidelines, under de bleachers. *Laissez le bon temp rouler, oui?* Dancin' all 'round?" her spoon twirled in the air like a dancer, a drip of melted cream slipping free and whirling to the floor.

Starnes inclined his head. He had seen such parties. Taken part in them when he was in high school and later in college. He even remembered this particular night, trying to dance with Della at a party, a victory *fais-do-do* down on the bayou, testing his repaired hip for the first time, trying to find himself after the months of surgeries and therapy and pain like he had never experienced before, mind numbing, sanity-stealing agony. And the next day, unable to get out of bed, the pain was so extreme.

"So much excitemen'," Serena said. "People dey screaming. Shouting. Drinking stuff from ice-chest all over. Purple Jesus. Ever hear a it?" she again gestured with the spoon.

Starnes nodded, but she went on as if he hadn't, her Cajun accent thickening as she spoke.

"Grain alcohol an grape juice, wid fruit floatin' all in it. Pineapple ring, apple slice, berry all kind. I wander from group to group, leave before anyone notice me and tell me to beat it. Somewhere along de way, someone hand me cup a PJ and I drank it all. Ate de fruit in the bottom. I didn't know."

She shook her head and a long strand of black hair fell forward from the ponytail, over her brow. She set down the bowl and laced her fingers in her lap.

"I didn't know. I drank another glass, mebe two. Found mysel' at dis one group. Boys and girls. Cheerleaders. Football players. Under de bleachers. I drunk as two cats, you unnerstan'? *Chokay.*"

Starnes drank, his mouth dry. Serena handed back his bowl, still nearly full and drank from her glass. Made a face. "Dis the real stuff? I like only Diet Coke."

"We're out. Sorry." The words sounded wooden, stiff. Serena didn't seem to notice. She glanced at L'ron. He nodded once at her as if to encourage her to continue.

"Some dem Cajun, I see dem dere. Cajun boy t'ree or two, I know from class. I join dem, sit on side in de dark. Quiet. Dey gots a fire and plenty beer, plenty Purple Jesus and I drinking dat PJ still." She shook her head again, her eyes dark pools of wonder and pain. Her voice was scratchy suddenly, and she drank the entire glass of Coke. Starnes refilled it.

"De fire it burn down low. I not see de girls leave. I not pay attention. I sittin' wid de boys by den and laughing at dey jokes, singin' dey songs. Cajun songs some of dem. I member 'La Pistache A Tante Nana,' and 'Gabriel's Waltz.' I sing loud wid dem boy. And den somet'ing happen."

Thunder rumbled again. A splash came from the bayou, a slithering splash of a small gator entering the water. Serena's eyes were wide, the whites showing all around. Tears glistened like rainwater over black stones. When she continued, it was a whisper.

"I on my back by de fire and my clothes tore off. An my sing turn to scream. An' de boys . . . de boys take turn wid me. All dem. All but one. Hurt me. Over and over. All night it seem. An' I see dis face. Dis one face. Far off all t'rough it. Cry wid me. He de only one dat not hurt me. He stan' back and he cry wid me. He tears big as mine."

"L'ron," Starnes said softly. To the side, L'ron said nothing, his gaze firmly on Serena, as if he held her up with his stare, sharing his strength. Serena spoke on, tears falling silently, her voice cracked and rough.

"After dey finish wid me, go off laughing, he find my clothes." Serena met L'ron's eyes in the night. "He'p me get dem on. Give me he shirt when mine all tore. Take me to Doc Boulanger. Call de police. Call my *daddy*." Serena looked beyond them both, her eyes filled with the past.

"My daddy come, all drunk he be, but he come. See me laying on de doctor table, blood and dirt and man-stuff all over me. Bruised and tore up bad. De police take him aside, out the doctor office. And when dey all come back in, he nose bleed. He face all beat. And he tell de police to get on out. Can hardly talk, he so beat up and so drunk. Say he not filin' charges on the de heroes a de Homecoming Game. His whore daughter only '*git what she deserve*', he say. Say she '*dirt trash*'. *Slut, whore*, he call me. My 'bein' wid all dem boy *bring him shame*. . . .'" Serena paused as her father's words left her mouth. "He say I ruin now."

Starnes tasted blood where he had bitten his lip as she spoke.

"I had no place to go. No one care for me. . . ." Serena's voice trailed off, shattered and ruined as her body had been that night so long ago. She sobbed softly, her hands clenching the cola glass so tightly Starnes thought she might crack it.

And Starnes. . . . Where had he been that night? At the Estate, living in the little guesthouse. And that particular night he'd taken his cane and, at Della's urging, he had gone out dancing. Partying. Trying to find some part of himself in the aftermath of the accident that killed his wife and child and nearly left him a cripple. Had he not been at the Estate recuperating, he would have been in New Orleans in school. His great opportunity. . . .

Courtesy of Old Man Deveraux, Starnes had abandoned his mother and sister, the women who depended on him, and left for college, then law school. Stayed away for all of Serena's growing up years. Stayed away so long that he forgot, or tried to, just how bad life with Henry Templar could be. He hadn't considered, hadn't conceived, his father's brutish cruelty to Serena when he finally left. He had seized his golden egg, his great opportunity, and taken off, found a new, better life for himself, leaving Serena to deal with . . . *him*. With the fact of a gang rape and no one to lean on. No one to help her.

And the police, the only refuge left for children, for victims of abuse, had beaten up an old drunk and convinced him not to press charges against the BOMCs who had won the game. Back then, more than twenty years ago, a young girl would have had no legal advocate, no rape crisis counselor. She would have had no one. Serena had been alone.

Rage boiled up in Starnes, white hot, a liquid fire, eating him out from the inside. There was no air for breath, no coolness within him, no place to run from Serena's pain as she quietly cried. He could hear himself pant, struggling to breathe past the anger lodged in his throat, in his chest. And Serena's eyes focused on him, watched him, suffering in the cooling air between them.

"Why you din come?" she asked softly. "When you hear, why you din come? Help me."

Starnes groaned so softly it was like the far off thunder rumbling. He had hated his father for so many years, so many decades, that they had all blended together into an immense, vast loathing, like a black, oily sea burning in a fierce storm. Malice and malevolence writhed within him, so intense that there were no words for the level of hatred he felt. And by making Starnes part of the lie about Serena, the old bastard had made him a part of that cruelty.

If his father were in the house right now, Starnes knew he would have gotten up from the porch, found his father, and cut his throat with the fine knife he now owned. The gift left by L'ron and Joubert Boutte. But there was no one to take the brunt of his rage. No one to pound into bloody meat. No one but himself.

Serena tilted her head. If she saw the tears on his face, heard the panting breaths, she didn't comment. "After my daddy say dem t'ings, den he leave. De police leave, too, grinnin' dey was. L'ron take me home to he gran-mere. Ol' woman, she live on de bayou. She take care a me for two, t'ree week. And den I go back home. Back to school. Back to de laughter and de comments and de name what dey call me now. Slut. Whore. Dem boys laughing when dey pass me in de hall. And you never come see me. Never one time."

28

ROSES BENEATH THE GRIME and LIGHTNING

Gen sat on the floor beneath the single tack room light, filthy cloths in each hand. Stabilized between her legs was the saddle she had ridden into the bayou and then left to dry. The old saddle was tough to clean, the leather aged and worn, resisting the soap she worked into the grain. Already her arms ached from the unaccustomed activity of riding hard and soaping hard. Pushing herself, ruining her manicure, breaking yet another nail off into the quick, she cleaned out a layer of grime that had lain in the carved petals of a rose for years. Slowly, the sheen of red and green pigments began to glow.

It had been a beautiful saddle once. A gift from her father on her fifteenth birthday. He had wanted her to ride like a lady, like her mother, English-style, upright and dainty, sitting on a flat hunt seat. She had wanted to ride riotous and wild, Western style, in jeans and T-shirt, barefoot most of the time, coated with sweat and bayou slime.

The saddle had been the Old Man's way of giving in to her stubbornness. Though she had not realized it at the time, and though her father had made them fight for every victory, he had eventually given in to most anything she and Lily had ever wanted. Including her desire to make it alone in New York. He had helped her, but in a way that wouldn't wound her pride. Till now. And now she was wounded all over, all the past scars sliced open and bleeding freshly. Her father wasn't the monster she had thought, and she didn't know how to deal with that knowledge.

Gen swiped at the tears burning her face. She was sunburned. *Sunburned.* Just like a kid too stupid to wear sunscreen. She knew better. But then the grownup Geneva Stone had gone missing. She had been misplaced somewhere in the last week and Gen was afraid she would never find her again. Was afraid she didn't want to. Sniffing at the mucous beneath her nose, she scrubbed into another rose, peeling back layers of filth.

Her boots, shiny with her efforts, sat side by side nearby, the rags she had dirtied balled up by their heels. She had rinsed out the boots when she arrived back at the barn from her ride and hung them upside down to drip-dry during supper. Now, though they would be a little stiff, they would not sour, and the leather was protected with a layer of mink oil.

She had, however, forgotten to rinse out the saddle blanket, and it stank to high heaven. If she had time, she would take all the blankets to a washerette tomorrow and launder them. She wondered if Sivana's Washerette and Beauty Salon was still open. As a teen she had whiled away hours there while horse blankets and warmers tumbled in an industrial-sized machine. Sivana kept the washer in tip-top shape, attracting all the women from miles around, giving them time for a permanent, a dye-job, or a haircut while they waited for the barn things to wash and dry. Now the salon was likely a Wiccan herb shop or a crystal healing store. Even in the deep South the old ways were dying, replaced with even older ways that the young thought were new.

Another nail broke. Blood welled up at the nail-bed. Asa had once kept a bucket of kerosene in a corner just for such accidents. A scratch or abrasion, or a broken nail, was instantly dunked into the bucket to sterilize it. "Better than any old doctor," he used to say. Of course, Della would see the wound at dinner and run to her herb garden. . . . The herb garden. . . . Gen paused, one rag held in the air as the drop of blood swelled and dripped. She really had forgotten all about that garden. No wonder Della was irritated earlier. And Della would take some sage and comfrey and brew up a poultice to pull out any poison. Gen smiled. It always worked. She never had a single infected wound as a child.

There was no kerosene bucket in the corner. Gen sucked at the offending place instead, tasting saddle soap, filth and the salty blood before going back to work.

A final rose grew beneath her ministrations, the last of seven, three on each side and one at the horn. She was almost done. Just a coating of mink oil and she would be finished.

"Geneva?"

She jumped, whirling, her rag-wrapped hands held up in

instinctive defense. The saddle wobbled between her legs.

Barry stood there, grinning at her.

Gen turned her back on him and repositioned the saddle. The mink oil cap was stuck and she wiped her hands on her filthy jeans to try again.

"I don't think I've ever seen you quite so dirty."

"Likely, because I haven't *been* this dirty in twenty-nine years."

"Likely," he said musingly. "I can't say as I've ever heard you use the word 'likely' to start a sentence, either. Very . . . rustic . . . of you."

Gen paused, an unwilling smile on her mouth. "You can take your teasing and stuff it. I dirtied this saddle and I am expected to clean it. Deverauxs clean up after themselves. Besides, I'm almost done."

The words *Deverauxs clean up after themselves,* stood out in her mind as she polished the leather, her back to her husband. Gen wondered if that was what the Old Man was doing about Billy Ray Spinella then and now. Cleaning up after himself. Headstrong old coot.

She scrubbed the mink oil into the tanned hide, buffing as she went, bringing the leather to a high gloss finish. The green leaves and red roses, the carved black-brown bullwhip twining through like ribbon, all glistened. She would have to buff it again in the morning to remove any oil that might work out of the grain. But it was as beautiful now as it had been the day she got it. Better, perhaps, as the leather had matured and the colors ripened with the years.

Finished, Gen stood and lifted the saddle back to its support. The boots she tucked beneath, just as she had when she was a kid. Leaving dirty boots in the barn had become a standard practice to keep "barn stuff" out of the house. Gathering up all the dirtied rags, Gen dumped them in the huge, stained sink, stoppered it, added degreaser soap, and ran water.

Barry still stood behind her, watching. She could feel his eyes on her as she scrubbed the greasy saddle soap and mink oil out of the rags and off her hands. Wringing each rag as it was done, she draped it across the line over the sink and went on to the next. When they were all clean—well, cleaner—she glopped a measure of the degreaser soap into her hands and began to work at the tough stains. Black rings circled each nail. The creases in her palms and across the backs of her hands were outlined in black grime, adding years to them. She rubbed the degreaser into her hands and massaged her skin, paying special attention to her ruined manicure, using the stiff-bristled brush kept on the sink-rim for that purpose. Most of the black came out, leaving her with only one or two nails that looked as if they belonged to a car mechanic.

And still, Barry stood waiting.

She dried her hands and walked barefoot to the door, where Barry stepped aside and let her pass. Leaving the light on, Gen walked to the stableyard and hopped up to sit on top of the fence, toes curled around the lower board. Barry followed, leaned his arms across the top rail, chin nestled on his forearms.

Out in the stableyard, a mare and colt stood, the mare watching the sky, the colt suckling. Hoss was in the stableyard, his size drawing her eye. Several other animals milled nearby, none down on the ground asleep, all scenting rain on the air. Gen whistled and Hoss tossed his head, pawing the earth. She had always liked big horses. Liked sitting up high, able to see the world, and feeling as if it belonged to her, at least while she was riding.

"Now I know why you spent so much time and money in salons when we first met. Getting all the barnyard dirt out of the crevices, and smoothing out the effects of going barefoot."

"You never went barefoot?"

"Good Jewish kid in New York or Copenhagen or Buenos Aires? Child of a diplomat? Never." There was a smile in his voice, the timbre thoughtful, remembering. It sent ripples of pleasure up her spine to hear it. Always had. "I never had a place to go barefoot, except Central Park, on visits to my grandmother. And my mother had strict rules about uncivilized behavior."

"I was uncivilized. My whole growing-up life I was uncivilized. I rode horses like a rodeo rider, swam in predator-infested swimming holes whenever I could get away with it, and hung out with rednecks, Redbones, Cajuns and barn hands."

She glanced at him, slit-eyed. "Even when I took ballet and elocution lessons, and those hateful social graces lessons with Madame Touffont, I was a rebellious, uncivilized kid."

"Madame Touffont. Sounds like a wax museum."

Gen watched clouds scud overhead, concealing the moon. "She looked like an escapee from a wax museum. A poor quality attempt at a wax mannequin, tossed out the back door. Kinda bedraggled looking, with white skin, gray eyes, red lips. She never could get the lipstick on straight, and it wavered up and down. She drank elderberry wine and was always going to the kitchen for a tipple during lessons. Lily and I thought she was a hoot. I don't know what the Old Man paid her, but it had to have been too much."

"I like your father."

Uncomfortable with thoughts of the Old Man, Gen shrugged. He wasn't what she had thought he was, and she had spent so many years hating him, that it was impossible to see him in a new, fresh light. Della expected her to make things right with him. Gen had no idea how she was going to do that, and wasn't certain she even wanted to.

"And I like Starnes."

Gen watched the clouds, silent.

"And I want you to come home, Geneva."

After a long moment Gen sighed, the sound full of longing and unexplored dreams. "I asked you—was it today? yesterday? —how many affairs you had over the years," Gen murmured. "You said 'none'. I gave you a chance to make things—" She stopped, having almost said, *to make things right.* "—to tell me the truth. You didn't. You lied to me, Barry."

Gen could feel him stiffening beside her, his head coming up as she spoke. "Barry Stone, a man as good as his word, at least in business. So trusted that even on Wall Street, his handshake is binding."

Her tone was deliberately mild, almost tranquil as she added, "But in his marriage, he was a liar and a cheat."

"Geneva—"

She smiled tightly, cutting him off with a glance, though her voice was still calm. "You seem to have forgotten Jacey Schwarchkopf." Barry fell silent hearing the name.

"You had an affair with Jacey two years after we married. It lasted almost three months and was over before I knew it had started." An unexpected spark of anger flared in her. Gen swallowed it down, recognizing an old, lost hurt. But here it was, blazing brilliantly, still alive in her. Breathing deeply, she continued. "Jacey came to me and told me all about it. Dates when the two of you were together, gifts you gave her."

"Gen, I—"

"And Mary Elizabeth Muncie, who worked in your office." Clouds from the south blocked out the moon, throwing the barnyard into darkness. The mare snorted and nudged her colt back toward the barn and the lean-to that offered shelter. Thunder boomed far off, a low, rolling sound.

"Today she might have sued you for sexual harassment and won. She lost her job when your affair ended. Lost her apartment." Gen was surprised at the sound of her voice, quavery and hesitant, with a vibrato of bitter, forgotten fury. Her chest was tight with old suffering, each breath a biting pain.

"When I heard about it, I contacted her. Wrote her a stellar recommendation on your private letterhead and sent her to AT&T for an interview. She got the job and now is a vice president. Or was before the last time they scaled down."

Out of her control, let loose at last, the old rage sparkled brightly, a glowing flame she thought had died. How could pain last so many years? Gen considered her anger, the bitterness that roiled just beneath the surface of her soul.

The wind picked up. Barry moved away from her in the darkness, suddenly edgy, like the horses. A storm was heading this way fast, lightning flickering through the cumulonimbus rising over the horizon.

"I'm sorry, Gen," he whispered, the sound almost lost in the quickening breeze. "I never meant to hurt you."

Gen tilted her head back, letting the wind lift the hair off her sweaty neck. Her throat sealed shut on her reply. *Sorry. He was sorry.* . . . Voice low, she said, "I lived with it for years, Barry, because I loved you so desperately. And, after all, you always came back to me. You always came home. And you were discreet, though I could name other names."

The anger glistened within, a diseased flame coiling through her. Gen hadn't conquered the old feelings. The bitterness. The shame. She hadn't even forgiven him, though she thought she had. She had merely hidden her agony away, even from herself.

She found the perception astonishing.

"And then, a few years ago, just after you had that prostate cancer scare, the pattern stopped. You seemed to settle down, to mellow a bit."

She took a breath of stormy air, filling her lungs with lightning-singed mist. Managed a smile, relishing the way the wind whipped at her. It seemed to steal a bit of the choking virulence, leaving immaculate where once had been fetid rage. She took a second breath, her chest expanding now without pain. Again she breathed, and the misery seemed to flow out through her mouth into the coming storm. When she spoke again, the words came easier.

"You were happy to be with me. And I was so very glad that I had waited you out like a good little wife, because I never wanted to be divorced, Barry. Never. And after growing up with the Old Man dominating his way roughshod over my life, I didn't have enough pride to need to salvage it. Not back then." She shook her head.

"But I've had enough, Barry Stone. I'm not going to let you ruin my health. And I'm not going to let you damage my soul ever again. You can have your son. I hope he makes you very happy. I even hope you decide to change your mind and marry his mother. A kid needs a mom."

"I want you back, Gen." The deep voice was tortured, rising as he spoke. *"I—want—you—back!"*

Lightning shot from the sky, blasting a tree on the far side of the bayou. Blinding. Deafening. Seeming to scorch deep into her, as if cauterizing an old wound. Sparks sizzled as the tree across the bayou caught fire, spiraling up in the wind. The horses that had not been let into the pasture for the night raced around the small stableyard, panicked, screaming in fear.

Suddenly, Gen felt a shimmering strength pulse through her. Bright as the lightning. Energy sang in her bloodstream, tingled in her fingers. Tossing back her tangled hair, she laughed into the wind, the sound half challenge, half recognition. She felt alive. More vibrant than she had in years. Gen jumped to the ground.

Sprinting to the barn door, she opened it, allowing the horses all inside, running before them, opening stall doors and securing them back against the barn walls. If lightning hit the barn, the animals would be able to escape back into the stableyard and its relative safety from possible fire. Dancing on her bare feet, protecting them from shod hooves that could crush and maim, she soothed the mama horse, who seemed especially spooked. The colt trotted back and forth beside her, into and out of the stall, adding to the mare's torment. Barry stood in the doorway, lit by successive bursts of lightning. And then the rain hit.

A Louisiana storm is a raging thing, always unexpected, frenzied in its first, sudden assault. Pounding and blustery and often cold, as the rising hot wind creates a downdraft that sucks icy air from the higher atmosphere down to earth. Gen's skin tightened in the sudden chill and she ran for the tack room, bare feet instantly frozen. Shoving Barry into the small room in front of her, she slammed the door, enclosing them in safety from the terrified milling horses, and from the wind and lightning outside.

The electricity was off, the switch not responding when she flipped it up. The room was tightly sealed, stuffy and dry with the door closed. Gen felt around for a flashlight and discovered one on the shelf with the OTC veterinary medicines, in the same place where it had always been kept. The batteries were good, flooding the tack room with light.

He looked ill at ease, and Barry Stone never looked uncertain. Gen laughed, the sound buoyant and only a bit shaken. "Storm," she said, happily.

Giddy, Gen held the light up against her chin, throwing her face into odd angles of shadow. "Want to tell ghost stories?"

"Stop that." He snatched the flashlight from her hand and pointed it at the ceiling. "Did you hear one word I just said? *One word?*"

"Yes. You want me back. Tough. *Now* want to tell ghost stories?"

Barry Stone, as unyielding as his name implied, ran a hand through his hair. The white strands stood upright in the lightning-rich air. Gen braced for a strike very close by, feeling the small hairs on her arms rise in anticipation. She hoped it didn't hit the barn. Barry's eyes went wide, as spooked as the horses.

"I love you Geneva Stone! I want you to be my wife. I want you to come home!"

"I am home!" she shouted back over the storm, startled with

her own vehemence. "I don't want to *be* Mrs. Barry Stone anymore. I want to be Ginny Deveraux for a while." Wind churned beneath the door and swirled around the dusty room, whispering through her hair. "And then I'll decide who I want to be next. But for now, I'm not coming back to you. I don't think I'll ever be coming back to you!"

"Damn it, Geneva!"

"Right, Barry. Damn it to hell and back," she shouted, laughing. "Go back to New York. I'll see you before I leave for the next shoot. We'll do lunch!" she laughed, capricious as the storm.

And then the lightning hit.

Directly overhead. It blasted the sight from her eyes, the sound from her voice. Horses screamed in terror. Barry dropped the flashlight, sending it rolling, wild shadows flickering everywhere. Raw power sizzled through the room, blanking out the light for a moment, leaving them in darkness. Barry swore. Gen laughed again, feeling more alive than she had in years.

The flashlight glowed weakly, and by its feeble illumination, Gen found the latch and let the storm into the room. Barry swore again, scrabbling on the floor for the flashlight. Gen braved the tempest.

The horses were too afraid to stay safely in the barn, yet it was too dangerous to let them loose. The storm was more violent than she had anticipated, lightning flashed again and again, hitting the ground nearby more often than not. Shaking the earth. If she let them lose, they could be struck by lightning or injured when dissipating electricity shot through the wet ground.

The mare was cowering in her stall, the colt still on its feet. Hoss was in the doorway, pawing the ground. The biggest animal, he was also the most dangerous. Leaving her camisole tucked into her jeans, Gen slipped her T-shirt off over her head and climbed the stall door, latched back near her. In a single movement, she jumped onto his back and smacked the T-shirt over his eyes.

The huge horse screamed, rose onto his hind legs, nearly tossing Gen from his back. He pawed the air once, and dropped again to all fours, standing rigid. The shirt over his eyes robbed the animal of vision, rendering him immobile. Gen held the T-shirt in place with one hand, using his mane to pull herself back up his body. She was breathing hard. Barry was still swearing, but was standing at Hoss' side.

"Lead him into a stall" she directed. "Get me a horse-blinder out of the tack room. I think they're in that old trunk under the window."

Barry did as she directed, looping a length of rope around Hoss' neck and leading him into the nearest stall. Locking the door behind himself, he disappeared a moment and reappeared holding two saddle blankets and one black fabric blinder. Gen shoved Hoss' ears through the holes cut especially for the purpose and tied it off under his jaw. Hoss was still standing rigid. Unmoving, stunned with fear and blindness.

Easing her T-shirt out from beneath the blinder, Gen slid from his back and into the barn. Straddling another broad back, she tossed her T-shirt over its eyes. Barry, understanding, raced back for more of the specially cut blindfolds and settled one over the horse's ears, tying it off and helping Gen down.

"You need to be wearing boots!"

"No shit!" she shouted back wildly, only half noticing that for once Barry didn't reprimand her cursing.

Two horses later, Gen went back into the mare's stall. The colt was down, curled beneath his mother's hooves. She didn't know if it was injured or not, but the mare was standing guard, blowing, nostrils flared, eyes rolling in the uncertain light. Between flashes, Gen studied the mare's position over her downed foal.

Taking another chance, Gen rushed the mare in the moments between strikes and tossed her shirt over the mare's head, ensuring her instant paralysis. Barry tied off the blinder and led her from the room while Gen knelt and felt over the downed colt. Something sticky met her fingers, and she knew the young animal was injured, though how badly she couldn't tell.

He put his velvety nose into her hand and blew, scenting her. Sitting in the dark, Gen stroked the wounded colt, murmured soothing words, and prayed for dawn which was surely hours away. Outside, the storm raged on, turbulent, a brutal onslaught. Icy air blew through the barn, chilling, biting into her exposed flesh.

Exhaustion pulled at her like frozen pincers, a numbing paralysis. The energy she had felt only moments before seemed to drain through her pores and settle into the straw at her feet. She drooped over the foal, a trembling in her fingers that spread upward into her soul.

It was over. Her marriage was really over.

"We're not finished with this, Geneva," Barry said in the darkness.

Rage blasted into her and was gone. *Wouldn't he even let her grieve in peace?*

Laughter burbled in her throat, but she knew the sound would be hysterical, out of control. Or dead sounding. She took a breath of the frigid air, forcing down the hysteria, trying to find a spark of life inside, of power. The foal rustled uneasily in the straw. There was nothing left inside her. Nothing. Gen spoke the words that would seal the divorce.

"Sure we are, Barry," she said dully. "Call your lawyer. He should, by now, have a copy of the settlement offer my attorney drew up."

Barry went tense in the flickering gloom, standing stiffly, his arms slightly bent as if ready to fight. She could see the tautness in his legs each time lightning flashed at the stall window. Gen almost smiled at the picture he made.

"What? Did you think I was taking half? New York might say I can have half, my lawyer might say I can have half, but I don't need half of everything, Barry."

Gen could feel him considering, evaluating, a business deal in the works already. Barry Stone had never passed up a good deal in his life.

"What do you want?" His tone was just a bit rough, losing some of its extraordinary flavor in the cautious question. Careful to seem less than eager, yet unable to hide his interest. And by God, caught off guard.

Gen grinned, understanding what her mind had been trying to tell her ever since Barry appeared on her guesthouse doorstep. Her husband's unexpected trip to bayou country came clear. She dipped her head and put her nose next to the colt's, breathing his breath. It was warm, milk-scented. Earthy. Gen wondered how long Barry's attorney had argued in order to get Barry to cancel this week's business appointments and fly south. She shook her head, swallowing down raw bitterness. *Men.*

The colt butted her with his head, demanding her attention. Her fingers resumed their stroking, and she bent her face to him again. Some of her tension eased away in the simple connection, animal to animal, breath to breath.

"I want a generous cash settlement and a monthly allowance for three years." She paused, unmoving, in the heavy gale, wind banging a loose board close by, horses shifting carefully in their sightless state. "I want the building that houses my studio free and clear. I want the beach house in Hilton Head and a permanent three-bedroom apartment in the resort in St. Croix, all insurance payments, assessments, and upkeep to be paid by you or your estate for forty years whether I die in that time or not.

"In return, I'll sign over to you fifty percent of my shares of Stone Enterprises and allow you my proxy votes for ten years on the remaining percentage, with a generous—very generous—buyout agreement should you want to take me over. So to speak," she added with a wry smile in her voice. Surprised that she could still smile.

"With half of my shares in your hands, and power of my voting proxies, you should be able to retain control of the companies. I'll make no claim on any of the African investments at all, and agree to leave my monies where they are currently invested. After the three year allowance is over, I'll begin to draw on the investments at the going rate. That's all I can remember at the moment, but there's nothing substantially different in the papers. I'm not asking for the moon, Barry. And I won't negotiate with you. It's a take-it-or-leave-it proposition."

Her husband was silent, his tension slipping away as he considered. Thunder boomed close by again, but the sound was less intense, less ferocious. The storm was blowing itself out. Rain, once pounding on the metal roof, now spattered down with less violence. The sky lightened as clouds ripped apart and the moon appeared for a moment. The barn was quiet, horses in their stalls standing still, each experiencing its own temporary blindness. The mare was tied in the wide central aisle, close enough to scent her foal. The colt snorted, bumped at Gen's face, and lay his head on her leg, breathing a sigh. Gen stroked his ears and down his nose, the skin softer than the finest suede.

Outside, the rain slashed one final time, ten seconds of

concluding fury, and then an almost silence. Soft sprinkles fell, plops of rainwater draining off roof and trees onto the ground. The quiet was deep after the battering of the wind and crashing of thunder.

Barry sighed. "You really mean to do this."

Gen smiled down at the liquid eyes of the small colt, now revealed in moonlight. He was staring up at her, trusting and adoring. Gen could see the black blood on his foreleg and knew she would need to call Asa or Olivia to bind it and check out the colt for other injuries. He was a beautiful animal, bay and black, with one white foreleg and hoof. Asa would never buy or keep a horse with white hooves, which were softer and more prone to fungus, more likely to split and crack in Louisiana's wet soil than black hooves. No white hooves, not in his barn. Asa would never keep this little beauty.

"Gen?"

"Yes. I mean to divorce you, Barry."

After a long silence he said, "I'll contact my attorney in the morning." His tone was resigned, morose. Gen didn't believe it for an instant. He had his business. His son. And free reign for the first time in years to cat around like a tom on the prowl. Oh God, how trite. How realistic.

"Barry?"

"Yes."

"I'm asking for a *big* allowance for the first three years."

He chuckled, the sound rich as cream in the semidarkness. Bending, he knelt in the straw beside her, bringing his face to within inches of hers. "I wouldn't have it any other way."

29

I'LL TAN YOUR BACKSIDE GOOD

Asa and Olivia drove up to the barn in Asa's battered Jeep, jumping out to inspect the damage and the horses they had left confined in the yard. Finding Gen and Barry in the barn, the horses subdued and the property undamaged set Asa to grumbling. It was a sound Gen remembered from her youth. Asa had always grumbled, mumbling under his breath in a continuous half-internal monologue.

Lighting lanterns Gen had forgotten were kept on hand for electrical outages, they entered each of the stalls and examined each animal, removing the cloth blinders and rewarding the horses with a handful of sweet-feed. Leaving the mare blindfolded in the main passageway, Asa knelt down in the straw beside Gen and felt over the colt. Eyes half-closed, his rough hands moved across the animal in sure, confident strokes. Satisfied that no bones were broken, he urged the colt to its feet, helping it stand. Gen, her knee once again refusing her commands, scuttled into a corner, out of the way.

The sound of small hooves brought the mare in the passageway alert, and she shrilled a warning, dancing even in her blind world. The colt bucked, trying to get to his dame. To prevent further injury, Olivia brought the mare into the stall and the colt nosed his way under her belly to suckle, satisfying both mother and child that all was right with the world. In the uncertain light of lanterns, Gen watched the two together, a small, empty ache in her soul.

Asa sent Olivia for supplies, the muttered order barely distinguishable from his continuous complaints. Leaving the mare blindfolded, he cleaned and wrapped the foal's foreleg, his movements deft and gentle, one arm holding the foal, one working with gauze and stretch bandage. The scent of witch-hazel and menthol were crisp in the damp hay-manure-sweat smells of the barn. Reassuring. Horsey. Familiar. Gen had sat through many nights with Asa in this barn while growing up, following orders or keeping out of the way as Asa directed. They had been teacher and pupil, almost friends; she had been safe with Asa. Tears darted into her eyes, making the lantern light prism and shadows prance.

As if hearing her thoughts, the old man looked up at her, piercing her with stern black-on-black eyes. "You done alright."

Gen closed her eyes a moment and a sound, part-sob-part-laugh, escaped her. Olivia, standing beside the mare, agreed.

The colt wriggled a long-legged gavotte, escaping Asa's arm, reaching higher in his mother's belly for nourishment and comfort. Asa's hands followed the movement, still checking for injury. "I don't pretend to know why you done stay away all them years. But. . . ." He pursed his lips as if the words tasted sour on his tongue. "But I reckon I'm glad you come home afore it's too late. See the Old Man. Make things—whatever was wrong—right."

Gen nodded. *I thought my father killed my mother and brother . . .* but she left the phrase unspoken. This was John Deveraux's friend. The words would have been a depravity to him.

Asa checked his watch, stood, and held out his hand to her. "It's near two-thirty. Go get yourself some sleep," he ordered, just as he had so many years ago. Gen made the same little half-miserable sound and dashed tears from her eyes. She took his hand and felt herself lifted to her feet as easily as when she was a girl. Some things hadn't changed.

Gen stepped slowly, careful of her knee. It held, but there was a crackling deep in the tissue proving that other things had changed drastically. She would pay for this night's work.

Gen and Olivia moved past the mare, taking the lanterns with them, leaving Asa alone with the horses in the dark stall. His big hands gentled the skittish mare, gravely voice murmured words of comfort; she snorted and took a bit of a treat from his hand beneath the cloth blindfold. And slowly, Asa untied and removed the dark fabric.

It was a dicey moment when one removed the blinder from any horse, restoring sight. Twice the risk with a mare protecting her foal. If not properly gentled, she might have kicked out, disabling Asa with a single strike. The mare snorted hard, shook herself, dislodging her foal for a moment. She waggled her head back and forth to show her displeasure, but refrained from baring her teeth or laying back her ears. Asa eased from the stall and latched it.

Too tired to make the trip to the guest cottage, too tired to even think, Gen propped herself against a wall, bare feet in the layers of straw and dust, and watched as Olivia and Asa shook out and folded the cloth blinders and replaced them in the tack room, along with meds and supplies. Shadows fluttered and raced one another as if searching for a way out of the barn. Lantern light turned every common object exotic and mysterious. A striped horse blanket tossed over a fence became bars in a jail, a pail on its side became a dark opening into the netherworld. Gen was so drained she couldn't even smile at her own whimsy.

Barry was still somewhere near. She could feel him, but she didn't turn to look. How strange this all must be to him, she thought. Fierce storms and middle-of-the-night horse rescues. Commonplace events from Gen's childhood.

Asa stood at Hoss' stall door, shook his head and muttered, "How she got this one blinded, I never know, little bitty thing like her."

Barry said softly from the darkness, "She pulled off her T-shirt, climbed a stall door in her bare feet, and jumped on his back. Tossed the shirt over his eyes and held on. Damnedest thing I ever saw her do." There was wonder in his voice, and Gen smiled.

Asa turned in the dim light and found her again, little more than a shadow. "You ever do anything like that again, and I'll tan your backside good. You won't sit for a week, unner'stand?"

Gen shook her head, too worn to speak.

"John Deveraux's girl ain't gone get hurt in my barn, no siree." Peace seemed to settle in her bones as he said the words. Old words, oft spoke, so long ago. "Thought I sent you to bed, girl."

Gen pushed away from the wall. Wobbly as the colt, she scuffled out of the barn and stopped at the main door. Barry was just behind her, his body warm in the cooler air after the storm. His arms came around her, pulling her back against him, an intimate warmth, a simple sense of safety. She leaned into his body and let him support her. They had been together for more than half her life. And she knew this was the last time they would stand so. This was the last loving embrace they would share. For the rest of her life.

Warmth. Horse-smell and man-smell, sweat and Barry's cologne, the moon above, its light blurred by wisps of cloud. The soft hairs of his arms brushing her skin. Rainwater trickling and splatting softly. An image intense and somehow desperate, burning itself into her mind like a brand. Gen breathed deep, saying goodbye to it all. And to a part of herself she had clung to for too long. She turned in his arms and lifted her face. He kissed her lips once, softly. The touch lingering, full of dead dreams and tattered hopes. And he let her go.

Gen moved away from the barn, shivering slightly in just her damp camisole and sweaty jeans. The wet barnyard soil was smooth and rich as syrup beneath her feet, splishing beneath her arches and up between her toes. Lovely feeling. Breezes touched her as softly as Barry's kiss, blowing chill bumps onto her skin. A night bird called far off. Whippoorwill. Gen smiled into the night.

Behind her, the barn lights blazed as power came back on, stealing the magic from the night. In her cottage, Gen showered yet again and crawled naked between damp sheets. She had left the cottage door open when she went to the barn, and the storm had blown in, soaking the old floorboards and the hooked rug, leaving everything within dank and cold to the touch. The power flickered and went out again. In the distance she could hear Asa cursing. Smiling, Gen slept.

◆　◆　◆

Starnes stared at himself in the mirror over his sink. Eyes red-rimmed and beard salted white through the dark mass. He scratched at the stubble, scrutinizing his face. Smile crinkles at the corners of his eyes had grown to caverns. The creases beside his nose had become canyons. "Jeeze," he whispered to himself. He looked old. He looked hung-over. He looked like he hadn't slept. All three true. And the beer, the caffeine, and the fury of the storm were only partly the cause of his sleeplessness. The other was the steady replay of Serena's voice, soft and curiously emotionless, telling him about the night that changed her life forever.

Starnes grunted, the sound rousing Bubba-Boy, who came from the kitchen, nails clicking on the wooden floor. She pushed her nose into him from behind, searching for a morning scratch. Still exploring his face, Starnes obliged her. Satisfied, she curled into the corner and lifted her back leg, searching now for a morning scratch in more personal places.

"Glad you didn't ask me to do that." Bubba ignored him.

It was five-twenty, still dark as pitch out, and he had to be at the Deveraux Estate by eight. He had two-and-half hours to find a way to feel human. Not that he was certain he ever could again. Stepping into the shower, he turned the water to cold, letting the strong spray wash away some of the stiffness left from a sleepless night, too much booze and too much pain. The stinging jets eased the worst of his body's misery. The ache in his soul would take something more.

Ginny.

Resting his head against the tiled wall, he sighed. As insensitive as a man from the stone age, all he could think of in his moment of misery was burying himself in the woman he loved. Finding solace in her body. *Ginny.*

He could admit it now. After last night he could admit anything. He had been waiting for her like a love-sick kid for three decades, his head in the sand like a fool.

And Serena. . . . His father had been rotten, heartless, vicious to the bone. And Starnes had been too busy and too selfish to watch over his baby sister, still living with the drunken sot and the ineffectual woman who birthed two helpless children.

Slamming off the water, Starnes raked a towel into the stall and vigorously dried himself. He thought about shaving, but why bother. Instead he pulled on a clean pair of jeans and a new white T-shirt, boots and his favorite sweat-stained hat. Picking up his briefcase, filling a bottle with tap water, he let Bubba-Boy out for her morning run and headed for the barn.

Sally-J was in her stall, standing half-asleep, hip-shot, big eyes slumberous and lazy. He fed her an apple and a half-can of feed. While she ate, he set her saddle and bridle across the stall door, groomed the mare quickly, checked her feet and saddled her.

Locking Bubba-Boy back in the house, he left the briefcase and a note on the hood of Herman's old truck, did a few stretches to loosen his hip and eased into the saddle. As the sun began to brighten the eastern horizon with a faint, pearl-gray sheen of light, Starnes headed along the bank downstream, the mare's hooves and birdcalls the only sounds.

It didn't occur to him to ask himself why he took Sally-J instead of the truck, which would have been easier. Some things were simply right. Deveraux Estate came into view, barn, outbuildings, grounds with overhanging live oaks dripping Spanish moss. Dark, ancient plantation house, seeming to move in the mist, revenant from another time. Poor boy come a calling.

He let Sally-J into the corral, stripped her of saddle and bridle. Other animals lifted sleepy, curious heads over stall doors. Leaving her alone, Starnes moved into a rising mist.

The door to Gen's cottage was open, six granddaddy-long-legs perched together on the screen door frame, huddled as if for warmth or for a *menage-a-six*. At the thought, fire blazed along Starnes' veins, heated his skin.

Sally-J called from the corral, letting him know she didn't appreciate being left alone with strange horses, insufficient morning food, and no treat after the early ride. He heard something heavy fall, and knew she had nosed her saddle off the whitewashed fence into the mud.

He ignored her. Listened only to the calling of the blood coursing through him.

He had waited all his life for this moment, this woman. In the distance, a whippoorwill issued a last plaintive call. A lonely, echoing plea.

Starnes reached out, touched the cold metal of the screen door handle. Droplets of moisture wet his fingers, cool morning dew that lay over the land. Looking back, he could see his footprints, dark against the silvered grass. Quietly, his boot heels kept off the wooden floor, he opened the door and entered the small cottage. Stopped. *What if Barry Stone was with her?* A wild dread coursed through him, wiping away his passion, replacing it with another need. *Ginny.*

But she was alone in the bed, huddled beneath the sheets and blankets, a small mound in the murky light. *"Ginny?"* he called, his voice softer than the whippoorwill. "Gen, it's Starnes."

She raised her head slowly from the pillows, slow lids blinking heavily in the dim light. Her hair was crushed on one side, wildly curly on the other. Her eyes were slightly bruised, as if she had been crying. She smiled. A pale arm slid from the blankets and lifted to him. An entreaty.

Boots, hat, and clothing seemed to fall from him and he took her hand. Her skin was warm in the cool dawn air. Gently, as if afraid he might wake or she might vanish, he slid between the sheets and gathered her against him. Soft woman-flesh, sleep-warm, compliant. She turned in his arms, wrapping her limbs around his chilled body, warming him, her head on his chest. And she fell asleep again, her breath little puffs against his skin. Stirring the hair curled there. Contented, Starnes closed his eyes, floating on the edge of sleep.

Asa, in the barnyard woke him, mild cursing, horse hooves pounding. Sally-J still voicing her complaints. Outside, the light was soft with late dawn, the air a pale pink, tasting of newness. Between the sheets, he breathed the scent of Gen, warm and moist and female, yet as familiar to him as his own. He believed he could have picked her out of a crowd of women blindfolded, simply by her remembered scent. He kissed her forehead, brushed aside the blonde curls. She smiled and lifted her lips for a kiss. *Did she think he was Barry?*

He kissed her mouth, careful of hurting her with the beard he hadn't shaved, tasted her sleep-touched skin. Wanting her. Oh God, wanting her. But wanting her to see *him*, to know who it was who kissed her lips, coiled a curl of hair around his thumb, slid his fingers along her scalp. Who it was who wanted her with a need like old pain.

She slipped a hand between them, running her fingers through the mat of hair on his chest, smiling softly. Tenderly, he caught her hair and nudged it back from her face, exposing an ear, delicate as a morning-glory bloom. He kissed it gently. "*Ah, me sha. . . . Je t'aime,*" he whispered. "I've always loved you."

Her smile spread and her hand drifted lower, nails against his lower belly. The skin there tightened with a quiver. He dipped his head and tasted the hollow at the base of her throat. Her skin was faintly salty, smelling of lemons and some exotic flower and horse. The same scent he had noticed when she stood in her father's study, crying. Her breath came faster as his hands slid around her hips. Slender, womanly curves, hips arched and rounded.

She kept her eyes closed, her palm moving across his scar, exploring his damaged hip with satiny fingertips. She whispered his name.

Desire flooded him, leaving him throbbing with need. *She knew him. Knew who it was who held her.*

She turned beneath him, guiding him, lifting her hips to fit them together. Her hands on his back, she urged him to hurry, hurry. With a rhythm old as time, he gripped her, and took her.

He watched her face in the growing light, her head thrown back, straining toward pleasure. A little cry of release, and her lashes fluttered. She gave tiny gasps, quick little breaths, and her fingers scraped down his chest, combing through the hair repeatedly as if in wonder.

He altered his rhythm, moving slowly against her. Raising up, he rested on braced arms, watching her, her skin like moonbeams on pearls, her hair a wild tangle. Her eyes still shut tight, breath coming faster.

He held back, moving slower, deeper, almost languidly, unmindful of the pain of his own desire. Body aching with withheld release, he gathered up a lifetime of waiting into this one moment, this one instant of need.

Her head arched back and she called his name. Shouting, he thrust deep, seeking his own release, as if he gave her his whole life, gave her everything he had, everything he was. Her eyes opened, gray as storm clouds.

"*Ginny,*" he whispered. He settled against her, gathering her into his arms. Enfolding her, warm and yielding. He was quivering and weak, his mind and vision blurred, overcome with the scent and sound, taste and feel of her. "Oh *Ginny,*" he whispered. "*Mon dieu.*"

He felt her lips curve into a smile against his shoulder. And suddenly she was asleep. Starnes laughed softly, settled her in his arms, and breathed her in. All of her. After so many years.

♦   ♦   ♦

Later, the light bright through the windows, he slipped from her and padded softly to the bathroom where he showered quickly and dressed, used her comb to neaten his hair. Holding his boots, he stepped away from the cottage, pausing in the damp grass to pull them on. The sheriff's car was already parked out front of the big house. He was late. And he didn't care.

Herman had brought his truck and his briefcase as Starnes had asked in his note, leaving a note of his own, laboriously printed, on the dash. Succinct and to the point.

I AINT YOU HOUSEBOY.

Grouchy old Frenchman. Starnes lifted his briefcase out of the truck and crumpled the note in his pocket. A glance told him that Sally-J and the saddle she had tipped into the mud were gone. Herman had ridden her back to the Templar Place.

The kitchen was empty and Starnes clomped up the stairs, his boots announcing his arrival. Mary Anne grinned at him, commiserating, as she ducked out of the sickroom. "The Old Man's got your name in his teeth. Been tearing it to shreds."

"Thanks for the warning," Starnes said, doffing his hat. Mary Anne blushed and disappeared into the nurse's room across the hall. Starnes pushed open John Deveraux's door.

"Asa tells me your horse was in the corral at dawn," the Old Man said the moment he entered. "And you look like shit."

Starnes grinned at the complaint and ignored the insult. "Sheriff, Mrs. Arceneaux, Deputy Stubbard. Sorry I'm late." He kissed Della on the cheek. "Morning, beautiful."

Della fired a canny look at him. "Beautiful? What you been up to Starnes-Boy?"

"Asa says you were in my daughter's cottage. That so?"

Della let out a whoop. "About time, and praise the Lord." She clapped her hands in delight.

Starnes lifted a brow, amused rather than embarrassed, his eyes on the occupant of the sickbed. "And if I was?"

Deveraux's brows met above his nose. His color darkened. "Some might say that's unethical behavior for a lawyer." He fought for breath, each one a little victory. His color returned to its usual shade of gray. "Sleeping with the daughter of a client."

"I'll be glad for you to find another attorney, Mr. Deveraux," Starnes said, dropping his briefcase on a table and taking a seat. "But frankly, I think you'll be dead and buried before you find one."

The Old Man barked with laughter, discarding his anger as quickly as he manufactured it. "I like her husband." he gasped, "but I like you better. Now, let's get this legal crap out of the way so I can die in peace."

◆　◆　◆

Eyes closed against the light, Gen rolled over in the soft bed, lifted her leg to scratch an insect bite on her calf. The smell of summer-damp and woman-warmth and man filled her nostrils and her eyes slitted open. Hands sliding out to either side, she touched cool sheets. He was gone, leaving only his scent on her body, and she breathed deeply detecting a whiff of horse and man-musk and bayou. In a way that spoke of childhood and security and contentment, she knew that she was home.

Smiling, Gen curled deeper into the mattress. Her left knee aching and tender, her shoulder muscles complaining, burning from the rodeo heroics of the night before, her back stiff from the morning's sleepy acrobatics. All-in-all, she felt pretty wonderful.

◆　◆　◆

Starnes listened to the stories again, this time with audio recording equipment, Mrs. Arceneaux with her dictating machine, and Deputy Stubbard with the parish's video camera recording every spoken nuance, every facial expression. A deposition in triplicate, the duplication needed because one of the group would soon be dead.

Feeling as though he were a spectator from a different dimension, observing through a thick glass or through some kind of quantum fog, Starnes sat though most of the repetitions only half aware, only half-listening. A sad tale, seen through the eyes of a different generation, a divided generation, where the whites perpetrated racism and violence, and blacks suffered in enforced silence.

Had the rape of Della and the death of Billy Ray Spinella taken place today, the Old Man might have been charged with manslaughter—or might not—and he might have gotten off entirely, if his lawyer were good enough, or his jury bad enough, or the evidence of self defense strong enough. Had the story come to light back in the sixties, Della could have been charged in the death of Billy Ray. Accessory or something. And if convicted, she would have done time at the very least. Now, it was all just sad. And the beginning of a media circus.

Near ten o'clock Mary Anne tapped on the door and let herself in, bringing in medication for the Old Man. Sheriff Pritchard stood quickly at her interruption, hands out to his sides as if directing traffic. "You can't come in now, miss. Sorry."

Mary Anne smiled sweetly at him and said, "Sorry yourself, bubba. I got medication for my patient, and unless you intend to take all medical responsibility for Mr. Deveraux, you'll let me give it to him." Without waiting for permission she sashayed past the astonished law officer and propped the medicine tray on the bedside table, her rounded bottom pointed at the door.

Beside her, the Old Man grinned and rolled over slightly, exposing his left hip and most of his butt toward the sheriff for the shot of pain medication she deftly administered. It was all Starnes could do to keep from laughing out loud when Pritchard turned quickly aside. No way did Starnes think the mooning was accidental. In fact, the patient's movements were so smooth he assumed the little scene was well planned.

"Mr. Deveraux, you was right, honey," the pert blonde said as she withdrew the needle from her patient's rump. " 'Bout them reporters?" She inspected the needle along its two-inch length and added casually, "We got us a couple vans outside already. I reckon I owe you that ten spot."

"Reporters? Well crap," Pritchard said brusquely and left the room.

Sliding his backside out of sight, John grunted, grinned, and said "We'll just say it's paid in full. I think it was worth every dime." Mary Anne tittered and Starnes was even more certain that the display of buttocks was intentional. Crazy old bastard.

Shaking his head, Starnes followed the sheriff out of the sickroom and across the hall. Standing in Gen's old bedroom, he peered out the window over Pritchard's shoulder to the right. In the yard were two news vans, a local station from New Orleans, and an MSNBC van.

"A leak somewhere in the sheriff's office?" Starnes asked with a calm he didn't feel. "That's surely the only explanation."

Pritchard was livid, the back of his neck shading into scarlet. He cursed under his breath, "Crap in a bucket. This'll be a media frenzy before the night is over." The sheriff's voice was gruff, but as he turned, Starnes caught a certain glint in his eyes. Calculating.

Though it was possible that Pritchard might not have planned a news conference for later today, though it was possible that the man might not have engineered the leak himself, Starnes could tell he was contemplating pithy sound bites, ready to turn this situation to his advantage any way he could. Starnes hated politicians. Every last corrupt one of them.

Starnes had known the news of the Old Man's confession would get out. It was too juicy. He had known it would create a stir, and that reporters would be looking for the story-behind-the-story, the real dirt. And because there was plenty to go around, Starnes had known it would be big, at least regionally. But he had hoped to have the Old Man in the grave before the story broke, and Gen on a plane to New York, and Della stashed away somewhere for her privacy. Now. . . . Barry Stone and his estranged wife were still in the house. Even the tabloids would be camped out on the lawn when they discovered that little tidbit. He could see the headlines. . . .

MURDER INVOLVING BILLIONAIRE or DIVORCE, MURDER with a subtitle reading COVER-UP PLOT? or LADY-KILLER, MURDER COVER-UP subtitled STONE AND DEVERAUX, MAID RAPED

All they would need to make it really sensational was the low-down on Barry Stone's illegitimate child, perhaps with a sidebar story on the kid's mother, and a second sidebar on Gen's attempts to have a child. Wouldn't that be just freaking dandy.

Starnes shook his head and followed the parish's foremost elected law officer back to the sickroom. Upon entering, he once again felt lethargic and attributed his mental fog to the burbling sound of oxygen and the stench of the dying man. He yawned, but it didn't help. He needed caffeine and lots of it.

Struggling to remain alert, Starnes sat forward on his side-chair, balancing some of his weight on his booted feet. Now if he started to drift off, he'd wake up when his center of gravity shifted. He hadn't been seated for more than five minutes of sworn testimony before Sheriff Pritchard asked the question Starnes had been waiting for.

"Now. Would you kindly tell about those blood stains you painted over, Mrs. LaPointe?"

"Don't answer that, Della," Starnes said quickly. Della's eyes narrowed at the officer.

"The blood stains left from when Mr. Deveraux beat Billy Ray Spinella unconscious after the alleged sexual attack?" the sheriff added.

The old woman smiled, her full lips widening, but the look she shot Pritchard was anything but congenial. "I'll allow as I painted over some brown stains in my own kitchen," she cocked her head, dark eyes crushing down on the sheriff, "several months after Billy Ray attacked me. No *alleged* 'bout it, less you calling me a liar. And I'll agree that them stains could have been A1, or gravy, or I reckon, just maybe, old blood . . . now that you mention it, Sheriff."

"And if the county was to bring a subpoena and have the paint scrapped off the section of wall where the alleged A1 Sauce splattered, what do you think we might find, Mrs. LaPointe?" Pritchard grinned, showing all his teeth.

Starnes tensed. He had discussed the possibility of this question with Della and suggested that it might be wise if she forgot the exact location of the section of wall she had painted over. Della had all but boxed his ears at the suggestion that she not tell the truth, but she had promised to think on it. Starnes had no idea if she had come up with a suitable response.

Della's eyes narrowed further at Pritchard and her lips made a soft moue as if she had tasted something foul. "Don't rightly 'member which section a wall that be, Sheriff. But I reckon you would find about forty years a paint, the remains a cleaning supplies, spackling where the Old Man had half the kitchen's walls repaired after my youngest girl's kitten finished sharpening her claws on it and such. That was back some twenty-two years ago," she said in an aside to Mrs. Arcenaux.

"I done forgot all about that till Bathsheba done remind me.

That kitty could a made a saint cuss. Clawed up that Sheetrock something fierce. Left the drapes alone, and the carpeting, but had herself a time on the wall above her food bowl. Made a terrible mess. Thought the Old Man was gone take her out and shoot her dead, but he had himself a soft spot for my little girl. Bathsheba a charmer, she was. Still is. And she did love her kitty-cat, claws and all.

"But I reckon you could look, Sheriff," Della smiled. "Wouldn't waste nothing but your time. And I wouldn't fuss 'bout it lessen you forgot to put all my walls back like they was before you started tearing into them. Yet and still, it do seem a shame to waste the parish's money on such."

Pritchard sat back, weighing the cost of such a search, the added expense of DNA match-up to the bones found in the grave with the Deverauxs, just in case the splatters were indeed blood, and the final possible use of the evidence in any future trial. Starnes had already calculated the pros and cons of a search and determined that Pritchard wouldn't bother. However, Jim Pritchard was unpredictable, and finding Billy Ray's blood on the wall would not look good for Della. When the sheriff went on with his questions, Starnes was relieved.

Della, wily as a whip, had answered just as he wanted her to. Smart woman, picking her way through legal landmines. But perhaps having to live powerless in a white-ruled world had taught her how to step carefully when the law was about. She and other peaceful folk had been forced to develop such survival skills. Learn, or do time, or die at the end of a lynch rope, the mantra for black people living in the sixties and earlier. And it wasn't much better today.

Shortly thereafter, the sheriff began to go over old ground again, repeating previously asked questions as if to trip up an unwary victim. But Starnes had little concern about Della's answers. She could outwit the sheriff with one arm tied behind her back. And the look she gave the helpless man when he persisted about the blood stains could have curdled milk. Starnes hoped that Stubbard had focused in real tight on the scene with the parish's video camera.

His hip began to ache slightly as the questions wore on, and Starnes wondered what Gen was doing about the news vans.

What Barry Stone was doing. He had a mental image of the big man curled in the trunk of a car escaping the property and the newshounds for New York and the security guards he undoubtedly had on retainer. It was a good image, the famous blue eyes squinched shut, knees curled up to his chin, arms wrapped around them. Bouncing over a rutted road. Really nice image, and Starnes smiled, changing his expression from one of amusement to one of encouragement as Della caught his eyes. Not that she was fooled. Not Della. She just lifted a brow and pursed her lips, a knowing look, sarcastic as hell. If he'd been wearing his hat, Starnes would have tipped it to her. What a woman.

They finally broke for lunch, which Della refused to fix. As she lumbered down the stairs to her private domain she called back up to the hopeful sheriff. "I is in court today, Sheriff Pritchard, in case you ain't noticed, and you can use the parish's money and order take-out for me just like you do for the white folk. Or you can go hungry. Take you own pick," she said.

The Old Man grinned into his fist at her words, and Starnes forced his own lips down. Too hungry to argue, Pritchard pulled out his cell phone and grudgingly ordered Chinese. He even sent Deputy Stubbard to pick it up. But it was clear that Pritchard considered it a real shame having missed out on a meal prepared by one of the parish's finest cooks.

Leaving the legal team, Starnes made a pit stop at the nurse's room for aspirin before heading downstairs to make a phone call from the Old Man's office. Walking out of the sickroom was like waking up from a dull dream. He had been sleepwalking for hours. The Old Man himself seemed none-the-worse for wear, his color no brighter and no grayer than usual. Perhaps he was enjoying his moment in the spotlight. But Starnes had plans to make and problems to see to—namely the news vans out front.

Slipping down the stairs he kissed Della on the cheek, led her in a quick succession of dance turns, twirling her around the kitchen floor, and moved on through the house. As he two-stepped down the hallway to the Old Man's office, he could hear her chuckling. "A charmer you is, Starnes-boy. A pure-T-charmer."

Throwing himself across the Old Man's leather couch, Starnes grabbed the old-time rotary phone and dialed from memory. As the phone rang in his ear, he remembered *Ginny* as he left her, her hair tousled on the pillow. He was smiling as the phone was picked up on the other end.

" 'Lo."

"Herman. I need a favor."

"You done use up all you favor today. *Saloprie!* What you t'ink I is bo? *C'est trop!* You want a yard boy—"

"It'll give you a chance to tote your shotgun in the face of reporters, and, most likely, get on the six o'clock news today."

The silence was telling.

"What it is I got to do?" The words were cautious, unwilling to be lured into anything that might be trouble he didn't want. As opposed to trouble he might want.

"Old Man Deveraux is giving a deposition today about an old murder. The media got hold of it somehow and they're parked out front, blocking the driveway, making a nuisance of themselves, ready to pounce on anyone unlucky enough to ride past. The Old Man will spring for protection."

"I ge't shoot any of 'em what come close to de house?"

"No. But you get to shout dirty words at them and fire into the air if they try to come to the door."

"Goo' enough. You want I should bring my old truck or come tru de bayou on Sally-J? Be a surprise, me coming from back de house."

"Sally-J sounds good. Oh, and Herman, if you haven't shaved today, don't."

Herman chuckled and Starnes could hear him scratching his briar-patch-of-a-beard. "I no even shower," he said as he hung up.

Starnes envisioned Herman, aromatic with last night's beer, garlic, and onion, beard scraggly and shirt untucked from his bib overalls, hair sticking wildly from the brim of his old hat above and boots unlaced and gaping open below, Herman should make a menacing enough figure to keep the news lice off the property. In less than half an hour the approach to the estate would be cleared and things would be back to normal. If Barry Stone wanted to leave then, he could. And good riddance.

30

BUTTING OUT

While Della and the assorted law officers ate at the long table in the kitchen, Gen slipped up the front stairs, the company stairs that were never used, yet had been kept waxed and shined as if Helena Deveraux still hosted parties every month. The long, hallway was subtly lit by sunlight from bedroom windows, striping the exotic carpet in bands of light and dark. Though he may not have entertained in over thirty years, the Old Man kept the place ornately decorated. Elegant.

Out of pride in the Deveraux heritage? Or in memory of Helena?

Tears pricked at her eyes. There was so much she didn't know. Gen paused, feet stilled on the thick carpeting. The guestrooms were further down the hall, and Barry's door was closed, the room beyond silent. She hadn't seen him since the storm. Since Starnes. . . . Her breath caught. Tears fought for control and for a moment won. Starnes. So much she didn't know.

Gen walked down the hallway to the Old Man's room. Turned the knob. Opened the door. Inside, the hiss of oxygen and the hum of a machine were the only sounds. Equipment, monitors, and a blood pressure cuff were stacked at the head of the bed, shades of blue, green, beige, and purple in jumbled disharmony.

Alone, except for the cat, the Old Man snored, his blowsy nurse occupied elsewhere. He looked old, lying on the bed, propped nearly upright by the pillows. Skin was a dusky gray, bagged around his jowls and wattled at his neck. The lime-green oxygen tubing pulled tightly around loose skin to the back of his head to the huge oxygen canister. His dark eyes were closed, his breathing stertorous. Gen closed the door and studied her father until Princess took exception to her presence and stood, walking up the Old Man's body and butting him in the nose.

Gen was smiling when he opened his eyes. "Good watch-cat," she said.

The Old Man grunted and pushed Princess to his lap, his eyes never wavering from her to the cat. There was no challenge there, no demanding glare, no anger, just an expectant curiosity, as if he actually wondered what she might have to say.

Slowly, Gen crossed the room, passed the foot of the bed to the window alcove, and sat in the armchair. It was low and deeply cushioned, just as when her mother was alive. The cold was brutal, chilling her skin into goose-flesh, purpling her fingertips. "I came to say I'm sorry."

The Old Man tilted his head. "You always were the brave one."

Gen almost snorted at the description.

"Brave," her father insisted, breath shallow, chest muscles shoving his ribs up and down with effort, struggling to fill his lungs with air. The effort was distinctly ineffective; he was drowning. Over the hiss of the oxygen, Gen could hear his lungs gurgle. "Went off to New-Damned-York City. Didn't even take the Templar kid. Could have. He told me, years later."

He looked at the glass of ice-water beside the bed and Gen lifted it, turning the straw to his lips. They were cracked from the hours of testimony, and had been smeared with something clear and gummy that stuck to the straw when he was finished.

"Get the afghan," he said, his voice stronger. It was an order, and, just as when she was a child, Gen obeyed instantly, wrapping the length of crochet around her. "You're cold," he added as an afterthought, and Gen realized that he was actually explaining one of his orders.

The soft yarn felt marvelous, and tears pricked again, her recent and tenacious enemy. If she gave in to them, would he call her a crybaby, as he so often had when she was a kid? "How did this conversation turn from my apology to you complimenting me?"

"I'm dying," he said gruffly. "Got things to say to you. I'm older, meaner, and bigger than you. I own this damned house, at least for a few more days," he glared. "I control everything and everyone in it, in case you forgot. So I go first. And if I say you're brave, then by-God, you are."

GWEN HUNTER

Gen laughed, the sound brittle, ratcheting. The Old Man was still ornery and querulous as ever, not that she had expected any different. "Yes, sir." Even she could hear the animosity in her tone, and her father grinned, showing teeth, recognizing the sound from her adolescent rebellion. There was a time when he would have swatted her for it. Now he just showed her his teeth, and she waited for him to say, *I'm amused, but not stupid. Tread carefully in my presence, little girl.* But instead of the old rejoinder, he went on.

"You went off to New York without a by-your-leave. Took me nine months to find you, and you half starving. Or would have if you hadn't hooked up with Stone. Knew you wouldn't take money from me." There was hint of pride in his tone and then it vanished. "Stubborn, too. Just like a *Deveraux*," he prodded, reminding her who she was, who he was. "So I made sure you were taken care of. I made a few phone calls. Artsy people your mother knew. Set up that showing in the gallery. Bought the pictures you took." Coughing interrupted his goading.

The confirmation, the boast, if that was what it was, made it all real, the fact that her initial success wasn't her own. She had gloried in her youthful achievements. Prided herself in her freedom from the Old Man's influence and financial backing. The Old Man's blood-money. Gen looked away, her hands crushing soft yarn.

"Pisses you off doesn't it?" he asked, his teeth showing a trace of bloody mucous that he licked away.

Gen swallowed down a reply. Even now, it was hard to be rude to him, impossible to be honest, to take over the conversation and tell him what she had come to say and then get out. She was facing fifty and still couldn't cuss out her old man. Old habits died a hard death, especially when they had been ingrained by liberal use of *whuppings* with a belt. Besides. What could she say? He was right. It *did* make her angry. And he *had* helped her all those years ago.

"You can hardly stand it that you ran away from home to get away from me, and yet . . ." more teeth, now with gums, "yet—I—made—you," he said distinctly.

Suddenly Gen laughed, a real laugh this time, strong and sharp, staccato, like bullets ricocheting off plate steel. Then she lifted an eyebrow, raised her chin, drawing on every bit of hauteur schooled in her by years with Barry Stone. "You got a good deal, Old Man. You should consider yourself lucky to have made such a fine investment. Those photographs are worth a fortune now. Do I get them when you croak?"

Her father barked with laughter, the sound of the laugh so much like hers that it startled them both. "That's the spirit, girl," he managed, eyes twinkling, before the coughing took him. A long strangling moment of convulsive contortions.

And Gen realized that her father had been proving his claim that he controlled everyone and everything on the Estate. Bullying her into the show of spirit. Wanting her to resist him. Wanting her to fight back. Cruel brute. Mean as the devil himself.

Brave, he had called her. Brave. And he had been proud of it. She watched him fight the disease that wanted him dead. Watched him fight just to take one more breath.

The coughing stopped, his breathing fainter, his chest working harder. As his color deepened, growing dark gray, his mouth opened and closed spasmodically. And something deep in his eyes changed as he struggled, twisted like a snake coiling back on itself. Something like astonishment and fury braided through with fear.

Gen waited, offering nothing, not hovering, not fluttering around. He would have hated that. If he wanted her help, he would ask for it. Finally he coughed one last horrific time, the sound vicious, seeming to tear something deep inside. His eyes closed at the fierce pain so she wouldn't see his suffering. Then, he seemed to catch his breath, enough to speak. Or perhaps he just decided to speak, breath or no. John Deveraux had never stopped for anything in his life, and she didn't expect for him to stop now until he was good and ready.

"Brave. Stubborn. Artsy like your mother. And you look like her. Been a credit to this family." Nodding his head emphatically he said, "I'm proud of you." The words came clearly and cleanly. No cutting tone, no mockery. Simply a statement of fact. A statement of pride.

And they shocked her to her core. The tears she had managed to control spilled over and shot down her cheeks like scalding oil.

"Stop it, girl."

Gen laughed again, softly this time, and wiped her face on the afghan.

"Hate a woman who cries."

"Breaks your heart, doesn't it?" she countered, her tone as demanding as his. Goading. Because it was what he wanted. She understood that now, for the first time. What John Deveraux wanted from his daughters was strength. Power. Spirit.

He grinned at her. "Now that you mention it. Yes."

"So now can I say I'm sorry?"

"Sure. Go ahead. Knock yourself out."

"I'm sorry I thought all these years that you killed Mama and Matthew."

He closed his eyes against the pain and she looked away. He would have hated that she saw. Saw the pain, the grief. As fresh as if his wife had just died. "Loved that woman," he whispered. "Never . . . never hurt her. Loved my son. Nearly killed me when they died."

Her tears fell harder, hot on her icy skin. "I thought. . . . Lily and I. . . . We both thought—"

"And I didn't have the courage to talk to you about it," he said.

Gen's eyes flew open, staring at the Old Man through a watery veil. *He had called her brave. . . .*

"Never had the guts to even say her name most days. Let you girls down. Weak."

"I—"

"Weak!" he insisted. "These days even a lily-livered CPA has the guts to talk to his kids. They call it sensitivity. Call it being in touch with your feminine side," John Deveraux mocked. "Call it whatever they want, I could never do it. I messed up with you girls, but you survived. And I'm proud of it." He lifted his head. Glared at her, black Deveraux eyes shooting sparks. "And you be proud of it, too. Hear me? Be proud of who you are. What you did with your life. What you'll do in the future." His breathing sped up, his chest working like a broken bellows.

"Hell, I lived a good life. Lived it the way I wanted, did what I wanted, took what I wanted, and somehow, by the grace of God, raised two strong, beautiful, brave daughters," he said resolutely.

"I may have screwed up royally in a lot of ways, but I must have done something right, too," he grated out. "Look at you!

You're a Deveraux through and through."

Gen laughed past the tears. "So does that mean you accept my apology?"

The Old Man laughed again, the sound so like her own. "Stubborn woman."

"Yeah," she said.

"Forgiven."

"Good. Then I forgive you for being a mean-old son-of-a-bitch for my entire life, cruel, hard-handed, and hard-hearted. So now are you gonna die? It always ends like that in the movies."

Before the Old Man could respond, Gen heard the sound of feet thudding on the stairs, the sheriff and the court people coming back from lunch. "I'll be back this evening," she said, and opened the door. Princess ran before her, tail twitching, agitated. Together, before Gen could be caught with a tear-streaked face, they slipped down the front stairs. But she saw Mary Anne peeking through the crack in the nurses' room door, her eyes huge and her mouth shut for once.

Gen wondered how the nursing staff knew when the Old Man was having problems. When he wanted them. He didn't have the breath to bellow as he had when she was a kid. Gen abruptly recalled a little beige box sitting beside the coil of green oxygen tubing at the head of the bed, one of the jumble of little boxes and rolls and equipment monitors. A baby monitor. She rounded the bottom of the stairs and paused. Mary Anne had heard the entire conversation. The Old Man had intended for her to hear, for some obscure reason. A witness to what? Her bitchiness? Her tears? His foul mouth?

His pride in her?

Or maybe he simply forgot it was on, got caught up in the moment, and never thought of the nurse listening to every word. But that would suppose he was getting old, was losing it in some way. Gen remembered the look in her father's eyes, fierce, determined, proud. She pushed on through the dining room and into the empty kitchen. She would never understand the Old Man. Never.

The kitchen smelled of Chinese spices and grease, and stacks of white paper boxes were piled beside the sink. Gen opened the fridge and pulled out the remaining three boxes, opened and tasted. Boiled rice, MuShu pork, and shrimp with lobster sauce. Odd combination, but it should heat up well enough. She found a plate and was filling it with mixed Chinese-American staples when Lily swayed down the family stairs.

She hadn't seen her sister for more than a few minutes each day, and Lily looked wan, her eye-makeup sleep-smudged. Her perfect chignon was slightly crushed on one side and a long crease marred her flawless left cheek. "Have a good nap?" Gen asked.

"Um. Got enough for me? I'm starved."

Gen pulled another stoneware plate from the cupboard and heated the rest of the Chinese while Lily poured tea and found stainless. They would find no "heathern chopsticks" in Della's kitchen, they both knew without even looking.

Silently, they ate, forks clicking. Someone had closed the air-conditioning vents to the kitchen and after the meal with the crowd and their accumulated body heat, the air was slightly warmer than a walk-in freezer. In Alaska, it might have been considered almost pleasant.

Mid-bite, Lily looked up and grinned. It wasn't the polished smile of the grown-up Lily, but the carefree, mischievous smile of the girl-Lily. Gen interpreted the smile instantly. It felt good, it felt right, for them to be together in the kitchen alone like this. It had been years.

She toasted with her glass and drank the tea. It was sweet. Della's sweet tea. Holding up the glass, she questioned as she chewed.

Lily shrugged. "Italians," she said through a mouth of pork and rice.

Gen grinned. *When in Rome. . . .*

"Want to talk?" Lily asked later, when, still silent, they had cleaned up the kitchen and washed the dishes that wouldn't fit in the dishwasher. "We could go to the guesthouse. You got a cat-with-the-cream-look written all over you. And I want to know who."

At Gen's blank look she said, "Barry or Starnes?"

◆　　◆　　◆

Starnes sat through the final hour of interrogations in intense misery. His hip was strumming with pain like a Spanish guitar in the hands of a master. Several times he was forced to stand and work his leg, moving through the physical therapy routine while the Q&A faltered around him. Pritchard rolled his eyes, the Old Man ignored him, and Della silently watched, knowing the level of his misery and the near-shame he experienced anytime he was forced to expose his suffering to the world. Just before the pain reached its zenith, the session was over and he was able to leave. Not even bothering with a professional leave-taking, he limped from the room, down the stairs, and outside to the single-dose packet of Demerol he kept locked in his truck for emergencies. The pain medication would leave him woozy and light-headed, but now that the deposition was over, that wouldn't matter. In fact, being a bit light-headed might help with the rest of his day.

As the medication went down dry, Serena-style, he lifted a hand to Herman and drove past the news vans that were parked along the road and down the street from the Deveraux Estate, taking back roads to the Templar Place. And his sister. He stopped at Izaguirre's Grocerette and Sundries for kitchen supplies and dinner, and by the time he cut the engine in the driveway the pain was easing, the glare of the setting sun was achieving an artificial luster brought on by medication. But his day from hell was nowhere near being over.

The house windows and the truck cab reverberated with the sound of Jimmy Hendrix blasting from Serena's speakers. She was home. Engine ticking, heat seeping into the cab, he dropped his head back and rested. Thank all that was holy for Demerol.

The deposition had gone much as he expected, no surprises, no glitches, and he was comfortably certain that no future legal charges would be leveled against Della. The Old Man had accomplished what he intended. He had protected his long time housekeeper and friend from the effects of his crime.

Not that Starnes' association with John Deveraux was finished. The Old Man had other crimes he wanted off his chest and he expected Starnes to be there for the confessions and the reparations. The sun dropped lower, throwing its blistering heat into the cab when Starnes opened the door. The sound of Hendrix was maddening. Taking his briefcase and gathering up the groceries, Starnes entered his clamorous house.

♦ ♦ ♦

"So, what are you going to do?"

"Do? About what?" Gen asked.

Lily rolled her eyes and finished off the sweet tea they had carried to the guesthouse. "You love the man?"

Gen paused. "I've always loved Starnes," she said softly. "But if you're asking about the future, he didn't . . . we didn't talk about it."

"What's to talk about," Lily said, her full lips lifting in a sensual smile.

Gen grinned and shook her head at her irrepressible sister. "It's not that simple—"

"Love is never simple, sister-mine. Love just is."

"I have a life in New York, Lily. I have a business. A job I love." Gen remembered the weight of a camera in her hands, the excitement of a perfectly framed shot, the feeling of power that came from control of the lighting, the props, the mannequins. The ache of longing was so intense she had to fight the surge of adrenaline, the urge to run to the little closet and pick up her camera, the need to photograph something, anything. She had a vision of the Old Man in his sickbed, his ravaged face caught in the lens. He would be furious, eyes blazing. It would be a wonderful shot. Her father dying, the very scent of death caught on film. It was a callous and insensitive thought, but it would be a fabulous photograph.

And then the realization hit her. *Oh, God. Her father was dying. Really dying.* She would be alone. No mother. No father. No husband or children. No one to run back to if life became overwhelming.

There isn't a place in my life for a man, the thought whispered. *There isn't a place in my life for anyone.* Even Barry had been relegated to the sidelines, his career or hers keeping them separated for weeks, sometimes months at a time. *There really isn't a place in my life for anyone.* Shock rolled through her.

Fighting back unanticipated fear, Gen said the first words that gathered in her throat. "I have a shoot in Maui in less than ten days, and I have to go, whether the Old Man is dead or not. I might not be here when he dies." *No one to run back to.*

Unexpectedly, Lily's eyes hardened. "Well, isn't that just too damn bad," she said harshly. "But why should that surprise me, you running off and leaving me with the Old Man. We were talking about Starnes, in case you don't remember." Lily pushed her tea glass away with disgust, hand trembling, her color rising. "And, so what if the Old Man isn't dead. Or if he is. So what? He maybe didn't kill Mama and Matthew, but he's still a heartless *bastard*." She leaned in, tears gathering. "He still beat me, beat us, too many times to count. I am *not* going to grieve over his death!" she hissed.

Lily was trembling, her face splotched red, her eyes bright with unshed tears, tears Gen couldn't understand, the sudden transformation from gossipy amusement to hostility. Tears concerning Starnes? Tears about the Old Man, for whom she had just refused to grieve?

Confused, Gen stared at her sister, stared as Lily changed before her eyes. She seemed to crumple and expand with every breath, the sound as rasping as the Old Man dying only yards away.

"I grieved over Mama. I grieved over you. *I will not grieve ever again!*" she said.

Gen knew that Lily's upset had little to do with their present conversation. Lily had children. Lily had a husband who literally worshiped the ground she walked on. Lily made sure that he did. No matter who died, Lily would never be alone. And yet, Lily sat there, fists clenching with unnamed emotion.

Gen could have a man, and a son, too, if she was willing to go back to Barry. And Starnes? He had come to her in the night and left just as easily. There was no equation that included him. "I travel thirty weeks a year," she said, to fill the silence between them, "with shoots in various parts of the world. Starnes. . . . Starnes. . . ."

Tears spilled over, carving scalding runnels through Lily's carefully applied makeup. A harsh breath jarred her frame. Gen stared at her sister in horror, sympathetic tears gathering in her own eyes. "Lily? This isn't about Starnes. Talk to me."

But in her mind she was thinking, *Even if I had a family, there would be no place in my life for them. No room.* Was that what had ultimately destroyed her marriage? Had there been no room in her life even for him? Her mind whirled, disconnected, a jumble of parts, with nothing whole as Lily seemed to fall apart before her eyes.

Her sister shook her head violently, swiped at her cheeks, hands shaking. A single sob tore from her, as if the cry severed her soul.

In a voice as broken as dry bayou mud, Lily said, "You could live here when the Old Man dies. In the Estate House." The words sounded hard, cold, though Gen knew her sister wasn't, and obstinate, which she was.

"That way, the kids could come down and stay anytime they wanted. You could fly back and forth to New York on day trips whenever you need to. And you could still have Starnes, if you want him," she added, as if tossing in a final bargaining chip.

"I don't live here anymore," Gen repeated, knowing that this was why Lily was upset, the fact that she didn't live here. And Gen didn't understand why that subject had upset her sister. "I don't live here anymore," she said haltingly. "I left here twenty-nine years ago!"

"I'm not talking about a little godforsaken town in the middle of the delta region," Lily said, fiercely. "I'm talking about a *person*. And you didn't *leave* here. You *ran away!*"

"So what does—?" A pulse of pure lightning thrummed through Gen. Nerveless, she stood. Thrusting her legs back. The side-chair clattered to the floor. "I—"

"You ran away! You ran away. And *you didn't take me with you!"*

Gen found the edge of the bed with numb knees and sat down hard on the mattress. The springs creaked slightly.

"You didn't take me with you!" The words rang in the small house. Suddenly cold, Gen put out her hands and gripped the coverlet, pulled it to her convulsively.

"You *left* me here with *him!"* Lily's head jerked toward the house, toward the Old Man's room, freeing long strands of black hair. They fell forward, clinging to her damp face. "And you would leave Starnes, too. Without ever talking to him about it. Without ever trying to find a way to make it work. You'd just *run away*," she said, the cry hoarse and cracked. "Run away again."

Gen's mouth opened but there were no words ready. She didn't know what to say. She shook her head. She wasn't running away. She wasn't. She was returning to a life she loved. And then the thought settled into her.

Lily had wanted to come with me? Away from the Estate? To New York? All those years ago. "Oh. Oh, God. . . ." she breathed. "Lily, I love you—"

"Stop." Lily held out a hand, palm between them like a wall. When she spoke, the words were tortured, forced past a throat closed with ancient pain. "You never even thought to ask me to come with you, did you? When you made plans to leave and go to New York. I never even crossed your mind."

"You were so young. In school. I couldn't have taken care of—"

"I was alone!" she howled, the sound of an animal wounded. "*Alone!*"

Gen, stunned beyond anything she ever felt, lifted her arms to her sister.

Lily rose stumbled to the bed and fell into her arms. Gen enfolded them both in the coverlet, soft cotton enveloping them, Lily's tears hot on her neck. She held her sister while she cried. "I never meant to." Gen's words died and then rose again, as if they had life. "I never meant to," she repeated, her own voice ruptured and painful. "Never, *ever* meant to leave you."

"I know," Lily said, her whisper rough. "I know. But you did. You left me alone. And now, you're planning to leave Starnes the same way."

"Lily. It's not the same. It's not." The words simply stopped. Then, " I'm so sorry Lily-love. I'm so sorry."

"I was so afraid when you left," she sobbed. "It was just me and him in this big old house. And he was angry. He was crazy, like a mad animal. And I was so alone. And you didn't come back. And you didn't even call."

"I'm sorry, *me sha.* I'm sorry," Gen rocked with her sister, still wadding the coverlet, filling in the open places, making a warm cocoon, their bodies locked, embracing old pain.

They rocked slowly as the sun angled down, throwing long shadows. Light flooded the guesthouse, picking out the tea glasses, a ribbon of clear water and melted ice in the tops of both. Illuminating the luggage, the clothing hanging from the open closet door, the piles of shoes and boots in the corner. It was all commonplace. Gen lived her life out of a suitcase.

On the porch, Princess stalked back and forth, back and forth, her tail a long crooked shadow. Twice, she jumped for the doorknob, paw swiping as she tried to find a way inside.

As the minutes passed, Lily calmed, her sobs slowing, her breathing becoming easier. Gen's own tears dried. Out of all the harsh words they had spoken and she had thought, Gen remembered certain lines clearly.

There isn't a place in my life for anyone.

I will not grieve, ever again!

No one to run back to if life becomes overwhelming.

She had indeed run away, leaving her young sister grieving under the iron fist of the Old Man. She had run away, crying her need for independence, her need for freedom. But in her selfish flight, she had abandoned her sister. And all the time, all those years ago, she had secretly been depending on her father as a place to run to if the going got hard. She was a fraud through and through. A fraud and a fool who didn't even know herself.

Lily sighed and sat back, using the sheet to wipe her face, smearing makeup across the white cotton and her cheeks.

"I look a fright, don't I?"

"What happened to the beautiful tears you usually cry? You can weep and sob and wail and never dribble a drop of mascara. Now you look a lot like I do when I cry."

"Oh, heavens, not that bad."

Gen laughed, that oh-so familiar tone of her father's laughter coming from her throat. The sound brought her up short, the laughter a wild untamed thing in the silence of the little house. It seemed to echo as it wafted away, and a silence settled between them. Gray eyes to dark, they measured one another, seeing the years, the changes differing lives had wrought in fine lines, age-dulled hair, softer physiques.

As Gen stared at her sister, a strange sense of peace washed through her, slow and thick as bayou water. Not the peace of slowing down or stopping or even resting. But the peace of excitement. The peace of being on a journey and watching for the sights around the next bend.

She was indeed her father's daughter. And her mother's. The child of a murderer father and a mentally ill, successfully suicidal mother. Some heritage. Soon, her last parent would be gone, taking the final remnants of strength and weakness with him, leaving her with a painful legacy, a revised and reshaped picture of herself. Brave, according to the Old Man. Capable. Valuable. If her father had left her with one thought today, it was that, above all, she was a Deveraux. And solely, wholly, herself.

"So. What are you going to do about Starnes?"

Gen lifted an eyebrow and grinned wickedly.

"Oh, my Lord. You're going to tell me to butt out."

Smiling, Gen said, "Yes. I am. Butt out, Sister-mine. And stay butted-out."

Resignedly, Lily shook her head. And then blew her nose on Gen's sheets.

◆　　◆　　◆

Starnes walked into the house, the vibrations of Hendrix jarring through his bones. The security blanket turned up full volume. But today, finally, he understood Serena's compulsion, her dependency on the noise. Or he understood at least a little of it.

Listening to Serena, and later to Serena and L'ron as they explained details of the attack and the aftermath, had explained so much, cleared up so many things about his sister. "Unexplore' territory," L'ron had called it. Places in the past he had refused to go. Perhaps been afraid to go. Pain and suffering were tight knots of yarn to be unraveled by a competent therapist, not a guilt-ridden older brother.

Stopping at the fridge, Starnes deposited two, two-liter Cokes, regular for him, diet for Serena. He opened a tall can of Chef Boyardee ravioli and dumped the contents into a microwave bowl, washed and tore fresh-picked mixed-greens for salads, and set them in bowls on a tray. When the ravioli was hot, he poured cola into iced glasses, put plates and forks together on the tray and a vinaigrette dressing beneath his arm with the two-liter bottle of Diet Coke, and carried it all to the screened porch. Setting the small table, he paused and looked out over the bayou. Hendrix was so loud, even the water seemed to pulsate.

Sighing, Starnes walked down the hallway to his sister's sanctum. He stood outside her door, one fist raised to knock, not knowing if Serena would hear him, not knowing if she was alone, not knowing if she would listen. There had been a time, years ago, when she had tried to tell him what he wanted to hear. He had been afraid then and had run away, buried his head in a court case.

His fist descended to the door in a ratta-tat-tat. There was no diminution of the volume on the other side, no response. After a long moment Hendrix changed key and played a riff that sounded like trains colliding. He knocked again. This time the door opened and the sound erupted into the hallway like a tidal-wave. Serena stood barefoot in the door, sleepy-eyed and tousled.

Starnes motioned and mouthed, *"Eat?"*, and when she nodded, he twisted one hand, brows raised in question, *"Turn down the volume?"*

His sister shrugged and went to the sound system, deftly decreasing the volume and changed CDs to Carley Simon. Mellow music rolled out like gentle waves, massaging his eardrums and he smiled. "Thanks."

"De rein," she mumbled. "You cook?"

"Ravioli and salads."

Serena perked up like a kid. She had always loved ravioli. "Chef or store brand?"

"The good stuff."

When she smiled this time, it was a high-wattage grin.

"Wash up, kiddo," he said. "Your hands look like you've been playing in the dirt."

When Serena joined him on the porch, she was washed and wearing a fresh T-shirt with Minnie Mouse on the front, clean jeans, and her hair was pulled back in a ponytail. Without acknowledging him, she dug into the rich, meaty pasta, licking tomato sauce from her lips with each bite. She ate as if ravenous, clearing away the entire plate of food in just minutes. Starnes tried to remember the last time he had fed her and realized that unless she had grabbed fast-food somewhere, it had been over a week since she had a meal. Surely L'ron had fed her when they went fishing. "This the first time you ate anything today?"

Serena thought, her fork held in mid-air and shrugged, before she ate into the salad. "Stuff's good, too," she said. "Raddichio?"

"Izaguirre's mixed greens."

"They good." She paused and drank the Diet Coke, draining

the glass and drinking half of the refill he poured before speaking again. "God, I hungry. L'ron fed me breakfast, but only fruit. *Fruit*, can you believe dat?"

"Some people actually eat fruit, you know," Starnes said, amused.

"Not dis girl. Steak, eggs, sausage and grits. Meat-and-potato girl, I am, and he know it, *oui*. Apples," she snorted. "Pears and strawberries. *Kiwi*. Did you know dat kiwi *green?!* Yuck." She shuddered and Starnes laughed before he sobered.

"We need to talk." The words came out thoughtlessly, hard and stiff. But Serena simply looked at him.

" 'Bout what?"

"About what we didn't say last night."

"And dat is?" Serena's eyes were slitted, suspicious.

"About," the word stuck in his mouth, "about Daddy."

Serena said nothing, her gaze sharp as broken glass.

"About why you always say that you killed him," he said. "Say that you killed Daddy."

"Some t'ings you don want to know, brozzer."

"Some things I have to know, Serena. And I figured out this morning that you never finished the story. Somehow you managed to leave something out. And I want you to tell me."

"No matter what dat be?" she asked, her voice suddenly cunning, expression harshly amused.

"No matter."

Serena stood and crossed to the swing, sat, measured him across the porch, the distance only a few feet, yet feeling like miles, or years, her face behind the fall of her hair like a daytime moon seen through heavy fog. She pushed off with one foot, the other tucked beneath her and she smiled, but it was a strange smile, full of something he wasn't certain that he wanted to see. When she spoke her voice was silken.

"Dat ole man turn up dead come spring. Fell off he pirogue. Fishin'. Broke he neck. *Accident*, dey rule it, but dey not able to 'splain dem finger mark on he neck. Dem *bruise*."

"He was murdered?" Starnes whispered.

Serena only looked at him, her eyes so deep he could have fallen in and never found his way out. The anger he had fought the night before seemed to twine about him, tentacles binding him tightly to this moment, this stygian darkness within himself. He had known it, somewhere deep in his soul. He had known his father had been murdered, and only waited to hear it confirmed. Ugly happiness danced with the anger inside. He was glad his father had been killed. Glad because that act so long ago freed him from having to do it himself. Primitive thoughts of death and vengeance and satisfaction surged within him.

He managed a single deep, painful breath. Then another, easier, less painful, staring into his sister's eyes. *His father had been murdered. . . .*

"And you know who killed him, don't you?" he said.

Still, she only looked at him. Silent. Giving him nothing. And then he knew. Knew it with a certainty that cut through the anger like a heated blade.

"L'ron killed Daddy, didn't he, Serena?" Starnes whispered haltingly. "L'ron. He almost told me so. Almost tells me so, every time I see him. Every time he tells me that he always takes care of you. . . ." Starnes sat back, his anger escaping like steam, curling around and vanishing. "I never listened." And then he fitted another piece of the puzzle. "L'ron killed Daddy out at Bayou *Je Vas Jamais Oublier.* Bayou *I Will Never Forget.*"

Still her eyes gave nothing away, and when she spoke, her voice was dead, as colorless as the bayou. "He refuse to take my part. Refuse to let L'ron and me file charges against de boys what rape me. Even when L'ron and I go together and ask him when he sober, a preacher-man." She stared hard at him, face cold. "Daddy fell fishing. He a good-for-nothing-Cajun-drunk. And he fell and he died. Dat all I got to say 'bout dat, so don' you ask me no more."

An emotion he could decipher filled her eyes, anger, righteous rage. A further truth smoldered beneath her fury. She threw back her head as if she might howl, a feral wolf, crying at the night. But it was words she spoke, and truth that leapt free. "L'ron only man ever stand up for me. Ever. Only man what try to stop him from hitting me. Only man. I never forget."

Conclusions raced through Starnes' mind like mist and fumes, frivolous and half-witted. *The rape changed you, changed your whole life. That's why you don't eat fruit, isn't it,* he wanted to say. *Why you eat meat-and-potatoes. Why you call yourself a slut, and act it, too. Why you live in this strange world you have made for yourself, all alone. Because Daddy let the crime against you go unpunished. Because you witnessed L'ron kill him for it.*

But Starnes said nothing. Nothing at all. And his anger was gone like smoke on the breeze.

31

WE ALL NEED SOMETHING

"I talked to the Old Man today."

Lily looked at her silently. She had washed off the remains of her makeup and applied a heavy coat of Gen's cooling moisturizer. Her face looked clean and open and vulnerable, now. Much like the little sister that Gen had left alone when she ran away to New York.

"I think you should talk to him, too."

"Why? What have I got to say to him? I changed his bedpan and fed him soup when he was too weak on the day I arrived. I did the daughterly thing. I played nursemaid. And I brought him his grandchildren. He got to meet my kids and get to know them. I broke every vow I ever made about the old goat. What else is there to do?"

"Forgive him."

Lily's eyes closed. She could have been praying, or trying not to curse. "I went to confession the other day," she said, her lips barely moving. "I forget when, now. It was just after I came here. And Father Tony had a few words to say to me on the lack of my ability to forgive."

"He said something similar to me. Something like, 'This family needs a lot of healing. Maybe it could start with you.' I almost spit in his face, it made me so mad."

Lily's lips curved up at the image, her eyes still shut. "You would never do anything so undignified. You'd just look down your nose and lift that arched brow and cut him dead. Just turn your back and walk off."

"Undignified? I rode a horse bigger than a moose through the bayou the other day and I was barefoot, had my hair in a ponytail, and stank like sour fish."

Lily laughed but when she spoke, her voice was tentative. "So what did you talk about? To the Old Man."

"I told him he was a mean, cruel, hard-fisted bastard. I told him I had hated him for most of my life. I told him that I believed he had killed Matthew and Mama."

"You said all that to him? To his face?"

"Most all of it. It runs together in my head now. But yeah. Most of it."

"And he didn't get out of bed and beat you half to death?"

"Clearing things up on his deathbed has compensations," Gen said. Lily laughed again, eyes closed, and Gen wondered what she was shutting out. "And then he asked my forgiveness."

Lily's eyelids twitched as if they wanted to pop open, amazed. They tightened closed. "And?"

"I forgave him."

Lily shuddered. "And you want me to do the same. Forgive him."

When Gen said nothing, Lily opened her eyes at last, the lids rising slowly as if it were an enormous battle, a battle between good and evil, between light and dark. Gen banished her whimsy, meeting her sister's black eyes.

"For my sake, right? So I won't carry around any excess baggage. Oprah stuff."

Gen shrugged, not certain why she knew Lily needed to forgive the Old Man, only certain that she did.

"You'll go with me?"

"Yes," Gen said. "I'll go with you."

◆   ◆   ◆

In the moments after the near revelations about Henry Templar's death, Starnes and Serena talked. For the first time ever, they talked about the past, almost like two normal siblings remembering difficult times. They talked about their father's funeral, their mother's funeral, each offering a word here, a memory there. They discussed in detail the town's reaction to the two deaths so close together, the town drunk's by accident, his wife's by heart failure. They discussed everything, including the fact that Serena had dropped out of school, run away, and moved into a commune of hippies living in Calcasieu Parish. Stayed there, more or less happily, until one Christmas when she came home, the Christmas she and Deon Hoffpauir met and moved in together. And everyone in three parishs knew what the outcome of that relationship had been. The infamous *bitten-off-penis* affair.

They were able to say almost anything to one another. By then, he would have given her anything; if words were what she wanted, he would share them with her. Starnes asked after the lives and occupations of the boys who had raped her. Oddly, Serena had kept up with the men and she wanted to talk.

One of the boys had died of suicide. One was a Baptist minister in a "holy-roller" church in Mississippi, or so she had heard. One was in jail. Two were lovers, living in New Orleans and operating a successful antiques shop. Some had just disappeared. Not one of the boys who had been part of the violence that night lived in town. No one except L'ron.

Starnes suggested the possibility of legal charges against the football players or even a civil suit, but they discarded both notions, one for reason of statute of limitations, the other for practicality. Who would believe it now after all these years? Who would care, but the two of them and perhaps L'ron. And when no walls were left between brother and sister, there came a sense of peace, a sense of healing. Finally, silence fell between them, companionable, easy. A soft silence of contentment, of relief.

The sun set early that night, beginning its long trek into winter, the day shorter than the one before, the night a hint cooler. The setting rays were gold, fuchsia, purple and orange, flaming on the bayou, a memory of the time it burned for real, with oil spilled by the negligent wildcatter. Starnes and Serena watched the false burn, reflections of sun and clouds upside-down on the surface, then gone as the water darkened. Watched it metamorphose from fire into water, like some prehistoric Celtic myth. Watched it change, as their world had changed in the last hours. Watched and waited.

After darkness was total, and fish and night birds swam and hunted, after mosquitoes had filled the air in swarms, Starnes spoke. "I want to get you some help, Serena. Professional help."

His sister snorted, the sound French and deep, echoing off the water. "Something we no try yet, brozzer?"

He nodded in the darkness. "One something. A blend of medication and talk therapy in a group home." When she didn't get up and walk away, didn't snort again, didn't laugh or curse him, he continued. "I spent part of last night looking some up on the Internet. Louisiana has several, one in New Orleans, that I think may offer you some . . ." he searched for the word. ". . . some healing. It's with a group of Carmelite nuns in a private, closed abbey. You can finish high school there, too. Get your GED." Serena was silent. "I called Father Tony. He said he would check into it. If you wanted."

Serena stretched, pulling her arms over her head, feet outstretched in unconscious exhaustion, and groaned with the movement. Barefoot and her pale, her arched feet looked delicate and impossibly tiny in the darkness. Her legs bent back again and the motion propelled the swing.

"It might be . . . wise," he said, choosing his words as if they rested among landmines, "if you got away. There are some questions about two men burned in a car not far from here. Questions about your possible involvement."

Still, his sister said nothing. Her silence was almost eerie and it took a moment before he realized why. The music had stopped, unnoticed, long ago. And Serena had not gone in to replenish the stack of CDs. Serena was sitting in the silence with him. "I can get you more information tomorrow. And if you are interested we could go see it. Visit, talk to the sisters."

After long minutes went by she said softly, "Find out what you can. About the nuns."

A sense of elation shot through him, clean and wild. An unrestrained happiness.

"And Starnes," her voice was a whisper on the night. " 'Bout them two burned men . . . I know 'bout them, yes. I was there."

The fragile happiness broke inside him like shattered crystal, the shards cutting deep. Half rising from the chair, his motion was arrested, frozen. "No. . . ." he whispered. "No," he stated more forcefully.

Focusing on his sister's face in the darkness was like focusing on air, on a reflection moving across the moon, her skin a white mask framed by dark-on-dark. Her face a pale smear, like the moon dancing in a sky gone mad. He remembered L'ron's comment about the small boot print found at the scene. He remembered that Serena had lost her boots on the bayou. Moving stiffly, Starnes sat back, his hip twinging a reminder of caution.

"I there, *oui*. Not when they die, but I was there when they burn. An' when I see dey name in de paper, I recognize dem both. Dey two de boys what rape me dat night. Ricky Hoggard and Glynwood Jarrett, call him Glinny in school. He play fullback."

The implications of his sister's words began to sink in. She had been there. And she had reason to want to see them both dead.

"I told you a few day ago that I was thumbing down to Byglass road. Father Tony stop and pick me up. Took me to confession. Remember?"

Starnes nodded in the darkness. Nearby, a fish jumped, its landing a smacking splatter. A bird called far off, a night jar, the echo a lonely sound.

"I had spend de night with Jimmy Mason down on Le Cou Bayou, partying and drinking with he friend. He got him a houseboat down dere wid a bar and a bath. Keep it dock near the Old Meranto Inn, he do. We party on it oft time."

"I thought that inn was out of business," Starnes said, his voice the calm, reasoning voice of a lawyer, at odds with the frenzied heartbeat of the brother battering his chest. "Years ago. The Meranto's both died in the fire that closed the inn."

"Jim-bo bought dat property, shut off damaged part, knock out doorways between de rooms and he live in rest of it. Not much to look at, but it keep de rain off his head."

Starnes could imagine the place. Cobbled together living space, Jerry-rigged plumbing, the kitchen a hotplate and microwave stuck in a corner. Tattered couches, battered furniture from the fifties, scuffed floors and a stench of cigarettes strong enough to choke a mule.

"Anyway, we party for a few day and then Jimmy, he run off de others and we go fishing on he johnboat. Stay too long on de water. Sun set. He running lights don't work, so we floating down de bayou in de dark, slapping at mosquito, drinking beer. And we see a fire start on shore. Jimmy, he pull de boat over and tie it off. And we gots out. I had to pee so it seem like a good idea. But it wasn't. We walk up to the road just in time to see a ute pull off."

"A what?"

"A ute. A utility vehicle," she explained as if to a child. "Like a Jeep Wagoneer, mebe. Dark color. Spraying mud wid it tire, it was getting out of dere in a hurry some. Jim-bo and me, we stick around. See men inside, burning. Burning black and crisp," she said, her voice a low burr of remembered shock.

"Some kind of stink it was. And we run back to de boat, silent-like, so de killer don't hear us. Only we get turn around in de dark and I fall in de bayou. Deep mud she was. Lose my boot, dem both. Jim-bo, he lose he hat. And we push off de johnboat and float on down Le Cou to de Inn. I shower off de bayou water and get all my thing together. Pack. By den, sun come up. I start walking, thumbing. And Father Tony, he come along. Take me to town."

Starnes' mind was flitting down legal pathways, considering this possibility, then that one. Serena had seen nothing that might be used for conviction, but the fact that she had run from the scene and not reported the deaths and the burning might make her an accessory after the fact, especially if later it was proved she knew the killers. And since his sister knew every low-life in three parishes, that would be a given. An accessory before the fact if it came out in a trial about the rape. Serena's violent history wouldn't help either.

No one in the parish was ever likely to forget that Serena had bitten off her lover's private parts. Someone might even locate Deon Hoffpauir, get him up on the stand to tell all he knew of her, with no regard to the fact that Deon had been beating her, forcing her to perform oral sex when she attacked him. "Did you and Jimmy ever speak of it again? The burning?"

"Not word one, no."

"So you don't know if he might have seen more in the darkness than you did? You don't know if he might have recognized the ute?"

Her shoulders lifted in the dark. Fell. An eloquent shrug.

"And you didn't tell L'ron?"

"No. I din tell L'ron."

Something in the tone caught his wondering mind. "Why? Why didn't you tell L'ron?" And then, he knew. "Because L'ron drives a black utility vehicle," he said softly. He remembered the black Jeep Wagoneer L'ron had driven to the house the night he cleaned out Serena's houseguests.

Serena neither agreed nor disagreed. She sat silently, shushing her feet against the porch floor, swinging.

"And you're afraid that since the two men in the burned car were some of the men who raped you. . . ." Starnes began putting it together in his mind, from little bits of information, a remembered glance, an odd tone. "And since he killed Daddy. . . . You're afraid that L'ron might still be avenging you," he concluded.

Serena shrugged again. "Roberto Freyouz. Call hem Berto in school. He commit suicide. So dey say. Two other disappear. Never be hear from again. Vanish, dem both. Another in prison, Jean Giroir, but I hear dere some question dat he de killer what kill his girlfrien'. Some question. I put dem fact all together and I wonder. 'Bout L'ron."

The old case flitted through his mind, the irregularities of Giroir's girlfriend's death and the original investigation. "But Serena. The question about his killing her wasn't about his guilt or innocence. He was found with the body. Blood and forensic evidence was conclusive. He had her blood matted into his hair. He killed her alright. The only *question* was whether the strangulation killed her before she bled out from the stab wounds. It was an open and shut case."

"Yes?" she said, her voice lifting. "You sure dat?"

"I'm sure. I remember reading about the case. Jean Giroir was high on meth when he killed her. He pled no contest and was sentenced to thirty-five years in state prison. And Roberto Freyouz. . . . Okay, I don't remember that one, but I'll bet it's not a questionable suicide. I'll check into it in the morning. If there's no question he killed himself, will you . . . will you consider telling L'ron about the deaths of the men in the car."

Serena watched him, her eyes measuring this new relationship that they seemed to be building. She cocked her head. "You be dere wid me?"

"Yes. I'll be with you. Promise."

"What you gone do 'bout L'ron killing Daddy?"

"What do you mean?"

"You gone have him arrested? Have him put in de jail?"

Starnes chuckled softly. "Let me guess," he said, knowing where Serena was going with the questions. "If I take you to Sheriff Pritchard, tell him all about our dear old Daddy's death, you'll have a sudden attack of amnesia and recant every word spoken tonight."

He could see Serena's teeth glow in the darkness. "That why dey call you de smart Templar," she said. "Right brainy, you. Me? I'm carraazy, taking medications for mental illness. Can't believe a word I say." Her chin jutted up, defiant. " 'Sides. I tell you nothing. *Pas* one lil' t'ing."

"No. You didn't. I'm not going to the sheriff, Serena. I should, but I'm not." His lips quirked up slightly. "But I may talk to L'ron about Daddy. About all this. That okay with you?"

"*Ouais*," she said in formal French. "*Merci beaucuop, mon frère.*" Surprisingly, she stood, came to him and bent, pressing her lips to his cheek. "Nite, bo."

Moments later the soft strains of violins drifted through the house. A Mozart sonata. Starnes didn't even know she owned classical music. But then, until tonight, he hadn't known much at all about Serena. *Co-dependent, you. . . .*

L'ron's diagnosis had been accurate. Maybe the cop could quit law enforcement and take up counseling. Or maybe he could go into the revenge business. His business card could read, "Been done wrong? I can fix it." Just as he had "fixed" Serena's problem with their father.

Starnes still didn't know how he was going to handle that little tidbit of information. As an officer of the court he was duty-bound to report what he knew of a crime, but he didn't know anything. Had his father pulled a gun on L'ron? Had there been an element of self defense? What would forensics show if an inquest were opened now? There was no ethical way to deal with this. And how in the name of all that was holy could he think of ethics when his sister was involved? Starnes went to Serena's room and tapped.

"*Oui*, Starnes?"

He opened the door. "Do you have a couple of dollars?"

She looked at him blankly, already dressed in the same virginal white gown she had worn before. "*Deux* dollar? Yeh."

"Give them to me, please."

Face puzzled, she reached for the jeans hanging over a chair and pulled out crumpled dollar bills. Starnes plucked out two. "One for you, one for L'ron," he said. "You both just hired me on retainer. Client confidentiality and client privilege. Nothing you say to me has to be reported . . . or at least a few laws on the books still say so. Enough for me to keep my mouth shut."

Serena grinned. "You work cheap."

"Keep it to yourself," he said in a mock-whisper.

Before sleep, Starnes activated his computer and printed off standard retainer contracts for Serena and for L'ron. His old friend might not know it, but he now had a semi-permanent attorney. That it was the son of the man he allegedly killed was pure irony. Starnes paused while making a list on his Things To Do pad.

L'ron Rebardi had killed his father.

He should have felt something, some kind of anger or sadness. Instead what he felt was akin to relief. Perhaps Gen had put it best to Father Tony. "*Some wounds are impossible to heal, Father. Some wounds actually bring the sufferer death.*"

She had been right. Henry Templar was a brutal, hard-drinking, hard-fisted child-abuser. In today's world, his children would have been put in foster care. L'ron Rebardi, a frightened teenager, had killed him, then gone on to make something good of his own life. He didn't deserve to do time for the death of a piece of scum. Starnes was rationalizing but it made him feel better. And he knew there was more left to be done to protect his friend.

Not quite midnight. Too late, he thought, but she would forgive him. He dialed Mare's home number.

She was awake but not glad to hear from him. "What the heck do you want?" she said.

His paralegal, and until recently, Lindsay's paralegal as well, Mare had been a part of his practice for decades, and had been angling to get him married since the moment they met. She thought she had found just the solution to his needs in Lindsay.

"Do you know that poor girl came in to the office and cleaned out her things—lock, stock, and barrel? And she cried the entire time she was there. She said you two were no longer engaged and that she couldn't work in the same office with you any more. You—broke—her—heart."

Starnes heard a pot bang down on the stove as she spoke. Mare had given up drinking coffee because it made her irritable. She claimed that drinking tea had a salubrious effect on her disposition. Starnes begged to differ but not when Mare was within hearing.

"I need something from you."

"I need a million dollars. We all need something. Lindsay needs an apology from you, but I bet she won't get it."

Starnes breathed a laugh into the phone and said, "I have a list of names for you and will have some more tomorrow. I need the current location of each and anything you can dig up on them in the next twenty-four hours."

Mare sipped her tea noisily. "Am I ever going to get you married off?"

"Later, Mare. This is work."

"Oh, *well,* then let's not do *anything* to get in the way of almighty *work,*" she said, the line dripping with sarcasm like moss dripped from oaks.

"It's work involving Serena."

"Well, why didn't you say so. Family comes first. You got that girl started on a good program yet?"

"I'm working on it. Seriously this time." Starnes heard pages rustling in the background.

"Give me what you got," she said.

Starnes called off all the names Serena had mentioned, and as many of the current locations and causes of deaths as he could remember. "They were members of the Moisson High School football team. And Mare, they ganged raped my sister with she was fifteen years old." Mare sucked in her breath but said nothing. "This is personal, but we're on retainer."

"I can't sleep. All I been doing around the office for the last week is filing my nails. I'll start on it tonight."

"You're a dream woman."

"Remember that when you sign my bonus check at Christmas. Anything else?"

"No. That should do it for now."

"Call Lindsay."

The phone went dead in his hands.

32

NO NEED TO GET CATTY

Gen woke with the sunrise and pulled the sheets over her head.
They still smelled like Starnes. Starnes who hadn't even spoken to
her yesterday after he left her. Not one word. Not even a phone
call. And he hadn't come to dinner with the family. Nothing.

Tossing the sheets and coverlet to the foot of the mattress, she
crawled out of bed and stripped off the linens. She needed to
move, needed to stretch, needed to feel a horse beneath her. She
needed to see Starnes, but that could wait. First, she had some
things to do.

She clomped into estate house wearing boots and a hat she
found in the back of her closet. She had a feeling it had belonged
to Starnes, left there after his recuperation, but perhaps that was
wishful thinking. The black cowboy hat had sat on the top shelf
for so many years that dust had formed layers, a nest of cobwebs
draping over it like lace. The hatband was crusty with old sweat
and a mouse had taken a few bites out of the brim at one time,
but the hat was still functional, if a little too large. It looked fine
after a good banging on the side of the guesthouse.

Gen stretched out on her father's old leather couch, holding
the heavy office phone, and called New York. Talking to Joachim
brought back memories of New York and Barry and created a
longing she refused to give in to. Barry was gone. Like Starnes, he
had slipped away, but he had at least said goodbye. Dressed in a
form-fitting Armanii, he stood at the door to the guesthouse, the
screen door between them, took his formal leave, and walked
away. Gen had watched silently as he climbed into a rattletrap
truck and was driven to the airport by the wicked-looking old
Cajun Starnes had found to guard the Estate.

She knew the divorce would go through. Knew her life with
her husband was over. Knew things would never be the same

again.

"Geneva?"

She jumped. "I'm here Jo. So, can you get the lights and the generator?"

"I said I could get them. Twice, I said I could get them. You're not listening," he grumbled. "Daydreaming or doing two things at once?"

"Sorry. I'll pay better attention," she said contritely. Slighting Jo was more dangerous than forgetting Barry's mother's birthday, which she had done once years ago. The old sayings about the guilt trips hosted by Jewish mothers were true in every particular, but Joachim could out-guilt even Mama Stone. She hurried to amend her faux-pas. "I don't know what I'd do without you, there, handling all the details, taking care of everything for me . . . while my father dies," she added for effect, enjoying the dialogue with Jo, so familiar she could have scripted it herself.

"Well, of course I take care of you. It's my job," he said, mollified, "and I'm very good at it. Oh, and speaking of taking care of you? I've hired you a housekeeper-chef. Her name is Jane Chen, and she starts the Monday we get back from Maui. She gets room and board and three hundred a week, which I thought was *outrageous* until I tasted this wonderful Teriyaki-style chicken dish. And I've been assured that her bird's nest soup is simply *in the grave*."

Gen knew that meant that the soup was even better than *to die for*. "Mmmm," she said. "Does she have her green card or am I harboring an illegal?"

There was a sharp silence on the other end as Jo ignored her question, and Gen shook her head. He'd do what he wanted, green card or no.

"The equipment is on hold at Waikiki for us, ready for pickup. The only problem is transportation to the site. I'm still waiting to hear back from *Captain Andy,*" he said disparagingly, "about the number of trips it will take to get all the equipment across the reef in shallow-draft boats. I'm hearing rumblings that transport costs will be higher than the bids."

"Did we add anything to the list we gave him back in March?"

"Not much. A few incidentals."

"Check with the tourism department and find a competing

company. We can rumble, too."

"Oh Geneva, dear girl, you are so evil. This is the reason I love working for you."

"This? Not the fantastic salary, the access to the beautiful models—and yes I mean the hardbodies—the travel, the great Christmas bonuses—"

"No reason to get catty," he sniffed. "You want me to arrange a flight back two days before the shoot so you can check over everything? Get back to civilization?"

"No. Book me a flight directly from here as late as possible. Even if you have to go on ahead and get the equipment moved without me."

The silence on the New York end was telling. "*You* want *me* to handle the transport of the equipment? *Me?* Listen, missy, you let me talk to the *savages* down there. They've hidden my Geneva and replaced her with an imposter."

"No need to get catty," she quoted back at him, laughing. "Let me know the flight details and call me if you have any problems you don't want to bother to handle."

"Geneva?" Jo always called her by her full first name.

"Yes?"

"Are you alright? I don't mean to be unkind, dear girl, but you do sound, well, different."

Different? Gen could have sworn he meant to say something else. For a moment she considered herself as Jo might see her were he in the room with her now, boots, jeans, and hat, feet propped on the couch arm, no makeup, hair in a ponytail. And how he might have seen her before she left New York for this trip into her past. God, how trite. "Nicer?" she asked wryly. "More gentle? A little less of a . . ." she fished for a word other than bitch, "control freak?"

"Your words, sweetie, not mine," he said in a sing-song. "But now that you mention it, yes."

Gen looked down her length, seeing broken nails, a not-quite-clean T-shirt. Years and an entire society away from her previous life. "Yes. I guess so. I am different. Talk to you later, Jo."

She made a half dozen other calls canceling lunch with friends in New York, got updates on two charitable boards she served on, and when she couldn't put it off any longer, she called her lawyer and told him to serve the papers on Barry. To end her marriage.

After the last phone call, Gen lay on the couch, her photos on the walls in the semi-dark room. Nothing in her life was as it had been only a few weeks before. Nothing. Gen remembered the young flight attendant on the 727, the boy with the Humphrey Bogart eyes. What was his name? Jack something. He had offered her a Margarita big enough to swim in. Would he even recognize her now? Would she care if he didn't?

Rolling off the couch, Gen slipped up the stairs to her sister's room. Lily was up, wearing a silk dressing gown, sitting beside the window, a cup of hot coffee steaming on the side table near her, a single rose in a vase and a crystal bowl of fruit untouched at hand. Lily had dark circles beneath her eyes, visible even through the concealer and makeup she had already applied.

"Didn't sleep?" Gen asked, taking a seat in the other side chair.

Lily shook her head. "Everything's changing." Her dark eyes met Gen's. "The kids love the Old Man. They want to live here, can you believe it? They want us to move here, Hollis and me. They called him last night and actually discussed the possibility with him!" She paused, her eyes growing red, her bottom lip caught between her teeth. "And you want me to forgive The Old Man. And then he's going to die."

Gen watched, waiting.

"We've spent our whole lives hating him and using that hatred as a springboard for every good thing we've ever done," Lily said wryly, "proving that we could do it, whatever it was, thumbing our noses at him, demonstrating to the world that we were nothing like him." A tear rolled down her face.

"Proving that we didn't need him or his money," Gen summed up. "All because we concluded that he killed our mother and Matthew. We stood on that assumption for our whole lives and it's been knocked out from under us. And now, we have to figure out who we are and how we're going to live. And it sucks."

When Lily reached for her cup, her hand trembled just as it had done the day before. "So. With all that in mind, are you going to force me to go see the Old Man now?"

Gen said, "You've never been afraid of anything in your whole life. Why start now?"

"I *was* afraid. I was *always* afraid. I was afraid of being alone. I still am." She dabbed at her eyes delicately, and Gen was pleased to see that Lily's upset wasn't enough to smear her mascara. It meant that things were still under control, unlike the previous night when she had let it all go and ended up blowing her nose on the sheets.

"Me, too. And I stand a lot better chance of being alone than you do, sister-mine. You have a husband and children. I now have no one. Except for you and yours."

"We'll always be here for you. You know that."

"I know. Which reminds me. Think Keri would like to go to Maui? Hang out with the beautiful people, watch them diet and binge and purge and complain about being fat when they weigh about half of what I do? Meet a few important people in the industry and see if they spot anything special about her?"

"Oh, heavens, she will *die*," Lily laughed, her voice stronger. "You mean it?"

"Yeah, I mean it. Get dressed. It's time to see dear old Dad."

♦   ♦   ♦

Starnes looked over the list of names, trying to see each as evidence, not as the identity of a boy who had raped his sister. Thirteen names. Not the whole team. Not even the total number who had played in the homecoming game. Just twelve boys who had attacked and brutalized Serena while L'ron watched, drunk and helpless, too young and afraid to intervene.

Mare had done good work, finding the addresses of almost all of them, whether they were under the ground or still living above it. Serena was right. There were a lot of missing and dead in the bunch.

Tilting back his head, he studied the ceiling over the old couch, the faxed documents lying across his stomach. Starnes knew that guilt could have led to Roberto Freyouz' suicide, and caused Jean Giroir to snap and kill his girlfriend. The same emotion could also have been involved in the death-by-cop of T'bo Hebert following a botched robbery of a 7-Eleven in Morgan City six years after graduation. Charles Stein, the minister of The Church of the Holy Spirit in Mississippi could have sought sanctuary in the ministry for the same reason. Though Starnes had no idea how violence would affect two young, impressionable, sexually ambivalent boys, he didn't think it would force a change of sexual orientation. It might help it along, however. Today, Micah Brehew and Steven Wilkerson had a thriving antiques business. Starnes wondered if they, or any of the others had heard from the two missing boys, Peter Mahoney and Josh Brenner.

He glanced over the list of names again, a sense of unease pricking at the back of his mind. Something about the names. But it, whatever it was, wouldn't come, mired in the backwaters of his brain. He knew better than to struggle with the thought, and let it go for the time being.

Starnes didn't know if the men still alive would talk about the rape. The statute of limitations had run out long ago. There was nothing that the law could do to any of them. Would that and perhaps a legal document promising silence and forgoing possible civil suits loosen any tongues?

Picking up his phone, Starnes dialed. Giving his name to the yat-voiced receptionist, Starnes added, "Tell them I'm Serena Templar's brother. Make sure they know that. And tell them I'm not calling to cause trouble."

If she was surprised, she didn't let it show. Instead she said simply, "Certainly, sir."

A long minute later a voice came on the line. He wasn't effete. He didn't sound gay, if gay even had a sound. He sounded resigned and a little hesitant. And just a bit afraid. "Micah Brehew, here. I wondered how many more years would go by before someone else would contact us about Serena. But I must admit, I didn't expect it to be *you*."

"Okay," Starnes said, drawing out the word uncertainly. So, no one had recently been in contact with the antiques store owners. But had they heard from someone else? Did they expect to hear from someone? Someone specific? Someone dangerous? And why *not* him? Starnes rolled to a sitting position, elbows on his knees, head hanging forward. "I have a feeling that we need to talk," Starnes said slowly, "you and Steven and I. Would you be willing to see me? I can be there in a little over—"

"*No!*"

Starnes wasn't surprised at the answer, only at the intensity of it.

"Why would we want to talk to you, brother of Serena Templar?"

Floundering, Starnes said, "Mutual self protection, perhaps?"

Micah paused. "Mutual?"

Starnes told Serena's story about the crispy critters she saw burning and explained how she might now have legal problems. Delicately, he illustrated the relationship between the two dead men and Serena, and with Micah and his partner, Steven. Picking his words was like walking through a swamp. His own feelings when speaking of Serena's ordeal were brittle and uncertain, yet, he had to take care not to libel, even with a truth, because he might not be able to prove Serena's allegations of gang rape in a court of law. And he wanted help from Micah, help that might result in putting Starnes' own best friend in jail.

It wasn't his best summation, being forced to leave out names, use euphemisms when he wanted to be crude and direct, and he was forced into the self control he exercised in a court of law. Through it all, Micah was silent. Starnes could hear him breathing.

At the end, Starnes said, "I am afraid that it's marginally possible that someone is killing off the twelve boys responsible for Serena's. . . . For Serena. And I want to know if anyone has approached you, warned you, threatened you in any way, with regard to that night."

Micah sighed. A second sigh followed right behind and Starnes realized that he was on speaker phone, a high-quality one that had left him no white-noise-clue. He'd likely been taped as well. Could he be any more stupid?

"We are willing to meet with you," the new voice said. "Provided that Sergeant L'ron Rebardi contacts us first."

Starnes sat back, the supple leather rustling beneath him. "L'ron?" His was one of the many names Starnes had avoided using, and hearing it now both threw him and caused his heart to jolt with dismay. "What does L'ron have to do with this?"

"You asked about a warning. L'ron came to us several years ago, telling us that we might one day be approached by someone," the new voice seemed to search for words, "dangerous. And if we were, we should contact the sergeant and have him with us during any meeting."

Starnes grinned broadly, the sense of relief like cold water on burned skin. That cleared his friend of suspicion, didn't it? Or did it only make it certain that L'ron would have first access to them? Letting them agonize over an attack whose schedule was entirely in his own hands. If so, that would make L'ron a first-rate sadist. And pathological, too. Couldn't be L'ron. Could it?

"So call L'ron," Starnes said. "But don't tell him who called you, only that someone did and that they're on their way to see you."

"And why would we want to do that?" Micah asked.

"In case L'ron is the one doing the killing." The words felt strange coming from his mouth, alien, like a creature bursting from a chest cavity in an old sifi movie.

Mood music filled his ear. Vivaldi. Starnes realized that he had been put on hold. Well, he didn't blame them for needing to talk that one over. It made him a bit sick at his stomach, too.

The music cut off mid-chord. "And why would L'ron be the one killing us off?"

"Steven, right?"

After a pause, he answered, his tone guarded. "Perhaps." Unwilling to give anything away. Starnes didn't blame him.

"He was there the night of the homecoming game. He's still alive. L'ron has made it his life work to take care of Serena. He loves her," Starnes ticked off the reasons why L'ron could be the killer. "He drives a black utility vehicle. A black ute was there when Ricky Hoggard and Glynwood Jarrett were killed, cut in pieces and set on fire in their car."

There was a shocked hiss on the New Orleans end.

"You didn't know how they died?"

"It wasn't exactly front page news in New Orleans," Steven-Perhaps said. "A killing in a podunk town. If it was there we missed it."

"And L'ron Rebardi never said one word about being in love with Serena Templar. Why should we believe you?"

"Ask him. He doesn't hide it. And, he has ties to another death, one I'm not at liberty to discuss with you." Henry Templar's death was not open for discussion, now or ever.

Vivaldi came back on, the rich strains coursing into him. To the side of his desk, the fax machine clicked on and whirred to life. Standing, Stares leaned over and read the message as it scrolled off.

> Final papers on Deveraux's will and testament
> messengered to you earlier. Arrive in 15.
> Stay put.
> Mare

"Templar," Stevens said briskly, "we need three hours. And you are not to come here. We will meet at the Sheriff's Department in Moisson. You know it?"

"I know it."

"We will call L'ron precisely one hour before we are to meet. You're to come alone. No one else. Understand?"

"Alone. I understand. You're taking precautions. I'll be there." Starnes hung up. "And what do I do if they're the killers?" It was possible that he had just screwed himself, except, if they were the bad guys, meeting at the combo PD/Sheriff's Department was not a really wise place to gun down an enemy. He didn't think that Micah Brehew and Steven Wilkerson sounded dumb.

"Only problem wid all dat is I gone be dere, too."

Starnes looked up to find Serena framed in the doorway of his office. Her long legs were encased in tight-fitting jeans, new boots peeked out beneath the belled legs, a thin white T-shirt stopped an inch above the low-slung waist. Two things were clear—she had left her room without changing the music, and she was wearing a bra. Both miracles.

She handed him a heavy white envelope, sealed and marked with a messenger company out of New Orleans. "This come while you on de phone. And I *am* going with you," she said clearly, dropping her Cajun to make a point.

He took the envelope. "Okay."

Getting the signatures on Jonathan Joseph Arcemont Deveraux's final will and testament was seriously anticlimactic. He signed with no complaints, no last minute changes or amendments, no more fires for Starnes to put out. In the end, the Old Man's signature was witnessed by Asa and Olivia Rogers, and two more hired hands. Redundant signatures, but Starnes liked to be thorough.

He didn't want to think why John was so cooperative. Starnes knew the Old Man didn't have much time, but the knowledge was cerebral, not something he had accepted. Not yet. The Old Man had simply always been there, a part of his life, for good or ill. The fact of his death was foreign, like a weird fetish discovered in some Asian archeological dig. Far away.

But John was gray now all the time, his breathing wet and shallow, painfully labored. The day-long deposition had tired him dangerously and he had not recovered. Then, too, there was the look in his eyes. Open and curious and ready. Almost eager.

When Starnes and the witnesses left the room, they passed Father Tony standing in the hallway. Though the priest spoke to each of them, he was in a hurry, and slipped into the sickroom with little fuss, his black bag in one hand, like a doctor making house calls. Starnes knew that this black bag contained the implements of the confession and the Mass. And the Last Rites. He had seen the bag before, when his mother passed away, in the hand of an older and more jaded priest.

When Starnes left the estate house, he looked toward the guesthouse, but the blinds were down over the windows and the door was shut. The air was surprisingly cool for early September, and Gen was most likely out riding. There was no time for seeing Gen even if she had been sitting on the swing expecting him.

Serena stood waiting at the truck, both doors open, her body resting against the leather seat, ankles crossed on the shell-crete, fanning herself. She had scarcely let him out of her sight, expecting him to ditch her before he left for the sheriff's department. She didn't understand that he had no intention of leaving her. Seeing Micah Brehew and Steven Wilkerson might be good for her. An intervention of sorts. Might start her on the road to some sort of healing. And then it might not. Starnes was taking a lot of chances today, flying by the seat of his pants.

"Get in," he said, tilting his hat up to see her face. "We'll ride by the Sheriff's Department and park awhile. See what we see."

Serena flashed him a grin that shouldn't have caused him pain. It was open and joyous and ready for a challenge, the sort of smile she might have worn had she not been brutalized when she was fifteen. He started the engine and pulled onto the road. He wanted his sister well. He wanted Gen to marry him and move into the bayou house. Pipe dreams? He hoped not.

Six miles later they parked under the shade of an old live oak, its branches twisted by wind and years into stationary writhing pythons. It was cool enough to sit in the cab, drinking iced Cokes from the best Coke machine in Moission, which just happened to be across the street from the Law Enforcement Center. Even on the hottest day, it kept cans so cold that ice floated to the top when popped.

L'ron's black ute was out of sight, parked in the fenced lot to the side of the building with the other officer's POVs, but he was on duty. A quick phone call had determined that. As they waited, Starnes studied his sister, sitting in the quiet cab, sipping her Diet Coke. No music. No sly smiles or innuendo. Just a woman, seemingly calm, waiting to see two of the men who had raped her long ago.

"So?" she asked, without turning her head to him.

"So, what?"

"So, do I got de *chocolat* on my face, or I pass?"

"You pass," he said with a grin. "In fact, you are a beautiful woman, Serena Templar. Stronger than I ever gave you credit for. And I am proud to be your brother."

Still she didn't turn or reply, didn't even smile, but her skin seemed to warm all over, as if she blushed with pleasure. And then her face fell, her eyes widening. Starnes followed her gaze.

He watched as a black ute pulled up to the front of the Sheriff's Department. It parked, the dark glass windows obscuring the driver within. As the door opened, a middle aged man slowly got out and stood, one foot on the running-board of the truck. He was dressed in khakis and a white shirt, tie loose at his neck, and he stared at the front doors as intently as the Templars stared at him. At the holster he wore strapped around his chest. A cop. Plainclothes detective?

Moving slowly, as if his muscles were operated from outside his body, he reached in and lifted out a navy sport coat, shrugged into it. Grasped a long black bag, a shotgun case, and shouldered it. Awkwardly, he entered the building.

33

"You know him?" Starnes asked softly, recognizing the face but not recalling the name, though he had seen the man before.

"*Oui.* I know hem."

"Cop?"

Serena said, "I see hem sometime. 'Round town." After a moment, she added, "And one time, long time pas'."

♦   ♦   ♦

Gen reined in Hoss and sat, looking at the Estate. The air was strangely cool for the first of September, the light casting a pellucid sheen, the sky overhead a crystal blue that looked as if some crazed artist had forgotten to paint in the perpetual gray haze of Louisiana mornings. The light and sky were more like southern Italy or a Pacific island, clear and beautiful, and adding a radiance to the landscape that it seldom had.

In the distance, farm machinery hummed like angry bees, birds called, though Gen had long forgotten which bird made the odd hooting sound and which made odd, metallic clicks. Hoss blew out through his nose in satisfaction, his big body settling beneath her. Bayou water plinked to the dust below, falling from the wet threads of the saddle girth.

Horses milled in the corral, Asa squatted beside a farrier bent over the back hoof of a black mare. Olivia held the placid mare's head, the fingers of one hand stroking through a tangled mane. By the condition of her coat, the mare had been out to pasture for a while, perhaps one of the brood mares kept on the Estate. Burrs and snarls and old mud mottled her coat.

If she had been bred, it was a recent pregnancy, her sides not swelled out, but then, Asa bred all his mares in season so he didn't have any out of season births to contend with. Asa preferred one month of birthing hell and eleven months of relative calm.

Laughter floated on the peculiar air. The two men stood and the farrier slapped the mare on her haunches, sending her ambling toward the other horses in the corral. Olivia jogged for another, but halfway across the open space, she stopped and looked at the Estate House. The men followed her stare. Gen nudged Hoss into a walk, then into a trot, guiding him toward the house.

A green Cadillac raced up the drive, tires squealing to a halt. Doc Boulanger dove from the Caddy even before it stopped moving. Asa turned and ran for the house, leaving his daughter and the farrier standing alone.

Gen kicked with one heel, lifted the reins and leaned forward, her legs gripping the horse beneath her. Hoss broke into a canter, and, feeling his rider's anxiety, into a hard gallop. Bent over Hoss' thickly arched neck, Gen passed Asa and rounded the house, pulling the horse to a stop, his haunches dropping sharply, his front legs stiffening into a skid of his own, digging into the turf of the lawn.

She threw herself from his back, taking the reins with her, over Hoss' head. Momentum propelled her into the brick wall. Looping the reins through the pitted metal of the old horse tie, she left Hoss shaking his head in irritation and tore inside. Gen stopped short, sweat trickling down her sides, staring through the darkness up the stairs. Della's weeping rang through the house.

◆　　◆　　◆

"Tell me about him."

Serena shook her head, no.

A ruby-colored Mercedes pulled past them and parked smoothly in the visitor parking. Two men, one in a dark suit, one in slacks, loafers, and pale pink polo shirt, stepped from the car. Together they paused, staring at the building and its glass front doors. If they spoke, Starnes couldn't see it, and they walked inside.

"Micah and Steven?"

Serena nodded, the motion hard and slightly uncoordinated.

"Then let's go inside," Starnes said softly.

The words seemed to freeze his sister. Prickly cold broke out on her arms. She set the can of Diet Coke in the drink holder, turned stiffly, opened the door and stepped away from the truck, leaving the door hanging open. Oddly enough, Serena moved just as the unknown man had, as if she were being operated from outside her body against her will.

Starnes slipped from the cab, closing the heavy door with effort. Rounding the truck, he closed the passenger door as well and followed Serena across the central grassy block with its bronze Confederate soldier and charging horse, and up the steps. The old wooden doors of the LEC had been replaced decades ago with glass and brass, now green with verdigris.

Starnes leaned past Serena and opened the outer door. His sister was quivering, her face white, splotches of color high on her cheeks. "You could stay in the truck," he said.

"No." She shook her head, moving as if palsied. "No."

Starnes opened the inner door and together they walked to the desk. A uniformed, elderly black man sat there, narrow eyes looking them over for weapons, contraband or signs of trouble. He was desiccated and gaunt—thin skin stretched over sharp cheekbones, eyes like honed iron in hollow sockets—and suspicious, all trust in his fellow man burned out of him.

"Sergeant Bollotte," Starnes said mildly, as he always did upon entering Bollotte's domain.

"Templar," Bollotte acknowledged. "You here for Rebardi and his little party?"

Starnes would not have referred to the meeting quite that way, but he agreed.

The officer glanced down at his notes and back up. "Interrogation room four."

Starnes lifted his brows in surprise, one hand closing involuntarily on Serena's arm. "Interrogation room?"

"You know where they are?" Bollotte asked, giving nothing away, not answering Starnes unspoken question.

"I can find it."

"Four," Bollotte repeated, his eyes more angry than usual.

One hand on Serena's arm in protection or warning, he wasn't certain which, Starnes moved to the back of the stationhouse, the sounds of the front desk fading and the sounds of the jail not yet heard. The interrogation rooms were isolated from the rest of the building in a nook that turned toward the courthouse next door and backed up to the records room. Starnes didn't like the idea of meeting in an interrogation room. Why not in L'ron's office? Why not in a conference room?

He turned the knob and pushed open the door to number four. Serena, a half step ahead of him, jerked back. Two men were in the dimly lit room, one in casual dress leaning against the one-way window overlooking interrogation room three, the suited one sitting with crossed knee in a straight-backed chair. Micah Brehew and Steven Wilkerson.

The men looked up, saw the Templars framed in the doorway and started, just as Serena had. Starnes' grip tightened. Four pairs of eyes met, measured, drew conclusions, all in the space of a breath, the moment carved and punctured with old pain and surprise.

Serena lifted her shoulder, pulling her arm free from Starnes' grasp. Planting booted feet, she hooked her thumbs into the front belt loops of her jeans and stared at the two men. "What in hell L'ron Rebardi got in he little brain? Old time reunion?" she demanded, her body vibrating like a tightly strung wire.

Serena didn't flinch. Didn't run. She fought with the only weapons she had. Her smart mouth. A stunned pride blossomed in Starnes. He could have hugged her.

The two men shared a quick glance and the one in the slacks stood, moving slowly, as he might if cornered by a rabid panther. Gray eyes were on Serena, but they flashed a moment at Starnes. "I'm Micah Brehew," he said.

Silent, Starnes stood in the hallway behind his sister, not touching her. He spread his arms and braced them on the doorjamb to either side of her, leaning in slightly, the posture both protective and threatening. "I'm Templar," he said.

"I ask you two a question," Serena said, her voice shuddering with leashed fury.

"We don't know. The old man at the entrance brought us back. We haven't seen Rebardi."

"Go on in Templar."

Starnes whirled. Pritchard stood in the hallway behind them, his face tight.

"Sergeant Rebardi thinks you two should join the . . . gentlemen."

Starnes heard and understood the faint pause. *Gentlemen* wasn't the sheriff's first descriptive choice. Starnes nudged an unwilling Serena into the room and felt the door close at his back. Pritchard had not followed them in. The latch didn't click. Whatever they were all here for, it wasn't to be detained. And where was L'ron?

The silence in the small room was suffocating, Serena electric as an angry eel. Moving as slowly as Micah had, Steven stood and introduced himself to Starnes. Starnes saw no reason to reply, simply studied the man as he might an especially large nutria rat squirming on the end of a spike.

"So?" Serena demanded.

Both men looked at her, shared that same quick glance, and looked back at her. Micah said, "I— We— We often talked about that . . . night. About what we might say to you if we ever . . . saw you again."

Serena tilted her head, the tendons standing out on her neck like braided rope. Starnes held his position behind her, watching her body language, the energy that steamed from her in malignant waves. "And?" she said.

"There was never anything good enough. Never enough words to . . . to make it up to you what we did. That night."

"That true," she said, her head jerking once up and down.

"And, 'I'm sorry', always sounded so useless," Steven said. "So stupid."

"It a start," Serena said, lifting her head in challenge. Then, "*Try it.*" The demand was unequivocal. Two pairs of eyes widened. Micah opened his mouth to speak.

A door scraped on tile, the sound loud and rough, amplified. All four of them jumped, Starnes' eyes racing from Micah, to the closed door behind him, to the speakers overhead. The light in interrogation room three came on. Shocked, Starnes watched the room.

L'ron's voice boomed through the speakers as he closed the door behind himself and the man who had carried the shotgun into the sheriff's department. "We got dem in here. I 'preciate you take a look."

"L'ron," Serena said, racing to the observation window.

Starnes caught her just before she plastered herself against the one-way glass. He didn't know what L'ron had planned here, but he didn't want an outline of Serena's body against the window to give anything away. Holding his sister against his chest, one arm around her waist, Starnes seated her in an armless desk-chair and took the chair beside her.

Glancing back at Steven and Micah, now positioned just behind them, Starnes saw the black box in the center of the table. Recording equipment. A single red light lit the face of the system. It was recording, but recording what? Whom? Who was that guy? *Damn L'ron Rebardi!* Starnes returned his attention to the window.

The light beyond exposed a table, chairs pushed against the far wall. The table was covered with a yellow flat bed sheet, a faded, floral, yard sale discard. The thin sheet covered what looked like a box and lumps of various sizes.

L'ron lifted the sheet and furled it around one arm before tossing it on a chair. On the table were two human skulls and hundreds of bones, from leg bones to what could have been toes, all laid out in neat lines. L'ron's bones, the ones he had once mentioned to Starnes. In plastic zip-lock bags were bits of leather, paper, shell casings, two sets of handcuffs, three shoes, folded bits of clothing: jeans, T-shirts, socks and briefs, all muddy and ragged. A knife, its blade rusted, its hilt half-rotted, was in a bag to the side, packets of silicate moisture-preventive in the bottom.

"Jeeez Louise," the man with L'ron said. "This what the sheriff got you looking into?"

"Yeah. I foun' dese bones. Most by happenstance. Luck. An' de sheriff, he been looking to make him another detective. He say I was to run wid de investigation and see what I fin'. But man, I got to tell you, I stumped."

The man slid the black shotgun case onto the table with a soft thump, freeing his hands. "Got any ID on them yet?"

Beside him, Serena was staring at the unknown man, shaking as if she had a fever. Starnes slipped an arm around her shoulders and she leaned into him for warmth, her body inexplicably cold. Bending down to her, Starnes whispered, "Who is he?"

When Serena didn't answer, Micah's soft voice complied. "Berto's daddy. Wasn't he a cop?"

"Yes. I think so," Steven answered.

L'ron rested back on a chair, one booted foot in the seat, his backside on the chair back. To a casual observer he might look relaxed, but Starnes noted the position of his hands, loose at his sides as if ready for violence, the tension in his full lips as he studied the cop a few feet away. "Two boys dey is, missing twenty year. Peter Mahoney and Josh Brenner. Turn out, dey classmates. Graduated same year as me."

Serena's breath shuddered, her chills worsened, and Starnes resisted the urge to pull her onto his lap and wrap her in his arms. He knew she would have fought that kind of contact. He wished he had a coat to slip around her, but he didn't. To protect her, all he had was his training and experience as lawyer and brother. He tried to clear his mind. "Berto?" he asked.

"Roberto Freyouz," came the response. "Yeah. I think that's his daddy."

Gently, like leaves falling from dying trees, the pieces fell into place in Starnes' mind. "Oh. Mary, Mother of God," he whispered.

"And you want me to do what?" Freyouz asked, voice amused, calm. Too calm.

"Take a look at dis evidence. I don' like what I think I seeing."

The door to room four opened and Pritchard stepped in, shutting it behind him. Quickly, he bent over the recorder and checked its status, glanced at the window and then at the four in the room with him. Straddling a chair, he sat next to Serena. Behind them, Micah and Steven stepped away as if distancing themselves from the sheriff.

"And what do you think you're seeing?" Freyouz' voice was silky now, the amusement almost taunting.

"I think I'm seeing the bones of two boys tortured to death. By a cop." L'ron's Cajun accent disappeared. His diction clear and unambiguous.

"And you think that, why?"

"Police issue handcuffs. The brand this department was using in the late seventies and early eighties. Spent .38 rounds, also what this department was using in that timeframe. As to the torture, there were wear marks and signs of inflammation on the wrist and ankle bones of both boys. The paleoanthropologist I consulted at the University of Houston considered the wear to be consistent with prolonged shackling. The skulls of both boys show fractures to teeth, occipital bones, and mandibles," L'ron said softly.

"Somebody beat them to death over a long period of time. Days. Weeks. Torture possibly administered with this," L'ron lifted one of the clear bags and offered it to Freyouz. The other cop didn't even glance at the bag, his eyes steady on L'ron. "And possibly carved them up with this." L'ron held up the knife, both bags in his left hand, his right hand unencumbered.

"Dr. Susan Methody, she say as how the boys got nicks on their bones. Nicks that could have been created if someone was trying to, say, skin them alive and they were fighting. Driving the blade into the bone over and over."

Freyouz was smiling faintly, right hand smoothing his leather holster. Pritchard tensed, then seemed to force himself to relax. "Rebardi's party, my back hind foot," he said softly.

"Well, you have the method," Freyouz said. "Part one of any good police investigation. Good work. Now?"

"Now I got to determine motive. And opportunity."

Freyouz nodded slowly, his head barely moving. "And?"

"And I think you had them both."

"Motive," Freyouz was smiling, his chest jerking with strangled laughter. "What motive could I have against two boys?"

"Friends of your son's."

"Friends of yours, too, for that matter." Freyouz unsnapped the thin leather strap holding the weapon secure. "On the football team, as I recall. You used to *party* together." The accent on the word *party* shrewd and sharp.

"Friends of Berto's. Friends who lived, when he died."

"All kinds of parties."

Beneath his hands, Starnes felt Serena's trembling intensify. He pulled her roughly to him, wrapping his arms around her. She didn't resist, instead, burying her head in his chest. Her tears soaked through to his skin in the instant before she returned her gaze to the window.

"Friends who, together, hurt Serena Templar. Raped her after a football game. Raped her, left her for dead. And when I got her to a doctor and called the police, who should show up but Berto Freyouz' daddy in his police uniform, to beat up an old drunk and convince him that his daughter was not worth the stain on the honor of the football *heroes*."

Freyouz lifted his right hand, drawing his weapon.

Pritchard stood, the high-pitched scrape of the chair like a small scream.

Serena jerked from Starnes' arms and whirled in her chair. "Don' you let him do dis!" she hissed to Pritchard. "Stop hem!"

L'ron grinned slowly, big horse-teeth showing something like pleasure. Or harsh satisfaction.

Freyouz gripped the weapon firmly in both hands.

"Shit," Pritchard said and ran from the room.

So this was Rebardi's party. *Son of a bitch.* Starnes stared at L'ron, looking for a Kevlar vest beneath his uniform shirt. Was it there? Was L'ron protected from a chest shot?

L'ron stood, moving languidly, watching the other cop. Carefully, he placed the bags on the table, freeing both hands.

Pritchard returned, the door to the hallway still open. Starnes could hear soft scrapes on the old tile. Someone else was outside. Pritchard stared at L'ron and Freyouz in indecision.

"Stop hem!" Serena demanded again.

"And Berto," L'ron said, "good boy he was till that night. He go to confession, and de priest tell him he got to go to de police and confess. But *you* de police. Overcome he was with he shame. And he take you gun and he shoot himself."

Silence followed the statement. Utter and complete. Serena stood, poised, as if prepared to throw herself through the glass.

"And you fall apart. Loose you wife. Start drinking. Crawl so far inside bottle, almost loose you job. And den one day you fin' Peter Mahoney and Josh Brenner, out fishing mebe, or swimming. And you take dem somewhere. Make dem disappear for real. And two week later you back on de job, you ol' self and everyone happy.

"Few month later, you career take off like a rocket on Mardi Gras. You de firs' one on de scene when Jean Giroir kill he girlfrien'. In fac' you call it in. And dat one case make you detective. When T'bo Hebert was kill in dat robbery attemp' you dere, too. Funny, ain't it? How you dere when dey all die or get into trouble?"

"And?" Freyouz' voice was hoarse, his eyes hard as black stone.

"And now a knife wid you initials on it found in de grave with two more boys. Friend of Berto. Friend dere dat night when dey all rape Serena Templar. You knife, Freyouz. Or Berto's. Got he initials carve on it."

"And you think you're going to charge me on this? Based on speculation and a set of initials? I reported the knife stolen years ago, Rebardi. Years ago." The weapon in Freyouz' hands turned toward L'ron.

Sheriff Pritchard stiffened and moved toward the entrance again, swearing under his breath. He slipped out, whispering something to the others in the hallway.

"Your cuffs. Your knife. Your blackjack. All reported stolen," L'ron said softly, his eyes on the gun pointed his way, his body loose and relaxed and ready for anything, his Cajun once again vanishing like a mirage. "Convenient. And I agree, explainable. All except for the fact that I dug them up in your old backyard. 6147 Lombarbi Way. The house you lived in when you still had your wife and your son. Before he died and she left you and you started swimming in a bottle.

"And, of course, there is the simple fact that you were identified leaving the scene where Ricky Hoggard and Glynwood Jarrett were burned after their bodies were dismembered. Both friends of Berto. Both involved in the rape of Serena Templar."

The weapon in Freyouz' hands lifted fractionally. He smiled as his finger tightened. The world seemed to slow. Starnes started to stand. Serena leapt for the window, screaming, *"No!"*

L'ron dove for the floor.

And Freyouz fired.

The air exploded. The amplified blast echoing in the small rooms and down the hallway.

Fired again. Glass shattered over them.

The door beside Freyouz slammed open. Pritchard flew across the room. Tackled Freyouz. Starnes grabbed Serena and drug her to the floor, throwing his body over hers, the sound of the second blast still ringing.

34

ALL GLUED UP, HOLDING DOWN THE GYM FLOOR

"And I agree that your mother and brother should be buried beside your father, in the family plot."

Gen's eyes were dry, her head held regally. "What will it take to make that happen?"

Father Tony looked down at the desktop in his small parish office, his face tightening. "The Church no longer accepts monetary compensation—"

"You mean bribes?"

His lips pursed into an unwilling grin. "You sound like your father."

Gen looked away. "Sorry."

"No, don't be. Your father always spoke his mind, said exactly what he meant. I admired that. And I know he wanted to be buried beside Helena. With your help, I think that's possible." Father Tony smiled gently. "When he died, her name was the last word he spoke." His face softened. "I think he would be proud that you want to do this for them all. Why don't we go take a look at your family plot and decide how you want things handled."

"And the funeral?" Lily asked.

"In these envelopes," he said handing each of them one. "Tomorrow at ten. I know it sounds fast, but he didn't want to wait. He wanted it over with. He planned his funeral ceremony months ago, wanting no fanfare, no excitement, just a simple service, closed casket, a few flowers, and memorial gifts to go to the parish soup kitchen."

Gen looked at the envelope in her hand. "My mother wanted to start a soup kitchen, years ago, for the immigrants moving into the area."

"Your father knew that. I don't think he would mind my telling you that he financed the startup of the kitchen in eighty-nine, paid for the renovations of the building, bought the appliances and the food for the first year. All anonymously. All because of your mother. He loved her," Father Tony said.

Gen tucked the envelope under her arm, gazing at the bare walls and the battered furniture of the priest's office. It needed a coat of paint and new carpet, but colorful cloth draped the windows and the chairs were comfortable, upholstered in a Western motif. Sounds of a basketball game echoed down the hallway from the gym. Signs of the good father's impact on a parish that needed him, just as her father had needed him when he lay dying.

"You want gray carpet?" she asked, not aware that she was going to speak until she heard the words. "I think that as part of a memorial to our father, my sister and I would like to see to the repainting of this office and your personal quarters. Lily?"

Her sister's brows lifted. "Of course. We *always* intended on *some sort* of memorial," she said, spearing Gen with a look. "Though I must admit we hadn't settled on what."

Gen smothered a smile. The memorial they had considered for years was to empty the Old Man's ashes in the parish dump. The alternative to that scenario was to add his ashes to mortar and re-tile the city YMCA restrooms. Controlling her expression, Gen said, "Yes. Well, we hadn't made the decision, but considering all we learned about Matthew and Mama, it seems like we should do something a bit more genteel than anything we had talked about before."

Lily rolled her eyes and crossed her legs, the slither of silk stockings vaguely mocking. Addressing the priest, she said, "You do know we hated the old bastard, don't you?"

Father Tony laughed, the sound French and boisterous. "I know that the Old Man enjoyed being a pain in the butt," he said, shocking Gen with the word. Priests didn't talk that way when she was a girl. Not at all. "And he succeeded most of the time. I also know that not all you two believed about your father was true."

Composing his face, Father Tony steepled his hands. He had long slender fingers and smooth rounded nails. A male model's hands. Gen instantly wanted to photograph him in the prayerful pose. Her father could have added it to his collection, she thought wryly.

"Healing after the passing of a parent is one of the most difficult things we do in life. It makes us look at who we are and where we came from. And then we have to address the issues we uncover, or run from them. I hope your father's passing will lead you both to address the central issues in your lives. I hope that, with the grace and help of God, you'll see your way to forgiveness and true peace. That would be the real memorial he would want."

Lily shook her head. "Gen may have forgiven—and maybe someday I'll able to forgive the old SOB—but our father was a violent, abusive, brutal man. I'll offer a cash memorial in lieu of the other plans we had made, but I won't promise to look for anything good in his life. Except that he finally died. Gen asked you a question. Gray carpet?"

Father Tony smiled and glanced away as if he knew something that they didn't. Well, he probably did. "Gray would be nice. But my personal quarters are fine. Your father had them redecorated last year when he redid the Estate House. If you want an appropriate memorial, we need a new floor in the parish church gym." His eyes sparkled with mischief. "Hardwood would be nice."

"Hardwood is fine. Gen will write you a check."

This time it was Gen's brows that went up. "I will? I mean, I will," she assured the priest, "but, I will?"

"You're the one rolling in money. Barry's money?" Lily reminded. "You pay the man for his floor and we'll take care of it between us after the estate is settled. Too bad the Old Man didn't get himself cremated. He'd look real good all glued up, holding down the gym floor."

"A service to his parish," Gen murmured.

Father Tony laughed.

The memorial went smoothly, the old church filled to capacity. People had heard the news of the death in the almost mystical way of many small towns, and family members and friends had driven or flown in from all across the state. The governor even sent a representative. And, as the Old Man had requested, the service was stately, simple, and quite short.

There were as many black faces in the crowd as there were

white, and Gen was surprised at the respect and genuine grief expressed by so many members of so many races. Many were Della's friends, Della's children and grandchildren. Many were strangers. And many were crying.

It appeared that everyone had forgotten that her father once beat a black man almost to death. That he was an object of conjecture and gossip his entire life. No one seemed to care that on the day of his funeral, a story broke in the local paper about a man John Deveraux killed and buried in his wife's grave. But then, Gen and her sister had been gone for a long time. It seemed their autocratic father had made peace with the town, had actually done some good for it.

As Father Tony talked about the man her father had been, and all the things he had done for the parish in his long life, Gen discovered her ambivalent feelings for her father were growing even more confused. She could see therapy in her future. At the thought, she could almost hear the Old Man say, "Quacks. The lot of 'em."

Two hours after the service, back at the Estate House, after the last guest had hugged or clasped hands and promised to pray or think about them, after they had warmly greeted and as quickly said goodbye to dozens they had not seen in nearly three decades, the sisters were finally alone in the house where they grew up. Keri and Destan were showing their stepfather the barn and the horses the Old Man had given them. Della was lying down in her room, putting her "old feets" up. The house was cool instead of viciously cold, and strangely empty.

Stretched out in the Old Man's office, the once perpetually-closed drapery open to the afternoon light, the sisters drank sweet tea with bruised mint leaves floating in the bottom. Gen studied her photographs on the wall, her mind blank and yet too full, too crowded to process anything new. She kicked the unopened newspapers off the sofa to make more room.

"I feel dull. I expected to feel happy, relieved, glad he was finally in the grave. Instead I feel dull," Lily said, half mumbling. She slumped in the recliner and lolled her head back. "Cheated. Maybe a little charred around the edges. As if things didn't go like I thought they would."

Gen nodded. It described exactly how she felt. As if all her circuits had been overloaded and now she was simply burned out and smoking. She slipped the red sandals off her feet and they thumped on the braided rug one at a time. The old leather couch comforted as she settled deeply into the worn cushion. Her red suit-skirt rose on her thighs. Gen crossed her ankles.

She had still not seen Starnes. He hadn't called. He hadn't shown up for the funeral.

The tickets for her flight to Maui had been delivered. In a snit the night before, she had called Jo at home and told him she was leaving. Immediately. She and Keri would be flying out in the morning. There was no reason to stay longer.

She was leaving. And Starnes . . . ? Wham, bam, thank you ma'am. Gen never would have believed it, but it appeared to be true. Just as she had been warned back in school, if you sleep with a boy, he won't respect you in the morning. He might not even look your way again. The ache Gen felt at his loss was stronger than the ache she felt for her father. Or for Barry.

"He's dead."

Gen jerked. Stilled. Realized that Lily was speaking of the Old Man.

"And now all we have to do is settle the Estate and we can say goodbye to this place forever," Lily said. She sounded puzzled, as if she wasn't certain that she was pleased at the fact. Taking her cue from Gen, Lily slipped off her pumps and raised the foot rest. She wiggled her toes, her face creased in confusion. "And then we could just leave."

Gen studied her sister. "We could. Or . . . You could live here, at least part of the year, you and the kids. It would make a great winter home, though the heat in summer sucks."

Lily ignored the comment about living here and grinned. "*Sucks?* What kind of language is that for a world famous photographer and socialite? It sounds like something my daughter would say when she thought I wasn't listening."

"Former socialite," Gen said, unbuttoning the top buttons of her blouse. "And it was hot as Hades at the graveside. I'm glad I was wearing cotton instead of silk."

"Will you come back when Mama and Matthew are reburied next to him?"

"I'll be here."

"And Starnes?"

"He lives here."

"But he hasn't called."

"No. He hasn't called."

"Stupid man."

"He is that."

"I heard gossip that he was involved with some legal matter about that sister of his. Maybe he's been too busy to call."

Gen glanced at her sister, all the derision she could muster in her eyes.

Lily raised a hand, palm out to stop her. "Good point. He could have *made* time to call. He didn't. So you're leaving in the morning?" Tears sprang to her eyes.

"No reason to stay. The Old Man is dead."

"I'll miss you."

"You could join us." When Lily's tears instantly dried and her black eyes flashed excitement, Gen added, "I'll send you a ticket. Destan, too, if he's interested. But don't think you'll land and be whisked to a four-star hotel by a limo. It's an overland, over-mountain, all day trek on horseback. Or you could take the ferry we have set up to provide us with mail. You'll be seasick for five hours after you land, but it's an easier route."

"Seasick?" Lily made a moue of distaste. "Desolate place?"

"No hot water. Only cold, and only when the generator is running."

"Yuck," Lily grimaced. "I'll think about it."

Gen chuckled. "It's the most beautiful place in the world. Seriously. Privately owned, well guarded by cliffs a thousand feet high. Very few people get the chance to see the lagoon from the water, let alone stay there for a few days. You shouldn't miss it if you don't have to."

"I'll think about it. No hot water? How do you stand it?"

Shaking her head, Gen rolled into a sitting position on the couch and stood. "I have to pack. Why don't we cook supper for Della tonight? Let her rest?"

Lily rolled her eyes. "Cook? How about Chinese?"

"Did I hear you two spoiled chil'rens say something about *Chinese?*" Della's voice floated down the hallway from the kitchen. "I hopes you wasn't talking about no food, 'cause of we got more fried chicken and ham slices and potato salad and macaroni-and-cheese and Jell-O than we can stand, lef' by them mourners." Della appeared in the doorway draped in her voluminous house-coat, her gray hair hanging in long ringlets.

Gen leaned down, and kissed Lily's cheek. "I love you, Sis. The Old Man's dying was hard, but I'm glad we cleared the air between us. For that alone, the trip was worth it. Of course if I gain five more pounds eating Southern Fried Funeral Cooking I may change my mind."

"Watch you mouth, you sassy thing. Get youself in here and eat some this food."

"I feel like I'm twelve again," Gen muttered to Lily, yet already obeying Della. Taking her sweet tea with her, she slipped back into her sandals and moved toward the kitchen. "Coming?"

"In a minute," Lily murmured. Dust motes swirled on the air as Gen left. The air-conditioner came on, its soft hum calming.

After a moment, Lily rose and went to the desk. Finding the number she wanted in the thin phone book, she lifted the receiver and dialed.

◆　◆　◆

Starnes drug himself into the house. It had been two days since he had changed clothes or showered. He still had Serena's dried blood crusted onto his shirt, a three-day-stubble, and bones that ached at the thought of another night spent on the recliner in her hospital room. The doctor had sent him home, finally, saying that there was nothing more he could do to help her.

She was out of the woods, medically speaking. The bullet had been removed, the bones in her shattered right shoulder had been put back into place and the severed artery leading to her right arm had been repaired. She had been given two units of blood and massive amounts of antibiotics. She was going to live. She had told him so herself in no uncertain terms and demanded some privacy. So he had come home to sleep in his own bed.

Bubba-Boy jumped all over him, as if she had been alone and starved for days instead of being cared for and fed by Herman. She followed him past the office with all its demanding, blinking lights, faxes, answering machines, and piled-up mail, past the kitchen with its lure of real food instead of hospital mush, and through the laundry where he stripped and tossed the bloody clothing into the washer. While he was in the shower, Bubba waited, a bundle of nervous happiness, whining all the time, her tail whirling in excitement, her back legs jumping up and down. It was only when he fell onto the mattress, one hand over the side to pet her that she finally calmed down. He fell asleep with one hand on her silky ears.

◆ ◆ ◆

"Strap yourself in. Want a movie?"

Keri was wide eyed, almost too excited to speak. "I've never flown first class before. Can I have a glass of wine?"

"No. But you can have any non-alcoholic drink you want. What do you think I am, a pushover?"

"I can hope, can't I?"

Gen rolled her eyes at Keri, who grinned unrepentantly, strapped herself in, and lay her head back as the 747's engines roared to life. Gen had waited until the last possible minute to board, hoping Starnes would show up to say goodbye. Would show up asking to come with her. *Would show up and ask her to stay?* She was honest enough to know that she wanted him, too, all her protestations to the contrary. Okay—so she hated the Estate. Or had. So she lived in New York, had a business and a life there. Most of that life had been Barry's life, not hers. Not really.

But Starnes hadn't come. Hadn't called. Lily had tried to detain them, tried to get her to book a later flight. Gen knew her sister had also been hoping that Starnes would show up. Maybe carrying a big bouquet of roses and a diamond ring. To Lily every good romance story had a diamond in it somewhere.

The 747 taxied down the runway. Gen turned her mind forcefully to the shoot in Maui.

◆ ◆ ◆

Starnes rolled over and cracked open his eyes. The clock by his bed said 1:05. It was too bright around the blinds to be one in the morning unless the bayou was on fire again. That made it afternoon. Bubba-Boy, sensing that he was finally awake, jumped onto the bed, landing on Starnes' bladder with her front paws.

"Get down, dog. Okay, okay. I'll let you out." Stumbling,

naked, Starnes made his way to the door and let the dog out before relieving himself and showering off the effects of twelve hours in the sack. He had work to do, a dying client to see, calls to make, and a woman to woo. Brushing his teeth, he hurried through his morning ritual and headed to the office for his messages.

It was the very first message that turned his world upside down. John Deveraux had died. The subsequent seven messages continued to inform him that his client had died, that a funeral had been planned, that John had been given a nice funeral, and had been buried. All without his knowing. A sick feeling gripped his stomach. Gen had gone through it alone. Without him. Had he even seen her since—

"Oh, crap."

He hadn't seen her since he left her bed. Hadn't called. Hadn't .... He checked his calendar. Days. He cursed softly.

He replayed the messages and sat through them all. All the messages about his client dying and being buried, knowing that he had abandoned Gen when she needed him most. The last two messages he listened to several times. It was Lily at her succinct best.

"Listen to me, you sorry son-of-a-bitch. I don't know where you've been the last two days, but my sister is leaving tomorrow. Leaving this place, and you, and me, too. And because of you, she may not ever come back. If you're worth two splatters in a spittoon, if you care about her in any way at all, you get your butt over here before she gets on that plane. It leaves at one PM." The disconnection had been a sharp, peeved click.

An instant later she spoke again. "Well, I see you had a good reason for dumping my sister and not showing up for the Old Man's funeral. You and L'ron Rebardi are plastered all over the front page of today's paper, solving the murders of Peter Mahoney and Josh Brenner, Ricky Hoggard and Glynwood Jarrett. And I see where Micah Brehew and Steven Wilkerson helped." Starnes could hear paper crinkling in the background. Newspaper?

"BMOCs who raped your sister," her voice softened for an instant. "That's tough. I'm sorry for her. Really. No woman should have to go through that." Then her voice roughened again.

"Not that you couldn't have found time to at least call Gen. She needed you and you weren't there. You little snot." Again the angry click at the end.

It was way past one now. Swearing again, steadily, Starnes finished dressing and shaving and went through his mail and made his calls, his anger and frustration building all afternoon. When he was finished, he stopped and poured a glass of wine, opened a can of his sister's ravioli and heated it in the microwave, the house silent and empty around him. He watched through the glass as the tomato sauce bubbled, the bowl of pasta rotating slowly.

It was 6:10. And he was alone. He had been alone all his life. He was alone now. He would be doubly alone when Serena was well enough to join the Carmelite nuns at the abbey for an extended time of therapy and healing, physical, mental, and spiritual. And then, if he was reading things right, she might be leaving him permanently when she married L'ron. The cop had refused to leave Serena in the hospital, had half-slept in an extra recliner a helpful nurse found, though two in one room had been crowded. He had scarcely left her side since the bullet had crashed through the one-way glass and hit her.

Starnes dropped his head. God, there had been so much blood. If L'ron hadn't been there, along with the other cops, to apply pressure and pack her into a car for a blue-light drive to the ER, she would be dead. The surgeon had told him so.

The scent of ravioli cooking filled the kitchen. The realizations hit him hard. His sister had nearly died. And Gen was gone.

He pounded the counter, cursing. It accomplished nothing, she was still gone, on Maui somewhere photographing models.

There was nothing he could have done differently, except that he could have called her. He was a thoughtless bastard, just like always. But this time, his was the heart he broke. The microwave dinged. The small light went out. Standing in the dim kitchen, Starnes considered his life. His future. Still cursing, he turned and left the house, grabbing his truck keys on the way.

"Where is she?"

"On Maui. Without you." Lily stood up from the table and the

salad she had been eating, and climbed the back stairs to the
family wing, her soft-soled ballerina slippers slapping haughtily on
each step.

Frustration mounting, he turned to Della. "Where. Is. She?"

Della stood and took her plate, carrying it to the sink, where
she rinsed it under the faucet before placing it in the dishwasher.

"Della! Damn it! Tell me where is *Ginny!*"

She turned slowly, her face as angry as he had ever seen it.
"Say *what?*"

Starnes snarled and crossed the kitchen in two strides.
Gripping her upper arms he said, "I intend to go find her, beg her
forgiveness, propose to her, and marry her."

"And if she don't want to come back here to live?"

"I can damn well paint anywhere."

"Watch your mouth," she said harshly. "And let me go, boy. I
ain't a woman what like to be manhandled."

Starnes released her and stepped back, sucking in great
draughts of air, fighting for a calm that had long deserted him.

"You want my baby?"

"Yes. I want her. I've always wanted her. I've just been too
stupid to know it."

" 'Nuff to live where she want to live?"

"Enough for almost anything. But, yes. Enough to live
wherever she wants to."

"Ummmm. Well, she din' tell me exactly where she be."

"She told *me*, however." Lily peeked down over the banister,
grinning. "I even have a first class ticket coming. And if you are
real, real, *real* nice to me, I'll let you have it."

35

BLISTERS AND HORSE SWEAT

Starnes eased up in the saddle to cool his sweat-soaked jeans. It had been years since he had spent so many hours on horseback and his hip had retaliated by sending waves of pain up and down his leg. He had been forced to stop and stretch four times in the last three hours; now the sun was dropping fast. His guide was a native Hawaiian cowboy, taciturn, uncommunicative, at first amused at his charge's misery, and now antsy about getting to the site before sunset. He kept saying that they were almost to the lagoon. Of course, they had been almost to the lagoon for over an hour. His inner thighs had blisters on their blisters.

If his torture hadn't been so great, Starnes might have enjoyed the spectacular views. The narrow trail wound through rainforest, along towering cliffs, offering glimpses of the blue ocean between crags—a purgatory that looked like paradise. All he wanted was to get off the small horse.

The scenery opened up, rainforest falling away. Water, a clear blue, streaked with lavender and shades of emerald, curled up to a black sand beach beneath a sky of peach, apricot, and fuchsia. Palms bowed away from the water and offered partial shade to six thatched-roof cottages set back from the beach. In the water was a rail-thin girl, surely no more than twelve, splashing and giggling in a high-pitched tone, an inflatable purple raft floating beside her.

Starnes slid from the horse and stood on one leg, his weight resting against the hot sweaty beast as he took in the sight. The light was stunning, a visual aria of color as the sun set, falling quickly into the ocean. Gen danced along the shore, shouting directions, encouragement, her camera before her face, her hair wild and curly and waving about her. Keri ran to her aunt bringing something, exchanging something, acting as assistant. The light was going. Today's shoot was almost over.

Feeling pain even worse than he expected, Starnes pulled himself back onto the small horse. If he was going to propose to the girl of his dreams, he would do it right, atop a horse and not limping like Hop Along Cassidy.

◆　◆　◆

"Okay. That's a wrap for today. Supper in half an hour and entertainment shortly after," she shouted, her voice raspy and spent. She always suffered following an outdoors shoot, her voice and skin feeling the effects of the elements. But it was worth it, just to see light like this.

She transferred the remaining film to an empty bag, so tired she could barely move. And unlike the models, she wasn't done for the day. She had to clean the salt-spray off her lenses and the UV filters tonight and package up the exposed film for the mail-boat to take back in the morning. She had to make sure that Joachim had checked the level of gasoline for the generators. She had to compare notes about other supplies and the next day's weather with Jo.

"Keri, go check on the chef and make sure snacks and drinks are ready, okay?"

"Uh. Aunt Gen. We got company."

At her odd tone, Gen looked up. And blinked. And he was still there. *Starnes. . . .*

Starnes smiled down at her from the back of a scruffy little horse, Cajun-black eyes glinting against the sun's final glare. "If I agree to marry you, do I get to travel to exotic places and watch you work?"

Keri's mouth fell open and stayed that way. She looked back and forth between them, her eyes as wide as her mouth.

The blood in Gen's veins congealed. She was paralyzed, rooted to the earth, as his words thrummed through her. *Marry?* Shock shivered along her skin. Her flesh drew into tight peaks with cold and fear and stunned disbelief. *Starnes? And, marry?*

She captured a breath of heated, salty air and threw back her head. A smile fought for a place on her lips. *Starnes. . . . He came. This time, he came.* "Did I miss something? Like . . . did I get drunk and propose marriage to you? Hmmm," she shook her head as if thinking, while her heart tripped unevenly in joy. "I don't think so." The fitful wind changed direction, whirling ocean spray and the smell of tired horse against her.

"You didn't?" Starnes looked puzzled and lifted a hand, his index finger tilting back his old black hat. Face turned slightly to the far ocean, he pursed his lips thinking. "You sure?"

"Yeah," she said. "I'm pretty sure."

"Hummmm." His gaze found hers again in a long caress.

Gen could have sworn that she felt the touch of his eyes against her face, tangled in her hair, warm against her skin. She shivered in the damp heat, not certain how she would respond. Even now, thousands of miles from the bayou. Thousands of miles. He had followed her. And she was still not, completely, certain.

"Well, in that case," Starnes said at last, his voice rough. "Would you marry me? I'd get down on one knee, but I'm afraid that if I try, I might fall facedown in the sand. And a prospective groom should always appear at his best until he snares the beauty he's after."

"He should?"

"Absolutely."

"Oh, Mama's gonna have a duck," Keri breathed, scarcely daring to move.

"Snares?"

"Figure of speech."

Gen didn't want to ask. Didn't want to spoil this perfect moment. But she wasn't a child anymore to take a gift horse without looking him over. "And we would live where?"

"Completely negotiable. But I do have a wonderful, refinished third-story apartment, to offer the bride, in the French Quarter, just down from the river, with a wonderful view and several *priceless* antiques," he waggled his brows as if comically offering her the moon on a half-shell like some Bourbon Street barker, "all within walking distance of my New Orleans office. I can add in a really nice house situated on the water on Bayou Incendie, with barn, barbecue pit, and enough square footage to lodge said bride's family and New York friends who might come visiting. It's a great place to honeymoon during the warm and breezy winter months."

"And the idea of New York?" she countered.

"I'm entering my midlife crisis" he said with a wry grin, resting an elbow on the saddle horn. "I'm ready for a change. New York sounds doable."

Gen shook her head. "You do know that I'm still legally married?"

"I know. I figure the day your divorce is final we can come back here and tie the knot. Tim, foreman back at the ranch, said he could get a priest in here. So, what do you say? Marry me?"

Gen laughed, turned on her heel in the wet sand. "I'll think about it." She glanced back over her shoulder. "A girl is supposed to keep a suitor waiting, you know."

"Aunt Gen!" Keri squealed. "No!"

They both ignored the girl.

Starnes nodded slowly, his hat moving up and down against the setting sun. "Miss High and Mighty Deveraux would do just that, I suppose," he said, his lips turning up and his dark eyes crinkling in the dying light.

"I'm glad you remembered. I intend to say yes by moonlight, with a glass of champagne in my hand, a midnight ocean breeze ruffling my hair, and a guitar strumming in the darkness."

Keri whooped, "We're gonna have a wedding!" she shouted, jumping up and down. "We're gonna have a wedding!"

Gen just lifted her camera and snapped a quick half dozen shots of Starnes Templar atop the horse. He was still smiling. So was she. Behind him, the sun slipped slowly into the sea.

The End

ABOUT THE AUTHOR

A native of Louisiana, Gwen Hunter now lives in South Carolina. She is the author of eleven novels including the acclaimed DeLande Saga novels and the Rhea Lynch, MD Series. Her novels have been published worldwide in seven languages.

Visit her official website at www.gwenhunter.com, for the latest news and contact information.